U0001496

How to
Speak and Write Correctly

像樣的英文
這樣寫，這樣說

用英文思考，掌握正確的文法與字彙
不再背公式，擺脫不道地的中式英文
中英對照

Joseph Devlin 約瑟・德夫林 著　楊雅琪 譯

目録

Contents

前　言

　　在籌備本拙作的過程中，作者設下一個目標，也就是：讓本書成為目標讀者能夠使用的作品，也就是那些沒有時間、機會、能力或意向去仔細閱讀既詳盡又深奧的修辭、文法和寫作專書的人。對他們來說，這樣的書好比封鎖在一個他們無力打開的鐵箱之中的黃金。本書並不自視甚高，這既不是一本解說文章體例教條的修辭指南，也不是闡述各種武斷規則與例外情況的文法書。本書僅盡力幫助一般人用一般性的語言妥善地表達自己。書中列出英文的大方向規則，遵循這些規則，讀者就能適當地用英文進行口說和寫作。除了提出許多英文特有的慣用語和表達方式之外，書中也列出一些常見錯誤和陷阱，讓讀者能夠了解並避免犯錯。

　　作者沒有想要感謝的特定人士，而是想要感謝曾經寫過相關主題的每一個人。

　　這本拙作有如語言道路上指向正確方向的路標。作者希望依循這個路標前進的人，能抵達正確口說與寫作的目的地。

INTRODUCTION

In the preparation of this little work the writer has kept one end in view, viz.: To make it serviceable for those for whom it is intended, that is, for those who have neither the time nor the opportunity, the learning nor the inclination, to peruse elaborate and abstruse treatises on Rhetoric, Grammar, and Composition. To them such works are as gold enclosed in chests of steel and locked beyond power of opening. This book has no pretension about it whatever,–it is neither a Manual of Rhetoric, expatiating on the dogmas of style, nor a Grammar full of arbitrary rules and exceptions. It is merely an effort to help ordinary, everyday people to express themselves in ordinary, everyday language, in a proper manner. Some broad rules are laid down, the observance of which will enable the reader to keep within the pale of propriety in oral and written language. Many idiomatic words and expressions, peculiar to the language, have been given, besides which a number of the common mistakes and pitfalls have been placed before the reader so that he may know and avoid them.

The writer has to acknowledge his indebtedness to no one in particular, but to all in *general* who have ever written on the subject.

The little book goes forth–a finger-post on the road of language pointing in the right direction. It is hoped that they who go according to its index will arrive at the goal of correct speaking and writing.

第一章
用語上的需求

Requirements of Speech

學習正確的英文口說和寫作是件相當簡單的事，因為要達成一般對話或溝通目的，只須用到大約兩千個不同的單字。僅只掌握兩千個單字，並知道這些單字的正確擺放位置，並不能讓我們成為英文大師，不過已經足夠讓我們正確地說與寫。你可能會說，比起字典裡收錄的詞彙量，兩千個單字根本不算什麼嘛！話說回來，從來沒有人用過字典裡所有的單字，就算你像《聖經》裡的瑪土撒拉（Methuselah）活到九百多歲，也用不著這麼多字。

近代版的大部頭字典有超過二十萬個單字，但只要其中的百分之一就足夠滿足所有需求了。當然了，你或許不這麼認為，也不甘於以通用名稱來稱呼事物。你或許野心勃勃想證明自己比別人優秀、展現豐富的學識，不過有時這麼做，反而突顯出你賣弄學問、孤陋寡聞。舉例來說，你或許不想直接稱鏟子（spade）為鏟子，寧可稱之為「用來磨去土壤表層的椎狀器具」（a spatulous device for abrading the surface of the soil）。不過，使用大家耳熟能詳、自老一輩起就在使用的簡單稱呼還是比較好，畢竟這種稱呼自古以來沿用至今，大家也都耳熟能詳。

明明用簡單、常見的字彙就能達成目的，卻偏要使用艱澀陌生的字彙，只會突顯你的無知。偉大的學者、作家和有禮貌的講者都使用簡單字彙。

先前說到只要兩千個字，就能滿足對話、通信和寫作的所有目的。不過，我們發現許多在社會上被認定為素質高、文雅、具有學識的人用的字更少，因為他們知道的單字沒有那麼多。現今

It is very easy to learn how to speak and write correctly, as for all purposes of ordinary conversation and communication, only about 2,000 different words are required. The mastery of just twenty hundred words, the knowing where to place them, will make us not masters of the English language, but masters of correct speaking and writing. Small number, you will say, compared with what is in the dictionary! But nobody ever uses all the words in the dictionary or could use them did he live to be the age of Methuselah, and there is no necessity for using them.

There are upwards of 200,000 words in the recent editions of the large dictionaries, but the one-hundredth part of this number will suffice for all your wants. Of course you may think not, and you may not be content to call things by their common names; you may be ambitious to show superiority over others and display your learning or, rather, your pedantry and lack of learning. For instance, you may not want to call a spade a spade. You may prefer to call it a spatulous device for abrading the surface of the soil. Better, however, to stick to the old familiar, simple name that your grandfather called it. It has stood the test of time, and old friends are always good friends.

To use a big word or a foreign word when a small one and a familiar one will answer the same purpose, is a sign of ignorance. Great scholars and writers and polite speakers use simple words.

To go back to the number necessary for all purposes of conversation correspondence and writing, 2,000, we find that a great many people who pass in society as being polished, refined and educated use less, for they know less. The greatest scholar alive hasn't

最偉大的學者能靈活運用的字不超過四千個，而且其中半數都沒有派上用場的機會。

莎士比亞是有史以來最傑出的才子，他的著作中有多達一萬五千個不同的字，但是其中有將近一萬個字，現在已經遭到淘汰或失去意義。

每個擁有一定智力的人，應該都能正確使用自己的母語。只要辛苦一下花點心思學習，就能獲得豐碩成果。

比較一下這兩種人之間的差異：一種是斯文有禮、知道如何正確挑選和使用單字的人；一種是粗野不文，說話刺耳、容易傷人的人。後者說話欠缺思考、文法錯誤百出、言詞荒誕不經，有他在場就令人不快，任誰都想敬而遠之。

只需要上幾堂課，你就能正確掌握英文文法，能在正式場合正確對談，或以書面恰當表達自己的想法和概念。

本書目的正是儘量以簡明扼要的方式，為讀者指引一條筆直的道路，點出必須避免的錯誤，協助讀者達到正確學習英文的目標。這不是一本文法書，而是一本指南，一個指向正確方向的無聲號誌。

more than four thousand different words at his command, and he never has occasion to use half the number.

In the works of Shakespeare, the most wonderful genius the world has ever known, there is the enormous number of 15,000 different words, but almost 10,000 of them are obsolete or meaningless today.

Every person of intelligence should be able to use his mother tongue correctly. It only requires a little pains, a little care, a little study to enable one to do so, and the recompense is great.

Consider the contrast between the well-bred, polite man who knows how to choose and use his words correctly and the underbred, vulgar boor, whose language grates upon the ear and jars the sensitiveness of the finer feelings. The blunders of the latter, his infringement of all the canons of grammar, his absurdities and monstrosities of language, make his very presence a pain, and one is glad to escape from his company.

The proper grammatical formation of the English language, so that one may acquit himself as a correct conversationalist in the best society or be able to write and express his thoughts and ideas upon paper in the right manner, may be acquired in a few lessons.

It is the purpose of this book, as briefly and concisely as possible, to direct the reader along a straight course, pointing out the mistakes he must avoid and giving him such assistance as will enable him to reach the goal of a correct knowledge of the English language. It is not a Grammar in any sense, but a guide, a silent signal-post pointing the way in the right direction.

英文詞類與其變化

所有英文單字可分為九大類別,稱為九大詞類,分別是:

① 冠詞

② 名詞

③ 形容詞

④ 代名詞

⑤ 動詞

⑥ 副詞

⑦ 介系詞

⑧ 連接詞

⑨ 感嘆詞

其中又以名詞最為重要,其他詞類多少都依附著名詞產生變化。名詞是任何人、物、地、思想或概念的名稱。名詞分為「**專有名詞**」和「**普通名詞**」兩種。普通名詞是某個族群或類別共有的名稱,像是「人」和「城市」;專有名詞則區別出族群或類別中的個體,像是「約翰」和「費城」。前者說的「人」是整個人類族群共有的名稱,「城市」則是所有集合大型人口的中心共有的名稱,但「約翰」代表人類中的特定個體,「費城」則代表了世界上所有城市中特定的一個。

名詞會因「人稱」、「數量」、「性別」和「格」產生詞形變化。**人稱**是指談話或書信中,發言者、聽者和所涉對象之間的

THE ENGLISH LANGUAGE IN A NUTSHELL

All the words in the English language are divided into nine great classes. These classes are called the Parts of Speech. They are Article, Noun, Adjective, Pronoun, Verb, Adverb, Preposition, Conjunction, and Interjection.

Of these, the Noun is the most important, as all the others are more or less dependent upon it. A Noun signifies the name of any person, place or thing, in fact, anything of which we can have either thought or idea. There are two kinds of Nouns, Proper and Common. Common Nouns are names which belong in common to a race or class, as *man, city*. Proper Nouns distinguish individual members of a race or class as *John, Philadelphia*. In the former case *man* is a name which belongs in common to the whole race of mankind, and *city* is also a name which is common to all large centres of population, but *John* signifies a particular individual of the race, while *Philadelphia* denotes a particular one from among the cities of the world.

Nouns are varied by Person, Number, Gender, and Case. Person is that relation existing between the speaker, those addressed and the subject under consideration, whether by discourse or correspondence. The Persons are *First*, *Second* and *Third* and they represent respectively the speaker, the person addressed and the person or thing mentioned or under consideration.

關係，分為第一、第二和第三人稱，分別代表發言者、聽者，以及受到提及或指涉的人、事、物。

數量是從一到多之間的區別。數量分為單數和複數，單數表示一，複數代表二及以上。英文名詞的複數形，一般是在單數形後面加 s 或 es 形成。

名詞的**性別**之於名詞的關係，相當於人的性別之於個體的關係。不過人的個體只分兩種性別，名詞則有四種，意即「陽性」、「陰性」、「中性」和「通性」。陽性代表所有雄性種類；陰性代表所有雌性種類；中性代表沒有生命的事物；通性代表有生命、但當下無法確定性別的生物，如魚、鼠、鳥等等。有時被我們認定為沒有生命、正確來說屬於中性的事物，可用「擬人」的修辭手法變成陽性或陰性，例如比喻太陽為 He is rising（他正昇起）；月亮為 She is setting（她正落下）。

格指出某個名詞與另一個名詞、動詞或介系詞的關係，分為主格、所有格和受格三種。主格是一個句子所談的主題，或主導動詞動作的主體；所有格表示擁有；受格則是指受到動詞的動作影響的人、事、物。

Number is the distinction of one from more than one. There are two numbers, singular and plural; the singular denotes one, the plural two or more. The plural is generally formed from the singular by the addition of *s* or *es*.

Gender has the same relation to nouns that sex has to individuals, but while there are only two sexes, there are four genders, viz., masculine, feminine, neuter and common. The masculine gender denotes all those of the male kind, the feminine gender all those of the female kind, the neuter gender denotes inanimate things or whatever is without life, and common gender is applied to animate beings, the sex of which for the time being is indeterminable, such as fish, mouse, bird, etc. Sometimes things which are without life as we conceive it and which, properly speaking, belong to the neuter gender, are, by a figure of speech called Personification, changed into either the masculine or feminine gender, as, for instance, we say of the sun, *He* is rising; of the moon, *She* is setting.

Case is the relation one noun bears to another or to a verb or to a preposition. There are three cases, the *Nominative*, the *Possessive* and the *Objective*. The nominative is the subject of which we are speaking or the agent which directs the action of the verb; the possessive case denotes possession, while the objective indicates the person or thing which is affected by the action of the verb.

詞類定義

冠詞是位於名詞前的單字，藉以顯示該名詞是用於限定或一般意義。冠詞分為 a／an 和 the 兩種。

形容詞是修飾名詞的字，藉以區別出該名詞的特徵或特性。

代名詞是代表或取代某個名詞的字，以免該名詞被過度重複。代名詞跟名詞一樣也有格、數量、性別和人稱之分。代名詞分為「人稱代名詞」、「關係代名詞」和「形容代名詞」三種。

動詞表示動作或正在做某事。動詞會因時態、語氣以及數量、人稱出現詞形變化，其中數量、人稱的變化完全由主詞決定。

副詞是修飾動詞、形容詞的字，有時也用來修飾其他副詞。

介系詞用於連接字詞，同時顯示這些字詞中所提到事物之間的關係。

連接詞是連結單字、片語、子句和句子的字。

感嘆詞是表達驚訝或突發情緒的字。

DEFINITIONS

An *Article* is a word placed before a noun to show whether the latter is used in a particular or general sense. There are but two articles, *a* or *an* and *the*.

An *Adjective* is a word which qualifies a noun, that is, which shows some distinguishing mark or characteristic belonging to the noun.

A *Pronoun* is a word used for or instead of a noun to keep us from repeating the same noun too often. Pronouns, like nouns, have case, number, gender and person. There are three kinds of pronouns, *personal*, *relative* and *adjective*.

A *verb* is a word which signifies action or the doing of something. A verb is inflected by tense and mood and by number and person, though the latter two belong strictly to the subject of the verb.

An *adverb* is a word which modifies a verb, an adjective and sometimes another adverb.

A *preposition* serves to connect words and to show the relation between the objects which the words express.

A *conjunction* is a word which joins words, phrases, clauses and sentences together.

An *interjection* is a word which expresses surprise or some sudden emotion of the mind.

英文三大要點

使用英文的三大要點是：純正、簡明和精確。

純正是指使用好的英文。不能使用任何俚語、粗話、遭淘汰的過時詞語、外來成語、模稜兩可的措詞，或任何不符文法的言詞。也不鼓勵使用新創字詞，除非該字詞已被最優秀的作者和演說家所採用。

簡明是指使用明確的言詞進行最清楚的思想表達，讓人對發言者或作者想要傳達的思想、概念不會產生任何誤解。嚴禁使用隱晦或擁有雙重意義的字詞，以及可能受到不同解讀的字詞。要達到簡明，文風必須一目了然、一聽即懂且面面俱到，避免任何花俏、迂腐、矯揉造作或過分修飾的風格。

精確要求簡潔、精準的表達方式，不要任何冗詞、贅述，風格要夠精鍊、清楚、簡單，好讓聽者或讀者立刻就懂發言者或作者的意思。一方面禁止所有複雜長句，另一方面也不允許太過短促的句子，目標是句子長度拿捏得當，以緊緊抓住聽者或讀者對於話語或文句的注意力。

THREE ESSENTIALS

The three essentials of the English language are: *Purity*, *Perspicuity* and *Precision*.

By *Purity* is signified the use of good English. It precludes the use of all slang words, vulgar phrases, obsolete terms, foreign idioms, ambiguous expressions or any ungrammatical language whatsoever. Neither does it sanction the use of any newly coined word until such word is adopted by the best writers and speakers.

Perspicuity demands the clearest expression of thought conveyed in unequivocal language, so that there may be no misunderstanding whatever of the thought or idea the speaker or writer wishes to convey. All ambiguous words, words of double meaning and words that might possibly be construed in a sense different from that intended, are strictly forbidden. Perspicuity requires a style at once clear and comprehensive and entirely free from pomp and pedantry and affectation or any straining after effect.

Precision requires concise and exact expression, free from redundancy and tautology, a style terse and clear and simple enough to enable the hearer or reader to comprehend immediately the meaning of the speaker or writer. It forbids, on the one hand, all long and involved sentences, and, on the other, those that are too short and abrupt. Its object is to strike the golden mean in such a way as to rivet the attention of the hearer or reader on the words uttered or written.

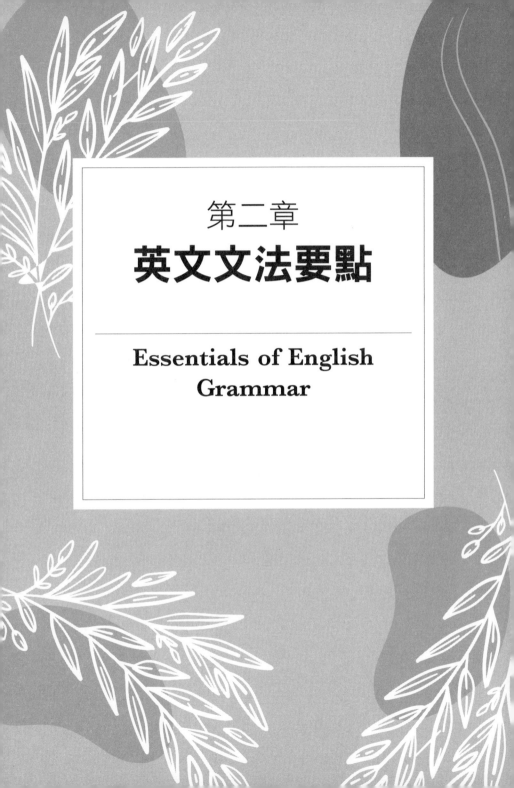

第二章
英文文法要點

Essentials of English Grammar

想要正確說寫英文，必須掌握文法的根本原則。即便大量閱讀大師著作，或與最優秀的演說家關係多好、多努力模仿他們，如果不懂正確句子架構的基本原則以及單字之間的關係，我們就會像鸚鵡一樣，只會重複自己聽到的東西，卻不理解其中意義。鸚鵡是沒有判斷能力的生物，當然無法理解語意，只會重複別人向牠說的話。因此，無論是不雅還是優美的句子，鸚鵡模仿起來一樣流利；同理可證，如果我們不懂文法，可能說出大錯特錯的句子，卻以為自己說得十分精準。

文法分類

文法有四大研究分類，意即：拼字學、語源學、句法學和韻律學。

拼字學——談字母和單字組合模式。

語源學——談各類單字和單字變化。

句法學——談句子中的單字串連和排列。

韻律學——談說讀方式和不同種類的韻文。

前三類與我們最為息息相關。

In order to speak and write the English language correctly, it is imperative that the fundamental principles of the Grammar be mastered, for no matter how much we may read of the best authors, no matter how much we may associate with and imitate the best speakers, if we do not know the underlying principles of the correct formation of sentences and the relation of words to one another, we will be to a great extent like the parrot, that merely repeats what it hears without understanding the import of what is said. Of course the parrot, being a creature without reason, cannot comprehend; it can simply repeat what is said to it, and as it utters phrases and sentences of profanity with as much facility as those of virtue, so by like analogy, when we do not understand the grammar of the language, we may be making egregious blunders while thinking we are speaking with the utmost accuracy.

DIVISIONS OF GRAMMAR

There are four great divisions of Grammar, viz.:

Orthography, *Etymology*, *Syntax*, and *Prosody*.

Orthography treats of letters and the mode of combining them into words.

Etymology treats of the various classes of words and the changes they undergo.

Syntax treats of the connection and arrangement of words in sentences.

Prosody treats of the manner of speaking and reading and the different kinds of verse.

The three first mentioned concern us most.

字母

　　字母是一種標誌或符號，每個字母代表一個可清楚發出的聲音。字母分為「母音字母」和「子音字母」。母音字母本身就能唸出明確的聲音；子音字母沒有母音字母協助時，則無法唸出聲音。母音字母為 a、e、i、o、u，而當 w 和 y 不在字首或音節之首時，也是母音字母。

音節與單字

　　音節是可一次說出的一個明確聲音。每個音節至少要有一個母音。一個單字含有一個或多個音節。

　　將單字拆成不同音節有許多規則，不過最好的規則是儘可能按照發音器官發出正確發音的方式來拆解音節。

九大詞類

冠詞　冠詞是位於名詞前的單字，用來顯示該名詞是用於限定或一般意義。

　　冠詞分為 a／an 和 the 兩種。a／an 稱為「不定冠詞」，它不指稱特定的人、事、物，而是指該名詞最廣泛的意義，所以 <u>a</u>

LETTERS

A *letter* is a mark or character used to represent an articulate sound. Letters are divided into *vowels* and *consonants*. A vowel is a letter which makes a distinct sound by itself. Consonants cannot be sounded without the aid of vowels. The vowels are *a*, *e*, *i*, *o*, *u*, and sometimes *w* and *y* when they do not begin a word or syllable.

SYLLABLES AND WORDS

A syllable is a distinct sound produced by a single effort of [Transcriber's note: 1-2 words illegible] shall, pig, dog. In every syllable there must be at least one vowel.

A word consists of one syllable or a combination of syllables.

Many rules are given for the dividing of words into syllables, but the best is to follow as closely as possible the divisions made by the organs of speech in properly pronouncing them.

THE PARTS OF SPEECH

ARTICLE

An Article is a word placed before a noun to show whether the noun is used in a particular or general sense.

man（一個人）是指任何人，無論他的種族為何。

the 稱為「定冠詞」，它指出特定人、事、物，所以 the man（這個人）是指某個特定的個人。

名詞 名詞是任何人、地、物的名稱，像是 John（約翰）、London（倫敦）、book（書本）。名詞分為「專有名詞」和「普通名詞」。

專有名詞是特定人、地、物的名稱；普通名詞是一整個類別或物種的名稱。名詞會因「數量」、「性別」和「格」而發生詞形變化。

數量的名詞變化表示該名詞代表一個或多個數量。

性別的名詞變化表示該名稱是指稱雄性、雌性、無生命物體，或無法分辨性別的事物。

格的名詞變化表示所描述的人、地、物狀態，例如是肯定句或問句的主詞、所指事物的擁有者或持有者，或是某個動作或一段關係的對象。

There are two articles, *a* or *an* and *the*. *A* or *an* is called the indefinite article because it does not point put any particular person or thing but indicates the noun in its widest sense; thus, *a* man means any man whatsoever of the species or race.

The is called the definite article because it points out some particular person or thing; thus, *the* man means some particular individual.

NOUN

A *noun* is the name of any person, place or thing as J*ohn, London, book.* Nouns are proper and common.

Proper nouns are names applied to *particular* persons or places.

Common nouns are names applied to a whole kind or species.

Nouns are inflected by *number, gender and case.*

Number is that inflection of the noun by which we indicate whether it represents one or more than one.

Gender is that inflection by which we signify whether the noun is the name of a male, a female, of an inanimate object or something which has no distinction of sex.

Case is that inflection of the noun which denotes the state of the person, place or thing represented, as the subject of an affirmation or question, the owner or possessor of something mentioned, or the object of an action or of a relation.

以下例句說明名詞詞形變化：

> John tore the leaves of Sarah's book.
> 約翰撕破莎拉的書的頁面。

句中的 book 代表單一物體，leaves 則代表同一類別裡的多個物體，兩者之間的區別是「數量」。John 是男性，Sarah 是女性，而 book 和 leaves 都是沒有性別之分的無生命物體，三者之間的區別是「性別」。另外，John 是撕破書頁的人，同時也是此句的主詞，而 Sarah 是書本的所有人，leaves 是被撕破的物體，book 是與 leaves 有關的物體，這些各自不同的狀態就是「格」。

形容詞 形容詞是修飾名詞的字，用以顯示或指出該名詞具有區別性的標記或特徵，例如 A black dog（一隻黑色的狗）。

形容詞有三種比較等級的形態，分別是「原級」、「比較級」和「最高級」。

原級是形容詞的單純形態，用於表達原有特質沒有增減的情況，例如：nice（好的）。

比較級是用於表達原有特質出現增減的形容詞形態，例如：nicer（更好的）。

最高級是用於表達原有特質出現最大程度增減的形容詞形態，例如：nicest（最好的）。

Thus in the example, "John tore the leaves of Sarah's book," the distinction between *book* which represents only one object and *leaves* which represent two or more objects of the same kind is called *Number*; the distinction of sex between *John*, a male, and *Sarah*, a female, and *book* and *leaves*, things which are inanimate and neither male nor female, is called *Gender*; and the distinction of state between *John*, the person who tore the book, and the subject of the affirmation, *Mary*, the owner of the book, *leaves* the objects torn, and *book* the object related to leaves, as the whole of which they were a part, is called *Case*.

ADJECTIVE

An adjective is a word which qualifies a noun, that is, shows or points out some distinguishing mark or feature of the noun; as, A *black* dog.

Adjectives have three forms called degrees of comparison, the *positive*, the *comparative* and the *superlative*.

The *positive* is the simple form of the adjective without expressing increase or diminution of the original quality: *nice*.

The *comparative* is that form of the adjective which expresses increase or diminution of the quality: *nicer*.

The *superlative* is that form which expresses the greatest increase or diminution of the quality: *nicest*.

另一種說明方式如下：

不做比較時，使用形容詞的原級形態，例如：

> a rich man
> 一位富翁

在做一對一或個體對群體的比較時，使用形容詞的比較級形態，例如：

> John is richer than James.
> 約翰比詹姆士富有。
>
> He is richer than all the men in Boston.
> 他比波士頓其他人來得富有。

在比較一個個體和其他多個個體時，使用形容詞的最高級形態，例如：

> John is the richest man in Boston.
> 約翰是波士頓最富有的人。

表達無法增減的特性或狀況的形容詞，只有原級形態，例如：a circular road（環形道路）；the chief end（首要目標）；an extreme measure（極端手段）。

形容詞的比較等級以兩種方式表示：在原級後面加 er（比較級）或 est（最高級），或在原級前面加 more（比較級）或 most（最高級）。以 handsome（英俊）為例，其比較級和最高級是

or

An adjective is in the positive form when it does not express comparison; as, "A *rich* man."

An adjective is in the comparative form when it expresses comparison between two or between one and a number taken collectively, as, "John is *richer* than James"; "he is *richer* than all the men in Boston."

An adjective is in the superlative form when it expresses a comparison between one and a number of individuals taken separately; as, "John is the *richest* man in Boston."

Adjectives expressive of properties or circumstances which cannot be increased have only the positive form; as, A *circular* road; the *chief* end; an *extreme* measure.

Adjectives are compared in two ways, either by adding *er* to the positive to form the comparative and *est* to the positive to form the superlative, or by prefixing *more* to the positive for the comparative handsomer、handsomest，或是 more handsome、most handsome。有兩個音節以上的形容詞，一般會在前面加 more 或 most 形成比較等級。

　　許多形容詞的比較等級呈現不規則變化，例如：bad、worse、worst（糟的、更糟的、最糟的）和 good、better、best（好的、更好的、最好的）。

代名詞　　代名詞是用來替代名詞的單字，例如：

> John gave his pen to James, and <u>he</u> lent <u>it</u> to Jane to write <u>her</u> copy with <u>it</u>.
> 約翰把自己的筆給了詹姆士，他把它借給珍去寫她的謄本。

如果沒有代名詞，這個句子就得寫成：

> John gave John's pen to James, and James lent the pen to Jane to write Jane's copy with the pen.

　　代名詞分為三種：「人稱代名詞」、「關係代名詞」和「形容代名詞」。

■ 人稱代名詞

　　顧名思義，是用來替代人、地、物的名稱，分為 I、you、he、she、it，其複數形是 we、you、they。I 是第一人稱，代表說

and *most* to the positive for the superlative; as, *handsome, handsomer, handsomest* or *handsome, more handsome, most handsome.* Adjectives of two or more syllables are generally compared by prefixing more and most.

Many adjectives are irregular in comparison; as, Bad, worse, worst; Good, better, best.

PRONOUN

A *pronoun* is a word used in place of a noun; as, "John gave his pen to James and *he* lent it to Jane to write *her* copy with it." Without the pronouns we would have to write this sentence—"John gave John's pen to James and James lent the pen to Jane to write Jane's copy with the pen."

There are three kinds of pronouns—Personal, Relative and Adjective Pronouns.

■ Personal Pronouns

Personal Pronouns are so called because they are used instead of the names of persons, places and things. The Personal Pronouns are *I, He, She*, and *It*, with their plurals, *We, You* and *They. I* is the pronoun of the first person because it represents the person speaking. *You* is the pronoun of the second person because it represents the person spoken to. *He, She, It* are the pronouns of the third person because they

話的人。you 是第二人稱,代表第一人稱說話的對象。he、she、it 是第三人稱,代表第一、第二人稱談論的對象。

代名詞跟名詞一樣,也有數量、性別和格之分。第一和第二人稱的性別顯而易見,因為他們代表說話者本身和說話者的對象。以下列出人稱代名詞的格變化:

第一人稱(男性或女性)

	單數	複數
主格	I	We
所有格	Mine	Our
受格	Me	Us

第二人稱(男性或女性)

	單數	複數
主格	You	You
所有格	Your	Your
受格	You	You

represent the persons or things of whom we are speaking.

Like nouns, the Personal Pronouns have number, gender and case. The gender of the first and second person is obvious, as they represent the person or persons speaking and those who are addressed. The personal pronouns are thus declined:

First Person, M. or F.

	Sing.	Plural.
N.	I	We
P.	Mine	Our
O.	Me	Us

Second Person, M. or F.

	Sing.	Plural.
N.	You	You
P.	Your	Your
O.	You	You

第三人稱（男性）

	單數	複數
主格	He	They
所有格	His	Their
受格	Him	Them

第三人稱（女性）

	單數	複數
主格	She	They
所有格	Her	Their
受格	Her	Them

第三人稱（中性）

	單數	複數
主格	It	They
所有格	Its	Their
受格	It	Them

Third Person, M.

	Sing.	Plural.
N.	He	They
P.	His	Their
O.	Him	Them

Third Person, F.

	Sing.	Plural.
N.	She	They
P.	Her	Their
O.	Her	Them

Third Person, Neuter.

	Sing.	Plural.
N.	It	They
P.	Its	Their
O.	It	Them

■ 關係代名詞

之所以稱為「關係」，是因為與前面的單字或片語有關聯，例如：

> The boy <u>who</u> told the truth 那個實話實說的男孩
>
> He has done well, <u>which</u> gives me great pleasure. 他做得很好，這讓我相當開心。

此處的 who 和 which 除了用來取代字詞之外，who 與男孩有直接關係，which 則與他做得很好這件事有直接關係。

關係代名詞所指稱的單字或片語稱為「先行詞」。關係代名詞包括 who、which、that 和 what。who 只能用來指人，例如：

> The man <u>who</u> was here 先前在這裡的這位男士

which 用來指低等動物或沒有生命的事物，例如：

> The horse <u>which</u> I sold 我賣掉的那匹馬
>
> The hat <u>which</u> I bought 我買的那頂帽子

that 可用來指人和事物，例如：

> The friend <u>that</u> helps 幫忙的那位朋友
>
> The bird <u>that</u> sings 那隻鳴唱的鳥
>
> The knife <u>that</u> cuts 那把切割用的刀子

■ Relative Pronouns

The *Relative* Pronouns are so called because they relate to some word or phrase going before; as, "The boy *who* told the truth;" "He has done well, *which* gives me great pleasure."

Here *who* and *which* are not only used in place of other words, but *who* refers immediately to boy, and *which* to the circumstance of his having done well.

The word or clause to which a relative pronoun refers is called the *Antecedent*.

The Relative Pronouns are *who, which, that* and *what*.

Who is applied to persons only; as, "The man *who* was here."

Which is applied to the lower animals and things without life; as, "The horse *which* I sold." "The hat *which* I bought."

That is applied to both persons and things; as, "The friend *that* helps." "The bird *that* sings." "The knife *that* cuts."

what 是複合關係代名詞，兼具先行詞與關係代名詞的功能，用法等同 that which，例如：

> I did <u>what</u> he desired = I did <u>that which</u> he desired 我照他想要的那樣去做

關係代名詞的單、複數形式相同。who 代表陽性或陰性；which 和 that 代表陽性、陰性或中性；what 是中性的關係代名詞。

that 和 what 沒有詞形變化。who 和 which 詞形變化為：

	Who			Which	
	單數	複數		單數	複數
主格	Who	Who	主格	Which	Which
所有格	Whose	Whose	所有格	Whose	Whose
受格	Whom	Whom	受格	Which	Which

who、which、what 用於問句時，稱為疑問代名詞。

What is a compound relative, including both the antecedent and the relative and is equivalent to *that which*; as, "I did *what* he desired," i. e. "I did *that which* he desired."

Relative pronouns have the singular and plural alike.

Who is either masculine or feminine; *which* and *that* are masculine, feminine or neuter; *what* as a relative pronoun is always neuter.

That and *what* are not inflected.

Who and *which* are thus declined:

	Who			Which	
	Sing.	Plural		Sing.	Plural
N.	Who	Who	N.	Which	Which
P.	Whose	Whose	P.	Whose	Whose
O.	Whom	Whom	O.	Which	Which

Who, *which* and *what* when used to ask questions are called *Interrogative Pronouns*.

■ 形容代名詞

兼具形容詞和代名詞的特性，可分為以下幾類：

一、**指示代名詞**：直接指稱某人或事物，包括 this、that 和其複數形 these、those。

二、**分配代名詞**：用於代表個體性，包括 each、every、either、neither。

三、**不定代名詞**：用於代表不指定性，包括 any、all、few、some、several、one、other、another、none。

四、**所有格代名詞**：表示擁有的狀態，包括 mine、yours、his、hers、its、ours、theirs。

動詞 　動詞是用於表示動作或在做某事的單字，也可以將它定義為用來肯定、命令或提問的字。

像是 John the table 這組字詞沒有明確的意義，不過一旦加進 strikes 這個動詞，則傳達一種肯定的意思，使句子變得完整、有意義。

沒有詞形變化的單純動詞，稱為原形動詞，例如 to love 中的 love 即為原形動詞。

動詞分為規則／不規則和及物／不及物。可在現在式後面加 ed 或 d（字尾是 e 時）以形成過去式的動詞，就是**規則動詞**。過去式不是以 ed 做結尾的動詞，則為**不規則動詞**。

■ Adjective Pronouns

Adjective Pronouns partake of the nature of adjectives and pronouns and are subdivided as follows:

Demonstrative Adjective Pronouns which directly point out the person or object. They are *this, that* with their plurals *these, those.*

Distributive Adjective Pronouns used distributively. They are *each, every, either, neither.*

Indefinite Adjective Pronouns used more or less indefinitely. They are *any, all, few, some, several, one, other, another, none.*

Possessive Adjective Pronouns denoting possession. They are *mine, yours, his, hers, its, ours, theirs.*

THE VERB

A *verb* is a word which implies action or the doing of something, or it may be defined as a word which affirms, commands or asks a question.

Thus, the words *John the table*, contain no assertion, but when the word *strikes* is introduced, something is affirmed, hence the word *strikes* is a verb and gives completeness and meaning to the group.

The simple form of the verb without inflection is called the *root* of the verb; e. g. *love* is the root of the verb, "To Love."

Verbs are *regular* or *irregular, transitive* or *intransitive.*

A verb is said to be *regular* when it forms the past tense by

　　及物動詞是指其動作會傳給或影響某人、事、物，例如：I struck the table.（我拍打桌子。）句中 struck 的動作影響了 table 這個物品，因此它是及物動詞。**不及物動詞**的動作只與主詞有關，例如：I walk / sit / run.（我走路／坐著／奔跑。）

　　不過，許多不及物動詞也可當成及物動詞使用，例如：I walk the horse.（我溜這匹馬），這裡的 walk 就是及物動詞。

　　動詞會因「數量」、「人稱」、「時態」、「語氣」出現詞形變化。主詞的數量和人稱會影響動詞的詞形，反映出該動作是由一個或多個主詞進行，或是由發言者、聽者或被談論者進行動作。

■ 時態

　　動詞的時態依照時間的劃分方式而定。時態分為「現在式」、「過去式」和「未來式」，這三大類時態各有子分類，藉以表達事件是正在發生、已經發生或是尚未發生。

■ 語氣

　　語氣簡單分為四種類別：「不定語氣」、「直述詞氣」、「祈使語氣」、「假設語氣」。

　　動詞的語氣表示行使該動作的模式或方式。如果以最廣泛的意義使用一個動詞，沒有指定人稱、數量或時間、地點，即為**不定語氣**。例如 to run（奔跑），其中沒有告知是誰在什麼時間或地點奔跑等資訊。

adding *ed* to the present or *d* if the verb ends in e. When its past tense does not end in *ed* it is said to be *irregular*.

A *transitive* verb is one the action of which passes over to or affects some object; as "I struck the table." Here the action of striking affected the object table, hence struck is a transitive verb.

An *intransitive* verb is one in which the action remains with the subject; as "*I walk*," "*I sit*," "*I run*."

Many intransitive verbs, however, can be used transitively; thus, "I *walk* the horse;" *walk* is here transitive.

Verbs are inflected by *number, person, tense* and *mood*.

Number and *person* as applied to the verb really belong to the subject; they are used with the verb to denote whether the assertion is made regarding one or more than one and whether it is made in reference to the person speaking, the person spoken to or the person or thing spoken about.

■ TENSE

In their tenses verbs follow the divisions of time. They have *present tense, past tense* and *future tense* with their variations to express the exact time of action as to an event happening, having happened or yet to happen.

■ MOOD

There are four simple moods–the *Infinitive*, the *Indicative*, the *Imperative* and the *Subjunctive*.

The Mood of a verb denotes the mode or manner in which it is

當動詞被用來指出、宣布、提問或做任何直接陳述時，就屬於**直述詞氣**，例如：The boy loves his book.（這個男孩喜愛他的書。）是與這個男孩有關的直接陳述。Do you have a pin?（你有別針嗎？）是一個尋求答案的簡單問句。

動詞用於表達命令或請求時，屬於**祈使語氣**，例如：

Go away. 走開。

Give me a penny. 給我一便士。

動詞用來表達疑問、猜測、不確定性，或未來某個動作須視狀況而定時，屬於**假設語氣**，例如：

If I come, he will stay. 如果我來，他就會留下。

許多文法學家會加上第五種語氣，稱為「潛在語氣」，來表達能力、可能性、權利、必要性、意志或職責。這種語氣需要搭配 may、can、ought、must 等助動詞，但這些都可以拆解成直述或假設語氣。以此句為例：

I may write if I choose. 要我選的話，我也許會寫。

有人會將 may write 歸類為潛在語氣，但事實上 I may write 這個子句是直述詞氣，第二個子句 if I choose 則表示條件，以此條件來決定進行「寫」這個動作，而不是決定「要不要寫」的自由。

used. Thus if it is used in its widest sense without reference to person or number, time or place, it is in the *Infinitive* Mood; as "To run." Here we are not told who does the running, when it is done, where it is done or anything about it.

When a verb is used to indicate or declare or ask a simple question or make any direct statement, it is in the *Indicative* Mood. "The boy loves his book." Here a direct statement is made concerning the boy. "Do you have a pin?" Here a simple question is asked which calls for an answer.

When the verb is used to express a command or entreaty it is in the *Imperative* Mood as, "Go away." "Give me a penny."

When the verb is used to express doubt, supposition or uncertainty or when some future action depends upon a contingency, it is in the subjunctive mood; as, "If I come, he will remain."

Many grammarians include a fifth mood called the *potential* to express *power, possibility, liberty, necessity, will* or *duty*. It is formed by means of the auxiliaries *may, can, ought* and *must*, but in all cases it can be resolved into the indicative or subjunctive. Thus, in "I may write if I choose," "may write" is by some classified as in the potential mood, but in reality the phrase *I may write* is an indicative one while the second clause, *if I choose*, is the expression of a condition upon which, not my liberty to write, depends, but my actual writing.

動詞有兩種分詞:現在分詞(或進行式分詞),有時稱為主動分詞,以 ing 為結尾;過去分詞(或完成式分詞),常稱為被動分詞,以 ed 或 d 為結尾。

動詞用在不定語氣時,具有名詞的性質;用在分詞形式時,具有形容詞的性質,例如:

> To rise early is healthful 早起有益健康
> An early rising man 早起的人
> The newly risen sun 剛升起的太陽

以 ing 結尾的分詞經常被當成名詞使用,等於動詞的不定語氣,例如:

> To rise early is healthful. = Rising early is healthful.

動詞的主要變化形分為現在式、過去式和過去分詞,例如:

現在式	過去式	過去分詞
Love	Loved	Loved

有些動詞缺少一個或以上的變化形,這類動詞稱為不完全變化動詞。

Verbs have two participles, the present or imperfect, sometimes called the *active* ending in *ing* and the past or perfect, often called the *passive*, ending in *ed* or *d*.

The *infinitive* expresses the sense of the verb in a substantive form, the participles in an adjective form; as "To rise early is healthful." "An early rising man." "The newly risen sun."

The participle in *ing* is frequently used as a substantive and consequently is equivalent to an infinitive; thus, "To rise early is healthful" and "Rising early is healthful" are the same.

The principal parts of a verb are the Present Indicative, Past Indicative and Past Participle; as:

Love	Loved	Loved

Sometimes one or more of these parts are wanting, and then the verb is said to be defective.

現在式	過去式	過去分詞
Can	Could	（從缺）
May	Might	（從缺）
Shall	Should	（從缺）
Will	Would	（從缺）
Ought	Ought	（從缺）

　　動詞也可分為「主要動詞」和「助動詞」。一個句子或子句如果沒有主要動詞，就不具明確性或肯定性。助動詞則必須與主要動詞的原形或分詞一起使用，比起使用一般時態和語氣，它能表達出更精確的時間和語氣，例如：

> I am writing an exercise; when I have finished it, I shall read it to the class.
> 我正在寫練習題，等我寫完，就會唸給全班聽。

　　如果沒有主要動詞 writing、finished、read，句子就沒有意義，而助動詞 am、have、shall 則讓意義更加明確，在傳達時間的概念上尤其清楚。

　　助動詞又稱「輔助動詞」，共有九種，也就是：be、have、do、shall、will、may、can、ought、must。之所以稱為助動詞，是因為它能協助形成複合時態。

Present	Past	Passive Participle
Can	Could	(Wanting)
May	Might	–
Shall	Should	–
Will	Would	–
Ought	Ought	–

Verbs may also be divided into *principal* and *auxiliary*. A *principal* verb is that without which a sentence or clause can contain no assertion or affirmation. An *auxiliary* is a verb joined to the root or participles of a principal verb to express time and manner with greater precision than can be done by the tenses and moods in their simple form.

Thus, the sentence, "I am writing an exercise; when I have finished it I shall read it to the class." has no meaning without the principal verbs *writing, finished read*; but the meaning is rendered more definite, especially with regard to time, by the auxiliary verbs *am, have, shall*.

There are nine auxiliary or helping verbs, viz., *Be, have, do, shall, will, may, can, ought*, and *must*. They are called helping verbs, because it is by their aid the compound tenses are formed.

▮ Be 動詞

Be 動詞是最重要的助動詞，共有以下變化形：am、is、are、was、were、be、being、been。

▮ 語態

在動詞形式中，**主動語態**表示主詞並非接受動作的一方，而是做出動作的一方，例如：

> The cat <u>catches</u> mice. 那隻貓捕捉老鼠。
>
> Charity <u>covers</u> a multitude of sins.
> 仁慈能遮掩許多罪。

當及物動詞的動作施加在主詞身上時，也就是當動詞的主詞是接受動作的一方時，該動詞為**被動語態**，例如：

> John was loved by his neighbors.
> 約翰受到鄰居的喜愛。

句中主詞 John 同時也是受到喜愛的受詞，該動詞的動作施加在他身上，因此複合動詞 was loved 為被動語態。在及物動詞的過去分詞前面加上 be 動詞相對應的變化形，即形成被動語態。

▮ 動詞變化形

動詞變化形是根據語態、語氣、時態、人稱和數量進行的詞形變化。

▊ TO BE

The verb *To Be* is the most important of the auxiliary verbs. It has eight parts, viz., *am, is, are, was, were, be, being* and *been*.

▊ VOICE

The *active voice* is that form of the verb which shows the Subject not being acted upon but acting; as, "The cat *catches* mice." "Charity *covers* a multitude of sins."

The *passive voice*: When the action signified by a transitive verb is thrown back upon the agent, that is to say, when the subject of the verb denotes the recipient of the action, the verb is said to be in the passive voice.

"John was loved by his neighbors." Here John the subject is also the object affected by the loving, the action of the verb is thrown back on him, hence the compound verb *was loved* is said to be in the *passive voice*. The passive voice is formed by putting the perfect participle of any *transitive* verb with any of the eleven parts of the verb *To Be*.

▊ CONJUGATION

The *conjugation* of a verb is its orderly arrangement in voices, moods, tenses, persons and numbers.

以下是動詞 love 的所有變化形：

一、主動語態

● 主要變化形

現在式	過去式	過去分詞
Love	Loved	Loved

● 不定語氣

To love

● 直述詞氣

現在式

	單數	複數
第一人稱	I love	We love
第二人稱	You love	You love
第三人稱	He loves	They love

Here is the complete conjugation of the verb "Love."

Active Voice

● PRINCIPAL PARTS

Present	Past	Past Participle
Love	Loved	Loved

● Infinitive Mood

To love

● Indicative Mood

PRESENT TENSE

	Sing.	Plural
1st person	I love	We love
2nd person	You love	You love
3rd person	He loves	They love

過去式

	單數	複數
第一人稱	I loved	We loved
第二人稱	You loved	You loved
第三人稱	He loved	They loved

未來式

	單數	複數
第一人稱	I will love	We will love
第二人稱	You will love	You will love
第三人稱	He will love	They will love

現在完成式

	單數	複數
第一人稱	I have loved	We have loved
第二人稱	You have loved	You have loved
第三人稱	He has loved	They have loved

PAST TENSE

	Sing.	Plural
1st person	I loved	We loved
2nd person	You loved	You loved
3rd person	He loved	They loved

FUTURE TENSE

	Sing.	Plural
1st person	I will love	We will love
2nd person	You will love	You will love
3rd person	He will love	They will love

PRESENT PERFECT TENSE

	Sing.	Plural
1st person	I have loved	We have loved
2nd person	You have loved	You have loved
3rd person	He has loved	They have loved

過去完成式

	單數	複數
第一人稱	I had loved	We had loved
第二人稱	You had loved	You had loved
第三人稱	He had loved	They had loved

未來完成式

	單數	複數
第一人稱	I will have loved	We will have loved
第二人稱	You will have loved	You will have loved
第三人稱	He will have loved	They will have loved

● 祈使語氣（限用現在式）

	單數	複數
第二人稱	Love (you)	Love (you)

PAST PERFECT TENSE

	Sing.	Plural
1st person	I had loved	We had loved
2nd person	You had loved	You had loved
3rd person	He had loved	They had loved

FUTURE PERFECT TENSE

	Sing.	Plural
1st person	I will have loved	We will have loved
2nd person	You will have loved	You will have loved
3rd person	He will have loved	They will have loved

● Imperative Mood (PRESENT TENSE ONLY)

	Sing.	Plural
2nd person	Love (you)	Love (you)

● 假設語氣

現在式

	單數	複數
第一人稱	If I love	If we love
第二人稱	If you love	If you love
第三人稱	If he loves	If they love

過去式

	單數	複數
第一人稱	If I loved	If we loved
第二人稱	If you loved	If you loved
第三人稱	If he loved	If they loved

現在完成式

	單數	複數
第一人稱	If I have loved	If we have loved
第二人稱	If you have loved	If you have loved
第三人稱	If he has loved	If they have loved

● Subjunctive Mood

PRESENT TENSE

	Sing.	Plural
1st person	If I love	If we love
2nd person	If you love	If you love
3rd person	If he loves	If they love

PAST TENSE

	Sing.	Plural
1st person	If I loved	If we loved
2nd person	If you loved	If you loved
3rd person	If he loved	If they loved

PRESENT PERFECT TENSE

	Sing.	Plural
1st person	If I have loved	If we have loved
2nd person	If you have loved	If you have loved
3rd person	If he has loved	If they have loved

過去完成式

	單數	複數
第一人稱	If I had loved	If we had loved
第二人稱	If you had loved	If you had loved
第三人稱	If he had loved	If they had loved

● 不定語氣

現在式	完成式
to love	to have loved

● 分詞

現在分詞	過去分詞	完成式分詞
Loving	Loved	Having loved

PAST PERFECT TENSE

	Sing.	Plural
1st person	If I had loved	If we had loved
2nd person	If you had loved	If you had loved
3rd person	If he had loved	If they had loved

● INFINITIVES

Present	Perfect
to love	to have loved

● PARTICIPLES

Present	Past	Perfect
Loving	Loved	Having loved

二、被動語態

● 直述詞氣

現在式

	單數	複數
第一人稱	I am loved	We are loved
第二人稱	You are loved	You are loved
第三人稱	He is loved	They are loved

過去式

	單數	複數
第一人稱	I was loved	We were loved
第二人稱	You were loved	You were loved
第三人稱	He was loved	They were loved

未來式

	單數	複數
第一人稱	I will be loved	We will be loved
第二人稱	You will be loved	You will be loved
第三人稱	He will be loved	They will be loved

Passive Voice

● Indicative Mood

PRESENT TENSE

	Sing.	Plural
1st person	I am loved	We are loved
2nd person	You are loved	You are loved
3rd person	He is loved	They are loved

PAST TENSE

	Sing.	Plural
1st person	I was loved	We were loved
2nd person	You were loved	You were loved
3rd person	He was loved	They were loved

FUTURE TENSE

	Sing.	Plural
1st person	I will be loved	We will be loved
2nd person	You will be loved	You will be loved
3rd person	He will be loved	They will be loved

現在完成式

	單數	複數
第一人稱	I have been loved	We have been loved
第二人稱	You have been loved	You have been loved
第三人稱	He has been loved	They have been loved

過去完成式

	單數	複數
第一人稱	I had been loved	We had been loved
第二人稱	You had been loved	You had been loved
第三人稱	He had been loved	They had been loved

PRESENT PERFECT TENSE

	Sing.	Plural
1st person	I have been loved	We have been loved
2nd person	You have been loved	You have been loved
3rd person	He has been loved	They have been loved

PAST PERFECT TENSE

	Sing.	Plural
1st person	I had been loved	We had been loved
2nd person	You had been loved	You had been loved
3rd person	He had been loved	They had been loved

未來完成式

	單數	複數
第一人稱	I will have been loved	We will have been loved
第二人稱	You will have been loved	You will have been loved
第三人稱	He will have been loved	They will have been loved

● 祈使語氣（限用現在式）

	單數	複數
第二人稱	Be loved	Be loved

● 假設語氣

現在式

	單數	複數
第一人稱	If I am loved	If we are loved
第二人稱	If you are loved	If you are loved
第三人稱	If he is loved	If they are loved

FUTURE PERFECT TENSE

	Sing.	Plural
1st person	I will have been loved	We will have been loved
2nd person	You will have been loved	You will have been loved
3rd person	He will have been loved	They will have been loved

● Imperative Mood (PRESENT TENSE ONLY)

	Sing.	Plural
2nd person	Be loved	Be loved

● Subjunctive Mood

PRESENT TENSE

	Sing.	Plural
1st person	If I am loved	If we are loved
2nd person	If you are loved	If you are loved
3rd person	If he is loved	If they are loved

過去式

	單數	複數
第一人稱	If I were loved	If they were loved
第二人稱	If you were loved	If you were loved
第三人稱	If he was loved	If they were loved

現在完成式

	單數	複數
第一人稱	If I have been loved	If we have been loved
第二人稱	If you have been loved	If you have been loved
第三人稱	If he has been loved	If they have been loved

過去完成式

	單數	複數
第一人稱	If I had been loved	If we had been loved
第二人稱	If you had been loved	If you had been loved
第三人稱	If he had been loved	If they had been loved

PAST TENSE

	Sing.	Plural
1st person	If I were loved	If they were loved
2nd person	If you were loved	If you were loved
3rd person	If he was loved	If they were loved

PRESENT PERFECT TENSE

	Sing.	Plural
1st person	If I have been loved	If we have been loved
2nd person	If you have been loved	If you have been loved
3rd person	If he has been loved	If they have been loved

PAST PERFECT TENSE

	Sing.	Plural
1st person	If I had been loved	If we had been loved
2nd person	If you had been loved	If you had been loved
3rd person	If he had been loved	If they had been loved

● 不定語氣

現在簡單式	現在完成式
to be loved	to have been loved

● 分詞

現在分詞	過去分詞	完成式分詞
Being loved	Been loved	Having been loved

請注意：以上第三人稱單數以 he 代表 he、she 和 it 的動詞變化。

副詞 副詞是修飾動詞、形容詞和其他副詞的字，例如：

He writes <u>well</u>. 他寫得很好。

句中的副詞 well 表示寫作的方式。另外，在以下例句中：

He is <u>remarkably</u> diligent. 他相當勤奮。
He works <u>very</u> faithfully. 他非常忠誠地工作。

● INFINITIVES

Present	Perfect
to be loved	to have been loved

● PARTICIPLES

Present	Past	Perfect
Being loved	Been loved	Having been loved

(N. B.– In the third person singular he is representative of the three personal pronouns of the third person, *He*, *She* and *It*.)

ADVERB

An *adverb* is a word which modifies a verb, an adjective or another adverb. Thus, in the example–"He writes *well*," the adverb shows the manner in which the writing is performed; in the examples–"He is remarkably diligent" and "He works very faithfully," the adverbs modify the adjective *diligent* and the other adverb *faithfully* by expressing the degree of diligence and faithfulness.

副詞 remarkably 修飾形容詞 diligent，very 則修飾另一個副詞 faithfully，藉以表達勤奮和忠誠的程度。

副詞主要是以一個字取代原本要用兩個以上的字描述的情況，例如：there 取代 in that place（在那個地方）；whence 取代 from what place（從什麼地方）；usefully 取代 in a useful manner（以有用的方式）。

副詞跟形容詞一樣，有時字尾會出現變化，藉以表示比較和不同程度的特質。

有些副詞在字尾加上 er 或 est，即可形成比較級或最高級，例如：soon、sooner、soonest（快地、更快地、最快地）。字尾是 ly 的副詞，則在前面加上 more 或 most 來比較，例如：nobly、more nobly、most nobly（高貴地、更高貴地、最高貴地）。

少數副詞的比較級和最高級形態是不規則的，例如：well、better、best（好地、更好地、最好地）。

介系詞 介系詞用於連接單字、子句和句子，以顯示這些元素之間的關係，例如：My hand is <u>on</u> the table.（我的手放在桌上。）句中的 on 顯示 hand 和 table 之間的關係。

介系詞又叫「前置詞」，之所以稱為「前置」，是因為它通常放在其他字前面，藉以指出這個字與另一個字之間的關聯。

Adverbs are chiefly used to express in one word what would otherwise require two or more words; thus, *There* signifies in that place; *whence*, from what place; *usefully*, in a useful manner.

Adverbs, like adjectives, are sometimes varied in their terminations to express comparison and different degrees of quality.

Some adverbs form the comparative and superlative by adding *er* and *est*; as, *soon, sooner, soonest*.

Adverbs which end in *ly* are compared by prefixing *more* and *most*; as, *nobly, more nobly, most nobly*.

A few adverbs are irregular in the formation of the comparative and superlative; *as, well, better, best*.

PREPOSITION

A *preposition* connects words, clauses, and sentences together and shows the relation between them. "My hand is on the table" shows relation between hand and table.

Prepositions are so called because they are generally placed *before* the words whose connection or relation with other words they point out.

連接詞 連接詞用於連結單字、子句和句子，例如：

> John <u>and</u> James 約翰和詹姆士
>
> My father <u>and</u> mother have come, <u>but</u> I have not seen them. 我父母已經來了，但我沒看見他們。

最常使用的連接詞為 and、also、either、or、neither、nor、though、yet、but、however、for、that、because、since、therefore、then、if、useless、lest。

感嘆詞 感嘆詞是表達突發情緒的單字，例如：

> <u>Ah</u>! There he comes. 啊！他來了。
>
> <u>Alas</u>! What shall I do? 哎呀！我該怎麼辦？

句中的 ah 表達驚訝，alas 則表達苦惱。

以驚嘆語氣表達時，名詞、形容詞、動詞和副詞也可當感嘆詞使用，例如：

> Nonsense! 胡說！
>
> Strange! 真奇怪！

目前已經列出所有詞類，並盡量簡短地描述每個詞類的功能。這些詞類同屬一個語族，彼此互有關係，不過緊密程度不

CONJUNCTION

A *conjunction* joins words, clauses and sentences; as "John *and* James." "My father and mother have come, *but* I have not seen them."

The conjunctions in most general use are *and, also; either, or; neither, nor; though, yet; but, however; for, that; because, since; therefore, then; if, unless, lest.*

INTERJECTION

An *interjection* is a word used to express some sudden emotion of the mind. Thus in the examples,–"Ah! there he comes; alas! what shall I do?" *ah*, expresses surprise, and *alas*, distress.

Nouns, adjectives, verbs and adverbs become interjections when they are uttered as exclamations, as, *nonsense! strange!* etc.

We have now enumerated the parts of speech and as briefly as possible stated the functions of each. As they all belong to the same family they are related to one another but some are in closer affinity than others. To point out the exact relationship and the dependency of one word on another is called *parsing* and in order that every etymological connection may be distinctly understood a brief resume of the foregoing essentials is here given:

The signification of the noun is *limited* to *one*, but to any *one* of the kind, by the *indefinite* article, and to some *particular* one, or some particular *number*, by the *definite* article.

一。說明某個字和另一個字之間的確切關係和依賴程度的研究，稱為「語法分析」。為了讓讀者清楚了解所有字源上的關係，以下針對前面的介紹進行重點整理：

名詞前面加上不定冠詞時，指任何一個人、事、物；若前面加上定冠詞，則指某個或某些特定人、事、物。

單數名詞代表一個人、事、物，複數名詞代表多於一的任何數量。名詞是雄性、雌性，或沒有性別之分的事物名稱。名詞代表肯定句、命令句或疑問句的主詞、事物的擁有者或持有者、動作的受詞，或是介系詞所表達的一段關係。

形容詞表達某個人、事、物具有區別性的特質。原級形容詞表達不具比較性的特質；比較級形容詞為一對一或個體對群體之間的比較；最高級形容詞為一個個體跟多個個體之間的比較。

代名詞用於代替名詞。人稱代名詞單純用於取代名詞；關係代名詞取代句子中的先行詞，並對先行詞具有特殊的指稱關係；形容代名詞是以形容詞的方式指稱其所代表的人、事、物。有些代名詞兼具名詞的功能，其中幾個是經常用於問句的疑問詞。

動詞可用來表達肯定和命令。不同的動詞變化形表達數量、人稱、時態和方式。在時態方面，肯定句分為現在式、過去式和未來式。以方式來說，肯定句分為直述詞氣（不確定條件是否已被滿足）、假設語氣（暗示條件未被滿足）、祈使語氣（表達命令或懇求）、或不定語氣（沒有肯定或命令的情況）。動詞也可用現在分詞或過去分詞，來表達行動、狀態正在進行或已經完成，現在分詞有時可以當作名詞使用，過去分詞有時可以當作形

Nouns, in one form, represent *one* of a kind, and in another, *any number* more than one; they are the *names of males*, or *females*, or of objects which are neither male nor female; and they represent the *subject* of an affirmation, a command or a question, the *owner* or *possessor* of a thing, or the *object* of an action, or of a relation expressed by a preposition.

Adjectives express the *qualities* which distinguish one person or thing from another; in one form they express quality *without* comparison; in another, they express comparison *between two*, or *between one* and a number taken collectively and in a third they express comparison between *one* and a *number* of others taken separately.

Pronouns are used in place of nouns; one class of them is used merely as the *substitutes* of *names*; the pronouns of another class have a peculiar *reference* to some *preceding* words in the *sentence*, of which they are the substitutes, and those of a third class refer adjectively to the persons or things they represent. Some pronouns are used for both the *name* and the *substitute*; and several are frequently employed in *asking questions*.

Affirmations and *commands* are expressed by the verb; and different inflections of the verb express *number, person, time* and *manner*. With regard to *time*, an affirmation may be *present* or *past* or *future*; with regard to manner, an affirmation may be *positive* or *conditional*, it being doubtful whether the condition is fulfilled or not, or it being implied that it is not fulfilled; the verb may express

容詞使用。

副詞用於修飾肯定句，有些副詞可以經由詞形變化，表示不同程度的修飾。

連接詞連結不同字詞；**介系詞**表達某個人、事、物與另一個人、事、物之間的關係；**感嘆詞**表達突發的情緒或驚訝。

有些單字因字義不同，有時屬於某個詞類，有時則屬於另一個詞類。例如：

> After a storm comes a calm. 暴風之後一片寧靜。

這裡的 calm 是名詞。

> It is a calm evening. 這是一個寧靜的夜晚。

這裡的 calm 是形容詞。

> Calm your fears. 平息你的恐懼。

這裡的 calm 是動詞。

以下用一個包含所有詞類的句子，進行語源分析：

> I now see the old man coming, but, alas, he has walked with much difficulty.
> 我看到那個老人走了過來，不過，哎呀，他的步履艱難。

command or *entreaty*; or the sense of the verb may be expressed *without affirming* or *commanding*. The verb also expresses that an action or state *is* or *was* going on, by a form which is also used sometimes as a noun, and sometimes to qualify nouns.

Affirmations are *modified* by *adverbs*, some of which can be inflected to express different degrees of modification.

Words are joined together by *conjunctions*; and the various *relations* which one thing bears to another are expressed by *prepositions. Sudden emotions* of the mind, and *exclamations* are expressed by *interjections.*

Some words according to meaning belong sometimes to one part of speech, sometimes to another. Thus, in "After a storm comes a *calm*," *calm* is a noun; in "It is a *calm* evening," *calm* is an adjective; and in "*Calm* your fears," *calm* is a verb.

The following sentence containing all the parts of speech is parsed etymologically:

"I now see the old man coming, but, alas, he has walked with much difficulty."

I, a personal pronoun, first person singular, masculine or feminine gender, nominative case, subject of the verb *see*.

now, an adverb of time modifying the verb *see*.

see, an irregular, transitive verb, indicative mood, present tense,

- I 是人稱代名詞，屬於第一人稱單數，代表男性或女性，屬於主格，是動詞 see 的主詞。
- now 是修飾動詞 see 的時間副詞。
- see 是不規則及物動詞，屬於直述詞氣，現在式，呼應 I 這個主格兼主詞，使用第一人稱單數形。
- the 是定冠詞，用來限定名詞 man。
- old 是原級形容詞，用來修飾名詞 man。
- man 是普通名詞，屬於第三人稱單數，代表男性，受到動詞 see 影響的受格。
- coming 是動詞 to come 的現在分詞（或進行式分詞），用來指涉名詞 man。
- but 是連接詞。
- alas 是感嘆詞，表達同情或悲傷。
- he 是人稱代名詞，屬於第三人稱單數，代表男性，屬於主格，是動詞 has walked 的主詞。
- has walked 是規則及物動詞，屬於直述詞氣，完成式，呼應 he 這個主格兼主詞，使用第三人稱單數形。
- with 是受到名詞 difficulty 影響的介系詞。
- much 是原級形容詞，修飾名詞 difficulty。
- difficulty 是普通名詞，屬於第三人稱單數，代表中性，是受到介系詞 with 影響的受格。

注意：much 一般來說是副詞，作為形容詞時的比較等級為：

原級	比較級	最高級
much	more	most

first person singular to agree with its nominative or subject *I*.

the, the definite article particularizing the noun man.

old, an adjective, positive degree, qualifying the noun man.

man, a common noun, 3rd person singular, masculine gender, objective case governed by the transitive verb *see*.

coming, the present or imperfect participle of the verb "to come" referring to the noun man.

but, a conjunction.

alas, an interjection, expressing pity or sorrow.

he, a personal pronoun, 3rd person singular, masculine gender, nominative case, subject of verb has walked.

has walked, a regular, intransitive verb, indicative mood, perfect tense, 3rd person singular to agree with its nominative or subject *he*.

with, a preposition, governing the noun difficulty.

much, an adjective, positive degree, qualifying the noun difficulty.

difficulty, a common noun, 3rd person singular, neuter gender, objective case governed by the preposition *with*.

N.B. *Much* is generally an adverb. As an adjective it is thus compared:

Positive	Comparative	Superlative
much	more	most

第三章
句子

The Sentence

句子由一組單字集結而成，排列為能夠傳達確切意義或意涵的組合，也就是說，句子能夠表達完整的思想或概念。無論句子多短，都必須包含一個限定動詞和一個引導該動詞的主詞或主體。

　　Birds fly（鳥兒飛翔）、Fish swim（魚兒悠游）、Men walk（人類行走），這些都是句子。

　　一個句子必定包含兩個部分：句子所描述的對象，以及對這個對象的描述。代表這個對象的字詞稱為「主詞」，用來描述該對象的字詞稱為「述詞」。在上述例句中，birds、fish、men 是主詞，fly、swim、walk 是述詞。

　　句子分為「單句」、「合句」、「複句」三類。

　　單句表達單一思想，由一個主詞和一個述詞組成，例如：Man is mortal（人是血肉之軀）。

　　合句由兩個以上具有相同重要性的單句組成，句中每個部分能獨立表達意思或受到理解，例如：

The men work in the fields, and the women work in the household.
男人在田裡幹活，女人在家裡工作。

也可寫成：

The men work in the fields, and the women in the household.

A sentence is an assemblage of words so arranged as to convey a determinate sense or meaning, in other words, to express a complete thought or idea. No matter how short, it must contain one finite verb and a subject or agent to direct the action of the verb.

"Birds fly;" "Fish swim;" "Men walk;" are sentences.

A sentence always contains two parts, something spoken about and something said about it. The word or words indicating what is spoken about form what is called the *subject* and the word or words indicating what is said about it form what is called the *predicate*.

In the sentences given, *birds, fish* and *men* are the subjects, while *fly, swim* and *walk* are the predicates.

There are three kinds of sentences, *simple, compound* and *complex*.

The *simple sentence* expresses a single thought and consists of one subject and one predicate, as, "Man is mortal."

A *compound sentence* consists of two or more simple sentences of equal importance the parts of which are either expressed or understood, as, "The men work in the fields and the women work in the household," or "The men work in the fields and the women in the household" or "The men and women work in the fields and in the household."

或者寫成：

The men and women work in the fields and in the household.

複句由兩個以上的單句組成，其中一個單句依賴另一個單句，以形成完整的意義，例如：

When he returns, I shall go on my vacation.
等他回來，我就要去度假了。

這裡的 when he returns 要仰賴另一個單句才有意義。

子句是複句中一個個別的部分，例如上一個例句中的 when he returns。

片語由兩個以上的單字組成，但不含限定動詞。沒有限定動詞，就無法肯定任何事情或傳遞概念，也就不構成句子。

不定語氣的動詞或沒有限定的分詞不能當成述詞。例如 I looking up the street 不是句子，因為沒有表達完整的動作。聽到 The dog running along the street 這樣的詞語時，我們會期待後面還會加上更多東西，以更明確地描述這隻狗，例如：

A *complex sentence* consists of two or more simple sentences so combined that one depends on the other to complete its meaning; as; "When he returns, I shall go on my vacation." Here the words, "when he returns" are dependent on the rest of the sentence for their meaning.

A *clause* is a separate part of a complex sentence, as "when he returns" in the last example.

A *phrase* consists of two or more words without a finite verb.

Without a finite verb we cannot affirm anything or convey an idea, therefore we can have no sentence.

Infinitives and participles which are the infinite parts of the verb cannot be predicates. "I looking up the street" is not a sentence, for it is not a complete action expressed.

The dog running along the street <u>bit</u>.
那隻沿街奔跑的狗會咬人。

The dog running along the street <u>barked</u>.
那隻沿街奔跑的狗吠叫。

The dog running along the street <u>fell dead</u>.
那隻沿街奔跑的狗倒地死亡。

The dog running along the street <u>was run over</u>.
那隻沿街奔跑的狗被輾過。

因此，每個句子一定要有一個限定動詞來限定主詞。

遇到及物動詞時，也就是當該動作發生會影響某個人、事、物時，受影響者稱為「受詞」，例如：Cain killed Abel.（該隱殺了亞伯），殺的動作影響了亞伯；The cat has caught a mouse.（這隻貓抓到了一隻老鼠），老鼠是「抓」這個動作的受詞。

句子中的單字排列

在單句中，單字的自然排列方式當然是**主詞→動詞→受詞**，在多數情況下沒有其他排列方式。以 The cat has caught a mouse 為例，我們不能寫成 The mouse has caught a cat，這樣一來意思就變了。另外一種排列方式是 A mouse, the cat has caught，這樣雖然看得懂，卻給人一種表達力欠佳、不太通順的感覺。

然而在長句中，除了主詞、動詞、受詞之外還有很多其他的

When we hear such an expression as "A dog running along the street," we wait for something more to be added, something more affirmed about the dog, whether he bit or barked or fell dead or was run over.

Thus in every sentence there must be a finite verb to limit the subject.

When the verb is transitive, that is, when the action cannot happen without affecting something, the thing affected is called the *object*. Thus in "Cain killed Abel" the action of the killing affected Abel. In "The cat has caught a mouse," mouse is the object of the catching.

ARRANGEMENT OF WORDS IN A SENTENCE

Of course in simple sentences the natural order of arrangement is subject–verb–object. In many cases no other form is possible. Thus in the sentence "The cat has caught a mouse," we cannot reverse it and say "The mouse has caught a cat" without destroying the meaning, and in any other form of arrangement, such as "A mouse, the cat has caught," we feel that while it is intelligible, it is a poor way of expressing the fact and one which jars upon us more or less.

字,這讓我們有更大的自由可做各種不同排列,以傳達最好的效果。這時要以簡明和精確為原則,進行適當的單字排列,並賦予句子結構特定的「文風」。

大多數人都很熟悉英國詩人湯瑪士・格雷（Thomas Gray）的不朽名作〈墓園輓歌〉中的這行詩句:

The ploughman homeward plods his weary way.
返家的農人步履蹣跚而沉重。

這句話有十八種不同的寫法,以下列舉其中幾種變化:

- Homeward the ploughman plods his weary way.
- The ploughman plods his weary way homeward.
- Plods homeward the ploughman his weary way.
- His weary way the ploughman homeward plods.
- Homeward his weary way plods the ploughman.
- Plods the ploughman his weary way homeward.
- His weary way the ploughman plods homeward.
- His wear way homeward the ploughman plods.
- The ploughman plods homeward his weary way.
- The ploughman his weary way plods homeward.

應該沒有其他排列方式會比這位詩人用的句子出色。當然,他是按照詩詞節奏和韻腳排列單字,上述變化方式則大多根據想要強調的字進行排列。

In longer sentences, however, when there are more words than what are barely necessary for subject, verb and object, we have greater freedom of arrangement and can so place the words as to give the best effect. The proper placing of words depends upon perspicuity and precision. These two combined give *style* to the structure.

Most people are familiar with Gray's line in the immortal *Elegy*–"The ploughman homeward plods his weary way." This line can be paraphrased to read 18 different ways. Here are a few variations:

Homeward the ploughman plods his weary way.
The ploughman plods his weary way homeward.
Plods homeward the ploughman his weary way.
His weary way the ploughman homeward plods.
Homeward his weary way plods the ploughman.
Plods the ploughman his weary way homeward.
His weary way the ploughman plods homeward.
His weary way homeward the ploughman plods.
The ploughman plods homeward his weary way.
The ploughman his weary way plods homeward.

and so on.

It is doubtful if any of the other forms are superior to the one used by the poet. Of course his arrangement was made to comply with the rhythm and rhyme of the verse. Most of the variations depend upon the emphasis we wish to place upon the different words.

在排列一般句子中的字詞時，不要忘了**句首**和**句尾**是吸引讀者注意力的重要位置。這兩個位置的單字比其他位置的單字更受到強調。

格雷的詩句所傳達的大意是一位疲憊的農人踏著沉重的步伐回家，但他的排列方式讓這個概念有了非常細微的差異。前述的各種變化方式中，有些讓人比較注意農人，有的強調踏著沉重步伐，有的則著重疲憊感。

既然句首和句尾是最重要的位置，自然要避免將無足輕重的字詞放在這兩個地方。在這兩個位置中，又以句尾更為重要，因此要放句中最重要的單字。千萬不要用 and、but、since、because 這類薄弱的單字作為句子的開頭，也不要以介系詞、薄弱的副詞或代名詞作為句子的結尾。

句中意思緊密相關的字詞應該放得近一點。忽略這個法則所造出的句子，雖然不至於讓人看不懂，卻顯得荒唐可笑。例如：

> Ten dollars reward is offered for information of any person injuring this property by order of the owner.

Ten dollars reward is offered 和 by order of the owner 應該放在一起，才是「主人下令提供十美元的懸賞，給通報破壞莊園者的消息的人」，原本的排列讓人誤以為破壞莊園是主人下的命令。

In arranging the words in an ordinary sentence we should not lose sight of the fact that the beginning and end are the important places for catching the attention of the reader. Words in these places have greater emphasis than elsewhere.

In Gray's line the general meaning conveyed is that a weary ploughman is plodding his way homeward, but according to the arrangement a very slight difference is effected in the idea. Some of the variations make us think more of the ploughman, others more of the plodding, and still others more of the weariness.

As the beginning and end of a sentence are the most important places, it naturally follows that small or insignificant words should be kept from these positions. Of the two places the end one is the more important, therefore, it really calls for the most important word in the sentence. Never commence a sentence with *And, But, Since, Because,* and other similar weak words and never end it with prepositions, small, weak adverbs or pronouns.

The parts of a sentence which are most closely connected with one another in meaning should be closely connected in order also. By ignoring this principle many sentences are made, if not nonsensical, really ridiculous and ludicrous. For instance: "Ten dollars reward is offered for information of any person injuring this property by order of the owner."

<u>This monument was erected</u> to the memory of John Jones, who was shot <u>by his affectionate brother</u>.

This monument was erected 和 by his affectionate 應該放在一起，才是「這座紀念碑是他情深義重的兄弟立的，以紀念被射殺的約翰‧瓊斯」，原本的排列易讓人誤以為約翰‧瓊斯是被他情深義重的兄弟所射殺。

在建構句子時，必須嚴格遵守文法規則。務必遵守一致性法則，也就是特定單字之間的一致性。

規則 1　動詞和主詞的人稱和單複數要一致，例如：I have、You have、He has，這些例子顯示動詞變化與主詞一致。單數主詞需要使用單數動詞，而複數主詞要使用複數動詞，如：

The boy writes. 這個男孩寫字。
The boys write. 這些男孩寫字。

動詞和主詞之間的一致性，容易因為下列情況混淆：

■ 集合名詞和一般名詞

集合名詞是一組被視為整體的人、事、物，例如 class（班級）、regiment（軍團）。強調整體中的個人或事物時用複數動詞，例如：

"This monument was erected to the memory of John Jones, who was shot by his affectionate brother."

In the construction of all sentences the grammatical rules must be inviolably observed. The laws of concord, that is, the agreement of certain words, must be obeyed.

1. The verb agrees with its subject in person and number.

"I have," "He has," show the variation of the verb to agree with the subject. A singular subject calls for a singular verb, a plural subject demands a verb in the plural; as, "The boy writes," "The boys write."

The agreement of a verb and its subject is often destroyed by confusing (1) collective and common nouns; (2) foreign and English nouns; (3) compound and simple subjects; (4) real and apparent subjects.

(1) A collective noun is a number of individuals or things regarded as a whole; as, *class, regiment.* When the individuals or things are prominently brought forward, use a plural verb; as The class *were* distinguished for ability. When the idea of the whole as a

> The class <u>were</u> distinguished for ability.
> 這個班上的學生能力傑出。

強調整體時用單數動詞，例如：

> The regiment <u>was</u> in camp.
> 這個軍團駐紮在營地。

■ 外來名詞和英文名詞

一般人有時很難分辨外來名詞的單複數，因此必須慎選動詞形式，這時應該查閱字典上的用法，例如：

> He was an <u>alumnus</u> of Harvard. 他是哈佛校友。
> They were <u>alumni</u> of Harvard. 他們是哈佛校友。

■ 複合主詞和單一主詞

當句子中有一個動詞，而主詞是兩個以上不同事物、以 and 相連時，用複數動詞，例如：

> Snow and rain <u>are</u> disagreeable. 雪和雨令人厭煩。

當主詞代表兩個以上相同事物、以 or 相連時，用單數動詞，例如：

> The man or the woman <u>is</u> to blame.
> 要怪這個男人或這個女人。

unit is under consideration employ a singular verb; as The regiment *was* in camp.

(2) It is sometimes hard for the ordinary individual to distinguish the plural from the singular in foreign nouns, therefore, he should be careful in the selection of the verb. He should look up the word and be guided accordingly. "He was an *alumnus* of Harvard." "They were *alumni* of Harvard."

(3) When a sentence with one verb has two or more subjects denoting different things, connected by *and*, the verb should be plural; as, "Snow and rain *are* disagreeable." When the subjects denote the same thing and are connected by *or* the verb should be singular; as, "The man or the woman is to blame."

■ 實際主詞和表象主詞

同一個動詞對上多個代表不同人稱或數量的主詞時，動詞要跟語意上最受到突顯的主詞一致，例如：

> He, and not you, <u>is</u> wrong. 錯的是他不是你。
>
> Whether he or I <u>am</u> to be blamed. 要怪他或我。

規則 2 千萬別把過去分詞和過去式混淆使用。這種錯誤相當常見，例如：

> （×）He done it.
> （○）He did it. 他做到了。
> （×）The jar was broke.
> （○）The jar was broken. 這只罐子破了。
> （×）He would have went.
> （○）He would have gone. 他本來會去的。

規則 3 要特別仔細區別主格和受格。在所有單字中，只有代名詞保有受詞原有的獨特格位字尾。記住受格會跟在及物動詞和介系詞後面，例如：

> （×）The boy who I sent to see you
> （○）The boy whom I sent to see you
>   我派去見你的那個男孩

這裡的 whom 是及物動詞 sent 的受格。

(4) When the same verb has more than one subject of different persons or numbers, it agrees with the most prominent in thought; as, "He, and not you, *is* wrong." "Whether he or I *am* to be blamed."

2. Never use the past participle for the past tense nor *vice versa*.

This mistake is a very common one. At every turn we hear "He done it" for "He did it." "The jar was broke" instead of broken. "He would have went" for "He would have gone," etc.

3. Take special care to distinguish between the nominative and objective case. The pronouns are the only words which retain the ancient distinctive case ending for the objective.

Remember that the objective case follows transitive verbs and prepositions. Don't say "The boy who I sent to see you," but "The boy whom I sent to see you." *Whom* is here the object of the transitive verb sent. Don't say "She bowed to him and I" but "She bowed to

（×）She bowed to him and I.
（○）She bowed to him and me. 她向他和我鞠躬。

這裡的 me 是跟在介系詞 to 後面的受格。

Between you and I 是常見說法，不過正確說法是 between you and me，因為 between 是介系詞，因此要用受格。

規則 4 小心使用關係代名詞 who、which 和 that。who 只能用於人，which 只能用於事物，例如：

The boy <u>who</u> was drowned 淹死的那個男孩
The umbrella <u>which</u> I lost 我弄丟的那把傘

that 可以用於人、事、物，例如：

The man <u>that</u> I saw 我看到的那個男人
The hat <u>that</u> I bought 我買的那頂帽子

規則 5 不要將最高級用於比較級，例如：

（×）He is the richest of the two.
（○）He is the richer of the two.
他是兩人中比較富有的那個。

him and me" since me is the objective case following the preposition *to* understood. "Between you and I" is a very common expression. It should be "Between you and me" since *between* is a preposition calling for the objective case.

---

4. Be careful in the use of the relative pronouns *who, which* and *that*.

Who refers only to persons; which only to things; as, "The boy who was drowned," "The umbrella which I lost." The relative *that* may refer to both persons and things; as, "The man *that* I saw." "The hat *that* I bought."

---

5. Don't use the superlative degree of the adjective for the comparative;

---

as "He is the richest of the two" for "He is the richer of the two."

其他常見的錯誤包括：

一、使用雙重比較級或最高級，例如：

（×）These apples are much <u>more</u> preferable.
這些蘋果更好。

（×）The <u>most</u> universal motive to business is gain.
做生意最共通的動機是為了賺錢。

preferable 是本身就具有比較意味的字，而 universal 本身就具有最高級意味。

二、比較分屬不同類別的事物，例如：

（×）There is no nicer <u>life</u> than a <u>teacher</u>.
沒有比老師更好的人生。

三、將某個事物放入非其所屬的類別，例如：

（×）The fairest of her daughters, Eve.
她的女兒中最美麗的，夏娃。

四、將某個對象排除在其歸屬的類別之外，例如：

（×）Caesar was braver than any ancient warrior.
凱薩比任何古代戰士都更英勇。

Other mistakes often made in this connection are:

(1) Using the double comparative and superlative; as, "These apples are much *more* preferable." "The most universal motive to business is gain."

(2) Comparing objects which belong to dissimilar classes; as "There is no nicer *life* than a *teacher*."

(3) Including objects in class to which they do not belong; as, "The fairest of her daughters, Eve."

(4) Excluding an object from a class to which it does belong; as, "Caesar was braver than any ancient warrior."

規則 6 別把形容詞和副詞混淆使用，例如：

（×）He acted <u>nice</u> towards me.
（○）He acted <u>nicely</u> towards me. 他對我很好。

（×）She looked <u>beautifully</u>.
（○）She looked <u>beautiful</u>. 她看起來很美。

規則 7 副詞儘量放得離其修飾的字詞近一點，例如：

He <u>walked</u> to the door <u>quickly</u>.
他快速走到那扇門。

寫成以下方式較佳：

He <u>walked</u> <u>quickly</u> to the door.

規則 8 除了要小心區別代名詞的主格和受格之外，使用上也
要避免模稜兩可的狀況。

　　在下面這段對話中，美國喜劇演員比利・威廉斯（Billy
Williams）向朋友波頓描述自己騎一匹屬於經紀人漢伯林的馬的
經歷，內容相當貼切地呈現忽略代名詞的指稱用法時，會鬧出什
麼樣的笑話。

6. Don't use an adjective for an adverb or an adverb for an adjective.

Don't say, "He acted *nice* towards me" but "He acted *nicely* toward me," and instead of saying "She looked *beautifully*" say "She looked *beautiful*."

7. Place the adverb as near as possible to the word it modifies.

Instead of saying, "He walked to the door quickly," say "He walked quickly to the door."

8. Not alone be careful to distinguish between the nominative and objective cases of the pronouns, but try to avoid ambiguity in their use.

The amusing effect of disregarding the reference of pronouns is well illustrated by Burton in the following story of Billy Williams, a comic actor who thus narrates his experience in riding a horse owned by Hamblin, the manager:

So down I goes to the stable with Tom Flynn, and told the man to put the saddle on him.

On Tom Flynn?

No, on the horse. So after talking with Tom Flynn awhile I mounted him.

What! mounted Tom Flynn?

No, the horse; and then I shook hands with him and rode off.

Shook hands with the horse, Billy?

No, with Tom Flynn; and then I rode off up the Bowery, and who should I meet but Tom Hamblin; so I got off and told the boy to hold him by the head.

What! hold Hamblin by the head?

No, the horse; and then we went and had a drink together.

「我跟湯姆·弗林走到馬廄，叫人在他背上安上馬鞍。」

「在弗林背上嗎？」

「不，在馬背上。跟弗林聊了一會兒後，我就騎上他。」

「什麼！騎上弗林嗎？」

「不，騎上馬。接著我跟他握手，然後騎走了。」

「跟馬握手嗎，比利？」

「不，跟弗林。我騎到包理街上，半路遇到漢伯林，我下馬叫人牽住他。」

「什麼！牽住漢伯林？」

「不，牽住馬。然後我們一起去喝一杯。」

"So down I goes to the stable with Tom Flynn, and told the man to put the saddle on him."

"On Tom Flynn?"

"No, on the horse. So after talking with Tom Flynn awhile I mounted him."

"What! mounted Tom Flynn?"

"No, the horse; and then I shook hands with him and rode off."

"Shook hands with the horse, Billy?"

"No, with Tom Flynn; and then I rode off up the Bowery, and who should I meet but Tom Hamblin; so I got off and told the boy to hold him by the head."

"What! hold Hamblin by the head?"

"No, the horse; and then we went and had a drink together."

What! you and the horse?	「什麼！你跟馬嗎？」
No, me and Hamblin; and after that I mounted him again and went out of town.	「不，我跟漢伯林。然後我又騎上他往城裡走去。」
What! mounted Hamblin again?	「什麼！騎上漢伯林？」
No, the horse; and when I got to Burnham, who should be there but Tom Flynn, he'd taken another horse and rode out ahead of me; so I told the hostler to tie him up.	「不，騎上馬。我走到伯罕街，半路巧遇弗林，他早就騎了另一匹馬超到我前面去了。所以我叫馬夫把他綁起來。」
Tie Tom Flynn up?	「把弗林綁起來？」
No, the horse; and we had a drink there.	「不，把馬綁起來。我們就在那裡喝酒。」
What! you and the horse?	「什麼！你跟馬嗎？」
No, me and Tom Flynn.	「不，我跟弗林。」

　　觀眾聽得瘋狂大笑，最後比利說了：「喂，每次我說馬，你就以為是漢伯林；每次我說漢伯林，你就以為是馬。再跟你說下去，我就被抓去吊死了。」

"What! you and the horse?"

"No, me and Hamblin; and after that I mounted him again and went out of town."

"What! mounted Hamblin again?"

"No, the horse; and when I got to Burnham, who should be there but Tom Flynn, he'd taken another horse and rode out ahead of me; so I told the hostler to tie him up."

"Tie Tom Flynn up?"

"No, the horse; and we had a drink there."

"What! you and the horse?"

"No, me and Tom Flynn."

Finding his auditors by this time in a horse laugh, Billy wound up with: "Now, look here, every time I say horse, you say Hamblin, and every time I say Hamblin you say horse: I'll be hanged if I tell you any more about it."

句型分類

根據一般句型原則，可分為兩大類句子：鬆散句和掉尾句。

鬆散句會先點出重點概念，接著列出幾個相關事實。英國作家丹尼爾·笛福（Daniel Defoe）以這類句型著稱。他先寫出主要聲明，接著加上附屬句子。以《魯賓遜漂流記》（Robinson Crusoe）為例，他一開場就寫道：

I was born in the year 1632 in the city of York, of a good family, though not of that country, my father being a foreigner or Bremen, who settled first at Hull; he got a good estate by merchandise, and leaving off his trade lived afterward at York, from whence he had married my mother, whose relations were named Robinson, a very good family in the country and from I was called Robinson Kreutznaer; but by the usual corruption of words in England, we are now called, nay, we call ourselves, and write our name Crusoe, and so my companions always called me.	我於 1632 年生在約克市一個上流社會家庭裡，不過我們不是本國人。父親來自德國不來梅市，他先是移居到赫爾市，經商發跡後就收掉生意，搬到約克市定居，並在那裡與我母親結婚。母親娘家姓魯賓遜，是當地望族，於是他們將我取名魯賓遜·克羅伊茨內爾。不過英國人經常唸錯外來語，我們的姓氏被喚為克羅索……不對，連我們自己也這麼說跟寫了，因此朋友都這麼叫我。

SENTENCE CLASSIFICATION

There are two great classes of sentences according to the general principles upon which they are founded. These are termed the *loose* and the *periodic*.

In the *loose* sentence the main idea is put first, and then follow several facts in connection with it. Defoe is an author particularly noted for this kind of sentence. He starts out with a leading declaration to which he adds several attendant connections. For instance in the opening of the story of *Robinson Crusoe* we read:

"I was born in the year 1632 in the city of York, of a good family, though not of that country, my father being a foreigner of Bremen, who settled first at Hull; he got a good estate by merchandise, and leaving off his trade lived afterward at York, from whence he had married my mother, whose relations were named Robinson, a very good family in the country and from I was called Robinson Kreutznaer; but by the usual corruption of words in England, we are now called, nay, we call ourselves, and write our name Crusoe, and so my companions always called me."

在**掉尾句**中，重點概念最後才出現，前面先列一連串相關介紹。這樣的句子通常會由 that、if、since、because 引導，例如：

<u>That</u> through his own folly and lack of circumspection, he should have been reduced to <u>such</u> circumstance <u>as</u> to be forced to become a beggar on the street, soliciting alms from those who had formerly been the recipients of his bounty, was a sore humiliation.	由於他自己的愚蠢和缺乏審慎，他本該淪落到被迫流落街頭乞討的處境，向那些原本受他慷慨相助的人乞求施捨，這真是奇恥大辱。

「鬆散」這兩個字容易讓許多人認為好的文章不該使用這種句子，實則未必如此。在許多情況中，鬆散句比掉尾句更佳。

相較於寫作，一般來說口說傾向使用鬆散型的句子，理由是若在談話時使用掉尾型的句子，聽者容易在聽到重點之前，就忘記前面的介紹性子句了。寫作時可以任意使用這兩類句子，不過在口說時，應該多用以直接陳述起頭的鬆散句。

至於句子的長度，主要取決於寫作的性質。不過，一般可能認為短句優於長句。現今最傑出的作家傾向使用簡潔明快的句子，以抓住讀者的注意力。這些作家以「言簡意賅」為座右銘，努力將許多意思塞進簡短的字數裡。當然也要避免過於精簡，

In the periodic sentence the main idea comes last and is preceded by a series of relative introductions. This kind of sentence is often introduced by such words as *that, if, since, because*. The following is an example: "That through his own folly and lack of circumspection he should have been reduced to such circumstances as to be forced to become a beggar on the streets, soliciting alms from those who had formerly been the recipients of his bounty, was a sore humiliation." On account of its name many are liable to think the *loose* sentence an undesirable form in good composition, but this should not be taken for granted. In many cases it is preferable to the periodic form.

As a general rule in speaking, as opposed to writing, the *loose* form is to be preferred, inasmuch as when the periodic is employed in discourse the listeners are apt to forget the introductory clauses before the final issue is reached. Both kinds are freely used in composition, but in speaking, the *loose*, which makes the direct statement at the beginning, should predominate. As to the length of sentences much depends on the nature of the composition. However the general rule may be laid down that short sentences are preferable to long ones. The tendency of the best writers of the present day is towards short, snappy, pithy sentences which rivet the attention of the reader. They adopt as their motto *multum in parvo* (much in little) and endeavor to pack a great deal in small space. Of course the extreme of brevity is to be avoided. Sentences can be too short, too jerky, too brittle to withstand the test of criticism. The long sentence has its place and a very important one. It is indispensable in argument and often is very

太過簡短倉促的句子禁不起評論的考驗。長句有它的重要用處。陳述論據時缺少不了長句，描述事物或介紹需要詳盡說明的一般原則時，也常用到長句。使用長句時，資淺的寫作者應該避免使用沉重冗長的句子。山繆·詹森（Samuel Johnson）和湯瑪士·卡萊爾（Thomas Carlyle）使用這類句子，不過記住，凡人無法揮舞巨人的鎚頭。詹森和卡萊爾是知識巨人，沒有幾個人能享有跟他們一樣的文學地位。新手不該追求這樣高深的寫作風格。在英文文風方面，最傑出的作家非約瑟夫·愛迪生（Joseph Addison）莫屬。湯瑪士·麥考利（Thomas Macaulay）曾說：「若你希望寫作風格博學精深卻不賣弄學問，優美而不顯浮誇，簡單而不失文雅，必得日夜研讀約瑟夫·愛迪生的著作。」除了優美的寫作風格之外，愛迪生簡約的文筆，再次突顯這條重要的文學原則：若能用簡單的字句表達同樣的意思，就別用艱澀的字句。

麥考利本身就是寫作風格優美、值得仿效的作家。他的作品就像一條清澈的小溪，正午陽光灑在上面，照得河床閃閃發亮，讓你可以看見、細數河中美麗的白石子。另一位作家奧利弗·戈德史密斯（Oliver Goldsmith）的簡約風格也相當令人著迷。初學者應該研讀這些作家的作品，將之視為寫作指南。這些作品禁得起時間考驗，至今尚無人超越，未來應該也不會有，因為他們的寫作在英文中已達近乎完美的境界。

除了文法結構之外，沒有特定的句子架構規則。最好的方式是學習最傑出的作家，這些語文大師會引領你安全走過寫作這條路。

necessary to description and also in introducing general principles which require elaboration. In employing the long sentence the inexperienced writer should not strain after the heavy, ponderous type. Johnson and Carlyle used such a type, but remember, an ordinary mortal cannot wield the sledge hammer of a giant. Johnson and Carlyle were intellectual giants and few can hope to stand on the same literary pedestal. The tyro in composition should never seek after the heavy style. The best of all authors in the English language for style is Addison. Macaulay says: "If you wish a style learned, but not pedantic, elegant but not ostentatious, simple yet refined, you must give your days and nights to the volumes of Joseph Addison." The simplicity, apart from the beauty of Addison's writings causes us to reiterate the literary command–"Never use a big word when a little one will convey the same or a similar meaning."

Macaulay himself is an elegant stylist to imitate. He is like a clear brook kissed by the noon-day sun in the shining bed of which you can see and count the beautiful white pebbles. Goldsmith is another writer whose simplicity of style charms. The beginner should study these writers, make their works his *vade mecum*, they have stood the test of time and there has been no improvement upon them yet, nor is there likely to be, for their writing is as perfect as it is possible to be in the English language. Apart from their grammatical construction there can be no fixed rules for the formation of sentences. The best plan is to follow the best authors and these masters of language will guide you safely along the way.

段落

段落是由一組句子所組成，這些句子彼此意思緊密相關，以達到一個共同的宗旨。段落不但將文章中不同部分的文字排出順序，也讓文章更添風味，就像聖誕布丁上的葡萄乾一樣。滿滿一頁沒有分段的印刷文字會讓讀者難以閱讀，不但使眼睛疲累，也容易因單調而感到厭倦。不過，分成幾個部分之後，就能大大減輕文章的沉重感，取而代之的輕盈感會賦予文章一種魅力，可以說能抓住讀者的目光。段落就像淺河中的踏腳石，讓步行者能輕易地一個接著一個跳上去，直到過河為止。不過，要是石頭彼此距離太遠，就有可能讓人在跨越時踩空並掉進河裡，在水中掙扎，直到再次站穩為止。寫作也是一樣，有了段落，讀者就能輕易從一個意思相關的部分讀到另一個部分，同時保持對主題的興趣，直到讀完為止。

段落中提及的事物必須有某種關聯性，也就是句子間的依存關係。例如，在同一個段落中，我們不能同時談論著火的房子和脫逃的馬，除非兩者有某種關聯性，我們不能接連這樣寫道：

The fire raged with fierce intensity, consuming the greater part of the large building in a short time. The horse took fright and wildly dashed down the street, scattering pedestrians in all directions.

熊熊燃燒的大火在短時間內吞噬這棟大型建築物的大半部分。這匹馬受到驚嚇，瘋狂地在街上奔馳，行人嚇得四處逃竄。

THE PARAGRAPH

The paragraph may be defined as a group of sentences that are closely related in thought and which serve one common purpose. Not only do they preserve the sequence of the different parts into which a composition is divided, but they give a certain spice to the matter like raisins in a plum pudding. A solid page of printed matter is distasteful to the reader; it taxes the eye and tends towards the weariness of monotony, but when it is broken up into sections it loses much of its heaviness and the consequent lightness gives it charm, as it were, to capture the reader.

Paragraphs are like stepping-stones on the bed of a shallow river, which enable the foot passenger to skip with ease from one to the other until he gets across; but if the stones are placed too far apart in attempting to span the distance one is liable to miss the mark and fall in the water and flounder about until he is again able to get a foothold. 'Tis the same with written language, the reader by means of paragraphs can easily pass from one portion of connected thought to another and keep up his interest in the subject until he gets to the end.

Throughout the paragraph there must be some connection in regard to the matter under consideration,–a sentence dependency. For instance, in the same paragraph we must not speak of a house on fire and a runaway horse unless there is some connection between the two. We must not write consecutively:

這兩個句子沒有關聯性，因此應該分成兩個個別的部分。但若寫成：

The fire raged with fierce intensity, consuming the greater part of the large building in a short time, and the horse taking fright at the flames dashed wildly down the street, scattering pedestrians in all directions.	熊熊燃燒的大火在短時間內吞噬這棟大型建築物的大半部分，而這匹馬受到火焰的驚嚇，瘋狂地在街上奔馳，行人嚇得四處逃竄。

這麼排列就自然了，這匹馬是因為火焰而受到驚嚇，因此兩件事放在同一個段落。

就跟句子中的單字排列一樣，段落中最重要的位置是開頭和結尾。因此，第一和最後一個句子在結構和語氣上必須能夠迫使讀者注意。一般建議第一句要簡短，而最後一句可長可短，但要強而有力。第一句的目的是「清楚」陳述一個論點，最後一句則應「加強」這個論點。好的作家習慣在段落結尾重述、呼應或應用開頭的陳述。

在多數情況下，段落可被視為主要句子的詳細闡述。主要思想或概念就像一個核心，段落的各個部分都圍繞著這個核心建構起來。針對任何一個簡單的句子，只要問自己幾個相關的問題，就能發展出脈絡。例如：The foreman gave the order（這位工頭下了這道命令），會令人想到「是什麼命令？」「給誰的命令？」

"The fire raged with fierce intensity, consuming the greater part of the large building in a short time." "The horse took fright and wildly dashed down the street scattering pedestrians in all directions." These two sentences have no connection and therefore should occupy separate and distinct places.

But when we say–"The fire raged with fierce intensity consuming the greater part of the large building in a short time and the horse taking fright at the flames dashed wildly down the street scattering pedestrians in all directions,"–there is a natural sequence, viz., the horse taking fright as a consequence of the flames and hence the two expressions are combined in one paragraph.

As in the case of words in sentences, the most important places in a paragraph are the beginning and the end. Accordingly the first sentence and the last should by virtue of their structure and nervous force, compel the reader's attention. It is usually advisable to make the first sentence short; the last sentence may be long or short, but in either case should be forcible. The object of the first sentence is to state a point *clearly*; the last sentence should *enforce* it.

It is a custom of good writers to make the conclusion of the paragraph a restatement or counterpart or application of the opening.

In most cases a paragraph may be regarded as the elaboration of the principal sentence. The leading thought or idea can be taken as a nucleus and around it constructed the different parts of the paragraph. Anyone can make a context for every simple sentence by asking himself questions in reference to the sentence. Thus–"The foreman

「為什麼要給這個命令？」「有什麼結果？」等等問題。根據主要句子回答這些問題，詳盡說明後就會形成一個完整段落。

細讀寫得好的段落，就會發現段落中包含幾個元素，每個元素都幫助描述、確認或加強該段落的整體思想或宗旨。而且從一個元素轉換到另一個元素的過程是很流暢、自然而明顯的，彷彿這些元素的組合渾然天成。如果情況相反，段落中有幾個元素沒有直接關聯，或無法讓讀者順暢地逐一閱讀，甚至不得不重新排列這些元素，才能理解段落的完整意思，那麼說這樣的段落結構有問題並不為過。

段落結構沒有特別的規則。最好的建議是仔細研讀最傑出作家的段落結構，惟有透過有意識或無意識地仿效最佳典範，才能掌握這門藝術。

在英文中，散文段落寫得最好的作家是麥考利；演說風格的最佳典範是愛德蒙・伯克（Edmund Burke）；描述和敘述文段落寫得最好的大師，大概就屬與戈德史密斯齊名的美國作家華盛頓・歐文（Washington Irving）了。

在印刷中，會以稱為「縮排」的方式來標示一個段落，也就是在段落的開頭從左邊頁緣縮進一段空格。

gave the order"–suggests at once several questions; "What was the order?" "to whom did he give it?" "why did he give it?" "what was the result?" etc. These questions when answered will depend upon the leading one and be an elaboration of it into a complete paragraph.

If we examine any good paragraph we shall find it made up of a number of items, each of which helps to illustrate, confirm or enforce the general thought or purpose of the paragraph. Also the transition from each item to the next is easy, natural and obvious; the items seem to come of themselves. If, on the other hand, we detect in a paragraph one or more items which have no direct bearing, or if we are unable to proceed readily from item to item, especially if we are obliged to rearrange the items before we can perceive their full significance, then we are justified in pronouncing the paragraph construction faulty.

No specific rules can be given as to the construction of paragraphs. The best advice is,–Study closely the paragraph structure of the best writers, for it is only through imitation, conscious or unconscious of the best models, that one can master the art.

The best paragraphist in the English language for the essay is Macaulay, the best model to follow for the oratorical style is Edmund Burke and for description and narration probably the greatest master of paragraph is the American Goldsmith, Washington Irving.

A paragraph is indicated in print by what is known as the indentation of the line, that is, by commencing it a space from the left margin.

第四章
比喻性語言

Figurative Language

在比喻性語言中，字詞的使用與其在一般言語中常見的意涵略有不同，其在語意的表達上較平常更生動、更令人印象深刻。比喻讓言語溝通更有效率，它美化、強化言語，有如在菜餚裡放了鹽巴一樣，增添言語的風韻和滋味。此外，比喻也能加強措辭的能量和張力，進而強烈引起閱聽者的注意和興趣。比喻分為四類，意即：

一、改變單字拼法的「拼字比喻」。
二、改變詞形的「語源比喻」。
三、改變語句結構的「句法比喻」。
四、改變思維模式的「修辭比喻」，意即有效的口語和書寫技巧。

最後一類比喻最為重要，它賦予言語一種結構和風格，使言語成為思想交流的適當媒介。因此，本書只介紹「修辭比喻」。

「修辭比喻」有各種分類方式，有些專家分得太細太多，反而顯得累贅不實用。其實，任何傳達思想的措辭，都可歸類為比喻。

最重要、也最常見的主要比喻法包括：明喻、隱喻、擬人、託寓、提喻、轉喻、詠嘆、誇飾、頓呼、想像描繪、對偶、層遞、雋語、設問和反諷。前四種依照「相似性」進行比喻，接下來六種以「相連性」進行比喻，最後五種以「對比性」進行比喻。

In *Figurative Language* we employ words in such a way that they differ somewhat from their ordinary signification in commonplace speech and convey our meaning in a more vivid and impressive manner than when we use them in their every-day sense. Figures make speech more effective, they beautify and emphasize it and give to it a relish and piquancy as salt does to food; besides they add energy and force to expression so that it irresistibly compels attention and interest. There are four kinds of figures, viz.: (1) Figures of Orthography which change the spelling of a word; (2) Figures of Etymology which change the form of words; (3) Figures of Syntax which change the construction of sentences; (4) Figures of Rhetoric or the art of speaking and writing effectively which change the mode of thought.

We shall only consider the last mentioned here as they are the most important, really giving to language the construction and style which make it a fitting medium for the intercommunication of ideas.

Figures of Rhetoric have been variously classified, some authorities extending the list to a useless length. The fact is that any form of expression which conveys thought may be classified as a Figure. The principal figures as well as the most important and those oftenest used are, *Simile, Metaphor, Personification, Allegory, Synechdoche, Metonymy, Exclamation, Hyperbole, Apostrophe, Vision, Antithesis, Climax, Epigram, Interrogation* and *Irony.*

The first four are founded on *resemblance*, the second six on *contiguity* and the third five, on *contrast*.

第四章

比喻性語言

明喻是指出一個事物如何像是另一個事物，藉此陳述物體、動作或關係的相似性。例如：

> In his awful anger he was like the storm-driven waves dashing against the rock.
> 他氣急敗壞，有如暴風掃起的狂浪般衝撞岩石。

明喻能更清楚地描述主體，以更有力的方式讓人對它留下印象。如：

> His memory is like wax to receive impressions and like marble to retain them.
> 他的記性有如蠟一般，容易對事情留下印象；又如大理石一樣，不易忘卻烙在記性中的事情。

這句話以強烈的方式闡述這個人的記性，而非單純只說 His memory is good（他的記性很好）。

然而，有些明喻的使用流於低俗淺薄。例如：

> His face was like a danger signal in a fog storm.
> 他的臉彷彿迷霧風暴中的危險信號。
>
> Her hair was like a furze-bush in bloom.
> 她的頭髮好像盛開中的金雀花叢。
>
> He was to his lady love as a poodle to its mistress.
> 他有如貴賓狗對女主人一樣愛著他的戀人。

A *Simile* (from the Latin *similis*, like), is the likening of one thing to another, a statement of the resemblance of objects, acts, or relations; as "In his awful anger he was *like* the storm-driven waves dashing against the rock." A simile makes the principal object plainer and impresses it more forcibly on the mind. "His memory is like wax to receive impressions and like marble to retain them." This brings out the leading idea as to the man's memory in a very forceful manner. Contrast it with the simple statement–"His memory is good."

Sometimes *Simile* is prostituted to a low and degrading use; as "His face was like a danger signal in a fog storm." "Her hair was like a furze-bush in bloom." "He was to his lady love as a poodle to its mistress."

千萬不可使用這樣低劣滑稽的明喻。要記住，單純的相似不叫明喻，例如將一座城市比作另一座就不是明喻。要能形成修辭學上的明喻，被用來比較的物品必須屬於不同的類別。不過，也要避免使用老套的明喻，像是把英雄比作獅子，這種比喻被用過太多次了。此外，明喻的使用不能顯得牽強附會，像是：

> Her head was glowing as the glorious god of day when he sets in a flambeau of splendor behind the purple-tinted hills of the West.
> 她的頭熠熠生輝，有如西邊透著紫色光澤的山丘背後，置身於輝煌火炬中的光榮太陽神一般。

　　這時不如不要比喻，直接說 She had fiery red hair（她有一頭火紅色的頭髮）還來得清楚多了。

　　隱喻是用來暗示相似性的字詞，但它不像明喻一樣將一個事物比作另一個，而是直接將動作或行動換成另一個。例如在形容虔誠的人時，明喻法會說：

> He is as a great pillar upholding the church.
> 他猶如一根撐起教會的偉大支柱。

隱喻法則會說：

> He is a great pillar upholding the church.
> 他是一根撐起教會的偉大支柱。

Such burlesque is never permissible. Mere *likeness*, it should be remembered, does not constitute a simile. For instance there is no simile when one city is compared to another. In order that there may be a rhetorical simile, the objects compared must be of different classes. Avoid the old *trite* similes such as comparing a hero to a lion. Such were played out long ago. And don't hunt for farfetched similes. Don't say "Her head was glowing as the glorious god of day when he sets in a flambeau of splendor behind the purple-tinted hills of the West." It is much better to do without such a simile and simply say "She had fiery red hair."

A *Metaphor* (from the Greek *metapherein*, to carry over or transfer), is a word used to *imply* a resemblance but instead of likening one object to another as in the *simile* we directly substitute the action or operation of one for another. If, of a religious man we say, "He is as a great pillar upholding the church," the expression is a *simile*, but if we say "He is a great pillar upholding the church" it is a metaphor.

隱喻是比明喻更鮮明生動的比喻。隱喻好比一幅圖畫，因此生動運用隱喻能讓文字栩栩如生。隱喻讓我們能為最抽象的概念賦予某種形態、色彩和生命。英文中充滿隱喻，人們經常使用卻不自知，以下列舉幾個隱喻的例子：

The <u>bed</u> of a river 河床

The <u>shoulder</u> of a hill 山肩

The <u>foot</u> of a mountain 山腳

The <u>hands</u> of a clock 時鐘指針

The <u>key</u> of a situation 形勢的關鍵

不要使用混合隱喻，也就是用不同的隱喻指稱同一個主題，例如：

Since it was <u>launched</u>, our project has met with much opposition, but while its <u>flight</u> has not reached the heights ambitioned, we are yet sanguine we shall <u>drive</u> it to success.
自從推出以來，我們的計畫就遭到諸多反對，儘管進度未達理想標準，我們仍樂觀認為能成功推動這項計畫。[1]

句中一開始用帶有「啟航」之意的 launch，將計畫比喻成船，然後用帶有「飛行」之意的 flight，將計畫比喻成鳥，最後用 drive 將計畫比喻成馬。

---

1 譯注：由於語言特性不同，此處譯文無法呈現英文隱喻，僅供參考句子意思。

The metaphor is a bolder and more lively figure than the simile. It is more like a picture and hence, the graphic use of metaphor is called "word-painting." It enables us to give to the most abstract ideas form, color and life. Our language is full of metaphors, and we very often use them quite unconsciously. For instance, when we speak of the *bed* of a river, the *shoulder* of a hill, the *foot* of a mountain, the *hands* of a clock, the key of a situation, we are using metaphors.

Don't use mixed metaphors, that is, different metaphors in relation to the same subject: "Since it was launched our project has met with much opposition, but while its flight has not reached the heights ambitioned, we are yet sanguine we shall drive it to success." Here our project begins as a *ship*, then becomes a *bird* and finally winds up as a *horse*.

擬人是將無生命的物體描述得彷彿有生命一樣，這種方式可說是最優美有效的比喻。

> The mountains <u>sing</u> together, the hills <u>rejoice</u>
> and <u>clap</u> their hands.
> 群山合唱，丘陵歡欣鼓掌。
>
> Earth <u>felt</u> the wound, and Nature from her seat,
> <u>Sighing</u>, through all her works, gave signs of
> woe.
> 地球感受到傷口；大自然從她的位置發出嘆息，透過她的運行傳達災禍的徵兆。

擬人相當仰賴生動的想像力，特別適合用於詩詞寫作。擬人區別為兩種形式：

一、賦予沒有生命的物體某種人格，例如上述例句。

二、賦予沒有生命的物體某種生命特質，例如：

> A <u>raging</u> storm 狂風暴雨
>
> An <u>angry</u> sea 怒海狂濤
>
> A <u>whistling</u> wind 嘯嘯風聲

在**託寓**這種表達形式中，文字象徵著某個東西。託寓與隱喻相當類似，它是一種持續進行的隱喻。

託寓、隱喻和明喻的共通點是都以相似性為依據，例如以下例句屬於明喻：

Personification (from the Latin *persona*, person, and *facere*, to make) is the treating of an inanimate object as if it were animate and is probably the most beautiful and effective of all the figures.

"The mountains *sing* together, the hills *rejoice* and *clap* their hands."

"Earth *felt* the wound; and Nature from her seat,

Sighing, through all her works, gave signs of woe."

Personification depends much on a vivid imagination and is adapted especially to poetical composition. It has two distinguishable forms: (1) when personality is ascribed to the inanimate as in the foregoing examples, and (2) when some quality of life is attributed to the inanimate; as, a *raging* storm; an *angry* sea; a *whistling* wind, etc.

An *Allegory* (from the Greek *allos*, other, and *agoreuein*, to speak), is a form of expression in which the words are symbolical of something. It is very closely allied to the metaphor, in fact is a continued metaphor.

Allegory, *metaphor* and *simile* have three points in common–they

> Ireland is like a thorn in the side of England.
> 愛爾蘭有如英國背上一根芒刺。

以下例句屬於隱喻：

> Ireland is a thorn in the side of England.
> 愛爾蘭是英國背上一根芒刺。

和以下段落比較：

Once a great giant sprang up out of the sea and lived on an island all by himself. On looking around he discovered a little girl on another small island nearby. He thought the little girl could be useful to him in many ways so he determined to make her subservient to his will. He commanded her, but she refused to obey, then he resorted to very harsh measures with the little girl, but she still remained obstinate and obdurate. He continued to oppress her until finally she rebelled and became as a thorn in his side to prick him for his evil attitude towards her.

從前有個龐大的巨人從海中躍出，獨自住在一座島上。他環顧四周，發現附近另一座小島上有一個小女孩。他認為這個小女孩對他會有很多用處，於是決定強迫她屈從自己的意思。他命令她，但她拒絕聽話，於是他對小女孩祭出相當嚴厲的手段，但她仍堅持不從。他繼續壓迫她，最後小女孩起身反抗，變成巨人背上的一根芒刺，刺痛著他，報復他的邪惡態度。

are all founded on resemblance. "Ireland is like a thorn in the side of England;" this is simile. "Ireland is a thorn in the side of England;" this is metaphor.

"Once a great giant sprang up out of the sea and lived on an island all by himself. On looking around he discovered a little girl on another small island near by. He thought the little girl could be useful to him in many ways so he determined to make her subservient to his will. He commanded her, but she refused to obey, then he resorted to very harsh measures with the little girl, but she still remained obstinate and obdurate. He continued to oppress her until finally she rebelled and became as a thorn in his side to prick him for his evil attitude towards her."

這段描述屬於託寓，巨人顯然代表英國，小女孩則代表愛爾蘭。這種暗示相當明顯，儘管文中沒有提及這兩個國家。奇怪的是，英文中寫得最完美的託寓，竟然出自一位幾乎目不識丁、未受教育的人之手，而且還是在地牢中寫的。在《天路歷程》（Pilgrim's Progress）裡，約翰・班揚（John Bunyan）這位沿街替人修補鍋具的工匠寫下有史以來最出色的託寓。另一個絕佳範例則是愛德蒙・史賓賽（Edmund Spenser）的《仙后》（The Faerie Queene）。

使用**提喻**來做比喻時，被比喻者的特質會大於或小於所使用的字詞的字面意思，意即我們會賦予物體一個名稱，這個名稱的字面意思表達了比原本更多或更少的特質。舉例來說，英文中會以 world（世界）來表示世界上一部分的人，這裡的 world 在中文則變成「世人」的意思，例如：

The <u>world</u> treated him badly. 世人待他不好。

這裡是以「全部」代表「部分」。不過最常見的提喻是以「部分」代表「全部」，例如：

I have twenty <u>heads</u> of cattle. 我有二十頭牛。

One of his <u>hands</u> was assassinated.
他的其中一個手下遭到刺殺。

hand 在這裡是指他的士兵或弟兄。

This is an allegory in which the giant plainly represents England and the little girl, Ireland; the implication is manifest though no mention is made of either country. Strange to say the most perfect allegory in the English language was written by an almost illiterate and ignorant man, and written too, in a dungeon cell. In the "Pilgrim's Progress," Bunyan, the itinerant tinker, has given us by far the best allegory ever penned. Another good one is "The Faerie Queen" by Edmund Spenser.

Synecdoche (from the Greek, *sun* with, and *ekdexesthai*, to receive), is a figure of speech which expresses either more or less than it literally denotes. By it we give to an object a name which literally expresses something more or something less than we intend. Thus: we speak of the world when we mean only a very limited number of the people who compose the world: as, "The world treated him badly." Here we use the whole for a part. But the most common form of this figure is that in which a part is used for the whole; as, "I have twenty head of cattle," "One of his *hands* was assassinated," meaning one of his men. "Twenty *sail* came into the harbor," meaning twenty ships. "This is a fine marble," meaning a marble statue.

Twenty <u>sail</u> came into the harbor.
二十艘船駛進港口。

這裡以 sail（帆）代表船。

This is a fine <u>marble</u>. 這座大理石雕相當不錯。

這裡以 marble（大理石）代表石雕。

轉喻是以伴隨的事物來指稱某物，換句話說，這種比喻是用某物的名稱代替另一個事物，因為兩者緊密相關，只要提到其中一個，就會讓人聯想到另一個。例如在描述酒鬼時可以說：

He loves the <u>bottle</u>. 他很貪杯。

這裡不是指此人喜歡酒瓶，而是裝在裡面的酒。一般來說，轉喻分為三個子類別：

一、把「結果」和「原因」互換，例如：

<u>Gray hairs</u> should be respected.
我們應該尊敬銀髮族。

這裡比喻老年。

He writes a fine <u>hand</u>. 他寫得一手好字。

這裡比喻手寫。

Metonymy (from the Greek *meta*, change, and *onyma*, a name) is the designation of an object by one of its accompaniments, in other words, it is a figure by which the name of one object is put for another when the two are so related that the mention of one readily suggests the other. Thus when we say of a drunkard "He loves the bottle" we do not mean that he loves the glass receptacle, but the liquor that it is supposed to contain. Metonymy, generally speaking, has, three subdivisions:

(1) when an effect is put for cause or *vice versa*: as "Gray *hairs* should be respected," meaning old age. "He writes a fine hand," that is, handwriting.

二、用「象徵者」代替「被象徵者」，例如：

The <u>pen</u> is mightier than the sword.
筆比劍更強大有力。

這裡表示文學力量更甚武力。

三、用「容器」代替「內容物」，例如：

The <u>House</u> was called to order.
議院被要求遵守議會秩序。

這裡指的是議院裡的成員。

使用**詠嘆**進行比喻時，說話者不陳述事實，而是表達驚訝或情緒。例如他在聽到一件悲傷或不幸的事時，不是說：

It is a sad story. 這是個悲傷的故事。

而是驚呼：

What a sad story! 多麼悲傷的故事啊！

詠嘆法可說是用口語表達感受，不過也能用在書寫形式中來表達情緒。例如在描述高聳的山時，可以寫道：

(2) when the *sign* is put for the *thing signified*; as, "The pen is mightier than the sword," meaning literary power is superior to military force.

(3) When the *container* is put for the thing contained; as "The *House* was called to order," meaning the members in the House.

Exclamation (from the Latin *ex*, out, and *clamare*, to cry), is a figure by which the speaker instead of stating a fact, simply utters an expression of surprise or emotion. For instance when he hears some harrowing tale of woe or misfortune instead of saying, "It is a sad story" he exclaims "What a sad story!"

Exclamation may be defined as the vocal expression of feeling, though it is also applied to written forms which are intended to express emotion. Thus in describing a towering mountain we can write "Heavens, what a piece of Nature's handiwork! How majestic! How sublime! How awe-inspiring in its colossal impressiveness!" This figure rather belongs to poetry and animated oratory than to the cold prose of every-day conversation and writing.

> Heavens, what a piece of Nature's handiwork!
> How majestic! How sublime! How awe-
> inspiring in its colossal impressiveness!
> 天啊，真是大自然的鬼斧神工之作！多麼雄偉！多麼壯
> 麗！其龐大的樣貌多麼令人敬畏！

這種比喻適合用於詩詞寫作和生動演說，較不適合用在冷靜的日常對話和散文寫作中。

誇飾是以誇張的陳述形式，將事物描繪得比原本更偉大或渺小、更好或更糟，目的是透過言過其實的方式，增加某個想法的效果。例句如下：

> He was so tall his head touched the clouds.
> 他好高，頭都碰到雲了。
>
> He was as thin as a poker.
> 他瘦得跟紙片一樣。
>
> He was so light that a breath might have blown
> him away.
> 他好輕，好像吹一下就會被吹走。

大部分的人容易過度使用這種比喻。我們多少都會語帶誇張，不過有些人不會適可而止，到了胡謅瞎扯的地步。誇飾要有限度，在一般口說和寫作中，要在合理的範圍內使用。

Hyperbole (from the Greek *hyper*, beyond, and *ballein*, to throw), is an exaggerated form of statement and simply consists in representing things to be either greater or less, better or worse than they really are. Its object is to make the thought more effective by overstating it. Here are some examples: "He was so tall his head touched the clouds." "He was as thin as a poker." "He was so light that a breath might have blown him away." Most people are liable to overwork this figure. We are all more or less given to exaggeration and some of us do not stop there, but proceed onward to falsehood and downright lying. There should be a limit to hyperbole, and in ordinary speech and writing it should be well qualified and kept within reasonable bounds.

頓呼是直接呼喚不在場的人，彷彿他在場一樣；直呼沒有生命的物體，彷彿它有生命似的；或直呼抽象的事物，彷彿它有人格。例如：

> O, illustrious Washington! Father of our Country! Could you visit us now!
> 噢，威名顯赫的華盛頓！吾等的國父！您現在能否探訪吾等！
>
> My Country tis of thee / Sweet land of liberty / Of thee I sing.
> 您是我的祖國，甜美的自由之土，我為您歌唱。
>
> O! Grave, where is thy Victory. O! Death, where is thy sting!
> 死亡啊！你的勝利在哪裡？死亡啊！你的毒刺在哪裡？

　　這種比喻與擬人十分相近。

　　想像描繪是指將過去、未來或遙遠的事物，敘述得有如當下就在眼前一樣。這種比喻能夠產生理想的臨場感，適合用於生動的描繪，例如：

> The old warrior looks down from the canvas and tells us to be men worthy of our sires.
> 這位老戰士從畫布中往下看，告訴我們要成為對得起陛下的男子漢。

　　《聖經》中有許多這種比喻的範例。《啟示錄》是對未來的想像描繪。最常使用這種比喻的作家是卡萊爾。

An *Apostrophe* (from the Greek *apo*, from, and *strephein*, to turn), is a direct address to the absent as present, to the inanimate as living, or to the abstract as personal. Thus:

"O, illustrious Washington! Father of our Country! Could you visit us now!"

"My Country tis of thee–
Sweet land of liberty,
Of thee I sing."

"O! Grave, where is thy Victory, O! Death where is thy sting!" This figure is very closely allied to Personification.

Vision (from the Latin *videre*, to see) consists in treating the past, the future, or the remote as if present in time or place. It is appropriate to animated description, as it produces the effect of an ideal presence. "The old warrior looks down from the canvas and tells us to be men worthy of our sires."

This figure is much exemplified in the Bible. The book of Revelation is a vision of the future. The author who uses the figure most is Carlyle.

對偶以對比方式來做比喻，意即將兩個不相似的事物並列，以突顯彼此反差，例如：

> Ring out the <u>old</u>, ring in the <u>new</u>.
> Ring out the <u>false</u>, ring in the <u>true</u>.
> 鈴聲送走舊歲，迎來新年。鈴聲送走虛妄，迎來真實。
>
> Let us be friends in peace, but enemies in war.
> 讓我們成為承平時期的朋友，戰爭時期的敵人。

　　以下這段關於蒸汽引擎的描述，是相當不錯的對句手法：

> It can engrave a seal and crush masses of obdurate metal before it; draw out, without breaking, a thread as fine as a gossamer; and lift up a ship of war like a bauble in the air; it can embroider muslin and forge anchors, cut steel into ribands, and impel loaded vessels against the fury of winds and waves.
>
> 它能雕刻印章，也能壓碎頑強的大塊金屬；它能連續不斷地抽出遊絲一般細的線，也能將戰艦像小玩意兒一樣高舉到空中。它能在平紋細布上繡花、鍛造船錨、將鋼材切成鋼片，並推動滿載貨物的船隻迎風破浪。

An *Antithesis* (from the Greek *anti*, against, and *tithenai*, to set) is founded on contrast; it consists in putting two unlike things in such a position that each will appear more striking by the contrast.

"Ring out the old, ring in the new,
Ring out the false, ring in the true."

"Let us be *friends* in peace, but *enemies* in war."

Here is a fine antithesis in the description of a steam engine–"It can engrave a seal and crush masses of obdurate metal before it; draw out, without breaking, a thread as fine as a gossamer; and lift up a ship of war like a bauble in the air; it can embroider muslin and forge anchors; cut steel into ribands, and impel loaded vessels against the fury of winds and waves."

層遞是將多個思想和概念一連串列出，其中每個概念都比上一個來得強烈、深刻，最後一個則加強前面所有概念的力度，例如：

> He risked truth, he risked honor, he risked fame, he risked all that men hold dear, yea, he risked life itself, and for what? For a creature who was not worthy to tie his shoe-latchets when he was his better self.
> 他賭上真相、賭上榮耀、賭上名聲、賭上人們所珍惜的一切事物，沒錯，他還賭上性命，為的是什麼？為的是一個連幫他綁鞋帶都不配的傢伙。

雋語原本是指紀念碑上的碑文，代表具有針對性的表達內容。現在雋語是指散文或詩詞中，存在明顯矛盾的陳述或短語，例如：

> Conspicuous for his absence.
> 他的缺席引起注意。
>
> Beauty when unadorned is most adorned.
> 樸實的美才是最華麗的。
>
> He was too foolish to commit folly.
> 他太蠢了，才不會做出什麼蠢事。
>
> He was so wealthy that he could not spare the money.
> 他有錢到一毛不拔。

Climax (from the Greek, *klimax*, a ladder), is an arrangement of thoughts and ideas in a series, each part of which gets stronger and more impressive until the last one, which emphasizes the force of all the preceding ones. "He risked truth, he risked honor, he risked fame, he risked all that men hold dear, yea, he risked life itself, and for what? For a creature who was not worthy to tie his shoe-latchets when he was his better self."

Epigram (from the Greek *epi*, upon, and *graphein*, to write), originally meant an inscription on a monument, hence it came to signify any pointed expression. It now means a statement or any brief saying in prose or poetry in which there is an apparent contradiction; as, "Conspicuous for his absence." "Beauty when unadorned is most adorned." "He was too foolish to commit folly." "He was so wealthy that he could not spare the money."

設問是透過提問來表達明確語意的比喻法，例如：

> Does God not show justice to all?
> 難道上帝不向眾人彰顯正義嗎？
>
> Is he not doing right in his course?
> 難道他的做法不好嗎？
>
> What can a man do under the circumstances?
> 在這些情況下，還能怎麼辦呢？

反諷是使用與想表達的意義相反的用語，目標是凸顯出情況的錯誤或荒謬。例如：

> You can always depend upon the word of a liar.
> 你永遠可以信賴騙子說的話。

反諷與「揶揄」（ridicule）、「譏諷」（derision）、「訕笑」（mockery）、「諷刺」（satire）、「挖苦」（sarcasm）相似。「揶揄」是帶有輕視意味的笑話，「譏諷」是帶有個人敵意的揶揄，「訕笑」是侮辱性的譏諷，「諷刺」是詼諧的訕笑，「挖苦」是刻薄的諷刺，「反諷」則是變相的諷刺。

還有許多其他比喻性語言，它們能讓言語增添滋味，讓文字發揮作用，藉以傳達不同於日常口說和寫作的普通語意。這些比喻的最高使用原則是「要跟口說與寫作內容的性質與宗旨同調」。

Interrogation (from the Latin *interrogatio*, a question), is a figure of speech in which an assertion is made by asking a question; as, "Does God not show justice to all?" "Is he not doing right in his course?" "What can a man do under the circumstances?"

Irony (from the Greek *eironcia*, dissimulation) is a form of expression in which the opposite is substituted for what is intended, with the end in view, that the falsity or absurdity may be apparent; as, "You can always *depend* upon the word of a liar."

Irony is cousin germain to *ridicule, derision, mockery, satire* and *sarcasm. Ridicule* implies laughter mingled with contempt; *derision* is ridicule from a personal feeling of hostility; *mockery* is insulting derision; *satire* is witty mockery; *sarcasm* is bitter satire and irony is disguised satire.

There are many other figures of speech which give piquancy to language and play upon words in such a way as to convey a meaning different from their ordinary signification in common every-day speech and writing. The golden rule for all is to *keep them in harmony with the character and purpose of speech and composition.*

第五章
標點符號

Punctuation

林德利‧莫瑞（Lindley Murray）和古爾德‧布朗（Goold Brown）曾經訂定一套嚴謹的標點符號規則，不過後來大多已被打破並且棄之不用。這些規則太過苛刻死板、流於瑣碎，對一般作文而言多少有些不切實際。而且在那之後，語言、文風和表達方式已大幅改變，人們不再使用艱澀複雜、意思隱晦的句子，也很少使用冗長累贅的詞語，更儘量避免模稜兩可的表達，以求語意上的精練、簡潔和明確，標點符號也因此簡化不少。除了依循特定使用規則之外，憑著自己對語言的精準品味和判斷來下標點符號的也大有人在。不過，標點符號還是有一定的守則，這些守則廢除不得，必須加以嚴格遵守。

　　標點符號的主要目的是標示文章中的文法關係，以及各個字句之間如何依附，而不是用來標示實際說話時的停頓語氣。口說語氣的標點與寫作使用的標點往往是不一樣的。不過，有些標點符號確實可以突顯表述時的修辭效果。

Lindley Murray and Goold Brown laid down cast-iron rules for punctuation, but most of them have been broken long since and thrown into the junk-heap of disuse. They were too rigid, too strict, went so much into *minutiae*, that they were more or less impractical to apply to ordinary composition. The manner of language, of style and of expression has considerably changed since then, the old abstruse complex sentence with its hidden meanings has been relegated to the shade, there is little of prolixity or long-drawn-out phrases, ambiguity of expression is avoided and the aim is toward terseness, brevity and clearness. Therefore, punctuation has been greatly simplified, to such an extent indeed, that it is now as much a matter of good taste and judgment as adherence to any fixed set of rules. Nevertheless there are laws governing it which cannot be abrogated, their principles must be rigidly and inviolably observed.

The chief end of punctuation is to mark the grammatical connection and the dependence of the parts of a composition, but not the actual pauses made in speaking. Very often the points used to denote the delivery of a passage differ from those used when the passage is written. Nevertheless, several of the punctuation marks serve to bring out the rhetorical force of expression.

標點符號

英文中的主要標點符號包括：

一、逗號（,）

二、分號（;）

三、冒號（:）

四、句號（.）

五、問號（?）

六、驚嘆號（!）

七、破折號（–）

八、括號（()）

九、引號（" "）

還有其他用來表示各種關係的標點符號，不過都與印刷用途有關，在此不多介紹。

上述標點符號中的前四者可稱為文法標點，後五者為修辭標點。

 必須使用標點符號時，可用逗號表示短暫的間隔。在英文中，逗號標示句子中的最小間隔，可以的話儘量不用。以下說明逗號用法。

■ 用逗號分開一連串單字或片語，例如：

The principal marks of punctuation are:

1. The Comma [,]

2. The Semicolon [;]

3. The Colon [:]

4. The Period [.]

5. The Interrogation [?]

6. The Exclamation [!]

7. The Dash [–]

8. The Parenthesis [()]

9. The Quotation [" "]

There are several other points or marks to indicate various relations, but properly speaking such come under the heading of Printer's Marks, some of which are treated elsewhere.

Of the above, the first four may be styled the grammatical points, and the remaining five, the rhetorical points.

The **Comma**: The office of the Comma is to show the slightest separation which calls for punctuation at all. It should be omitted whenever possible. It is used to mark the least divisions of a sentence.

■ A series of words or phrases has its parts separated by commas:

"Lying, trickery, chicanery, perjury, were natural to him." "The brave, daring, faithful soldier died facing the foe."

> Lying, trickery, chicanery, and perjury, were natural to him.
> 撒謊、欺騙、狡辯和作偽證是他的本性。[2]

> The brave, daring, faithful soldier died facing the foe.
> 這位英勇、大膽又忠誠的士兵捨生迎敵。

如果這一連串的單字或片語是成對存在的，就得兩兩用逗號分開，例如：

> Rich and poor, learned and unlearned, black and white, Christian and Jew, Mohammedan and Buddhist must pass through the same gate.
> 富人和窮人、博學的和未受教育的、黑人和白人、基督教徒和猶太教徒、伊斯蘭教徒與佛教徒，都得通過同一扇大門。

■ 在短引用句前面加上逗號，例如：

> It was Patrick Henry who said, "Give me liberty or give me death."
> 說出「不自由，毋寧死」這句話的是派崔克・亨利。

■ 句子的主詞是子句或長片語時，要在主詞後面加上逗號，例如：

> That he has no reverence for the God I love, proves his insincerity.
> 他對我所敬愛的神毫無敬意，證實他的偽善。

---

2 譯注：中、英標點符號方式有所不同，譯文僅為參考，使用上應以英文為依據。

If the series is in pairs, commas separate the pairs: "Rich and poor, learned and unlearned, black and white, Christian and Jew, Mohammedan and Buddhist must pass through the same gate."

■ A comma is used before a short quotation:

"It was Patrick Henry who said, 'Give me liberty or give me death.'"

■ When the subject of the sentence is a clause or a long phrase, a comma is used after such subject:

"That he has no reverence for the God I love, proves his insincerity." "Simulated piety, with a black coat and a sanctimonious look, does not proclaim a Christian."

> Simulated piety, with a black coat and a sanctimonious look, does not proclaim a Christian.
> 用黑色大衣和虛偽的聖潔外表假裝虔誠，不代表就是基督徒。

■ 附帶說明的句子前後皆應加逗號，例如：

> The old man, as a general rule, takes a morning walk.
> 這位老人一向在晨間散步。

■ 同位語要用逗號隔開，例如：

> McKinley, the President, was assassinated.
> 麥金利總統遇刺。

■ 非限定關係子句需要用逗號，例如：

> The book, which is the simplest, is often the most profound.
> 最簡單的書往往最深奧。

■ 同一個主詞有一連串修飾字詞時，每段字詞後面必須加上逗號，例如：

> Electricity lights our dwellings and streets, pulls cars, drives the engines of our mills and factories.
> 電力點亮住家和街道、拉動車子、驅動工坊和工廠的引擎。

■ An expression used parenthetically should be inclosed by commas:

"The old man, as a general rule, takes a morning walk."

■ Words in apposition are set off by commas:

"McKinley, the President, was assassinated."

■ Relative clauses, if not restrictive, require commas:

"The book, which is the simplest, is often the most profound."

■ In continued sentences each should be followed by a comma:

"Electricity lights our dwellings and streets, pulls cars, trains, drives the engines of our mills and factories."

■ 以逗號取代被省略的動詞，例如：

Lincoln was a great statesman; Grant, a great soldier.
林肯是偉大的政治家；葛蘭特則是偉大的軍人。

■ 在說話對象後面加上逗號，例如：

John, you are a good man. 約翰，你是一個好人。

■ 在數字的讀法中，會以逗號作為千位的分隔符號，例如：

Mountains 25,000 feet high 高兩千五百呎的群山

1,000,000 dollars 一百萬美元

分號 標示比逗號更明確的間隔，一般用於合句中，分開各個單句，用法如下。

■ 分號經常用於進行對比，例如：

Gladstone was great as a statesman; he was sublime as a man.
身為一位政治家，格萊斯頓很偉大；身為一個普通人，他也相當崇高。

■ When a verb is omitted a comma takes its place:

"Lincoln was a great statesman; Grant, a great soldier."

■ The subject of address is followed by a comma

"John, you are a good man."

■ In numeration, commas are used to express periods of three figures:

"Mountains 25,000 feet high; 1,000,000 dollars."

The *Semicolon* marks a slighter connection than the comma. It is generally confined to separating the parts of compound sentences.

■ It is much used in contrasts:

"Gladstone was great as a statesman; he was sublime as a man."

■ 合句中各個單句若有不同的主詞，則以分號隔開，例如：

> The power of England relies upon the wisdom of her statesmen; the power of America upon the strength of her army and navy.
> 英國的力量在其政治家的智慧；美國的力量在其陸軍和海軍。

冒號 除了在慣用場合之外，冒號的使用幾乎已經過時。用法如下：

■ 句子後面若介紹一長段文字，通常會在該句後面加上冒號，例如：

> The cheers having subsided, Mr. Bryan spoke as follows:
> 待掌聲止息，布萊恩先生開始演說以下內容：

■ 在相關議題的說明或解釋內容前面加上冒號，例如：

> This is the meaning of the term:
> 以下是這個用語的意思：

■ 正式介紹直接引言時，會在引言前放上冒號，例如：

> The great orator made this funny remark:
> 這位偉大的演說家講了這麼一段有趣的話：

■ The Semicolon is used between the parts of all compound sentences in which the grammatical subject of the second part is different from that of the first:

"The power of England relies upon the wisdom of her statesmen; the power of America upon the strength of her army and navy."

The **Colon** except in conventional uses is practically obsolete.

■ It is generally put at the end of a sentence introducing a long quotation:

"The cheers having subsided, Mr. Bryan spoke as follows:"

■ It is placed before an explanation or illustration of the subject under consideration:

"This is the meaning of the term:"

■ A direct quotation formally introduced is generally preceded by a colon:

"The great orator made this funny remark:"

■ 書名的主標題若與副標題或次要標題並列排放，且未使用連接詞 or 時，則會使用冒號，例如：

> Acoustics: the Science of Sound
> 《聲學：聲音的科學》

■ 信件開頭的問候語會用冒號，例如：

> Sir: 先生：
> My dear Sir: 親愛的先生：
> Gentlemen: 紳士們：
> Dear Mr. Jones: 親愛的瓊斯先生：

■ 用於介紹前面已經提過的事情的多項細節，例如：

> The boy's excuses for being late were: firstly, he did not know the time, secondly, he was sent on an errand, and thirdly, he tripped on a rock and fell by the wayside.
> 這個男孩遲到的藉口包括：第一，他忘記時間了；第二，他被叫去跑腿；第三，他被石頭絆倒，所以就放棄了。

句號 是最簡單的標點符號，單純用於標示完整的非問句或驚嘆句的結束。其用法如下：

■ 用於語意完整的句子後面，例如：

■ The colon is often used in the title of books when the secondary or subtitle is in apposition to the leading one and when the conjunction *or* is omitted:

"Acoustics: the Science of Sound."

■ It is used after the salutation in the beginning of letters:

"Sir: My dear Sir: Gentlemen: Dear Mr. Jones:" etc. In this connection a dash very often follows the colon.

■ It is sometimes used to introduce details of a group of things already referred to in the mass:

"The boy's excuses for being late were: firstly, he did not know the time, secondly, he was sent on an errand, thirdly, he tripped on a rock and fell by the wayside."

The **Period** is the simplest punctuation mark. It is simply used to mark the end of a complete sentence that is neither interrogative nor exclamatory.

■ After every sentence conveying a complete meaning:

"Birds fly." "Plants grow." "Man is mortal."

Birds fly. 鳥飛。

Plants grow. 植物生長。

Man is mortal. 人是血肉之軀。

■ 用於縮寫之後，例如：

Rt. Rev. T. C. Alexander 亞歷山大主教牧師

D. D. 神學博士

L. L. D. 法學博士

問號 用於提出問題。用法如下：

■ 即便未必會得到答案，每個需要回答的句子後面都須加上問號，例如：

Who has not heard of Napoleon?
誰沒聽說過拿破崙？

■ 多個問句有一個共同的從屬關係時，在最後一個問句後面加上一個問號即可，例如：

Where now are the playthings and friends of my boyhood; the laughing boys; the winsome girls; the fond neighbors whom I loved?
我兒時的玩具和朋友、歡笑的男孩們、迷人的女孩們、可愛的鄰居們都到哪裡去了？

■ In abbreviations: after every abbreviated word:

Rt. Rev. T. C. Alexander, D.D., L.L.D.

The *Mark of Interrogation* is used to ask or suggest a question.

■ Every question admitting of an answer, even when it is not expected, should be followed by the mark of interrogation:

"Who has not heard of Napoleon?"

■ When several questions have a common dependence they should be followed by one mark of interrogation at the end of the series:

"Where now are the playthings and friends of my boyhood; the laughing boys; the winsome girls; the fond neighbors whom I loved?"

■ 問號常以插入方式表達懷疑，例如：

> In 1893 (?), Gladstone became converted to
> Home Rule for Ireland.
> 在1893年（？），格萊斯頓轉而支持愛爾蘭自治運動。

驚嘆號 驚嘆號的主要目的是表示某種情緒，應該儘量少用，在散文中尤其如此。用法如下：

■ 驚嘆號一般放在感嘆詞或表達感嘆的子句後面，例如：

> Alas! I am forsaken. 哎呀！我被拋棄了。
>
> What a lovely landscape! 多麼美麗的風景啊！

■ 表達強烈情緒時使用驚嘆號，例如：

> Charge, Chester, charge! On, Stanley, on!
> 衝啊，切斯特，衝啊！前進，史丹利，前進！

■ 非常強烈的情緒可用兩個驚嘆號表示，例如：

> Assist him!! I would rather assist Satan!!
> 幫他！！我寧願去幫撒旦！！

■ The mark is often used parenthetically to suggest doubt:

"In 1893 (?) Gladstone became converted to Home Rule for Ireland."

The *Exclamation* point should be sparingly used, particularly in prose. Its chief use is to denote emotion of some kind.

■ It is generally employed with interjections or clauses used as interjections:

"Alas! I am forsaken." "What a lovely landscape!"

■ Expressions of strong emotion call for the exclamation:

"Charge, Chester, charge! On, Stanley, on!"

■ When the emotion is very strong double exclamation points may be used:

"Assist him!! I would rather assist Satan!!"

破折號 一般僅用於句子突然出現中斷的情況，是最常遭到誤用的標點符號。用法如下：

■ 用於構句或情感突然改變時，例如：

> The Heroes of the Civil War—how we cherish them.
> 南北戰爭的英雄們——我們多麼珍惜他們啊。
>
> He was a fine fellow—in his own opinion.
> 他是一個好人——他自己這麼認為。

■ 為了演說效果而重複某個字句時，可用破折號來引導重複的部分，例如：

> Shakespeare was the greatest of all poets—Shakespeare, the intellectual ocean whose waves washed the continents of all thought.
> 莎士比亞是所有詩人中最偉大的——莎士比亞是知識之海，其浪潮席捲所有思想大陸。

■ 句子結束但語氣欲言又止時，可用破折號來表達，例如：

> He is an excellent man, but—
> 他這個人很優秀，可是——

The *Dash* is generally confined to cases where there is a sudden break from the general run of the passage. Of all the punctuation marks it is the most misused.

■ It is employed to denote sudden change in the construction or sentiment:

"The Heroes of the Civil War–how we cherish them." "He was a fine fellow–in his own opinion."

■ When a word or expression is repeated for oratorical effect, a dash is used to introduce the repetition:

"Shakespeare was the greatest of all poets–Shakespeare, the intellectual ocean whose waves washed the continents of all thought."

■ The Dash is used to indicate a conclusion without expressing it:

"He is an excellent man, but–"

■ 用於表示事情出乎意外，或結局不符合事情的自然發展時，例如：

> He delved deep into the bowels of the earth and found instead of the hidden treasure–a button.
> 他深入地底，發現的卻不是祕寶——是一個鈕扣。

■ 用於表示省略的數字，例如：

1908-9 代表 1908 和 1909 年；Matthew VII:5-8 代表《馬太福音》第十二章五到八節。

■ 省略 namely、that is 等單字時，可用破折號來代替，例如：

> He excelled in three branches–arithmetic, algebra, and geometry.
> 他在三個數學科目表現特別優秀——算術、代數和幾何學。

■ 不想寫出完整的單字時，可用破折號代表被省略的字母，粗俗藝瀆的字眼尤其會用這種表達方式，例如：

> He is somewhat of a r–l (rascal).
> 他有點流氓。

■ 引文和出處之間通常會放破折號，例如：

> "All the world's a stage."–Shakespeare
> 「世界即是舞台。」——莎士比亞

■ It is used to indicate what is not expected or what is not the natural outcome of what has gone before:

"He delved deep into the bowels of the earth and found instead of the hidden treasure–a button."

■ It is used to denote the omission of letters or figures:

"J–n J–s" for John Jones; 1908-9 for 1908 and 1909; Matthew VII:5-8 for Matthew VII:5, 6, 7, and 8.

■ When an ellipsis of the words, *namely*, *that is*, etc., takes place, the dash is used to supply them:

"He excelled in three branches–arithmetic, algebra, and geometry."

■ A dash is used to denote the omission of part of a word when it is undesirable to write the full word:

He is somewhat of a r–l (rascal). This is especially the case in profane words.

■ Between a citation and the authority for it there is generally a dash:

"All the world's a stage."–*Shakespeare*.

■ 多個問句和回答放在相同段落時，應以破折號分
　開，例如：

> Are you a good boy? Yes, Sir.–Do you love study? I do.
> 你是好孩子嗎？是的，先生。——你喜歡讀書嗎？喜歡。

括號 用於標示句子中的插入語，這種插入語用於說明句子的意思，但與句子沒有必要關聯，即便省略也無礙句子的完整性。盡量不要使用括號，因為這代表帶入本來不屬於這個句子的內容。括號的用法如下：

■ 破壞句子一致性的字詞應放在括號內，例如：

> We cannot believe a liar (and Jones is one), even when he speaks the truth.
> 我們無法相信騙子（瓊斯就是一個騙子），即使他說了真話。

■ 在演說的逐字稿中，括號用來代表聽眾表達認同或
　否定的插入語，例如：

> The masses must not submit to the tyranny of the classes (hear, hear), we must show the trust magnates (groans), that they cannot ride rough-shod over our dearest rights (cheers).
> 大家不要屈服於階級的專橫（說得好，說得好），我們必須讓信託業的大亨們看看（呻吟），他們不能壓榨我們最寶貴的權利（歡呼聲）。

■ When questions and answers are put in the same paragraph they should be separated by dashes:

"Are you a good boy? Yes, Sir.–Do you love study? I do."

Marks of Parenthesis are used to separate expressions inserted in the body of a sentence, which are illustrative of the meaning, but have no essential connection with the sentence, and could be done without. They should be used as little as possible for they show that something is being brought into a sentence that does not belong to it.

■ When the unity of a sentence is broken the words causing the break should be enclosed in parenthesis:

"We cannot believe a liar (and Jones is one), even when he speaks the truth."

■ In reports of speeches marks of parenthesis are used to denote interpolations of approval or disapproval by the audience:

"The masses must not submit to the tyranny of the classes (hear, hear), we must show the trust magnates (groans), that they cannot ride rough-shod over our dearest rights (cheers);" "If the gentleman from Ohio (Mr. Brown), will not be our spokesman, we must select another. (A voice, Get Robinson)."

> If the gentleman from Ohio (Mr. Brown), will not be our spokesman, we must select another (A voice, Get Robinson).
> 如果這位俄亥俄州來的紳士（布朗先生）無法擔任我們的發言人，我們必須另選一位（有人說找羅賓森吧）。

在不需要逗號的句子中使用括號時，兩邊括號「前面不必」加上標點符號。用在需要逗號的句子中時，如果括號中的內容與整個句子有關，兩邊括號「前面必須」加上逗號。如果括號中的內容與某個單字或短子句有關，則左括號「前面不加」逗號，右括號「後面要加」逗號。

引號 引號用於表示其內容引述自他人，用法如下：

■ 直接引述句的前後應該加上引號，例如：

> Abraham Lincoln said, "I shall make this land too hot for the feet of slaves."
> 亞伯拉罕・林肯說：「我將把這片土地變得如此炎熱，教奴隸制度無立足之地。」

■ 引述句中另有別的引述句時，最裡面的句子要用單引號，例如：

> Franklin said, "Most men come to believe 'honesty is the best policy.'"
> 富蘭克林說：「大部分的人都相信『誠實才是上策』。」

When a parenthesis is inserted in the sentence where no comma is required, no point should be used before either parenthesis. When inserted at a place requiring a comma, if the parenthetical matter relates to the whole sentence, a comma should be used before each parenthesis; if it relates to a single word, or short clause, no stop should come before it, but a comma should be put after the closing parenthesis.

The ***Quotation marks*** are used to show that the words enclosed by them are borrowed.

◼ A direct quotation should be enclosed within the quotation marks:

Abraham Lincoln said, "I shall make this land too hot for the feet of slaves."

◼ When a quotation is embraced within another, the contained quotation has only single marks:

Franklin said, "Most men come to believe 'honesty is the best policy.'"

■ 引述內容由好幾個段落組成時，每個段落前面都要加上引號。

撇號 （'）應標成逗號的樣子（只是位置在上面），而非引號或雙逗號的形式。撇號又稱省略號，被刪除或省略的字母通常是 e。其用法如下：

■ 撇號的主要用途是表示所有格。

所有單數名詞（包含普通和專有名詞）和字尾不是 s 的複數名詞，在字尾加上撇號和 s 即為所有格。這條規則的唯二例外是在詩詞中為了符合格律，可以省略 s，某些聖經短語也會省略 s，例如：

> For goodness' sake 看在上帝的份上
> For conscience' sake 看在良心的份上
> For Jesus' sake 看在耶穌的份上

這些片語習慣省略 s，現在也已成為慣用語了。

所有以 s 結尾的複數名詞在字尾加撇號即為所有格，例如：Boys'（男孩們的）、Horses'（馬兒們的）。

人稱代名詞的所有格不使用撇號，例如：Our（我們的）、Your（你們的）、Their（他們的）。

■ When a quotation consists of several paragraphs the quotation marks should precede each paragraph.

The **Apostrophe** should come under the comma rather than under the quotation marks or double comma. The letter elided or turned away is generally an *e*.

■ The principal use of the apostrophe is to denote the possessive case.

All nouns in the singular number whether proper names or not, and all nouns in the plural ending with any other letter than *s*, form the possessive by the addition of the apostrophe and the letter *s*. The only exceptions to this rule are, that, by poetical license the additional *s* may be elided in poetry for sake of the metre, and in the scriptural phrases "For goodness' sake." "For conscience' sake," "For Jesus' sake," etc. Custom has done away with the *s* and these phrases are now idioms of the language. All plural nouns ending in s form the possessive by the addition of the apostrophe only as boys', horses'. The possessive case of the personal pronouns never take the apostrophe, as our, your, their.

■ 在詩詞或一般對話中，撇號標示被省略的音節，例如：

> I've = I have 我已
>
> You're = you are 你是
>
> You'll = you will 你將

■ 有時為了將單字縮寫，必須去除幾個字母，這時就以撇號代替被省略的字母，例如：

> cont'd = continued 接續

■ 在表述日期時，如果已經知道是在哪個世紀，或是為了避免數字重複，可用撇號表示被省略的年份，例如：

> The Spirit of '76
> 76 年的精神

> I served in the army during the years 1895, '96, '97, '98 and '99.
> 我於 1895、96、97、98、99 年在陸軍服役。

■ In poetry and familiar dialogue the apostrophe marks the elision of a syllable,

as, "I've for I have"; "You're for you are"; "you'll for you will," etc.

■ Sometimes it is necessary to abbreviate a word by leaving out several letters.In such case the apostrophe takes the place of the omitted letters

as, "cont'd for continued."

■ The apostrophe is used to denote the elision of the century in dates, where the century is understood or to save the repetition of a series of figures,

as, "The Spirit of '76"; "I served in the army during the years 1895, '96, '97, '98 and '99."

大寫字母

　　大寫字母用於強調或區別出句子中的某些單字，藉此吸引讀者注意。有些作家，尤其是卡萊爾，經常使用大寫字母，已經到了濫用的程度。應該依照以下規則，僅在適當處使用大寫字母。

■ 在所有書寫格式中，每個句子第一個單字的首字母要大寫，例如：

> Time flies. 時光飛逝。
>
> My dear friends. 親愛的朋友。

■ 直接引言要以大寫開頭，例如：

> Dewey said, "Fire, when you're ready, Gridley!"
> 杜威說：「你準備好就發射，格里德利！」

■ 直接問句要以大寫為開頭，例如：

> Let me ask you, "How old are you?"
> 讓我問你一句：「你幾歲？」

CAPITAL LETTERS

Capital letters are used to give emphasis to or call attention to certain words to distinguish them from the context. Some authors, notably Carlyle, make such use of Capitals that it degenerates into an abuse. They should only be used in their proper places as given below.

■ The first word of every sentence, in fact the first word in writing of any kind should begin with a capital;

as, "Time flies." "My dear friend."

■ Every direct quotation should begin with a capital;

"Dewey said, 'Fire, when you're ready, Gridley!'"

■ Every direct question commences with a capital;

"Let me ask you, 'How old are you?'"

■ 每個詩句要以大寫為開頭，例如：

> Breathes there a man with soul so dead.
> 那人還在呼吸，靈魂卻已死去。

■ 每個標上序數的子句都要以大寫為開頭，例如：

> The witness asserts: (1) That he saw the man attacked; (2) That he saw him fall; (3) That he saw his assailant flee.
> 目擊證人聲稱：一，他看到這名男子遭到攻擊；二，他看到他倒地；三，他看到攻擊者逃逸。

■ 在書名中，名詞、代名詞、形容詞和副詞應以大寫為開頭，例如：

> Johnson's Lives of the Poets
> 強森的《詩人生平》

■ 羅馬數字須全大寫，例如：

> I, II, III, V, X, L, C, D, M
> 一、二、三、五、十、五十、一百、五百、一千

■ 專有名詞以大寫開頭，例如：

> Jones（瓊斯）、Johnson（強森）、Caesar（凱薩）、Mark Antony（馬克・安東尼）、England（英格蘭）、Pacific（太平洋）、Christmas（聖誕節）。

■ Every line of poetry begins with a capital;

"Breathes there a man with soul so dead."

■ Every numbered clause calls for a capital:

"The witness asserts: (1) That he saw the man attacked; (2) That he saw him fall; (3) That he saw his assailant flee."

■ In the titles of books, nouns, pronouns, adjectives and adverbs should begin with a capital;

as, "Johnson's Lives of the Poets."

■ In the Roman notation numbers are denoted by capitals;

as, I II III V X L C D M–1, 2, 3, 5, 10, 50, 100, 500, 1000.

■ Proper names begin with a capital;

as, "Jones, Johnson, Caesar, Mark Antony, England, Pacific, Christmas."

山、海、河等字做一般用途時為普通名詞，因此毋須大寫。但若加上形容詞或修飾語來指出特定物體，則為專有名詞，因此需要大寫，例如：Mississippi River（密西西比河）、North Sea（北海）、Allegheny Mountains（阿列格尼山脈）。同樣的，東、西、南、北等方位基點用於區分一個國家的特定區域時，需用大寫，例如：

> The North fought against the South.
> 北方與南方作戰。

在由專有名詞和普通名詞組成的複合字裡，普通名詞放在前面時須大寫，放在連字號後面則應小寫，例如：Post-Homeric（後荷馬時期）、Sunday-school（主日學）。

■ 專有名詞的衍生單字要以大寫為開頭，例如：

> American（美國人）、Irish（愛爾蘭人）、Christian（基督徒）、Americanize（美國化）、Christianize（基督教化）

按此原則，政黨、宗教派別和思想學派也要以大寫為開頭，例如：Republican（共和黨）、Democrat（民主黨）、Whig（輝格黨）、Catholic（天主教徒）、Presbyterian（長老教徒）、Rationalists（理性主義者）、Free Thinkers（自由思想家）。

■ 尊稱和政治職位的頭銜要以大寫開頭，例如：

> President（總統）、Chairman（主席）、Governor（州長）、Alderman（市議員）

Such words as river, sea, mountain, etc., when used generally are common, not proper nouns, and require no capital. But when such are used with an adjective or adjunct to specify a particular object they become proper names, and therefore require a capital; as, "Mississippi River, North Sea, Alleghany Mountains," etc. In like manner the cardinal points north, south, east and west, when they are used to distinguish regions of a country are capitals; as, "The North fought against the South."

When a proper name is compounded with another word, the part which is not a proper name begins with a capital if it precedes, but with a small letter if it follows, the hyphen; as "Post-Homeric," "Sunday-school."

■ Words derived from proper names require a Capital;

as, "American, Irish, Christian, Americanize, Christianize."

In this connection the names of political parties, religious sects and schools of thought begin with capitals; as, "Republican, Democrat, Whig, Catholic, Presbyterian, Rationalists, Free Thinkers."

■ The titles of honorable, state and political offices begin with a capital;

as, "President, Chairman, Governor, Alderman."

■ **學程和學位頭銜的縮寫要大寫，例如：**

> LL. D.（法學博士）、M. A.（碩士）、B. S.（學士）

授予學位的學習場所也要大寫，例如：Harvard University（哈佛大學）、Manhattan College（曼哈頓學院）。

■ **神父、女修道院院長、弟兄、姐妹、叔叔、阿姨等稱謂後面若有專有名詞，則須大寫，例如：**

Father Abraham（亞伯拉罕神父）、Mother Eddy（愛蒂院長）、Brother John（約翰弟兄）、Sister Jane（珍妮姐妹）、Uncle Jacob（雅各叔叔）、Aunt Eliza（伊莉莎阿姨）。神父這個詞若用於表示早期基督教作家，要以大寫為開頭，例如：

> Augustine was one of the learned Fathers of the Church. 奧古斯丁是教會中學識淵博的神父之一。

■ **上帝的各種稱呼要用大寫，例如：**

> God（上帝）、Lord（主）、Creator（造物者）、Providence（神）、Almighty（全能的神）、The Deity（天主）、Heavenly Father（天父）、Holy One（聖潔的神）

按此規則，指稱救世主的名詞也要大寫，例如：Jesus Christ（耶穌基督）、Son of God（神之子）、Man of Galilee（加利利人）、The Crucified（被釘十字架者）、The Anointed One（受

■ The abbreviations of learned titles and college degrees call for capitals;

as, "LL.D., M.A., B.S.," etc. Also the seats of learning conferring such degrees as, "Harvard University, Manhattan College," etc.

■ When such relative words as father, mother, brother, sister, uncle, aunt, etc., precede a proper name, they are written and printed with capitals;

as, Father Abraham, Mother Eddy, Brother John, Sister Jane, Uncle Jacob, Aunt Eliza. Father, when used to denote the early Christian writer, is begun with a capital; "Augustine was one of the learned Fathers of the Church."

■ The names applied to the Supreme Being begin with capitals:

"God, Lord, Creator, Providence, Almighty, The Deity, Heavenly Father, Holy One." In this respect the names applied to the Saviour also require capitals: "Jesus Christ, Son of God, Man of Galilee, The Crucified, The Anointed One." Also the designations of Biblical characters as "Lily of Israel, Rose of Sharon, Comfortress of the Afflicted, Help of Christians, Prince of the Apostles, Star of the Sea,"

膏者）。《聖經》人物的稱呼也要大寫，例如 Lily of Israel（以色列的百合）、Rose of Sharon（沙崙的玫瑰）、Comfortness of the Afflicted（苦難者的慰藉）、Help of Christians（進教之佑）、Prince of the Apostles（宗徒之長）、Star of the Sea（海星聖母）。上帝和基督的代名詞也要大寫，例如：His work、The work of Him（祂的工）。

■《聖經》及其相關著作的各種名稱要大寫，例如：

Holy Writ（聖文書）、The Sacred Book、Holy Book（聖書）、God's Word（上帝之語）、Old Testament（舊約）、New Testament（新約）、Gospel of St. Matthew（馬太福音）、Seven Penitential Psalms（悔罪詩）。

■ 源自《聖經》或聖經人物的表述要大寫，例如：

Water of Life（生命的活水）、Hope of Men（人類的希望）、Help of Christians（進教之佑）、Scourge of Nations（國之禍害）。

■《聖經》中的惡者名稱要大寫，例如：

Beelzebub（別西卜）、Prince of Darkness（黑暗王子）、Satan（撒旦）、King of Hell（地獄之王）、Devil（惡魔）、Incarnate Fiend（惡魔化身）、Tempter of Men（誘惑人類者）、Father of Lies（謊言之父）、Hater of Good（仇善者）。

etc. Pronouns referring to God and Christ take capitals; as, "His work, The work of Him, etc."

■ Expressions used to designate the Bible or any particular division of it begin with a capital;

as, "Holy Writ, The Sacred Book, Holy Book, God's Word, Old Testament, New Testament, Gospel of St. Matthew, Seven Penitential Psalms."

■ Expressions based upon the Bible or in reference to Biblical characters begin with a capital:

"Water of Life, Hope of Men, Help of Christians, Scourge of Nations."

■ The names applied to the Evil One require capitals:

"Beelzebub, Prince of Darkness, Satan, King of Hell, Devil, Incarnate Fiend, Tempter of Men, Father of Lies, Hater of Good."

■ 具有特殊重要性，尤其是代表重大歷史事件的名稱要大寫，例如：

　　The Revolutionary（美國革命）、The Civil War（南北戰爭）、The Middle Age（中古時期）、The Age of Iron（鐵器時代）。

■ 某個種族的重大歷史事件名稱要大寫，例如：

　　The Flood（大洪水）、Magna Charta（大憲章）、Declaration of Independence（獨立宣言）。

■ 星期、月份和季節的名稱要大寫，例如：

　　Monday（星期一）、March（三月）、Autumn（秋季）。

■ 代名詞 I 一定要大寫，所有用來表示驚訝的感嘆詞也都要以大寫開頭，例如：

　　Alas! He is gone. 哎呀！他走了。
　　Ah! I pitied him. 啊！我憐憫他。

■ Words of very special importance, especially those which stand out as the names of leading events in history, have capitals;

as, "The Revolution, The Civil War, The Middle Ages, The Age of Iron," etc.

■ Terms which refer to great events in the history of the race require capitals;

"The Flood, Magna Charta, Declaration of Independence."

■ The names of the days of the week and the months of the year and the seasons are commenced with capitals:

"Monday, March, Autumn."

■ The Pronoun *I* and the interjection *O* always require the use of capitals. In fact all the interjections when uttered as exclamations commence with capitals:

"Alas! he is gone." "Ah! I pitied him."

■ 所有化名、虛構和用於區別的名字要用大寫，例如：

The Wizard of the North（北方巫師）、Paul Pry（愛打聽消息的保羅）、The Northern Gael（北蓋爾人）、Sandy Sanderson（「桑帝」珊德森）、Poor Robin（可憐的羅賓）。

■ 在擬人法中，沒有生命的事物被賦予生命和行動時，被擬人化的名詞或物體要大寫，例如：

The starry Night shook the dews from her wings.
綴滿星辰的黑夜抖落翅膀上的露珠。

Mild-eyed Day appeared.
雙眼溫和的白日出現了。

The Oak said to the Beech, "I am stronger than you."
橡樹對山毛櫸說：「我比你強壯」。

■ All *noms-de-guerre*, assumed names, as well as names given for distinction, call for capitals,

as, "The Wizard of the North," "Paul Pry," "The Northern Gael," "Sandy Sanderson," "Poor Robin," etc.

■ In personification, that is, when inanimate things are represented as endowed with life and action, the noun or object personified begins with a capital;

as, "The starry Night shook the dews from her wings." "Mild-eyed Day appeared," "The Oak said to the Beech, 'I am stronger than you.'"

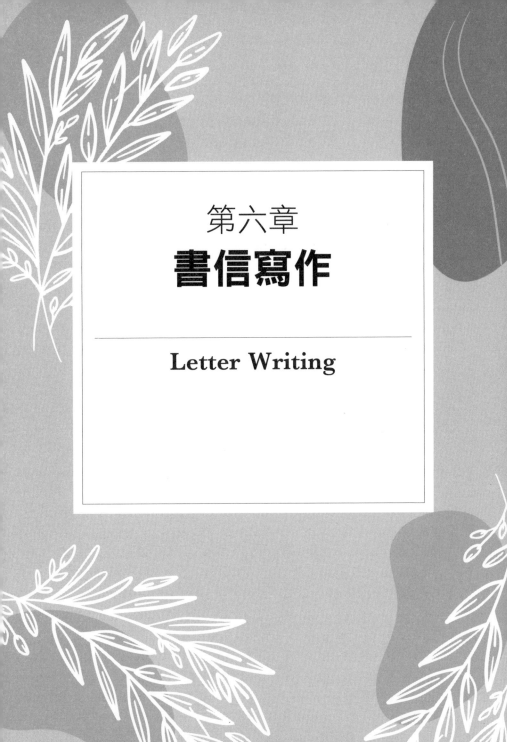

第六章
書信寫作

Letter Writing

許多人似乎認為書信寫作非常簡單易學，實則不然。書信寫作是最困難的一種寫作類型，要有很多耐性、下很多功夫，才能掌握它的精髓。事實上，能寫出完美英文書信的人少之又少。書信被視為一種直接談話的形式，因此又可稱為遠距離的對話。有形形色色的人懷著各種心境和情緒，在各種時候、就各種可能的主題，寫信給各式各樣社會背景相異、擁有不同人生目標的人，因此實在無法訂定一套制式規則來規範書信的長度、文風或主題，只能針對書信範圍和目的提供普遍性的建議，並列出在習慣上和往例中所認可的書信形式。

每個會寫字的人都應該了解書信寫作的原則，畢竟人人都會碰上需要寫信給遠方親友的時候，卻不見得會遇到需要進行其他類型寫作的情況。

在過去，目不識丁的鄉下人如果要跟親友通信，會請到處替人授課的教師代筆，但這麼做的缺點是得向收信人以外的人透露祕密，私密話語往往因此曝光。

Many people seem to regard letter-writing as a very simple and easily acquired branch, but on the contrary it is one of the most difficult forms of composition and requires much patience and labor to master its details. In fact there are very few perfect letter-writers in the language. It constitutes the direct form of speech and may be called conversation at a distance. Its forms are so varied by every conceivable topic written at all times by all kinds of persons in all kinds of moods and tempers and addressed to all kinds of persons of varying degrees in society and of different pursuits in life, that no fixed rules can be laid down to regulate its length, style or subject matter. Only general suggestions can be made in regard to scope and purpose, and the forms of indicting set forth which custom and precedent have sanctioned.

The principles of letter-writing should be understood by everybody who has any knowledge of written language, for almost everybody at some time or other has necessity to address some friend or acquaintance at a distance, whereas comparatively few are called upon to direct their efforts towards any other kind of composition.

Formerly the illiterate countryman, when he had occasion to communicate with friends or relations, called in the peripatetic schoolmaster as his amanuensis, but this had one draw-back–secrets had to be poured into an ear other than that for which they were intended, and often the confidence was betrayed.

如今教育普及，幾乎沒有需要請人代寫私密信件的情況。現在很少有人不識字到無法讀寫的地步。無論教育程度多低，最好還是自己寫信，而非請人代勞。即便寫出下面這樣錯字百出、構句有問題的書信，但仍能看出寫信者立意良善，努力自己寫信而非請人代勞：

> Deer fren, i lift up my pen to let ye no that i hove been sik for the past 3 weeks, hopping this will findye the same…
> 親愛的朋友，我提筆寫信讓你知道我病了三個禮拜，希望你一切安好……

書信的本質、主旨和語調取決於寫信目的、寫信者和收信者。風格要輕鬆或正式、平鋪直敘或辭藻華麗、輕鬆或嚴肅、愉快或沉重、多愁善感或實事求是，都取決於這三個條件。

書信寫作的最高準則是自然簡單，不應過分修飾，而要單純寫下寫信者腦中浮現的想法和概念。我們都不喜歡聽人說話拘謹、字句計較，同樣地，寫信拘謹、字句計較也會讓讀者感到乏味。輕鬆、對話般的信反而可以馬上抓住讀者的注意。

Now, that education is abroad in the land, there is seldom any occasion for any person to call upon the service of another to compose and write a personal letter. Very few now-a-days are so grossly illiterate as not to be able to read and write. No matter how crude his effort may be it is better for any one to write his own letters than trust to another. Even if he should commence, "deer fren, i lift up my pen to let ye no that i hove been sik for the past 3 weeks, hopping this will findye the same," his spelling and construction can be excused in view of the fact that his intention is good, and that he is doing his best to serve his own turn without depending upon others.

The nature, substance and tone of any letter depend upon the occasion that calls it forth, upon the person writing it and upon the person for whom it is intended. Whether it should be easy or formal in style, plain or ornate, light or serious, gay or grave, sentimental or matter-of-fact depend upon these three circumstances.

In letter writing the first and most important requisites are to be natural and simple; there should be no straining after effect, but simply a spontaneous out-pouring of thoughts and ideas as they naturally occur to the writer. We are repelled by a person who is stiff and labored in his conversation and in the same way the stiff and labored letter bores the reader. Whereas if it is light and in a conversational vein it immediately engages his attention.

The letter which is written with the greatest facility is the best kind of letter because it naturally expresses what is in the writer, he has not to search for his words, they flow in a perfect unison with

以最流暢方式寫下的信是最佳信件，因為它自然地表達出寫信者心裡的話，文字沒有經過精挑細選，而是自然流瀉出來，且完全符合寫信者想要溝通的想法。寫信告訴朋友自己怎麼度過週日時光時，並不需要琢磨用字遣詞或研究成語來取悅或打動朋友，只要像在當面聊天那樣，告訴他你在這天做了什麼、跟誰去了哪裡，發生了什麼大事，就能寫成一封自然、適合用於書信往來的信了。

書信類型不同，適合的寫作風格也不同，不過讓書信讀來自然的關鍵都是一樣的：寫信者不該試著在信中傳達出跟自己身分不符合的形象。一個學識有限的普通街道清潔工若想模仿大學教授，寫出散發文學氣息的書信，是既傻又徒勞無功的作法。他或許頭腦也很好，但受教程度不高，欠缺社會賦予的學養洗鍊。因此，他在寫信時，無論溝通對象是誰，都應記住大家只會期待他寫出同樣等級的信，不會預期他寫出切斯特菲爾德勳爵（Lord Chesterfield）或格萊斯頓首相（William Gladstone）的語法及用字。儘管如此，他仍應記住寫信對象是誰。如果寫信對象是大主教、教會顯要或政府官員，字詞要跟寫信給朋友時有所不同，既不能直呼大主教的名諱，也不能出現平常對熟人、朋友使用的親密用語。不過，要寫信給大主教和寫信給一般人一樣，都不需要豐富的學養。這位清潔工只需要知道稱謂的形式，以及如何善用自己有限的字彙即可。相關範例如下：

the ideas he desires to communicate. When you write to your friend John Browne to tell him how you spent Sunday you have not to look around for the words, or study set phrases with a view to please or impress Browne, you just tell him the same as if he were present before you, how you spent the day, where you were, with whom you associated and the chief incidents that occurred during the time. Thus, you write natural and it is such writing that is adapted to epistolary correspondence.

There are different kinds of letters, each calling for a different style of address and composition, nevertheless the natural key should be maintained in all, that is to say, the writer should never attempt to convey an impression that he is other than what he is. It would be silly as well as vain for the common street laborer of a limited education to try to put on literary airs and emulate a college professor; he may have as good a brain, but it is not as well developed by education, and he lacks the polish which society confers. When writing a letter the street laborer should bear in mind that only the letter of a street-laborer is expected from him, no matter to whom his communication may be addressed and that neither the grammar nor the diction of a Chesterfield or Gladstone is looked for in his language. Still the writer should keep in mind the person to whom he is writing. If it is to an Archbishop or some other great dignitary of Church or state it certainly should be couched in terms different from those he uses to John Browne, his intimate friend. Just as he cannot say "Dear John" to an Archbishop, no more can he address him in the familiar words

17 Second Avenue,
New York City.
January 1st, 1910.

Most Rev. P. A. Jordan,
Archbishop of New York.

Most Rev. and dear Sir:
While sweeping the crossing at Fifth Avenue and 50th street on last Wednesday morning, I found the enclosed Fifty Dollar Bill, when I am sending to you in the hope that it may be restored to the rightful owner.
I beg you will acknowledge receipt, and should the owner be found I trust you will notify me, so that I may claim some reward for my honesty.
I am, Most Rev. and dear Sir,

Very respectfully yours,
Thomas Jones.

第二大道十七號，
紐約市，
一九一〇年一月一日

P. A. 約旦大主教，
紐約市大主教

大主教，親愛的先生：
上週三早上我在清掃第五大道與五十街的十字路口時，發現附在此信中的五十美元紙鈔。我將鈔票寄給您，希望您將它還給失主。
請您確認收到此信，如找到失主，相信您能通知我，好讓我向失主請求償金，以回報我的拾金不昧。
向您致上崇高敬意，大主教，親愛的先生，

湯瑪仕・瓊斯

he uses to his friend of everyday acquaintance and companionship. Yet there is no great learning required to write to an Archbishop, no more than to an ordinary individual. All the laborer needs to know is the form of address and how to properly utilize his limited vocabulary to the best advantage. Here is the form for such a letter:

17 Second Avenue,
New York City.
January 1st, 1910.

Most Rev. P. A. Jordan,
Archbishop of New York.

Most Rev. and dear Sir:
While sweeping the crossing at Fifth Avenue and 50th street on last Wednesday morning, I found the enclosed Fifty Dollar Bill, which I am sending to you in the hope that it may be restored to the rightful owner.
I beg you will acknowledge receipt and should the owner be found I trust you will notify me, so that I may claim some reward for my honesty.
I am, Most Rev. and dear Sir,

Very respectfully yours,
Thomas Jones.

Observe the brevity of the letter. Jones makes no suggestions to the Archbishop how to find the owner, for he knows the course the Archbishop will adopt, of having the finding of the bill announced from the Church pulpits. Could Jones himself find the owner there

這封信相當簡明扼要。瓊斯並沒建議大主教如何找尋失主，因為他知道大主教會在教堂布道的場合公布找到這張鈔票的事情。要是瓊斯自己就能找到失主，就沒必要勞煩大主教了。

這封信確實不同於他會寫給朋友的信，不過信件內容簡單、不逾矩且平鋪直述，沒有華麗辭藻和艱澀深奧的字彙點綴，一針見血地點出信件目的。

書信可分為寫給親友、寫給商業夥伴、以公務人員的正式身分撰寫、為了教學目的撰寫，以及報導當前日常事件的信件。

親友書信是最常見的書信類型，其文風和形式取決於寫信者和收信者之間的關係和親密程度。親屬和摯友之間的書信，開頭和結尾能以最親密的對話形式寫成，語氣可以熱情或打趣，不過千萬不要逾越應有的規矩和禮儀。記住，書信跟對話不同，對話只會給意圖的對象聽到，但書信卻有可能被不相關的人看到。因此，千萬不要寫下任何讓他人看了會有損你的人格或本性的文字。你的用語可以歡樂、打趣、詼諧，流露自己的情感，但不可流於低俗，最重要的是，絕對不要使用在道德上有半點不得體的文字。

would be no occasion to apply to the Archbishop.

This letter, it is true, is different from that which he would send to Browne. Nevertheless it is simple without being familiar, is just a plain statement, and is as much to the point for its purpose as if it were garnished with rhetoric and "words of learned length and thundering sound."

Letters may be divided into those of friendship, acquaintanceship, those of business relations, those written in an official capacity by public servants, those designed to teach, and those which give accounts of the daily happenings on the stage of life, in other words, news letters.

Letters of friendship are the most common and their style and form depend upon the degree of relationship and intimacy existing between the writers and those addressed. Between relatives and intimate friends the beginning and end may be in the most familiar form of conversation, either affectionate or playful. They should, however, never overstep the boundaries of decency and propriety, for it is well to remember that, unlike conversation, which only is heard by the ears for which it is intended, written words may come under eyes other than those for whom they were designed. Therefore, it is well never to write anything which the world may not read without detriment to your character or your instincts. You can be joyful, playful, jocose, give vent to your feelings, but never stoop to low language and, above all, to language savoring in the slightest degree of moral impropriety.

商業書信涉及商業利益，因此是最重要的書信類型。人們通常透過書信往來判斷一個人或一家公司的商業性格。在許多情況中，給人留下不良印象的反而不是開發業務、爭取商業利益和累積客戶，而是信件。模稜兩可、馬虎隨便的用語對成功的事業是不利的。商業書信應該簡明扼要、直截了當，最重要的是要誠實，不要給人錯誤印象，或提出無法履行的誘因。商業書信跟商業行為一樣，誠實往往是上策。

　　官方信函幾乎全以正式形式寫成。語氣必須清晰、簡潔、莊重，讓收信者對國家法規和機構產生應有的尊重。

　　教學書信是自成一格的書信類型，是以書信形式寫成的文學作品。某些最傑出的作家會採用這種寫作形式，加以突顯其思想和概念的重要性，最著名的例子是切斯特菲爾德勳爵的《禮儀之書》（The Fine Gentleman's Etiquette），該書的內容是由好幾封給兒子的書信組成。

　　新聞信函是寄給報社，描述當前世界大事、典禮和事件的書信。一些當代最傑出的作家正是文字記者，他們以輕鬆流暢的風格，寫下簡單易讀、詼諧豐富的文章，讓讀者饒富興趣地一口氣從頭讀到尾。

Business letters are of the utmost importance on account of the interests involved. The business character of a man or of a firm is often judged by the correspondence. On many occasions letters instead of developing trade and business interests and gaining clientele, predispose people unfavorably towards those whom they are designed to benefit. Ambiguous, slip-shod language is a detriment to success. Business letters should be clear, concise, to the point and, above all, honest, giving no wrong impressions or holding out any inducements that cannot be fulfilled. In business letters, just as in business conduct, honesty is always the best policy.

Official letters are mostly always formal. They should possess clearness, brevity and dignity of tone to impress the receivers with the proper respect for the national laws and institutions.

Letters designed to teach or *didactic letters* are in a class all by themselves. They are simply literature in the form of letters and are employed by some of the best writers to give their thoughts and ideas a greater emphasis. The most conspicuous example of this kind of composition is the book on Etiquette by Lord Chesterfield, which took the form of a series of letters to his son.

News letters are accounts of world happenings and descriptions of ceremonies and events sent into the newspapers. Some of the best authors of our time are newspaper men who write in an easy flowing style which is most readable, full of humor and fancy and which carries one along with breathless interest from beginning to end.

The principal parts of a letter are (1) the *heading* or introduction;

　　書信結構包含四個主要部分：信頭（開場介紹）、正文（信件主文）、署名（結語和簽名）和信封上的地址。書信正文取決於信件本質和寫信者與收信者之間的關係，因此沒有特定形式或規則；其他三個部分則有特定規則，這些規則是約定俗成的用法，因此必須加以認識。

信頭

　　英文信頭包括兩個部分，意即收信人地址、寫信日期、收信人稱呼語，例如：

73 New Street, Newark, N.J., February 1st, 1910.	新街 73 號， 紐瓦克市，紐澤西州， 1910 年 2 月 1 日，
Messr. Gin and Co., New York Gentlemen:	紐約金恩公司的 諸位先生 紳士們：

　　收信人地址絕對不能省略，一定要寫上收信人所在的城市、街道和門牌號碼。此外，除非該座城市是知名大城，不會跟其他同名或名字相近的城市搞混，否則一定要寫上州的縮寫，就像上述例子中的 Newark, N.J. 一樣，因為俄亥俄州也有一個紐瓦

(2) the *body* or substance of the letter; (3) the *subscription* or closing expression and signature; (4) the *address* or direction on the envelope. For the *body* of a letter no forms or rules can be laid down as it altogether depends on the nature of the letter and the relationship between the writer and the person addressed. There are certain rules which govern the other three features and which custom has sanctioned. Every one should be acquainted with these rules.

THE HEADING

The *Heading* has three parts, viz., the name of the place, the date of writing and the designation of the person or persons addressed; thus:

73 New Street,
Newark, N. J.,
February 1st, 1910.

Messr. Ginn and Co.,
New York
Gentlemen:

The name of the place should never be omitted; in cities, street and number should always be given, and except when the city is large and very conspicuous, so that there can be no question as to its identity with another of the same or similar name, the abbreviation of the State should be appended, as in the above, Newark, N. J. There is

克市。許多信件因沒有遵守這個規則而被寄丟。每封信件都要標上**日期**，特別是商業書信。在商業書信中，日期不能標在信尾，不過親友書信則是可以。**收信人稱呼語**各有不同，就看通信者之間的關係為何。親友書信依交情或親密程度，有各種不同起頭方式，例如：

My dear Wife: 親愛的妻子：

My dear Husband: 親愛的丈夫：

My dear Friend: 親愛的朋友：

My darling Mother: 親愛的母親：

My dearest Love: 我最心愛的人：

Dear Aunt: 親愛的阿姨：

Dear Uncle: 親愛的叔叔：

Dear George: 親愛的喬治：

較不親密的正式稱呼語可使用以下例子：

Dear Sir: 親愛的先生：

My dear Sir: 我親愛的先生：

Dear Mr. Smith: 親愛的史密斯先生：

Dear Madam: 親愛的女士：

another Newark in the State of Ohio. Owing to failure to comply with this rule many letters go astray. The *date* should be on every letter, especially business letters. The date should never be put at the bottom in a business letter, but in friendly letters this may be done. The *designation* of the person or persons addressed differs according to the relations of the correspondents. Letters of friendship may begin in many ways according to the degrees of friendship or intimacy. Thus:

My dear Wife:

My dear Husband:

My dear Friend:

My darling Mother:

My dearest Love:

Dear Aunt:

Dear Uncle:

Dear George: etc.

To mark a lesser degree of intimacy such formal designations as the following may be employed:

Dear Sir:

My dear Sir:

Dear Mr. Smith:

Dear Madam: etc.

沒有學位或頭銜的一般人稱為 Mr. 或 Mrs.，稱呼語是 Dear Sir 或 Dear Madam。任何年齡的未婚女性在信封上的稱謂是 Miss，但在信裡的稱呼語是 Dear Madam。

在稱呼某公司的各位先生時，用 Mr. 的複數 Messrs，其相對應的稱呼語是 Dear Sirs 或 Gentlemen。

在英國會用 Esq. 代替 Mr. 來表示地位略高的人，在美國有時會這麼使用，但這種用語基本上已經過時。美國的風俗民情不會這麼使用。真的要用時，也只會用來指稱律師和治安官。

署名

署名又稱信尾，是由敬辭或暱稱和簽名組成。用語的使用取決於信件雙方的關係。夫妻或情人之間的書信可以下列例子做為書信結語：

Yours lovingly, 你的愛人
Yours affectionately, 你的摯愛
Devotedly yours, 你唯一的愛
Ever yours, 永遠愛你的

Ordinary people with no degrees or titles are addressed as Mr. and Mrs. and are designed Dear Sir: Dear Madam: and an unmarried woman of any age is addressed on the envelope as Miss So-and-so, but always designed in the letter as

Dear Madam:

The plural of Mr. as in addressing a firm is *Messrs*, and the corresponding salutation is *Dear Sirs*: or *Gentlemen*:

In England *Esq.* is used for *Mr.* as a mark of slight superiority and in this country it is sometimes used, but it is practically obsolete. Custom is against it and American sentiment as well. If it is used it should be only applied to lawyers and justices of the peace.

SUBSCRIPTION

The *Subscription* or ending of a letter consists of the term of respect or affection and the signature. The term depends upon the relation of the person addressed. Letters of friendship can close with such expressions as:

> Yours lovingly,
> Yours affectionately,
> Devotedly yours,
> Ever yours, etc.

夫妻和情人之間應避免使用過分親暱的結語，像是 Your own Darling（你的寶貝）、Your own Dovey（你的親親）和其他濃情蜜意的愚蠢結語，這讓書信顯得膚淺。即使不用荒誕可笑的用語，也能強烈表達愛意。

署名的正式表達方式包括：

Yours Sincerely, 敬上
Yours truly, 謹上
Respectfully yours, 肅此

這些用語可以稍作一些變化，表達寫信人對收信人的風度或態度，例如：

Very sincerely yours, 誠心敬上
Very respectfully yours, 誠心肅此
With deep respect yours, 誠心肅此
Yours very truly, 誠心謹上

請勿使用下列過分熱情的複雜用語，例如：

In the meantime with the highest respect, I am yours to command,
致上最高敬意，在下任您差遣

I have the honor to be, Sir, Your humble Servant,
先生，身為您謙卑的僕人實屬榮幸

as between husbands and wives or between lovers. Such gushing terminations as Your Own Darling, Your own Dovey and other pet and silly endings should be avoided, as they denote shallowness. Love can be strongly expressed without dipping into the nonsensical and the farcical.

Formal expressions of Subscription are:

>Yours Sincerely,
>
>Yours truly,
>
>Respectfully yours,

and the like, and these may be varied to denote the exact bearing or attitude the writer wishes to assume to the person addressed: as,

>Very sincerely yours,
>
>Very respectfully yours,
>
>With deep respect yours,
>
>Yours very truly, etc.

Such elaborate endings as

"In the meantime with the highest respect, I am yours to command,"

"I have the honor to be, Sir, Your humble Servant,"

> With great expression of esteem, I am sincerely yours,
> 謹以崇高敬意敬上
>
> Believe me, my dear Sir, Ever faithfully yours,
> 相信我，親愛的先生，我永遠忠誠地屬於您

最好不要使用這類用語做為正式書信的結語。如果你要寫信告訴萊恩先生說你有房子要賣，在描述房子和說明賣屋條件後，簡單這麼署名即可：

> Your obedient servant, 您順從的僕人
>
> Yours very truly, 誠心謹上
>
> Yours with respect, 敬重謹上
>
> James Wilson. 詹姆斯・威爾森

不要說你有此榮幸如何如何，或要對方相信你如何如何。你要表達的重點是你有房子要賣，你以誠摯、尊重的態度面對這位潛在客戶。

署名不要縮寫，例如：Y'rs Resp'fly。另外，也要明確表示自己的性別，例如：

> Yours truly,
> John Field
> （約翰・菲爾德謹上）

"With great expression of esteem, I am Sincerely yours,"

"Believe me, my dear Sir, Ever faithfully yours,"

are condemned as savoring too much of affectation.

It is better to finish formal letters without any such qualifying remarks. If you are writing to Mr. Ryan to tell him that you have a house for sale, after describing the house and stating the terms simply sign yourself

> Your obedient Servant
>
> Yours very truly,
>
> Yours with respect,
>
> James Wilson.

Don't say you have the honor to be anything or ask him to believe anything, all you want to tell him is that you have a house for sale and that you are sincere, or hold him in respect as a prospective customer.

Don't abbreviate the signature as: *Y'rs Resp'fly* and always make your sex obvious. Write plainly

> Yours truly,
>
> *John Field*

and not *J. Field*, so that the person to whom you send it may not take you for Jane Field. It is always best to write the first name in full.

不要寫成 J. Field，免得收信人誤以為你是 Jane Field（珍·菲爾德）。最好完整寫上全名。

如果你要寄信表達敬意或感謝他人善意，可以用與你獲得的善意相當的結語：

> Yours gratefully, 敬謝
> Yours very gratefully, 誠心敬謝

一般習慣用法並不會在自己的名字後面加上學位或頭銜，除非你是爵士、伯爵或公爵，而且人們只認識你的頭銜。美國沒有這類頭銜，因此沒有必要考量這點。別用下列署名方式：

> Sincerely yours,
> Obadiah Jackson, M.A./L.L. D.
> 奧巴迪亞·傑克森碩士／法學博士敬上

如果你是碩士或法學博士，不用大肆宣傳，人們一般也會知道。許多人——特別是神職人員——喜歡在自己的名字後面加上名譽學位以示炫耀。不須經過考試就能獲頒的名譽學位就不必拿出來講了，畢竟許多愚者都有這種要他靠頭腦肯定拿不到的學位。

If you are sending a letter acknowledging a compliment or some kindness done you may say, *Yours gratefully,* or *Yours very gratefully,* in proportion to the act of kindness received.

It is not customary to sign letters of degrees or titles after your name, except you are a lord, earl or duke and only known by the title, but as we have no such titles in America it is unnecessary to bring this matter into consideration. Don't sign yourself,

> Sincerely yours,
>
> Obadiah Jackson, M.A. or L.L. D.

If you're an M. A. or an L.L. D. people generally know it without your sounding your own trumpet. Many people, and especially clergymen, are fond of flaunting after their names degrees they have received *honoris causa*, that is, degrees as a mark of honor, without examination. Such degrees should be kept in the background. Many a deadhead has these degrees which he could never have earned by brain work.

地址

書信地址包含收信人姓名、稱謂和住所地點：

Mr. Hugh Black	休・布萊克先生
112 Southgate Street,	南門街 112 號，
Altoona,	阿爾圖納市，
Pa.	賓州

　　親密朋友通常會給彼此取暱稱，像是小名或綽號等。這在對話中可以隨意使用，但在任何情況下，信封上千萬不能出現這樣的暱稱。信封上的署名一定要用符合禮儀的正確名稱，彷彿出自陌生人之筆。寫信封時，唯一會遇到難題的是稱謂。男性稱謂是 Mr.，已婚女性稱謂是 Mrs.，未婚女性稱謂是 Miss，就連男孩都要稱為 Master（少爺）。一個以上的男性稱為 Messrs，一個以上的女性有時會用 Mesdames。如果收信人有頭銜，加上去會比較有禮貌，但是不要重疊使用頭銜，例如我們可以這麼寫：

> Robert Stitt, M.D., 醫學博士羅勃・史迪特

但不能這麼寫：

> Dr. Robert Stitt, M.D., 醫學博士羅勃・史迪特醫生

ADDRESS

The *address* of a letter consists of the name, the title and the residence.

> Mr. Hugh Black,
> 112 Southgate Street,
> Altoona,
> Pa.

Intimate friends have often familiar names for each other, such as pet names, nicknames, etc., which they use in the freedom of conversation, but such names should never, under any circumstances, appear on the envelope. The subscription on the envelope should be always written with propriety and correctness and as if penned by an entire stranger. The only difficulty in the envelope inscription is the title. Every man is entitled to *Mr.* and every lady to *Mrs.* and every unmarried lady to *Miss.* Even a boy is entitled to *Master.* When more than one is addressed the title is *Messrs. Mesdames* is sometimes written of women. If the person addressed has a title it is courteous to use it, but titles never must be duplicated. Thus, we can write

Robert Stitt, M. D., but never
Dr. Robert Stitt, M. D, or

或：

Mr. Robert Stitt, M.D. 醫學博士羅勃‧史迪特先生

寫信給醫學博士時，最好是用 M.D.（醫學博士）來表示他的專業，以與 Dr.（博士）做為區分，應該要寫為 Robert Stitt, M.D.,（醫學博士羅勃‧史迪特），而非 Dr. Robert Stitt,（羅勃‧史迪特博士）。

寫信給神職人員時，即便對方有其他頭銜，仍要保留 Rev.，例如：

Rev. Tracy Tooke, LL. D. 法學博士崔西‧圖克牧師

對方有一個以上的頭銜時，習慣上只會寫主要的頭銜，因此不會像下面這樣，列出山繆‧麥康牧師的所有學位：

Rev. Samuel MacComb, B.A, M. A., B. Sc., Ph.D., LL. D., D. D.

而是會寫為：

Rev. Samuel MacComb, LL. D.

這邊加上 LL. D. 會比 D. D. 更好，因為大多牧師都有神學博士的頭銜，而有法學博士頭銜的牧師相對較少。

Mr. Robert Stitt, M. D.

In writing to a medical doctor it is well to indicate his profession by the letters M. D. so as to differentiate him from a D. D. It is better to write Robert Stitt, M. D., than Dr. Robert Stitt.

In the case of clergymen the prefix Rev. is retained even when they have other titles; as

Rev. Tracy Tooke, LL. D.

When a person has more titles than one it is customary to only give him the leading one. Thus instead of writing Rev. Samuel MacComb, B. A., M. A., B. Sc., Ph. D., LL. D., D. D. the form employed is Rev. Samuel MacComb, LL. D. LL. D. is appended in preference to D. D. because in most cases the "Rev." implies a "D. D." while comparatively few with the prefix "Rev." are entitled to "LL. D."

尊稱州長、法官、國會成員和其他政府官員時，可用 Hon. 代替 Mr. 和 Esq.，因此會寫：

Hon. Skifkins, 尊敬的史基弗金斯

而不會寫：

Hon. Mr. Josiah Snifkins 尊敬的史基弗金斯先生

或：

Hon. Josiah Snifkins, Esq. 尊敬的史基弗金斯先生

Hon. 雖然經常用在州長的姓名前面，不過州長的稱謂應該是 Excellency，例如：

His Excellency, Charles E. Hughes, Albany, N. Y.	察爾斯・E・休斯閣下， 阿爾巴尼市， 紐約州

寫信給總統時，信封上的署名應該是：

To the President, Executive Mansion, Washington, D. C.	致總統， 總統官邸， 華盛頓特區

In the case of *Honorables* such as Governors, Judges, Members of Congress, and others of the Civil Government the prefix "Hon." does away with *Mr.* and *Esq.* Thus we write Hon. Josiah Snifkins, not Hon. Mr. Josiah Snifkins or Hon. Josiah Snifkins, Esq.

Though this prefix *Hon.* is also often applied to Governors they should be addressed as Excellency. For instance:

His Excellency,
Charles E. Hughes,
Albany,
N. Y.

In writing to the President the superscription on the envelope should be

To the President,
Executive Mansion,
Washington, D. C.

對於醫師、律師等專業人士和正當獲頒大學學位的人，可在信封上以其頭銜稱呼之，例如：

Jonathan Janeway, M. D.
強納森‧簡威，醫學博士

Hubert Houston, B. L.
賀伯特‧休士頓，法學士

Matthew Marks, M. A.
馬修‧馬克斯，碩士

收信人地址應該完整、清楚，包括城市、鄉鎮、街道和門牌號碼，而且筆跡必須清晰易讀。如果州的縮寫易與其他州的混淆弄錯，則應寫上完整州名。信封上的地址不要像信頭上那樣寫成同一行，而是要將每段訊息拆成不同行，例如：

Liberty, Sullivan County, New York	自由村， 沙利文郡， 紐約州

215 Minna St., San Francisco, California	米納街 215 號， 舊金山市， 加州

Professional men such as doctors and lawyers as well as those having legitimately earned College Degrees may be addressed on the envelopes by their titles, as

> Jonathan Janeway, M. D.
>
> Hubert Houston, B. L.
>
> Matthew Marks, M. A., etc.

The residence of the person addressed should be plainly written out in full. The street and numbers should be given and the city or town written very legibly. If the abbreviation of the State is liable to be confounded or confused with that of another then the full name of the State should be written. In writing the residence on the envelope, instead of putting it all in one line as is done at the head of a letter, each item of the residence forms a separate line. Thus,

> Liberty,
> Sullivan County,
> New York.

> 215 Minna St.,
> San Francisco,
> California.

信封右上角應保留郵戳空間。姓名和稱謂應該放在介於信封頂端和底端之間的中間位置。姓名不要寫在過於偏右或偏左的位置，而是寫在中間位置，姓名頭尾跟信封兩邊的距離要相等。

寫給知名大企業或政府官員時，有時習慣將街道和門牌號碼省略，例如：

Messrs. Seigel, Copper Co., New York City.	諸位先生，西格爾庫柏公司，紐約市

Hon. William J. Gaynor, New York City.	尊敬的威廉·J·蓋納，紐約市

短箋

「短箋」可以說是簡短的信函，主要是指邀請函、接受函、婉拒函和介紹函。在現代寫作禮儀中，短箋是非正式寫作；卡片的寫作禮儀已經取代拘謹正式的書信，因此非正式短箋已成常規。晚餐和宴會邀約現在多半都是寫在卡片上。婉拒函會寫在拜訪卡上寄回，上面簡單寫上「婉拒」兩個字。邀請卡和邀請函底下方通常會寫 R. S. V. P.，這是法文「敬請回覆」的縮寫，不過其實沒有必要在邀請卡上寫這個，因為每個有教養的人都知道應

There should be left a space for the postage stamp in the upper right hand corner. The name and title should occupy a line that is about central between the top of the envelope and the bottom. The name should neither be too much to right or left but located in the centre, the beginning and end at equal distances from either end.

In writing to large business concerns which are well known or to public or city officials it is sometimes customary to leave out number and street. Thus,

Messrs. Seigel, Cooper Co.,
New York City,

Hon. William J. Gaynor,
New York City.

NOTES

Notes may be regarded as letters in miniature confined chiefly to invitations, acceptances, regrets and introductions, and modern etiquette tends towards informality in their composition. Card etiquette, in fact, has taken the place of ceremonious correspondence and informal notes are now the rule. Invitations to dinner and receptions are now mostly written on cards. "Regrets" are sent back on visiting cards with just the one word *"Regrets"* plainly written

短箋

該回覆他人邀請。

不要在短箋信封上寫上 addressed（寄給）這個字。

由朋友遞送的短箋不要密封。

不要將短箋寫在明信片上。

以下是常見的短箋形式：

■ 正式邀請函：

Mr. and Mrs. Henry Wagstaff request the honor of Mr. McAdoo's presence on Friday evening, June 15th, at 8 o'clock to meet the Governor of the Fort. 19 Woodbine Terrace June 8th, 1910.	亨利・瓦格斯塔夫夫婦敬邀麥克阿杜先生於六月十五日週五晚間八點與州長會面。 伍班露台 19 號 1910 年 6 月 8 日

這是需要著晚禮服出席的正式宴會邀請函。以下麥克阿杜先生以第三人稱回覆：

thereon. Often on cards and notes of invitation we find the letters R. S. V. P. at the bottom. These letters stand for the French *repondez s'il vous plait*, which means "Reply, if you please," but there is no necessity to put this on an invitation card as every well-bred person knows that a reply is expected.

Don't write the word *addressed* on the envelope of a note.

Don't *seal* a note delivered by a friend.

Don't write a note on a postal card.

Here are a few common forms:

■ FORMAL INVITATIONS

Mr. and Mrs. Henry Wagstaff request the honor of Mr. McAdoo's presence on Friday evening, June 15th, at 8 o'clock to meet the Governor of the Fort.

19 Woodbine Terrace
June 8th, 1910.

This is an invitation to a formal reception calling for evening dress. Here is Mr. McAdoo's reply in the third person:

Mr. McAdoo presents his compliments to Mr. and Mrs. Henry Wagstaff and accepts with great pleasure their invitation to meet the Governor of the Fort on the evening of June 15th.

215 Beacon Street,
June 10th, 1910.

麥克阿杜先生向亨利‧瓦格斯塔夫夫婦致意,同時欣然接受兩位邀請,於6月15日晚上與州長會面。

培根街215號
1910年6月10日

麥克阿杜先生也可用以下方式婉拒:

Mr. McAdoo regrets that owing to a prior engagement, he must forego the honor of paying his respects to Mr. and Mrs. Wagstaff and the Governor of the Fort on the evening of June 15th.

215 Beacon Street,
June 10th, 1910.

麥克阿杜先生遺憾表示由於事先另有安排,因此必須放棄在6月15日晚上向亨利‧瓦格斯塔夫夫婦和州長致意的榮幸。

培根街215號
1910年6月10日

> Mr. McAdoo presents his compliments to
> Mr. and Mrs. Henry Wagstaff and accepts with
> great pleasure their invitation to meet the
> Governor of the Fort on the evening of June
> fifteenth.
>
> 215 Beacon Street,
> June 10th, 1910.

Here is how Mr. McAdoo might decline the invitation:

> Mr. McAdoo regrets that owing to a prior
> engagement he must forego the honor of paying
> his respects to Mr. and Mrs. Wagstaff and the
> Governor of the Fort on the evening of June
> fifteenth.
>
> 215 Beacon St.,
> June 10th, 1910.

以下是寫給傑瑞米亞・雷諾茲的短箋：

Mr. and Mrs. Oldham at home on Wednesday evening October 9th from seven to eleven. 21 Ashland Avenue, October 5th	歐漢夫婦 10 月 9 日週三晚上七點至十一點在家。 艾許蘭大道 21 號 10 月 5 日

雷諾茲先生回覆如下：

Mr. Reynolds accepts with high appreciation the honor of Mr. and Mrs. Oldham's invitation for Wednesday evening October 9th. Windsor Hotel October 7th	雷諾茲先生接受並誠心感謝歐漢夫婦 10 月 9 日週三晚上的邀約。 溫瑟飯店 10 月 7 日

或是：

Mr. Reynolds regrets that his duties render it impossible for him to accept Mr. and Mrs. Oldham's kind invitation for the evening of October 9th. Windsor Hotel October 7th	雷諾茲先生遺憾表示因職務在身，無法接受歐漢夫婦 10 月 9 日晚上的親切邀約。 溫瑟飯店 10 月 7 日

Here is a note addressed, say to Mr. Jeremiah Reynolds.

Mr. and Mrs. Oldham at home on Wednesday
evening October ninth from seven to eleven.

21 Ashland Avenue,
October 5th.

Mr. Reynolds makes reply:

Mr. Reynolds accepts with high appreciation
the honor of Mr. and Mrs. Oldham's invitation
for Wednesday evening October ninth.

Windsor Hotel
October 7th

or

Mr. Reynolds regrets that his duties render
it impossible for him to accept Mr. and Mrs.
Oldham's kind invitation for the evening of
October ninth.

Windsor Hotel,
October 7th,

有時較不正式的邀請函會寫在特別設計的小短箋上寄出，寫短箋者也會以第一人稱取代第三人稱來稱呼自己，例如：

360 Pine St., Dec. 11th, 1910. Dear Mr. Saintsbury: Mr. Johnson and I should be much pleased to have you dine with us and a few friends next Thursday, the fifteenth, at half past seven. Yours sincerely, Emma Burnside.	松樹街 360 號 1910 年 12 月 11 日 親愛的聖斯伯里先生， 強森先生和我敬邀您下週四（十五日）七點半與我們和幾位朋友一同用餐。 艾瑪・伯恩賽德敬上

聖斯伯里先生的回覆是：

57 Carlyle Strand Dec. 13th, 1910. Dear Mrs. Burnside: Let me accept very appreciatively your invitation to dine with Mr. Burnside and you on next Thursday, the fifteenth, at half past seven. Yours sincerely, Henry Saintsbury.	卡萊爾濱街 57 號， 1910 年 12 月 13 日 親愛的伯恩賽德夫人： 我接受並誠心感謝兩位邀請我下週四（十五日）七點半與伯恩賽德先生和您一同用餐。 亨利・聖斯伯里敬上。

Sometimes less informal invitations are sent on small specially designed note paper in which the first person takes the place of the third. Thus

360 Pine St.,
Dec. 11th, 1910.

Dear Mr. Saintsbury:
Mr. Johnson and I should be much pleased to have you dine with us and a few friends next Thursday, the fifteenth, at half past seven.

Yours sincerely,
Emma Burnside.

Mr. Saintsbury's reply:

57 Carlyle Strand
Dec. 13th, 1910.

Dear Mrs. Burnside:
Let me accept very appreciatively your invitation to dine with Mr. Burnside and you on next Thursday, the fifteenth, at half past seven.

Yours sincerely,
Henry Saintsbury.

介紹函

　　寫介紹函時必須慎重，因為寫者實際上是在為被介紹者做擔保。以下是介紹函範例：

603 Lexington Ave., New York City, June 15th, 1910.	萊辛頓大道 603 號， 紐約市， 1910 年 6 月 15 日
Rev. Cyrus C. Wiley, D. D., Newark, N. J.	神學博士賽洛斯・C・ 魏萊牧師 紐瓦克市，紐澤西州
My dear Dr. Wiley: I take the liberty of presenting to you my friend, Stacy Redfern, M. D., a young practitioner, who is anxious to locate in Newark. I have known him many years and can vouch for his integrity and professional standing. Any courtesy and kindness which you may show him will be very much appreciated by me.	親愛的魏萊牧師： 謹向您介紹我的朋友史戴西・瑞芬醫師。他是一位年輕的執業醫師，最近急著移居紐瓦克市。我與他熟識多年，可以擔保他的正直和專業地位。請您以禮善待他，我將感激不盡。
Very sincerely yours, Franklin Jewett.	誠心敬上 富蘭克林・朱威特

NOTES OF INTRODUCTION

Notes of introduction should be very circumspect as the writers are in reality vouching for those whom they introduce. Here is a specimen of such a note.

603 Lexington Ave.,
New York City,
June 15th, 1910.

Rev. Cyrus C. Wiley, D. D.,
Newark, N. J.

My dear Dr. Wiley:
I take the liberty of presenting to you my friend, Stacy Redfern, M. D., a young practitioner, who is anxious to locate in Newark. I have known him many years and can vouch for his integrity and professional standing. Any courtesy and kindness which you may show him will be very much appreciated by me.

Very sincerely yours,
Franklin Jewett.

第七章
錯誤

Errors

在下列範例中，括弧內的單字是多餘的，應該省略：[3]

1. Fill the glass (full).
倒滿杯子（到滿）。

2. They appeared to be talking (together) on private affairs.
他們好像（一起）在談私事。

3. I saw the boy and his sister (both) in the garden.
我看到那個男孩跟他姐姐（兩人都）在花園。

4. He went into the country last week and returned (back) yesterday.
他上個禮拜去鄉下，昨天返家（回來）。

5. They followed (after) him, but could not overtake him.
他們尾隨他（之後），卻無法追上他。

6. The same sentiments may be found throughout (the whole of) the book.
同樣的觀點貫穿（整本）全書。

7. I was very ill every day (of my life) last week.
上個禮拜我（人生中的）每天都很不舒服。

8. That was the (sum and) substance of his discourse.
那些就是他的演講的（重點和）主旨。

3　譯注：中、英文文法有所不同，譯文僅為參考，使用上應以英文為依據。

In the following examples the word or words in parentheses are uncalled for and should be omitted:

1. Fill the glass (full).

2. They appeared to be talking (together) on private affairs.

3. I saw the boy and his sister (both) in the garden.

4. He went into the country last week and returned (back) yesterday.

5. They followed (after) him, but could not overtake him.

6. The same sentiments may be found throughout (the whole of) the book.

7. I was very ill every day (of my life) last week.

8. That was the (sum and) substance of his discourse.

9. He took wine and water and mixed them (both) together.
他把酒和水（兩者都）混在一起。

10. He descended (down) the steps to the cellar.
他（往下）走下階梯來到地窖。

11. He fell (down) from the top of the house.
他從屋頂跌落（下來）。

12. I hope you will return (again) soon.
希望你很快就會（再次）回來。

13. The things he took away he restored (again).
他（再次）奪回自己被奪走的東西。

14. The thief who stole my watch was compelled to restore it (back again).
偷走我的手錶的小偷被迫把手錶（再次）歸還。

15. It is equally (the same) to me whether I have it today or tomorrow.
今天或明天拿到，對我來講（同樣）沒差。

16. She said, (says she) the report is false; and he replied, (says he) if it be not correct I have been misinformed.
她說：「這份報告是錯誤的，」（她這麼說道）；他回：「如果報告不正確，那麼我被誤導了。」（他這麼回答）

9. He took wine and water and mixed them (both) together.

10. He descended (down) the steps to the cellar.

11. He fell (down) from the top of the house.

12. I hope you will return (again) soon.

13. The things he took away he restored (again).

14. The thief who stole my watch was compelled to restore it (back again).

15. It is equally (the same) to me whether I have it today or tomorrow.

16. She said, (says she) the report is false; and he replied, (says he) if it be not correct I have been misinformed.

17. I took my place in the cars (for) to go to New York.
我坐上車子（以便）前往紐約。

18. They need not (to) call upon him.
他們不必（去）打給他。

19. Nothing (else) but that would satisfy him.
除了這個之外，沒有（別的）東西能夠滿足他。

20. Whenever I ride in the cars, I (always) find it prejudicial to my health.
我每次坐車（總是）都會覺得這樣有害健康。

21. He was the first (of all) at the meeting.
他是（所有人中）第一個來開會的。

22. He was the tallest of (all) the brothers.
他是（所有）兄弟中最高的。

23. You are the tallest of (all) your family.
你是家裡（所有人當中）長最高的。

24. Whenever I pass the house he is (always) at the door.
我每次經過這間房子，他（總是）都在門邊。

25. The rain has penetrated (through) the roof.
雨水穿透（進入）屋頂。

26. Besides my uncle and aunt, there was (also) my grandfather at the church.
除了叔叔嬸嬸之外，（還有）我的爺爺也在教堂。

17. I took my place in the cars (for) to go to New York.

18. They need not (to) call upon him.

19. Nothing (else) but that would satisfy him.

20. Whenever I ride in the cars I (always) find it prejudicial to my health.

21. He was the first (of all) at the meeting.

22. He was the tallest of (all) the brothers.

23. You are the tallest of (all) your family.

24. Whenever I pass the house he is (always) at the door.

25. The rain has penetrated (through) the roof.

26. Besides my uncle and aunt there was (also) my grandfather at the church.

27. It should (ever) be your constant endeavor to please your family.
你應該（一直）不斷努力取悅你的家人。

28. If it is true as you have heard (then) his situation is indeed pitiful.
如果你聽說的是真的，（那麼）他的處境確實令人同情。

29. Either this (here) man or that (there) woman has (got) it.
不是（這邊）這個男人，就是（那邊）那個女人拿到了。

30. Where is the fire (at)?
火災在哪裡？

31. Did you sleep in church? Not that I know (of).
你在教會上睡著了嗎？就我所知是沒有。

32. I have never before (in my life) met (with) such a stupid man.
我（人生中）從沒遇過這麼笨的人。

33. (For) why did he postpone it?
他為（了）什麼延期呢？

34. Because (why) he could not attend.
（為什麼）是因為他無法參加。

35. What age is he? (Why) I don't know.
他幾歲？（哎呀）我不知道。

27. It should (ever) be your constant endeavor to please your family.

28. If it is true as you have heard (then) his situation is indeed pitiful.

29. Either this (here) man or that (there) woman has (got) it.

30. Where is the fire (at)?

31. Did you sleep in church? Not that I know (of).

32. I have never before (in my life) met (with) such a stupid man.

33. (For) why did he postpone it?

34. Because (why) he could not attend.

35. What age is he? (Why) I don't know.

36. He called on me (for) to ask my opinion.
他拜託我（為了）問我的意見。）

37. I don't know where I am (at).
我不知道我在哪裡。

38. I looked in (at) the window.
我看向窗內。

39. I passed (by) the house.
我經過這間房子。

40. He (always) came every Sunday.
他（總是）每個星期天都來。

41. Moreover, (also) we wish to say he was in error.
再說，我們（也）想說他錯了。

42. It is not long (ago) since he was here.
他才剛來這裡（不久）。

43. Two men went into the wood (in order) to cut (down) trees.
兩個人到森林裡（為了）砍（倒）樹。

　　贅述相關範例不勝枚舉。新聞寫作常會出現贅字，有時甚至是整組不必要的字詞，其實不必多此一舉，也能理解或說明寫作內容。

36. He called on me (for) to ask my opinion.

37. I don't know where I am (at).

38. I looked in (at) the window.

39. I passed (by) the house.

40. He (always) came every Sunday.

41. Moreover, (also) we wish to say he was in error.

42. It is not long (ago) since he was here.

43. Two men went into the wood (in order) to cut (down) trees.

Further examples of redundancy might be multiplied. It is very common in newspaper writing where not alone single words but entire phrases are sometimes brought in, which are unnecessary to the sense or explanation of what is written.

權威作家犯的文法錯誤

即便最優秀的演說家和作家，也難免會有失足的時候。許多我們公認具有權威性、絕對不會出錯的作家，多少也曾犯下基本文法錯誤，違反九大詞類中一種或多種詞類的規則；有些甚至徹底打破每一種詞類的規則，其威望依舊穩如泰山，持續受到眾人景仰。麥考利就曾經亂用冠詞。他寫道：

> That <u>a</u> historian should not record trifles is perfectly true.
> 史學家不應記載旁枝末節之事，此言確實不假。

這裡的冠詞應該用 an。[4]

狄更斯也曾用錯冠詞。他將《魯賓遜漂流記》喻為 <u>an</u> universally popular book（廣受歡迎之作），這裡的冠詞應該用 a。[5]

一直以來，演說家和作家在處理名詞和代名詞之間的關係時也經常犯錯。例如亨利・海拉姆（Henry Hallam）在《歐洲文學》（Literature of Europe）中寫道：

> No one as yet had exhibited the structure of the human kidneys, Vesalius having only examined <u>them</u> in dogs.
> 迄今尚未有人展示人類腎臟結構，維薩留斯也只在狗的體內檢視過它們而已。

4　以h為字首但重音節不在h，或h不發音且第二個字母為母音時，不定冠詞用an。此為舊時用法，現代用法多用a。

5　universally的字首雖為母音字母u，但發音是以子音字母j的發音為首，故不定冠詞用a。

GRAMMATICAL ERRORS OF STANDARD AUTHORS

Even the best speakers and writers are sometimes caught napping. Many of our standard authors to whom we have been accustomed to look up as infallible have sinned more or less against the fundamental principles of grammar by breaking the rules regarding one or more of the nine parts of speech. In fact some of them have recklessly trespassed against all nine, and still they sit on their pedestals of fame for the admiration of the crowd. Macaulay mistreated the article. He wrote, "That *a* historian should not record trifles is perfectly true." He should have used *an*.

Dickens also used the article incorrectly. He refers to "Robinson Crusoe" as "*an* universally popular book," instead of *a* universally popular book.

The relation between nouns and pronouns has always been a stumbling block to speakers and writers. Hallam in his *Literature of Europe* writes, "No one as yet had exhibited the structure of the human kidneys, Vesalius having only examined them in dogs." This means that Vesalius examined human kidneys in dogs.

用這樣的方式描述，意思就變成「維薩留斯在狗的體內檢查『人類』腎臟」了。正確寫法應該是：

No one had as yet exhibited the kidneys in human beings, Vesalius having examine <u>such organs</u> in dogs only.
迄今尚未有人展示人類腎臟，維薩留斯也只檢視過狗的腎臟而已。

亞瑟‧赫爾布斯爵士（Sir Arthur Helps）在評論狄更斯時寫道：

I knew a brother author of his who received such criticisms from him (Dickens) very lately and profited by <u>it</u>.
我知道他有一位作家朋友最近受到他（狄更斯）的批評指教，因而獲益匪淺。

這裡應該要用 them 取代 it，跟複數形的 criticisms 才有一致性。

以下還有幾個傑出作家用錯代名詞的例子：

Sir Thomas Moore in general so writes it, although not many others so late as <u>him</u>.
整體來說，湯瑪士‧摩爾爵士是這麼寫的，儘管沒有多少人像他一樣遲到。——理察‧切尼維克斯‧川奇，《古今英文》

這裡應該用 he 取代 him。

The sentence should have been, "No one had as yet exhibited the kidneys in human beings, Vesalius having examined such organs in dogs only."

Sir Arthur Helps in writing of Dickens, states–"I knew a brother author of his who received such criticisms from him (Dickens) very lately and profited by *it*." Instead of *it* the word should be *them* to agree with criticisms.

Here are a few other pronominal errors from leading authors:

"Sir Thomas Moore in general so writes it, although not many others so late as *him*." Should be *he*.–Trench's *English Past and Present*.

What should we gain by it but that we should speedily become as poor as <u>them</u>.
除了應該盡快變得跟他們一樣貧窮之外，我們還應該從中得到什麼？——阿奇博爾德‧艾利森爵士，《論麥考利》

這裡應該用 they 取代 them。

If the King gives us leave, you or I may as lawfully preach, as <u>them</u> that do.
倘若國王准許我們離開，你我也許能合法宣揚此事，正如他們一樣。——湯瑪士‧霍布斯，《英國內戰史》

這裡應該用 they 或 those 取代 them。

The drift of all his sermons was, to prepare the Jews for the reception of a prophet, mightier than <u>him</u>, and whose shoes he was not worthy to bear.
他布道的重點是讓猶太人做好準備，接受一個比他更加偉大、他連為其提鞋都不配的先知。——法蘭西斯‧亞特伯里，《數個場合與主題的布道與演說》

這裡應該用 he 取代 him。

Phalaris, who was so much older than <u>her</u>...
法拉里斯比她年長許多……——李察‧本特利，《論法拉里斯》

這裡應該用 she 取代 her。

"What should we gain by it but that we should speedily become as poor as *them*." Should be *they*.–Alison's *Essay on Macaulay*.

"If the king gives us leave you or I may as lawfully preach, as *them* that do." Should be *they* or *those*, the latter having persons understood.–Hobbes's *History of Civil Wars*.

"The drift of all his sermons was, to prepare the Jews for the reception of a prophet, mightier than *him*, and whose shoes he was not worthy to bear." Should be than *he*.–Atterbury's *Sermons*.

"Phalaris, who was so much older than *her*." Should be *she*.–Bentley's *Dissertation on Phalaris*.

King Charles, and more than <u>him</u>, the duke and the Popish faction were at liberty to form new schemes.

除了查理國王之外，公爵和教皇派系的人也得以蘊釀新的陰謀。——亨利·聖約翰，《論黨派》

這裡應該用 he 取代 him。

We contributed a third more than the Dutch, who were obliged to the same proportion more than <u>us</u>.

我們的捐款比荷蘭人多三分之一，他們理應捐得比我們多。——強納森·史威夫特，《盟友的行為》

這裡應該用 we 取代 us.

上述範例都是把該用主格代名詞的地方用成受格代名詞。

Let <u>thou</u> and <u>I</u> the battle try.

汝與吾試著戰鬥。——作者不詳

這裡的 let 是主導動詞，後面要加受格，因此不能用 thou and I，要用 you and me。

Forever in this humble cell, let <u>thee</u> and <u>I</u>, my fair one, dwell.

讓汝與吾——吾之情人——永遠樓居這座簡陋牢房中。——馬修·普瑞爾

這裡應該用受格 you and me 取代 thee and I。

"King Charles, and more than *him*, the duke and the Popish faction were at liberty to form new schemes." Should be than *he.*–Bolingbroke's *Dissertations on Parties.*

"We contributed a third more than the Dutch, who were obliged to the same proportion more than *us*." Should be than *we.*–Swift's *Conduct of the Allies.*

In all the above examples the objective cases of the pronouns have been used while the construction calls for nominative cases.

"Let *thou* and *I* the battle try"–*Anon.*

Here *let* is the governing verb and requires an objective case after it; therefore instead of *thou* and *I*, the words should be *you (sing.)* and *me.*

"Forever in this humble cell, Let thee and I, my fair one, dwell"–*Prior.*

Here *thee* and *I* should be the objectives *you* and *me.*

作家最容易在關係代名詞的使用上栽觔斗。就連《聖經》也有誤譯關係代名詞的情形：

> <u>Whom</u> do men say that I am?
> 眾人說我是誰？——《馬太福音》
>
> <u>Whom</u> think ye that I am?
> 汝等認為我是誰？——《使徒行傳》

上述兩例都應以 Who 取代 Whom，因為它不是受到 say 或 think 主導的受格，而是依附 am 的主格。

> <u>Who</u> should I meet at the coffee house t'other night, but my old friend?
> 那晚我在咖啡館巧遇的，正是我的老友。——理察·史帝爾爵士
>
> It is another pattern of this answerer's fair dealing, to give us hints that the author is dead, and yet lay the suspicion upon somebody, I know not <u>who</u>, in the country.
> 這是答話者另一種巧妙的回答模式，暗示我們作者已經死了，卻把嫌疑指向國內某個我不知道的人。——史威夫特，《桶之物語》
>
> My son is going to be married to I don't know <u>who</u>.
> 我兒子要娶一個我不知道是誰的人。——戈德史密斯，《善良的人》

上述例子中的 who 應該改成受格 whom。

The use of the relative pronoun trips the greatest number of authors. Even in the Bible we find the relative wrongly translated:

Whom do men say that I am?–*St. Matthew.*

Whom think ye that I am?–*Acts of the Apostles.*

Who should be written in both cases because the word is not in the objective governed by *say* or *think*, but in the nominative dependent on the verb *am*.

"*Who* should I meet at the coffee house t'other night, but my old friend?"–*Steele.*

"It is another pattern of this answerer's fair dealing, to give us hints that the author is dead, and yet lay the suspicion upon somebody, I know not *who*, in the country."–Swift's *Tale of a Tub.*

"My son is going to be married to I don't know *who*."–Goldsmith's *Good-natured Man.*

The nominative *who* in the above examples should be the objective *whom*.

許多偉大作家胡亂使用比較級形容詞。

> Of two forms of the same word, use the <u>fittest</u>.
> 在同一個單字的兩種形式中，使用最適合的那個。——
> 墨瑞爾

這位作者想要提供良好的建議，卻做了不良示範。這裡應該使用比較級 fitter。

本身具備比較級或最高級意涵的形容詞，毋須在前面加上 more／most，或在字尾加上 er／est。以下例子違反這條規則：

> Money is the most universal incitement of human misery.
> 金錢是造成人類苦難最普遍的因素。——愛德華·吉本，《羅馬帝國興衰史》
>
> The <u>chiefest</u> of which was known by the name of Archon among the Grecians.
> 其中最首要的是希臘人所稱的「執政官」。——約翰·德萊頓，《普魯塔克的生活》
>
> The <u>chiefest</u> and largest are removed to certain magazines they call libraries.
> 其中最首要、最大的被挪到他們稱為圖書館的倉庫裡。——史威夫特，《書之戰》

Many of the great writers have played havoc with the adjective in the indiscriminate use of the degrees of comparison.

"Of two forms of the same word, use the fittest."–*Morell*.

The author here in *trying* to give good advice sets a bad example. He should have used the comparative degree, "Fitter."

Adjectives which have a comparative or superlative signification do not admit the addition of the words *more, most,* or the terminations, *er, est,* hence the following examples break this rule:

"Money is the *most universal* incitement of human misery."– Gibbon's *Decline and Fall*.

"The *chiefest* of which was known by the name of Archon among the Grecians."–Dryden's *Life of Plutarch*.

"The *chiefest* and largest are removed to certain magazines they call libraries."–Swift's *Battle of the Books*.

The two <u>chiefest</u> properties of air, its gravity and elastic force, have been discovered by mechanical experiments.

透過力學實驗，我們已經發現空氣的兩個最首要特性：重力和彈力。——約翰·阿布諾特

From these various causes, which in greater or <u>lesser</u> degree, affected every individual in the colony, the indignation of the people became general.

上述各原因或多或少影響了該殖民地的每一個人，引發人民的普遍憤慨。——威廉·羅勃森，《美國史》

The <u>extremest</u> parts of the earth were meditating a submission.

世界最盡頭之處的人民正在考慮是否歸順。——亞特伯里，《數個場合與主題的布道與演說》

The last are indeed <u>more preferable</u> because they are founded on some new knowledge or improvement in the mind of man.

最後幾個確實是更適合的，因為其以新知或人類心智的進步為基礎。——愛迪生，《旁觀者》

下列例子在該用比較級的地方用成最高級。只比較兩件事物時，必須使用比較級的形式。

This was in reality <u>the easiest</u> manner of the two.

事實上，這確實是兩種方式中最簡單的。——夏夫茨伯里伯爵，《給作家的建議》

The two *chiefest* properties of air, its gravity and elastic force, have been discovered by mechanical experiments.–*Arbuthno*.

"From these various causes, which in greater or *lesser* degree, affected every individual in the colony, the indignation of the people became general."–Robertson's *History of America*.

"The *extremest* parts of the earth were meditating a submission."–Atterbury's *Sermons*.

"The last are indeed *more preferable* because they are founded on some new knowledge or improvement in the mind of man."–Addison, *Spectator*.

In these examples the superlative is wrongly used for the comparative. When only two objects are compared the comparative form must be used.

"This was in reality the *easiest* manner of the two."–Shaftesbury's *Advice to an Author*.

In every well-formed mind, this second desire seems to be the <u>strongest</u> of the two.
對於每個心智健全的人來說，第二種渴望似乎是兩種當中最強烈的。——亞當·史密斯，《道德情操論》

「不可能性」本身沒有比較級，以下例子卻這麼形容：

As it was impossible they should know the words, thoughts and secret actions of all men, so it was <u>more impossible</u> they should pass judgment on them according to these things.
知道所有人的談話、思想和私底下的行動已經是不可能的事了，要依此評斷他們就更不可能了。——惠特比，《基督教之必要》

不少作家在應該使用副詞的地方用了形容詞，例如：

I shall endeavor to live hereafter <u>suitable</u> to a man in my station.
今後我將努力過著適合我這樣地位的人的生活。——愛迪生

I can never think so very <u>mean</u> of him.
我絕無法如此刻薄地評論他這個人。——本特利，《論法拉里斯》

His expectations run high and the fund to supply them is <u>extreme</u> scanty.
他的期望很高，支持這些期望的資金卻嚴重不足。——納森尼爾·蘭卡斯特（Nathaniel Lancaster），《論謹慎》（The Plan of an Essay Upon Delicacy）

"In every well formed mind this second desire seems to be the *strongest* of the two."–Smith's *Theory of Moral Sentiments.*

Of impossibility there are no degrees of comparison, yet we find the following:

"As it was impossible they should know the words, thoughts and secret actions of all men, so it was *more impossible* they should pass judgment on them according to these things."–Whitby's *Necessity of the Christian Religion.*

A great number of authors employ adjectives for adverbs. Thus we find:

"I shall endeavor to live hereafter *suitable* to a man in my station."–*Addison.*

"I can never think so very *mean* of him."–Bentley's *Dissertation* on Phalaris.

"His expectations run high and the fund to supply them is *extreme* scanty."–*Lancaster's Essay on Delicacy.*

在動詞的使用上，最常見的錯誤是主詞與動詞之間不一致。主詞與動詞位置距離很遠時最常出現這種錯誤，當動詞後面馬上跟著另一個數量不同的名詞時尤其容易讓人混淆。跟在 either、or、neither、nor，以及 much、more、many、everyone、each 後面的主詞和動詞，經常出現不一致的狀況。以下是作家們曾經犯過的筆誤（括號中為應該使用的正確用法）：

The terms in which the sale of a patent <u>were</u> (was) communicated to the public.
我們已向民眾溝通出售專利的條款了。——朱尼厄斯，《朱尼厄斯的信》

The richness of her arms and apparel <u>were</u> (was) conspicuous.
她雙手及全身穿金戴銀，真是引人注目。——吉本，《羅馬帝國興衰史》

Everyone of this grotesque family <u>were</u> (was) the creatures of national genius.
這個古怪家族中的每一個人都是國之英才。——埃薩克·迪斯雷利

He knows not what spleen, languor or listlessness <u>are</u> (is).
他不知憤懣、疲倦或懶怠。——休·布萊爾，《布道》

Each of these words <u>imply</u> (implies), some pursuit or object relinquished.
一字一句都暗示放棄某種夢想或目標。——布萊爾，《布道》

The commonest error in the use of the verb is the disregard of the concord between the verb and its subject. This occurs most frequently when the subject and the verb are widely separated, especially if some other noun of a different number immediately precedes the verb. False concords occur very often after *either, or, neither, nor,* and *much, more, many, everyone, each.* Here are a few authors' slips:

"The terms in which the sale of a patent *were* communicated to the public."–Junius's *Letters*.

"The richness of her arms and apparel *were* conspicuous."–Gibbon's *Decline and Fall*.

"Everyone of this grotesque family *were* the creatures of national genius."–D'Israeli.

"He knows not what spleen, languor or listlessness *are*."–Blair's Sermons.

"Each of these words *imply*, some pursuit or object relinquished."–*Ibid*.

Magnus, with four thousand of his supposed accomplices, <u>were</u> (was) put to death.
馬格努斯——連同四千個可能的同夥——被處死刑。
——吉本

No nation gives greater encouragements to learning than we do; yet at the same time <u>none are</u> (none is) so injudicious in the application.
沒有國家比我們祭出更多鼓勵學習的措施，而且沒有一項措施在實施上是不審慎的。——戈德史密斯

<u>There is</u> (are) <u>two or three</u> of us have seen strange sights.
我們當中有兩三人看到異象。——莎士比亞

該用過去式的地方不能用成過去分詞，但學問淵博的拜倫勳爵（Lord Byron）卻忽略這點。他在《塔索的哀嘆》（Lament of Tasso）中這麼寫道：

And with my years, my soul <u>begun</u> (began) <u>to pant</u> With feelings of strange tumult and soft pain.
隨著年歲增長，我的靈瑰因奇怪的騷動和輕柔的疼痛而開始喘息

李察・薩維奇（Richard Savage）在《流浪者》（Wanderer）中也犯下雙重錯誤：

From liberty each nobler science <u>sprung</u> (sprang), A Bacon brighten'd and a Spenser <u>sung</u> (sang).
在自由的風氣下，各個高尚的學者紛紛崛起，培根和斯賓賽大鳴大放。

"Magnus, with four thousand of his supposed accomplices *were* put to death."–*Gibbon*.

"No nation gives greater encouragements to learning than we do; yet at the same time *none are* so injudicious in the application."–*Goldsmith*.

"*There's two* or *three* of us have seen strange sights."–*Shakespeare*.

The past participle should not be used for the past tense, yet the learned Byron overlooked this fact. He thus writes in the *Lament of Tasso*:

"And with my years my soul *begun to pant* With feelings of strange tumult and soft pain."

Here is another example from Savage's *Wanderer* in which there is double sinning:

"From liberty each nobler science *sprung*, A Bacon brighten'd and a Spenser *sung*."

其他違反分詞使用規則的例子如下：

Every book ought to be read with the same spirit
and in the same manner as it is <u>writ</u> (written).
作者以什麼樣的精神和方式寫書，讀者就該以同樣的精
神和方式閱讀。──亨利·菲爾丁，《湯姆·瓊斯》

The Court of Augustus had not <u>wore</u> (worn) off
the manners of the republic.
奧古斯都法庭無損共和國的禮儀。──大衛·休謨，《道
德、政治與文學論文集》

Moses tells us that the fountains of the earth
were <u>broke</u> (broken) open or <u>clove</u> (cloven)
asunder.
摩西告訴我們陸地的泉源已被破開或劈裂。──湯瑪
仕·柏內特

... re-establishment of a free constitution, when
it has been <u>shook</u> (shaken) by the iniquity of
former administrations.
當憲法遭受前朝政府惡意破壞時，則要重新建立自由憲
法。──博林布魯克子爵

In this respect, the seeds of future divisions were
<u>sowed</u> (sown) abundantly.
因而大量播下引發日後分歧的種子。──博林布魯克子爵

以下例子在該使用不定語氣的地方用成現在分詞：

It is easy <u>distinguishing</u> the rude fragment of a
rock from the splinter of a statue.
要分辨出天然的岩石碎片與雕像碎塊並不困難。

Other breaches in regard to the participles occur in the following:

"Every book ought to be read with the same spirit and in the same manner as it is *writ*."–Fielding's *Tom Jones*.

"The Court of Augustus had not *wore* off the manners of the republic."–Hume's *Essays*.

"Moses tells us that the fountains of the earth were *broke* open or clove asunder."–Burnet.

"... re-establishment of a free constitution when it has been *shook* by the iniquity of former administrations."–*Bolingbroke*.

"In this respect the seeds of future divisions were *sowed* abundantly."–*Ibid*.

In the following example the present participle is used for the infinitive mood:

"It is easy *distinguishing* the rude fragment of a rock from the splinter of a statue."–Gilfillan's *Literary Portraits*.

這裡的 distinguishing 應該改成 to distinguish。

即使是最優秀的作家也經常用錯副詞。副詞 rather 常被用錯
地方。特倫奇大主教在《古今英文》中寫道：

It _rather_ modified the structure of our sentences
than the elements of our vocabulary.

這句應該寫成：

It modified the structure of our sentences _rather
than_ the elements of our vocabulary.
它修飾了句子結構而非字彙元素。

萊斯利・史蒂芬（Leslie Stephens）在撰寫詹森博士（Dr.
Johnson）的生平記事裡這麼寫道：

So far as his mode of teaching goes, he is _rather_
a disciple of Socrates than of St. Paul or Wesley.

這句應該寫成：

So far as his mode of teaching goes, he is a
disciple of Socrates _rather than_ of St. Paul or
Wesley.
就他的教學模式來看，他是蘇格拉底的弟子而非聖保羅
或魏斯理的弟子。

Distinguishing here should be replaced by *to distinguish*.

Adverbial mistakes often occur in the best writers. The adverb *rather* is a word very frequently misplaced. Archbishop Trench in his "English Past and Present" writes, "It *rather* modified the structure of our sentences than the elements of our vocabulary." This should have been written,–"It modified the structure of our sentences *rather than* the elements of our vocabulary."

"So far as his mode of teaching goes he is *rather* a disciple of Socrates than of St. Paul or Wesley." Thus writes Leslie Stephens of Dr. Johnson. He should have written, " So far as his mode of teaching goes he is a disciple of Socrates *rather* than of St. Paul or Wesley."

有些最優秀的作家經常用錯介系詞。某些名詞、形容詞和動詞後面必須使用特定的介系詞，例如 different from（有別於）、prevail upon（說服某人）、averse to（不利於）、accord with（與……一致）等都是固定用法。

下列例子中劃底線的介系詞應該替換成括號中的介系詞：

He found the greatest difficulty of (in) writing.
他發現寫作最是困難。——休謨，《英國史》

If policy can prevail upon (over) force
假如政策能夠戰勝武力——愛迪生

He made the discovery and communicated to (with) his friends.
他有了發現，並跟朋友交流這項發現。——史威夫特，《桶之物語》

Every office of command should be intrusted to persons on (in) whom the parliament shall confide.[6]
每個指揮單位都應託付給國會信任的人。——麥考利

幾位最受讚譽的作家將介系詞放在句尾，因而違反了寫作規範。例如卡萊爾在研究羅勃·伯恩斯（Robert Burns）的書中寫道：

Our own contributions to it, we are aware, can be but scanty and feeble; but we offer them with good will, and trust they may meet with acceptance from those they are intended for.
我們深知自己對這個領域的貢獻微不足道，但我們滿懷善意做出這些貢獻，也相信目標讀者或許能接受之。

6　intrust為entrust的另一種拼法，一般多用entrust。

The preposition is a part of speech which is often wrongly used by some of the best writers. Certain nouns, adjectives and verbs require particular prepositions after them, for instance, the word *different* always takes the preposition *from* after it; *prevail* takes *upon*; *averse* takes *to*; *accord* takes *with*, and so on.

In the following examples the prepositions in parentheses are the ones that should have been used:

"He found the greatest difficulty *of* (in) writing."–Hume's *History of England*.

"If policy can prevail *upon* (over) force."–*Addison*.

"He made the discovery and communicated *to* (with) his friends."–Swift's *Tale of a Tub*.

"Every office of command should be intrusted to persons *on* (in) whom the parliament shall confide."–*Macaulay*.

Several of the most celebrated writers infringe the canons of style by placing prepositions at the end of sentences. For instance Carlyle, in referring to the Study of Burns, writes:–"Our own contributions to it, we are aware, can be but scanty and feeble; but we offer them with good will, and trust they may meet with acceptance from those they are intended *for*."

這裡應該寫成 from whom they are intended 即可。

Most writers have some one vein which they
peculiarly and obviously excel <u>in</u>.——威廉·閔托

這句應該寫成：

Most writers have some one vein <u>in</u> which they
peculiarly and obviously excel.
多數作家都自有一個特別且明顯出眾的特色。

許多作家會用多餘的字詞來重複相同的想法和概念，稱為贅述。

Notwithstanding which, <u>however</u>, poor Polly
embraced them all around.
然而儘管如此，可憐的波莉仍然一一擁抱他們。——狄
更斯

I judged that they would <u>mutually</u> find each
other.
我認為他們會互相找到彼此。——克洛克特

... as having created a <u>joint</u> partnership between
the two Powers in the Morocco question.
……已在摩洛哥問題上建立兩個大國之間的聯合夥伴關
係。——《時代雜誌》

The only sensible position <u>there seems to be</u> is to
frankly acknowledge our ignorance of what lies
beyond.
看來唯一明智的作法，似乎是坦承我們對之後的發展一
無所知。——《每日電訊報》

–"for whom they are intended," he should have written.

"Most writers have some one vein which they peculiarly and obviously excel in."–*William Minto*.

This sentence should read–Most writers have some one vein in which they peculiarly and obviously excel.

Many authors use redundant words which repeat the same thought and idea. This is called tautology.

"Notwithstanding which (however) poor Polly embraced them all around."–*Dickens*.

"I judged that they would (mutually) find each other."–*Crockett*.

"....as having created a (joint) partnership between the two Powers in the Morocco question."–*The Times*.

"The only sensible position (there seems to be) is to frankly acknowledge our ignorance of what lies beyond."–*Daily Telegraph*.

Lord Rosebery has not budged from his position–splendid, no doubt–of <u>lonely</u> isolation.
羅斯貝里勳爵並未擺脫他對孤單的孤立立場——真不愧是光榮的孤立政策。——《時代雜誌》

Miss Fox was <u>often</u> in the habit of assuring Mrs. Chick.
福克斯小姐總是習慣讓奇克女士放心。——狄更斯

The deck <u>it</u> was their field of fame.
甲板是他們的名人堂。——湯瑪仕・坎貝爾

He had come up one morning, as was now <u>frequently</u> his wont...
有天早上他過來，就像他經常的習慣那樣……——安東尼・特洛勒普

The counselors of the Sultan <u>continue to</u> remain sceptical.
蘇丹的顧問們依然持續感到懷疑。——《時代雜誌》

Seriously, <u>and apart from jesting</u>, this is no light matter.
說認真的，我沒在開玩笑，這件事情非同小可。——沃爾特・白芝浩

To get back to your own country with <u>the consciousness that you go back with</u> the sense of duty well done.
你返回自己的國家，是帶著你已善盡職責的意識返國。——哈爾斯伯里勳爵

The Peresviet lost both her fighting-tops and <u>in appearance</u> look the most damaged of all the ships.
佩雷斯維特號的兩座戰鬥檣樓都被摧毀，外表上看起來是所有船艦中受創最嚴重的。——《時代雜誌》

"Lord Rosebery has not budged from his position–splendid, no doubt,–of (lonely) isolation."–*The Times*.

"Miss Fox was (often) in the habit of assuring Mrs. Chick."–*Dickens*.

"The deck (it) was their field of fame."–*Campbell*.

"He had come up one morning, as was now (frequently) his wont,"–*Trollope*.

The counsellors of the Sultan (continue to) remain sceptical.–*The Times*.

Seriously, (and apart from jesting), this is no light matter.–*Bagehot*.

To go back to your own country with (the consciousness that you go back with) the sense of duty well done.–*Lord Halsbury*.

The *Peresviet* lost both her fighting-tops and (in appearance) looked the most damaged of all the ships.–*The Times*.

> Counsel admitted that, that was a fair suggestion
> to make, but he submitted that it was borne out
> by the <u>surrounding</u> circumstances.
> 律師承認這是一個合理的建議，但他認為周遭狀況都能
> 證實這點。——《時代雜誌》

另一種添加不必要的單字或片語的狀況稱為「遁辭」，是指明明沒有必要，言詞卻拐彎抹角，除了填補篇幅外毫無作用。這種作法就好像一個人不走直線到達要去的地方，反而非要先繞一大圈才走到一樣。例如下列這句引言：

> Pope professed to have learned his poetry from
> Dryden, whom, whenever an opportunity
> was presented, he praised through the whole
> period of his existence with unvaried liberality;
> and perhaps his character may receive some
> illustration, of a comparison he instituted
> between him and the man whose pupil he was.
> 教皇自稱向德萊頓學習詩歌，只要一有機會，便從頭到尾千篇一律地大力讚揚德萊頓，比較他和這個他拜其為師的男人，或許可以讓他的性格獲得一些說明。

這句話可以省略許多冗詞，精簡成以下句子：

> Pope professed himself the pupil of Dryden,
> whom he lost no opportunity of praising; and
> his character may be illustrated by a comparison
> with his master.
> 教皇自稱是德萊頓的弟子，不放過任何讚揚德萊頓的機會，與他的老師做比較，或許可以說明他的性格。

Counsel admitted that, that was a fair suggestion to make, but he submitted that it was borne out by the (surrounding) circumstances.– *Ibid.*

Another unnecessary use of words and phrases is that which is termed circumlocution, a going around the bush when there is no occasion for it, save to fill space. It may be likened to a person walking the distance of two sides of a triangle to reach the objective point. For instance in the quotation: "Pope professed to have learned his poetry from Dryden, whom, whenever an opportunity was presented, he praised through the whole period of his existence with unvaried liberality; and perhaps his character may receive some illustration, of a comparison he instituted between him and the man whose pupil he was" much of the verbiage may be eliminated and the sentence thus condensed:

"Pope professed himself the pupil of Dryden, whom he lost no opportunity of praising; and his character may be illustrated by a comparison with his master."

His life was brought to a close in 1910 at an age
not far from the one fixed by the sacred writer
as the term of human existence.
他的生命在 1910 年畫下句點，過世時的年齡跟這位神
聖的作家所設定的人類生存期限相去不遠。

這句話可以簡單寫為：

His life was brought to a close at the age of
seventy.
他的生命在七十歲那年畫下句點。

寫成下面這句更好：

He died at the age of seventy. 他於七十歲死亡。

The day was intensely cold, so cold in fact that
the thermometer crept down to the zero mark.
這天天寒地凍，冷到溫度計下探到了零度的標記。

這句可以寫成：

The day was so cold the thermometer registered
zero.
這天冷到溫度計都標示零度了。

　　許多作家使用遁辭只是為了填白，也就是填補空間，或者
是在撰寫不熟悉或不懂的主題時遇到問題。年輕作家應該避免如
此，學著以清晰的表達方式，儘量簡潔地闡述自己的想法和概念。

"His life was brought to a close in 1910 at an age not far from the one fixed by the sacred writer as the term of human existence."

This in brevity can be put, "His life was brought to a close at the age of seventy;" or, better yet, "He died at the age of seventy."

"The day was intensely cold, so cold in fact that the thermometer crept down to the zero mark," can be expressed: "The day was so cold the thermometer registered zero."

Many authors resort to circumlocution for the purpose of "padding," that is, filling space, or when they strike a snag in writing upon subjects of which they know little or nothing. The young writer should steer clear of it and learn to express his thoughts and ideas as briefly as possible commensurate with lucidity of expression.

Volumes of errors in fact, in grammar, diction and general style,

　　許多偉大作家的作品都可挑出一堆事實、文法、措辭或整體風格上的錯誤，這清楚證明了沒有人是絕對不會出錯的，最優秀的作家有時也會犯錯。不過，這些錯誤大多是粗心或倉促之下犯的，不是因為這些作家欠缺這方面的知識。

　　一般來說，學者在寫作時可能出錯，不過在口說時很少如此。其實，許多能言善道、說話從不出錯的人，在寫作時卻不懂最基本的文法原則，也不知道如何正確寫出句子。這樣的人從小就習慣聽到正確的口說語言，因此使用適當的字句，對他已是習慣成自然的事了。不管是對的還是錯的東西，小孩都學得很快，他的大腦可塑性很高，這時在腦裡留下印象的事物，會讓他記上一輩子。就連鸚鵡都能學會使用適當的語言，只要對著鸚鵡說：Two and two make four.（二加二等於四。）牠絕對不會說成：Two and two makes four. 但寫作就不一樣了。如果不懂基本的文法原則，我們可能透過與傑出講者有所交流，口語上說得很正確，卻無法寫出正確的語言。即使只是寫封普通的信，也得知道書信結構的原則，以及單字之間的關係。因此，每個人至少都要了解自己母語的基本文法知識。

could be selected from the works of the great writers, a fact which eloquently testifies that no one is infallible and that the very best is liable to err at times. However, most of the erring in the case of these writers arises from carelessness or hurry, not from a lack of knowledge.

As a general rule it is in writing that the scholar is liable to slip; in oral speech he seldom makes a blunder. In fact, there are many people who are perfect masters of speech–who never make a blunder in conversation, yet who are ignorant of the very principles of grammar and would not know how to write a sentence correctly on paper. Such persons have been accustomed from infancy to hear the language spoken correctly and so the use of the proper words and forms becomes a second nature to them. A child can learn what is right as easy as what is wrong and whatever impressions are made on the mind when it is plastic will remain there. Even a parrot can be taught the proper use of language. Repeat to a parrot "Two and two *make* four" and it never will say "two and two *makes* four."

In writing, however, it is different. Without a knowledge of the fundamentals of grammar we may be able to speak correctly from association with good speakers, but without such a knowledge we cannot hope to write the language correctly. To write even a common letter we must know the principles of construction, the relationship of one word to another. Therefore, it is necessary for everybody to understand at least the essentials of the grammar of his own language.

第八章
應該避免的
常見錯誤
Pitfalls to Avoid

主詞、動詞一致性

在英文中，動詞常跟真正的主格或主詞中間隔了好幾個字，這時容易依照離動詞最近的主詞來做變化。以下幾個例子顯示，就連傑出作家有時也會誤入這類陷阱：

> The partition which the two ministers made of the powers of government <u>were</u> singularly happy.
> 兩位部長對政府權力的劃分感到格外高興。

這裡應該用 was，跟主詞 partition 才會一致。

> One at least of the qualities which fit it for training ordinary men <u>unfit</u> it for training an extraordinary man.
> 在適合用於訓練凡夫俗子的素質中，至少有一項不適合用於訓練非凡之士。

這裡應該用 unfits，跟主詞 one 才會一致。

> The Tibetans have engaged to exclude from their country those dangerous influences whose appearance <u>were</u> the chief cause of our action.
> 藏人努力將危險的影響勢力逐出國外，正是因為出現這些勢力，我們才會採取行動。

這裡應該用 was，跟 appearance 才會一致。

ATTRACTION

Very often the verb is separated from its real nominative or subject by several intervening words and in such cases one is liable to make the verb agree with the subject nearest to it. Here are a few examples showing that the leading writers now and then take a tumble into this pitfall:

1. "The partition which the two ministers made of the powers of government *were* singularly happy."–*Macaulay.*

(Should be *was* to agree with its subject, *partition.*)

2. "One at least of the qualities which fit it for training ordinary men *unfit* it for *training* an extraordinary man."–*Bagehot.*

(Should be *unfits* to agree with subject *one.*)

3. "The Tibetans have engaged to exclude from their country those dangerous influences whose appearance were the chief cause of our action."–*The Times.*

(Should be *was* to agree with *appearance.*)

An immense amount of confusion and difference
<u>prevail</u> in these days.
這些日子以來，各處普遍出現許多困惑和分歧。

這裡應該用 prevails，跟 amount 才會一致。

省略

這類錯誤主要是介系詞被省略了。

His objection (to) and condoning of the boy's
course, seemed to say the least, paradoxical.
他一方面反對這個男孩的作法，另一方面卻又縱容他，
實在自相矛盾。

objection 後面應該加上介系詞 to。

Many men of brilliant parts are crushed by force
of circumstances and their genius (is) forever
lost to the world.
許多優秀的人被大環境的勢力壓垮，他們的聰明才智從
此消失在這世界上。

有人認為 genius 後面少了動詞 are，不過這樣不符合文法，
正確的動詞應該是 is。

4. "An immense amount of confusion and indifference *prevail* in these days."–*Telegraph*.

(Should be *prevails* to agree with amount.)

ELLIPSIS

Errors in ellipsis occur chiefly with prepositions.

His objection and condoning of the boy's course, seemed to say the least, paradoxical.

(The preposition *to* should come after objection.)

Many men of brilliant parts are crushed by force of circumstances and their genius forever lost to the world.

(Some maintain that the missing verb after genius is *are*, but such is ungrammatical. In such cases the right verb should be always expressed: as–their genius *is* forever lost to the world.)

One

用不定形容代名詞 one 來代替某人時，容易讓人混淆。在這種用法中，one 並非特指某一個人，因此在句子或表述中使用 one 時，必須從頭到尾都用 one 來代替所指稱的主詞，例如：

One must mind one's own business if one wishes to succeed.
如欲成功，必得管好自己之事。

這個句子看似囉嗦且拙劣，卻是正確的寫法。千萬不能寫成：

One must mind his business if he wished to succeed.

這裡的主詞沒有特別指稱某一個人，因此不能只用代表男性的代名詞。不過，any one 就不一樣了，你可以這麼描述：

If any one sins, he should acknowledge it; let him not try to hide it by another sin.
有過錯必得承認，別試著用另一個過錯掩飾之。

ONE

The indefinite adjective pronoun *one* when put in place of a personal substantive is liable to raise confusion. When a sentence or expression is begun with the impersonal *one* the word must be used throughout in all references to the subject. Thus, "One must mind one's own business if one wishes to succeed" may seem prolix and awkward, nevertheless it is the proper form. You must not say–"One must mind his business if he wishes to succeed," for the subject is impersonal and therefore cannot exclusively take the masculine pronoun. With *any one* it is different. You may say–"If *any one* sins he should acknowledge it; let him not try to hide it by another sin."

Only

　　無論學養高低，大多數人使用這個單字時都容易犯錯。only 可能是最常被誤用的單字，隨著它在句中的位置不同，句子的意思也跟著不同，例如：

I <u>only</u> struck him that time.

　　這句意思是那次我「只有」打他，沒有踢他或用其他方式欺負他。如果移動 only 的位置，寫成：

I struck him <u>only</u> that time.

　　意思變成我「只有」那次打他，其他時候並沒打他。如果再次移動 only，寫成：

I struck <u>only</u> him that time.

　　意思變成那次我「只有」打他一個人。

　　在口說時，我們可以加強語氣，向聽者表達我們的意思，但在寫作時就沒辦法了，只能透過這個字的位置來傳達意思。使用 only 的首要規則，是 only 所要修飾或限定的字詞、片語必須緊跟在 only 之後。

ONLY

This is a word that is a pitfall to the most of us whether learned or unlearned. Probably it is the most indiscriminately used word in the language. From the different positions it is made to occupy in a sentence it can relatively change the meaning. For instance in the sentence–"I *only* struck him that time," the meaning to be inferred is, that the only thing I did to him was to *strike* him, not kick or otherwise abuse him. But if the only is shifted, so as to make the sentence read–"I struck him *only* that time" the meaning conveyed is, that only on that occasion and at no other time did I strike him. If another shift is made to–"I struck *only* him that time," the meaning is again altered so that it signifies he was the only person I struck.

In speaking we can by emphasis impress our meaning on our hearers, but in writing we have nothing to depend upon but the position of the word in the sentence. The best rule in regard to *only* is to place it *immediately before* the word or phrase it modifies or limits.

Alone

　這也是一個容易造成意思不明、改變語意的單字。用它取代前面例句中的 only，就會發現語意取決於這個字在句子中的位置：

I alone struck him at that time.

意思是只有我打他，沒有別人。

寫成：

I struck him alone at that time.

必須解釋成只有他被我打。

寫成：

I struck him at that time alone.

意思變成我只有那次打他。

　因此，在使用 alone 時，也要遵循跟 only 相同的規則。

ALONE

It is another word which creates ambiguity and alters meaning. If we substitute it for only in the preceding example the meaning of the sentence will depend upon the arrangement. Thus "I *alone* struck him at that time" signifies that I and no other struck him. When the sentence reads "I struck him *alone* at that time" it must be interpreted that he was the only person that received a blow. Again if it is made to read "I struck him at that time *alone*" the sense conveyed is that that was the only occasion on which I struck him. The rule which governs the correct use of *only* is also applicable to *alone*.

Other 和 Another

　　如果誤用這兩個單字，容易使語意跟原本要表達的意思相差
甚遠，例如：

> I have nothing to do with that <u>other</u> rascal
> across the street.
> 我跟對街另一個流氓沒有關係。

　　等於是說我自己也是一個流氓。

> I sent the dispatch to my friend, but <u>another</u>
> villain intercepted it.
> 我發了一封急件給我朋友，但另一個惡棍把它截走了。

　　顯然在說我朋友也是一個惡棍。

　　如果不用這些字就能表達意思，最好省略不用，就像上面兩
個例子。真的要用時，就要把意思表達清楚，只要讓用到這兩個
字的句子或片語不用仰賴上下文就能理解，便能讓意思變得清
楚。

OTHER AND ANOTHER

These are words which often give to expressions a meaning far from that intended. Thus, "I have *nothing* to do with that *other* rascal across the street," certainly means that I am a rascal myself. "I sent the despatch to my friend, but another villain intercepted it," clearly signifies that my friend is a villain.

A good plan is to omit these words when they can be readily done without, as in the above examples, but when it is necessary to use them make your meaning clear. You can do this by making each sentence or phrase in which they occur independent of contextual aid.

合併使用 and 和關係代名詞

千萬不能像這樣合併使用 and 和關係代名詞：

> That is the dog I meant <u>and which</u> I know is of
> pure breed.
> 我說的就是那種狗，我知道那是純種狗。

這是相當常見的錯誤。如果前面的句子或子句也有一個相對
應的關係代名詞，則可以使用 and，以下便是正確寫法：

> There is the dog which I meant and which I
> know is of pure breed.
> 我提到那種狗，我知道那種狗是純種的。

主詞不明的分詞

通常分詞或分詞片語修飾離它最近的主詞。如果句中只有一
個主詞和多個分詞，除了另有明確修飾對象的分詞外，所有分詞
都是用來修飾這個主詞，例如：

> John, working in the field all day and getting
> thirsty, drank from the running stream.
> 在田裡走了一天，口渴了的約翰喝起流動的溪水。

AND WITH THE RELATIVE

Never use *and* with the *relative* in this manner: "That is the dog I meant *and which* I know is of pure breed." This is an error quite common. The use of *and* is permissible when there is a parallel relative in the preceding sentence or clause. Thus: "There is the dog which I meant and which I know is of pure breed" is quite correct.

LOOSE PARTICIPLES

A participle or participial phrase is naturally referred to the nearest nominative. If only one nominative is expressed it claims all the participles that are not by the construction of the sentence otherwise fixed. "John, working in the field all day and getting thirsty, drank from the running stream." Here the participles *working* and *getting* clearly refer to John. But in the sentence, "Swept along by the mob I could not save him," the participle as it were is lying around loose and may be taken to refer to either the person speaking or to the

這裡的 working 和 getting 顯然都是在講約翰。但在以下例句中：

Swept along by the mob, I could not save him.
被暴民襲擊，我救不了他。

這個分詞的位置鬆散，因此有可能是修飾說這句話的人，或修飾句中談到的人。它的意思可能是說我被暴民襲擊，因此救不了他，也有可能是說我試著去救的這個人被暴民襲擊。

Going into the store, the roof fell.
走進店裡時，屋頂塌了下來。

這可以被解讀為是屋頂走進店裡時自己塌了下來。當然，這句原本想要傳達的意思是某人或某些人走進店裡時，屋頂正好塌了下來。

所有使用分詞的句子都應清楚表述，排除所有可能造成語意不清的狀況。分詞的位置必須讓人不會質疑它究竟是要指稱哪個主詞。一般建議加上相關字詞，以便讓語意變得清楚。

person spoken about. It may mean that I was swept along by the mob or the individual whom I tried to save was swept along.

"Going into the store the roof fell" can be taken that it was the roof which was going into the store when it fell. Of course the meaning intended is that some person or persons were going into the store just as the roof fell.

In all sentence construction with participles there should be such clearness as to preclude all possibility of ambiguity. The participle should be so placed that there can be no doubt as to the noun to which it refers. Often it is advisable to supply such words as will make the meaning obvious.

構句一致性

有時會發生句首與句尾文法結構完全不同的情況，這可能是因為句子寫到後面就忘了前面的構句，長句尤其容易發生這種情況，例如：

> Honesty, integrity and square-dealing will bring anybody much better through life than the absence of <u>either</u>.
> 誠實、正直和公平會讓人生過得比缺乏兩者中的其中一種來得順利。

這裡從 than 之後的構句一致性就中斷了。在此用 either 一字表示寫者忘記前面寫了三種特質，而非只有兩種。這個句子有三種可能的意思：缺乏其中一種特質、缺乏其中兩種特質，或缺乏全部三種特質。用 either 意味著兩者中的一個，絕不可用來指三者之中的任何一個。出現上述的句構錯誤時，可以將句子拆開，用不同的文法句型進行重組，例如：

> Honesty, integrity and square-dealing will bring a man much better through life than a lack of these qualities which are almost essential to success.
> 誠實、正直和公平等成功要素，會讓人生過得比沒有這些要素更順利。

BROKEN CONSTRUCTION

Sometimes the beginning of a sentence presents quite a different grammatical construction from its end. This arises from the fact probably, that the beginning is lost sight of before the end is reached. This occurs frequently in long sentences. Thus: "Honesty, integrity and square-dealing will bring anybody much better through life than the absence of either." Here the construction is broken at *than*. The use of *either*, only used in referring to one of two, shows that the fact is forgotten that three qualities and not two are under consideration. Any one of the three meanings might be intended in the sentence, viz., absence of any one quality, absence of any two of the qualities or absence of the whole three qualities. Either denotes one or the other of two and should never be applied to any one of more than two. When we fall into the error of constructing such sentences as above, we should take them apart and reconstruct them in a different grammatical form. Thus, "Honesty, integrity and square-dealing will bring a man much better through life than a lack of these qualities which are almost essential to success."

雙重否定

　　務必記住在英文中，使用兩個否定詞會相互抵消否定意涵，變成肯定的意思。如果原本想說自己對某事一無所知，卻說成：

> I <u>don't</u> know <u>nothing</u> about it.

　　反正會適得其反，意思變成自己知道這件事。這句應該寫成：

> I don't know <u>anything</u> about it.

　　若想要表達「沒人問他的意見」，卻寫成：

> He was <u>not</u> asked to give <u>no</u> opinion.

　　這句話與原意完全相反，表示確實有人問他的意見。這種情況屢見不鮮，因此使用雙重否定時要特別謹慎，這是相常容易落入的陷阱，寫的人往往犯了錯卻不自知，直到被人批評了才發現。

DOUBLE NEGATIVE

It must be remembered that two negatives in the English language destroy each other and are equivalent to an affirmative. Thus "I *don't* know *nothing* about it" is intended to convey, that I am ignorant of the matter under consideration, but it defeats its own purpose, inasmuch as the use of nothing implies that I know something about it. The sentence should read—"I don't know anything about it."

Often we hear such expressions as "He was *not* asked to give *no* opinion," expressing the very opposite of what is intended. This sentence implies that he was asked to give his opinion. The double negative, therefore, should be carefully avoided, for it is insidious and is liable to slip in and the writer remain unconscious of its presence until the eye of the critic detects it.

第一人稱代名詞

寫作時儘量少用第一人稱代名詞。別用第一人稱代名詞提出道歉，也千萬別使用下列用語：

> In my opinion 就我的觀點來說
> As far as I can see 以我目前來看
> It appears to me 在我看來
> I believe 我認為

既然作者是你，整篇文章本來就是在表達你的觀點，因此沒有必要一直強調或突顯自己。再說，I 帶有自負的意味，因此應該儘量避免使用。只有在陳述非一般人持有的見解，且可能會遭到反對時，才可使用第一人稱。

時態呼應性

兩個動詞相互依存時，兩者的時態之間也必須相互呼應，例如：

> I <u>will</u> have much pleasure in accepting your kind invitation.
> 我將相當高興地接受你親切的邀請。

FIRST PERSONAL PRONOUN

The use of the first personal pronoun should be avoided as much as possible in composition. Don't introduce it by way of apology and never use such expressions as "In my opinion," "As far as I can see," "It appears to me," "I believe," etc. In what you write, the whole composition is expressive of your views, since you are the author, therefore, there is no necessity for you to accentuate or emphasize yourself at certain portions of it.

Moreover, the big *I's* savor of egotism! Steer clear of them as far as you can. The only place where the first person is permissible is in passages where you are stating a view that is not generally held and which is likely to meet with opposition.

SEQUENCE OF TENSES

When two verbs depend on each other their tenses must have a definite relation to each other. "I will have much pleasure in accepting your kind invitation" is wrong, unless you really mean that just now you decline though by-and-by you intend to accept; or unless you mean that you do accept now, though you have no pleasure in doing so, but look forward to be more pleased by-and-by. In fact the sequence of the compound tenses puzzle experienced writers. The best

這樣寫是錯的，除非你想表達的是你剛剛才拒絕邀請，不過等一下就會接受；或者你現在接受邀請，但是不太高興，不過等一下應該會更高興地接受。

其實，經驗豐富的作家也會搞混複合時態的呼應。最好的方法是回想你所談的這件事發生的時間點，再用你在「當時」會自然用的時態，例如：

> I should have liked to have gone to see the circus.
> 我本來想去看了馬戲團的。

想要找出適當的時態呼應性，就要問自己「本來想去」（I should have liked）做什麼？這時答案自然會是「看馬戲團」（to go to see the circus）而不是「看了馬戲團」（to have gone to see the circus），因為後者的意思是「在過去某個時間點，我想要『已經看過馬戲團了』」，但這並非我的意思。我的意思是「在我講這件事的時候，我希望我已經看過馬戲團了」。I should have liked 這段話帶我回到過去還有機會看馬戲團的時候，在當時的時間點，「看馬戲團」這件事是現在式。整段解釋可以分析為一個簡單問題：「我當時想做什麼」（What should I have liked at that moment），答案是：「看馬戲團」（to go to see the circus），因此寫成：I should have liked to go to see the circus. 這樣的時態呼應才是對的。

如果句中某個動詞是過去式，而又有另一個動詞發生在比這前者更早的時間，這時另一個動詞必須使用不定詞的完成式，例如：

plan is to go back in thought to the time in question and use the tense you would *then* naturally use. Now in the sentence "I should have liked to have gone to see the circus" the way to find out the proper sequence is to ask yourself the question–what is it I "should have liked" to do? and the plain answer is "to go to see the circus." I cannot answer–"To have gone to see the circus" for that would imply that at a certain moment I would have liked to be in the position of having gone to the circus. But I do not mean this; I mean that at the moment at which I am speaking I wish I had gone to see the circus. The verbal phrase *I should have liked* carries me back to the time when there was a chance of seeing the circus and once back at the time, the going to the circus is a thing of the present. This whole explanation resolves itself into the simple question,–what should I have liked *at that time*, and the answer is "to go to see the circus," therefore this is the proper sequence, and the expression should be "I should have liked to go to see the circus."

He appeared <u>to have seen</u> better days.
他看起來風光不再。

不過下列例子則**不可**使用不定詞的完成式：

（○）I expected to <u>meet</u> him.
我當時預期見到他。

（×）I expected to <u>have met</u> him.
我當時預期見過他了。

（○）We intended to <u>visit</u> you.
我們當時打算拜訪你。

（×）We intended to <u>have visited</u> you.
我們當時打算拜訪過你了。

（○）I hoped they would <u>arrive</u>.
我當時希望他們會抵達。

（×）I hoped they would <u>have arrived</u>.
我當時希望他們抵達了。

（○）I thought I should <u>catch</u> the bird.
我當時以為我應該抓那隻鳥。

（×）I thought I should <u>have caught</u> the bird.
我當時以為我應該已經抓那隻鳥了。

（○）I had intended to <u>go</u> to the meeting.
我當時打算去開會。

（×）I had intended to <u>have gone</u> to the
meeting.
我當時打算去開過會了。

If we wish to speak of something relating to a time *prior* to that indicated in the past tense we must use the perfect tense of the infinitive; as, "He appeared to have seen better days." We should say "I expected to *meet him*," not "I expected to *have met him*." "We intended to *visit* you," not "*to have visited* you." "I hoped they *would* arrive," not "I hoped they *would have* arrived." "I thought I should *catch* the bird," not "I thought I should *have caught* the bird." "I had intended *to go* to the meeting," not "I had intended to *have gone* to the meeting."

Between 和 Among

這兩個介系詞常被隨便交替使用。between 指的是只在兩者之間，among 則是在多於兩者之間。如果有兩個人在平分錢，要說：

The money was equally divided <u>between</u> them.
他們兩個把錢平均分了。

如果多於兩個人在平分錢，要說：

They money was equally divided <u>among</u> them.
他們幾個把錢平均分了。

Less 和 Fewer

less 用於修飾不可數名詞的分量，fewer 用於修飾可數名詞的數目，例如：

（×）No man has <u>less</u> virtues.
（○）No man has <u>fewer</u> virtues. 人有更多美德。

（×）The farmer had some oats and a <u>fewer</u>
quantity of wheat.
（○）The farmer had some oats and a <u>less</u>
quantity of wheat.
這位農夫有一些燕麥和分量更少的小麥。

BETWEEN–AMONG

These prepositions are often carelessly interchanged. *Between* has reference to two objects only, *among* to more than two. "The money was equally divided between them" is right when there are only two, but if there are more than two it should be "the money was equally divided among them."

LESS–FEWER

Less refers is quantity, *fewer* to number. "No man has *less* virtues" should be "No man has *fewer* virtues." "The farmer had some oats and a *fewer* quantity of wheat" should be "the farmer had some oats and a *less* quantity of wheat."

Further
和
Farther

Each
other
和
One
another

Further 和 Farther

further 一般表示程度，farther 表示距離。下列兩個句子皆為正確：

I need no <u>further</u> supply.
我不需要更多的補給。

I have walked <u>farther</u> than you.
我走得比你更遠。

Each other 和 One another

each other 用於兩個人的情況，one another 用於超過兩個人的情況。下列兩個句子皆為正確：

Jones and Smith quarreled; they struck <u>each other</u>.
瓊斯和史密斯起了口角；他們互毆。

Jones, Smith and Brown quarreled; they struck one another.
瓊斯、史密斯和布朗起了口角；他們打成一團。

下列兩個句子皆為錯誤：

The two boys teach one another.
這兩個男孩互相教導。

The three girls love each other.
這三個女孩喜愛彼此。

FURTHER–FARTHER

Further is commonly used to denote quantity, *farther* to denote distance. "I have walked *farther* than you," "I need no *further* supply" are correct.

EACH OTHER–ONE ANOTHER

Each other refers to two, *one another* to more than two. "Jones and Smith quarreled; they struck each other" is correct. "Jones, Smith and Brown quarreled; they struck one another" is also correct. Don't say, "The two boys teach one another" nor "The three girls love each other."

Each ／ Every ／ Either ／ Neither

這幾個單字經常被用錯地方。each 用於「兩個或以上」的人、事、物，表示該數量中「各自獨立的每個個體」。every 用於「超過兩個」的人、事、物，表示該數量中「所有個體」。either 代表「兩者之中的任何一個」，**不能**用來同時包括兩者。neither 是 either 的負面表述，用於兩個被分別看待的個體，代表兩者皆非。

下列例子說明這些單字的正確用法：

Each man of the crew received a reward.
每位工作人員都獲得獎賞。

Every man in the regiment displayed bravery.
軍團中的每一個人都展現勇氣。

We can walk on either side of the street.
我們可以走在街道兩邊的任何一邊。

Neither of the two is to blame.
兩者都不應被責怪。

EACH, EVERY, EITHER, NEITHER

These words are continually misapplied. *Each* can be applied to two or any higher number of objects to signify *every one* of the number *independently*. *Every* requires *more than two* to be spoken of and denotes all the *persons* or *things* taken *separately*. *Either* denotes *one or the other of two*, and should not be used to include both. *Neither* is the negative of either, denoting not the other, and not the one, and relating to *two persons* or *things* considered separately.

The following examples illustrate the correct usage of these words:

Each man of the crew received a reward.

Every man in the regiment displayed bravery.

We can walk on *either* side of the street.

Neither of the two is to blame.

Neither ... nor ...

用 neither... nor... 連接兩個單數主詞時，要用單數動詞，例如：

<u>Neither</u> John <u>nor</u> James <u>was</u> there.
約翰或詹姆士都不在。

句中的 be 動詞不能用 were。

None

習慣上，none 後面用單數或複數動詞皆可，例如：

None <u>is</u> so blind as he who will not see.
沒有人跟不願看的人一樣盲目。

None <u>are</u> so blind as they who will not see.
沒有人跟不願看的人一樣盲目。

不過，none 是 no one 的縮寫，因此用單數動詞比較好。

NEITHER–NOR

When two singular subjects are connected by *neither, nor* use a singular verb; as, "*Neither* John *nor* James was there," not *were* there.

NONE

Custom Has sanctioned the use of this word both with a singular and plural; as–"None *is* so blind as he who will not see" and "None *are* so blind as they who will not see." However, as it is a contraction of *no one* it is better to use the singular verb.

Rise ╱ Raise

這兩個動詞常被混淆。rise 有以下幾個意思：

一、「向上移動或傳遞」，例如：to rise from bed（起床）。

二、「增加價值」，例如：stocks rise（股價上漲）。

三、「提升身分或等級」，例如：politicians rise（政治人物崛起）；they have risen to honor（他們已經邁向榮耀）。

raise 有以下幾個意思：

一、「舉起」，例如：I raise the table.（我抬起桌子。）

二、「提拔」，例如：He raised his servant.（他給他的僕人升職。）

三、「提高」，例如：The baker raised the price of bread.（烘焙師提高了麵包的價格。）

Lay ╱ Lie

及物動詞 lay 跟不及物動詞 lie 的過去式 lay 常被混淆，不過兩者意思天差地遠。不及物動詞 to lie 是指躺下或休息，後面不能直接加受詞，只能先接介系詞再接受詞，例如：

RISE–RAISE

These verbs are very often confounded. *Rise* is to move or pass upward in any manner; as to "rise from bed;" to increase in value, to improve in position or rank, as "stocks rise;" "politicians rise;" "they have risen to honor."

Raise is to lift up, to exalt, to enhance, as "I raise the table;" "He raised his servant;" "The baker raised the price of *bread*."

LAY–LIE

The transitive verb *lay*, and *lay*, the past tense of the neuter verb *lie*, are often confounded, though quite different in meaning. The neuter verb t*o lie*, meaning to lie down or rest, cannot take the objective after it except with a preposition. We can say "He *lies* on the ground," but we cannot say "He *lies* the ground," since the verb is

（○）He <u>lies on</u> the ground. 他躺在地上。

（×）He lies the ground.

與 lie 不同的是，lay 是及物動詞，有「放置」的意思，因此後面可以直接加受詞，例如：

I <u>lay</u> a wager. 我下了賭注。

I <u>laid</u> the carpet. 我鋪了地毯。

描述沒有生命的物體放在某個地方時，要用 lie 而不是 lay，例如：

It <u>lies</u> on the floor. 它放在地板上。

A knife <u>lies</u> on the table. 一把刀子放在桌上。

描述人把東西放在某個地方時，要用 lay 而不是 lie，例如：

He <u>lays</u> the knife on the table.

他把刀子放在桌上。

lie 的過去式是 lay，過去分詞是 lain：

He <u>lay</u> on the bed. 他曾躺在床上。

He <u>has lain</u> on the bed. 他已經躺在床上。

另外，也可以如此用 lay 描述自己：

neuter and intransitive and, as such, cannot have a direct object. With *lay* it is different. *Lay* is a transitive verb, therefore it takes a direct object after it; as "I *lay* a wager," "I *laid* the carpet," etc.

Of a carpet or any inanimate subject we should say, "It *lies* on the floor," "A knife *lies* on the table," not *lays*. But of a person we say–"He *lays* the knife on the table," not "He *lies*–." *Lay* being the past tense of the neuter to lie (down) we should say, "He *lay* on the bed," and *lain* being its past participle we must also say "He has *lain* on the bed."

We can say "I lay myself down." "He laid himself down" and such expressions.

It is imperative to remember in using these verbs that to *lay* means *to do* something, and to lie means *to be in a state of rest.*

Lay／
Lie

Say I／
I said

In／
Into

I lay myself down. 我讓自己躺下。
He laid himself down. 他曾讓自己躺下。

使用這兩個動詞時，記得 to lay 是指做一個動作，而 to lie
是指處於一種休息狀態。

Says I／I said

Says I 是粗俗用語，不要使用，I said 才是正確的形式。

In／Into

務必謹慎辨別這兩個介系詞的意思，不要交替使用。In 表
示某人或某物位於某個地方，無論該人或該物是處於移動或靜止
狀態；Into 則有「進入」的意思，例如：

（×）He went in the room.
（○）He went into the room. 他走進房間。
（×）My brother is into the navy.
（○）My brother is in the navy. 我兄弟在海軍。

SAYS I–I SAID

"*Says I*" is a vulgarism; don't use it. "I said" is correct form.

IN–INTO

Be careful to distinguish the meaning of these two little prepositions and don't interchange them. Don't say "He went *in* the room" nor "My brother is *into* the navy." *In* denotes the place where a person or thing, whether at rest or in motion, is present; and *into* denotes entrance. "He went *into* the room;" "My brother is *in* the navy" are correct.

Eat ／ Ate

不要將這兩者混淆。eat 是現在式，ate 是過去式。I eat the bread 代表吃麵包的動作正在持續；I ate the bread 代表吃的動作已經結束。eaten 是過去分詞，但常被誤用為 eat，因此在使用上必須注意。

過去式／過去分詞

粗心大意的說話者和寫作者最容易在不規則動詞（又稱強變化動詞）的過去式和過去分詞上犯錯。若要避免出錯，必須了解動詞的主要變化形式，這點並不困難，因為不規則動詞只有幾百個，日常生活中會用到的又更少了。以下是一些最常被用錯的動詞形式：

EAT–ATE

Don't confound the two. *Eat* is present, *ate* is past. "I *eat* the bread" means that I am continuing the eating; "I *ate* the bread" means that the act of eating is past. *Eaten* is the perfect participle, but often *eat* is used instead, and as it has the same pronunciation (et) of *ate*, care should be taken to distinguish the past tense, I *ate* from the perfect *I have eaten (eat)*.

PAST TENSE–PAST PARTICIPLE

The interchange of these two parts of the irregular or so-called *strong* verbs is, perhaps, the breach oftenest committed by careless speakers and writers. To avoid mistakes it is requisite to know the principal parts of these verbs, and this knowledge is very easy of acquirement, as there are not more than a couple of hundred of such verbs, and of this number but a small part is in daily use. Here are some of the most common blunders:

錯誤	正確
I seen	I saw
I done it	I did it
I drunk	I drank
I begun	I began
I rung	I rang
I run	I ran
I sung	I sang
I have chose	I have chosen
I have drove	I have driven
I have wore	I have worn
I have trod	I have trodden
I have shook	I have shaken
I have fell	I have fallen
I have drank	I have drunk
I have began	I have begun
I have rang	I have rung
I have rose	I have risen
I have spoke	I have spoken
I have broke	I have broken
It has froze	It has frozen
It has blowed	It has blown
It has flew（形容鳥）	It has flown

"I seen" for "I saw;"

"I done it" for "I did it;"

"I drunk" for "I drank;"

"I begun" for "I began;"

"I rung" for "I rang;"

"I run" for "I ran;"

"I sung" for "I sang;"

"I have chose" for "I have chosen;"

"I have drove" for "I have driven;"

"I have wore" for "I have worn;"

"I have trod" for "I have trodden;"

"I have shook" for "I have shaken;"

"I have fell" for "I have fallen;"

"I have drank" for "I have drunk;"

"I have began" for "I have begun;"

"I have rang" for "I have rung;"

"I have rose" for "I have risen;"

"I have spoke" for "I have spoken;"

"I have broke" for "I have broken;"

"It has froze" for "It has frozen;"

"It has blowed" for "It has blown;"

"It has flew" (of a bird) for "It has flown."

注意：To hang 當作「吊起／掛起」時，過去式和過去分詞都是 hung；當作「吊死／絞死」時，過去式和過去分詞都是 hanged，例如：

He was <u>hanged</u>.
他被吊死了。

An animal carcass was <u>hung</u>.
一具動物屍體被吊起來。

The beef was <u>hung</u> dry.
這塊牛肉被吊起來風乾。

The coat was <u>hung</u> on a hook.
這件大衣掛在勾子上。

介系詞和受格

務必記得介系詞後面一定要接受格，例如：

（×）between you and I
（○）between you and me 你我之間

不能用兩個介系詞描述同一個受格，除非這兩個介系詞之間有直接的關係，例如：

（×）He was refused admission to and forcibly ejected from the school.
（○）He was refused admission to the school and forcibly ejected from it.
他被拒絕入學，並被強制逐出學校。

N. B.–The past tense and past participle of *To Hang* is *hanged* or *hung*. When you are talking about a man meeting death on the gallows, say "He was hanged"; when you are talking about the carcass of an animal say, "It was hung," as "The beef was hung dry." Also say your coat "*was* hung on a hook."

PREPOSITIONS AND THE OBJECTIVE CASE

Don't forget that prepositions always take the objective case. Don't say "Between you and *I*"; say "Between you and *me*."

Two prepositions should not govern *one objective* unless there is an immediate connection between them. "He was refused admission to and forcibly ejected from the school" should be "He was refused admission to the school and forcibly ejected from it."

Summon
/
Summons

Unde-
niable /
Unexcep-
tionable

Summon / Summons

Summon（傳喚／召喚）是動詞，summons（傳喚／召喚／傳票）是單數名詞（複數為 summonses），例如：

（×）I shall summons him.
（○）I shall summon him. 我將傳喚他。
（×）I shall get a summon for him.
（○）I shall get a summons for him.
我會幫他拿傳票。

Undeniable / Unexceptionable

undeniable 是指無論好壞都無可否認，unexceptionable 是指無可挑剔。因此若想表達某人個性很好，應該如此表述：

（×）My brother has an undeniable character.
（○）My brother has an unexceptionable character.
我兄弟的個性無可挑剔。

SUMMON–SUMMONS

Don't say "I shall summons him," but "I shall summon him." *Summon* is a verb, *summons*, a noun.

It is correct to say "I shall get a *summons* for him," not a *summon*.

UNDENIABLE–UNEXCEPTIONABLE

"My brother has an undeniable character" is wrong if I wish to convey the idea that he has a good character. The expression should be in that case "My brother has an unexceptionable character." An *undeniable* character is a character that cannot be denied, whether bad or good. An unexceptionable character is one to which no one can take exception.

代名詞

代名詞常被錯誤使用，例如：

（×）Let you and I go.
（○）Let you and me go. 放你和我走。
（×）Let we and them go.
（○）Let us and them go. 放他們和我們走。

let 是及物動詞，因此後面要接受格。

（×）Give me them flowers.
（○）Give me those flowers. 把那些花給我。
（×）I mean them three.
（○）I mean those three. 我是指那三個。

them 是人稱代名詞的受格，不能當指示形容代名詞使用。

（×）I am as strong as him.
（○）I am as strong as he. 我跟他一樣強壯。
（×）I am younger than her.
（○）I am younger than she. 我比她年輕。
（×）He can write better than me.
（○）He can write better than I. 他能寫得比我好。

上述三個例子錯將該用主格的地方用成受格 him、her 和 me。

THE PRONOUNS

Very many mistakes occur in the use of the pronouns. "Let you and I go" should be "Let you and *me* go." "Let we and them go" should be "Let us and them go." The verb let is transitive and therefore takes the objective case.

"Give me *them* flowers" should be "Give me *those* flowers"; "I mean *them* three" should be "I mean those three." Them is the objective case of the personal pronoun and cannot be used adjectively like the demonstrative adjective pronoun. "I am as strong as *him*" should be "I am as strong as he"; "I am younger than *her*" should be "I am younger than *she*;" "He can write better than *me*" should be "He can write better than *I*," for in these examples the objective cases *him*, *her* and *me* are used wrongfully for the nominatives. After each of the misapplied pronouns a verb is understood of which each pronoun is the subject. Thus, "I am as strong as he (is)." "I am younger than she (is)." "He can write better than I (can)."

不過，只要知道這些代名詞後面原本應該要加什麼動詞，就能了解這些代名詞都應該使用主格形式，例如：

> I am as strong as he (is).
> I am younger than she (is).
> He can write better than I (can).

千萬不要說 It is me，要說 It is I（是我）。這邊的 be 動詞 is 是跟著前面的主詞 it 做變化，因此不管後面是哪個代名詞，動詞都是用 is。

另外，在問句中，be 動詞前面的代名詞格位要與主詞的格位一致，換句話說，主格 I 要用主格 who 來提問，受格 me、him、her、its、you、them 要用受格 whom 來提問：

> （×）Whom do you think I am?
> （○）Who do you think I am? 你認為我是誰？
> （×）Who do they suppose me to be?
> （○）Whom do they suppose me to be?
>   他們以為我是誰？

與介系詞並用時，一定要用關係代名詞的受格：

> （×）Who do you take me for?
> （○）Whom do you take me for?
>   你當我是什麼人？
> （×）Who did you give the apple to?
> （○）Whom did you give the apple to?
>   你把蘋果給了誰？

Don't say "*It is me;*" say "*It is I*" The verb *To Be* of which is is a part takes the same case after it that it has before it. This holds good in all situations as well as with pronouns.

The verb *To Be* also requires the pronouns joined to it to be in the same case as a pronoun asking a question; The nominative *I* requires the nominative *who* and the objectives *me, him, her, its, you, them*, require the objective *whom*.

"*Whom* do you think I am?" should be "*Who* do you think I am?" and "*Who* do they suppose me to be?" should be "*Whom* do they suppose me to be?" The objective form of the Relative should be always used, in connection with a preposition. "*Who* do you take me for?" should be "*Whom* do, etc." "*Who* did you give the apple to?" should be "*Whom* did you give the apple to," but as pointed out elsewhere the preposition should never end a sentence, therefore, it is better to say, "*To whom* did you give the apple?"

不過，之前說過不要將介系詞放在句尾，因此這樣表述比較好：

To whom did you give the apple?

及物動詞後面一定要用代名詞的受格：

（×）He and they we have seen.
（○）Him and them we have seen.
我們見過他和他們了。

That／So

以下句子應使用 so，而不是 that：

（×）It was that painful it made him cry.
（○）It was so painful it made him cry.
他痛到哭了出來。

These／Those

kind 和 sort 都是單數名詞，因此要用單數代名詞 this 和 that。

（×）These kind
（○）This kind 這一種
（×）Those sort
（○）That sort 那一類

After transitive verbs always use the objective cases of the pronouns. For "*He* and *they* we have seen," say "*Him* and *them* we have seen."

THAT FOR SO

"The hurt it was that painful it made him cry," say "so painful."

THESE–THOSE

Don't say, *These kind*; *those sort*. *Kind* and *sort* are each singular and require the singular pronouns *this* and *that*.

使用這類指示形容代名詞時，記住 this 和 these 是指鄰近的東西，that 和 those 是指較遠的東西，例如：

> This book（離我較近的書）
> That book（離我較遠的書）
> These boys（離我較近的一群男孩）
> Those boys（離我較遠的一群男孩）

Flee ∕ Fly

這兩者是完全不一樣的動詞，不能交替使用。flee 的主要動詞變化形式是 flee／fled／fled，fly 是 fly／flew／flown。flee 一般是指逃離危險，fly 是指像鳥一樣飛翔，例如：

> （×）He has flown from the place.
> 他飛離那個地方。
> （○）He has fled from the place.
> 他逃離那個地方。
> （○）A bird has flown from the place.
> 一隻鳥飛離那個地方。

In connection with these demonstrative adjective pronouns remember that *this* and *these* refer to what is near at hand, *that* and *those* to what is more distant; as, *this book* (near me), *that book* (over there), *these* boys (near), *those* boys (at a distance).

FLEE–FLY

These are two separate verbs and must not be interchanged. The principal parts of *flee* are *flee, fled, fled*; those of *fly* are *fly, flew, flown*. *To flee* is generally used in the meaning of getting out of danger. *To fly* means to soar as a bird. To say of a man "He *has flown* from the place" is wrong; it should be "He *has fled* from the place." We can say with propriety that "A bird has *flown* from the place."

Through / Throughout

（×）He is well known <u>through</u> the land.
他透過全國各地廣為人知。

（○）He is well known throughout the land.
他在全國各地廣為人知。

Vocation / Avocation

這兩個字拼法相似，但不能用錯。vocation 是某人賴以為生的工作、事業或職業，avocation 是有別於前述工作、事業或職業的嗜好或消遣，例如：

His vocation was the law; his avocation, farming.
他的職業是法律相關領域，嗜好則是務農。

THROUGH–THROUGHOUT

Don't say "He is well known through the land," but "He is well known throughout the land."

VOCATION AND AVOCATION

Don't mistake these two words so nearly alike. Vocation is the employment, business or profession one follows for a living; avocation is some pursuit or occupation which diverts the person from such employment, business or profession. Thus

"His vocation was the law, his avocation, farming."

Was／Were

　　在假設語氣中，單數主詞要用複數 be 動詞 were，因此要說 If I were（如果我是）而不是 If I was。代名詞 you 的複數 be 動詞一定是用 were，但這裡的 you 也有可能是指單數的你，因此一定要用 you were 而不是 you was。If I was him 是常見的表述方式，但這個句子有雙重錯誤，一個是動詞沒有反映出假設語氣，另一個是第二個代名詞誤用成受格。正確說法應該是 If I were he（如果我是他）。這也符合前面說過的 be 動詞規則：be 動詞前、後的代名詞格位必須一致。在這個例子中，be 動詞 were 前面的代名詞是用主格 I，因此後面的代名詞也要用主格 he。

A／An

　　以母音字母為首的名詞，其冠詞要用 an。以 h 為首的名詞，如果為了諧音或聽起來順耳的緣故而 h 不發音，其冠詞也要用 an，例如：an apple、an orange、an heir、an honor。

WAS–WERE

In the subjunctive mood the plural form *were* should be used with a singular subject; as, "If I *were*," not *was*. Remember the plural form of the personal pronoun *you* always takes *were*, though it may denote but one. Thus, "*You were*," never "*you was*." "*If I was him*" is a very common expression. Note the two mistakes in it–that of the verb implying a condition, and that of the objective case of the pronoun. It should read *If I were he*. This is another illustration of the rule regarding the verb To Be, taking the same case after it as before it; were is part of the verb *To Be*, therefore as the nominative (I) goes before it, the nominative (he) should come after it.

A OR AN

A becomes *an* before a vowel or before *h* mute for the sake of euphony or agreeable sound to the ear. *An apple, an orange, an heir, an honor,* etc.

第九章
文字風格

Style

盡可能用有效的形式呈現個人想法，以在讀者心中留下深刻印象，是每個寫作者的目標。有的人也許懷有崇高想法和概念，卻無法用吸引人的方式表達出來，以致無法充分發揮他的才智，沒能留名青史；也有人才能平庸，卻靠著流暢文筆吸引目光，為自己贏得令同輩欣羨的地位。

　　我們在日常生活中都看過才智過人之士受到冷落，能力平庸之輩卻獲選擔任要職。前者無法讓人留下深刻印象，縱使他們懷有偉大思想和概念，這些思想和概念卻被鎖在他們腦中，像囚犯一般拚命想要逃脫。它們欠缺打開監獄大門的語言之鑰，只好一直受到封鎖。

　　許多人之所以終生沒沒無聞，對社會或自己貢獻甚少，就是因為無法將內心想法表達出來並善加利用。充分發揮自己的能力是每個人的職責，這不只是為了圖利個人，更是為了造福他人。不一定要有深厚學問或造詣才能做到這點，只要克盡本分，工人跟哲學家一樣有用。也未必得多才多藝才行，善用一項才能遠勝過錯用十項才能。有的人只靠一項才能，卻比多才多藝的同輩中人成就更高；有的人只賺一塊錢，卻比手頭擁有二十塊錢的人發展得更好；也常有貧窮的人過得比百萬富翁更加舒適。一切都取決於個人。只要善用造物主所賦予的能力，並依循上帝和自然的法則生活，就是在履行自己在宇宙中被分配到的職責。換句話說，只要將自己的能力做最大的發揮，就是一個有用的人。

　　一個智商和教育程度普通的人若想將能力做最大發揮，必須要能透過口說和寫作正確地表達自我，也就是說要能明智地傳達

It is the object of every writer to put his thoughts into as effective form as possible so as to make a good impression on the reader. A person may have noble thoughts and ideas but be unable to express them in such a way as to appeal to others, consequently he cannot exert the full force of his intellectuality nor leave the imprint of his character upon his time, whereas many a man but indifferently gifted may wield such a facile pen as to attract attention and win for himself an envious place among his contemporaries.

In everyday life one sees illustrations of men of excellent mentality being cast aside and ones of mediocre or in some cases, little, if any, ability chosen to fill important places. The former are unable to impress their personality; they have great thoughts, great ideas, but these thoughts and ideas are locked up in their brains and are like prisoners behind the bars struggling to get free. The key of language which would open the door is wanting, hence they have to remain locked up.

Many a man has to pass through the world unheard of and of little benefit to it or himself, simply because he cannot bring out what is in him and make it subservient to his will. It is the duty of every one to develop his best, not only for the benefit of himself but for the good of his fellow men. It is not at all necessary to have great learning or acquirements, the laborer is as useful in his own place as the philosopher in his; nor is it necessary to have many talents. One talent rightly used is much better than ten wrongly used. Often a man can do more with one than his contemporary can do with ten,

個人想法，好讓頭腦最簡單的人也能理解。演說者或寫作者傳達自己想法的方式稱為「文風」。文風的定義是「一個人透過語言這項媒介表達個人概念的特定方式」。文風取決於一個人在傳達意思時的用字遣詞和文字排列。幾乎不會有哪兩個人寫作風格完全相同，用一樣的方式表達個人想法，就像不會有哪兩個人長得一模一樣，像用同一個模子刻出來的那樣。

就像口音和語調人人各有不同，人在使用的語言構成上也有差異。若派兩名記者去報導同一場火災，雖然兩人描述同一項事實，但描述時的用語則不盡相同。其中一名記者的表達風格會不同於另一名記者。

你可以這麼描述上次在慈善舞會上看到的紅髮女舞者：

The ruby Circe, with the Titian locks glowing like the oriflamme which surrounds the golden god of day as he sinks to rest amid the crimson glory of the burnished West, gave a divine exhibition of the Terpsichorean art which thrilled the souls of the multitude.

這位如紅寶石般充滿魅力的女子披著一頭橙紅秀髮，光芒之耀眼有如一面金焰旗，在金色日神落到西方的深紅光輝中歇息時包圍著袖，她以神乎其技的舞蹈藝術演出讓眾人靈魂為之振奮。

而你也可以簡單地說：

The red-haired lady danced very well and pleased the audience.

這名紅髮女子舞技出色，觀眾看得十分開心。

often a man can make one dollar go farther than twenty in the hands of his neighbor, often the poor man lives more comfortably than the millionaire. All depends upon the individual himself. If he make right use of what the Creator has given him and live according to the laws of God and nature he is fulfilling his allotted place in the universal scheme of creation, in other words, when he does his best, he is living up to the standard of a useful manhood.

Now in order to do his best a man of ordinary intelligence and education should be able to express himself correctly both in speaking and writing, that is, he should be able to convey his thoughts in an intelligent manner which the simplest can understand. The manner in which a speaker or writer conveys his thoughts is known as his Style. In other words *Style* may be defined as the peculiar manner in which a man expresses his conceptions through the medium of language. It depends upon the choice of words and their arrangement to convey a meaning. Scarcely any two writers have exactly the same style, that is to say, express their ideas after the same peculiar form, just as no two mortals are fashioned by nature in the same mould, so that one is an exact counterpart of the other.

Just as men differ in the accent and tones of their voices, so do they differ in the construction of their language.

Two reporters sent out on the same mission, say to report a fire, will verbally differ in their accounts though materially both descriptions will be the same as far as the leading facts are concerned. One will express himself in a style *different* from the other.

第一種文風堆砌辭藻、華而不實，仰賴浮誇累贅以製造效果，第二種文風則顯得簡單自然，當然是比較好的描述方式。避免使用第一種風格，它會讓人覺得作者是個膚淺、無知、缺乏經驗的人。現在新聞報導已經不用這種風格了，即便最浮誇的專欄也不再容忍這種風格。現今普遍捨棄矯揉造作、賣弄學問的文風。

努力追求令人愉悅的風格是每個演說者和寫作者的責任，如此便能為人所接納，而非遭到排擠。人們之所以對某個主題產生興趣，除了主題本身之外，也要看這個主題是以什麼方式呈現。有的作者會把它寫得引人入勝，有的則寫得令人反感。例如同樣一段歷史，有的史學家把它描寫得有如乾枯的木乃伊般枯燥無味、令人作嘔，有的則能妙筆生花，描寫得生動活潑，不只讀來宜人，也能令讀者著迷。

If you are asked to describe the dancing of a red-haired lady at the last charity ball you can either say–"The ruby Circe, with the Titian locks glowing like the oriflamme which surrounds the golden god of day as he sinks to rest amid the crimson glory of the burnished West, gave a divine exhibition of the Terpsichorean art which thrilled the souls of the multitude" or, you can simply say–"The red-haired lady danced very well and pleased the audience."

The former is a specimen of the ultra florid or bombastic style which may be said to depend upon the pomposity of verbosity for its effect, the latter is a specimen of simple *natural* Style. Needless to say it is to be preferred. The other should be avoided. It stamps the writer as a person of shallowness, ignorance and inexperience. It has been eliminated from the newspapers. Even the most flatulent of yellow sheets no longer tolerate it in their columns. Affectation and pedantry in style are now universally condemned.

It is the duty of every speaker and writer to labor after a pleasing style. It gains him an entrance where he would otherwise be debarred. Often the interest of a subject depends as much on the way it is presented as on the subject itself. One writer will make it attractive, another repulsive. For instance take a passage in history. Treated by one historian it is like a desiccated mummy, dry, dull, disgusting, while under the spell of another it is, as it were, galvanized into a virile living thing which not only pleases but captivates the reader.

措辭

文風的第一要項是用字遣辭，也就是**措辭**，指口說和寫作時所選用的字詞、片語。無論從什麼觀點來看，文筆好的祕訣在於在對的地方使用對的字詞。要做到這點，就一定要了解所使用的字詞的真正意思。許多同義詞看似意思一樣，可以交替使用，但仔細分析就會發現每個字的意思明顯不同。例如 grief 和 sorrow 都有「悲痛、哀傷」之意，看似相同，實則不然。grief 是主動的，sorrow 多少帶點被動意味；grief 由外在困境和不幸所引發，sorrow 則通常是自身行為造成的後果；grief 通常是喧嘩而激動的，sorrow 則是輕聲而退卻的；grief 是外顯的，sorrow 則維持冷靜。

如果不確定某個單字的確切意思，就要馬上查字典。有些偉大學者有時也會搞不清楚簡單字詞的意思、拼法或發音。只要遇到不熟的單字就標示起來，直到了解它的意思和用法。閱讀最優秀的書籍和語言專家的著作，研究他們如何使用字詞，將這些字詞用在句中何處，向讀者傳達什麼樣的意思。跟學養好的人相處。仔細聆聽能言善道者的說話內容，試著模仿他們的表達方式。如果他們用了你不了解的字詞，不要恥於發問。的確，你只需要小小的字彙量就能傳達想法，不過字彙量多有其好處。一個人住時，一個小鍋就夠你做菜吃了，而且比大鍋來得方便好用，但當朋友或鄰居來作客時就需要大上許多的鍋子，這時家裡有的話會比較好，才不會因傢俬太少而感到丟臉。

DICTION

The first requisite of style is *choice of words*, and this comes under the head of *Diction*, the property of style which has reference to the words and phrases used in speaking and writing. The secret of literary skill from any standpoint consists in putting the right word in the right place. In order to do this it is imperative to know the meaning of the words we use, their exact literal meaning. Many synonymous words are seemingly interchangeable and appear as if the same meaning were applicable to three or four of them at the same time, but when all such words are reduced to a final analysis it is clearly seen that there is a marked difference in their meaning. For instance *grief* and *sorrow* seem to be identical, but they are not. *Grief* is active, *sorrow* is more or less passive; *grief* is caused by troubles and misfortunes which come to us from the outside, while *sorrow* is often the consequence of our own acts. *Grief* is frequently loud and violent, *sorrow* is always quiet and retiring. *Grief* shouts, *sorrow* remains calm.

If you are not sure of the exact meaning of a word look it up immediately in the dictionary. Sometimes some of our great scholars are puzzled over simple words in regard to meaning, spelling or pronunciation. Whenever you meet a strange word note it down until you discover its meaning and use. Read the best books you can get, books written by men and women who are acknowledged masters of

　　儘量擴充自己的字彙量，現在用不到的單字就先記在腦海深處，需要時才好派上用場。隨身攜帶筆記本，寫下自己不懂或一知半解的單字，以便有時間時查字典學習。

純正度

　　文風的**純正度**是指使用標準、普遍、時下的字詞，意思就是當前最具權威人士所用、全體人民而非特定族群所用，以及當前經常被使用的字詞。用字遣詞有兩個指導原則，意即「用得對」和「用得好」。「用得對」是指字詞的正確性，「用得好」是指所用的字詞是否符合目的。不要使用過時、太過新穎或方言的字詞。

　　以下是英文風格的九大誡條：

一、不要使用外來語。

二、能用短字表達意思就不要用長字，例如用 fire 表示火災比用 conflagration 更好。

三、不要使用技術用語或只有某個領域的專家才懂的字詞，除非你是專門寫給這些人看的。

四、不要使用俚語。

五、寫散文時不要使用詩詞用字或陳舊字詞，例如：lore（學識）、e'er（從來）、morn（早晨）、yea（是）、nay（否）、verily（真正地）、peradventure（或許）。

六、不要使用陳腔濫調的單字和表述。

language, and study how they use their words, where they place them in the sentences, and the meanings they convey to the readers. Mix in good society. Listen attentively to good talkers and try to imitate their manner of expression. If a word is used you do not understand, don't be ashamed to ask its meaning.

True, a small vocabulary will carry you through, but it is an advantage to have a large one. When you live alone a little pot serves just as well as a large one to cook your victuals and it is handy and convenient, but when your friends or neighbors come to dine with you, you will need a much larger pot and it is better to have it in store, so that you will not be put to shame for your scantiness of furnishings.

Get as many words as you possibly can–if you don't need them now, pack them away in the garrets of your brain so that you can call upon them if you require them. Keep a note book, jot down the words you don't understand or clearly understand and consult the dictionary when you get time.

PURITY

Purity of style consists in using words which are reputable, national and present, which means that the words are in current use by the best authorities, that they are used throughout the nation and not confined to one particular part, and that they are words in constant use at the present time.

七、不要使用尚未廣受使用的報媒用語。

八、不要使用不合文法的字詞和用詞，例如：I ain't、he don't。

九、不要使用模稜兩可的字詞或片語，例如：

He showed me all about the house.
他帶我參觀整間房子／他給我看房子的所有資料。

不要再用陳腔濫調的字詞和過度使用的庸俗明喻和隱喻。下列用語已經被太多人用到爛了：

sweet sixteen 甜蜜十六歲

the Almighty dollar 萬能的美元

Uncle Sam 山姆大叔

on the fence 立場未定

the Glorious Fourth 光輝的七月四日

Young America 年輕的美國

the lords of creation 創造之神

the rising generation 崛起的世代

the weaker sex 較弱的性別

the weaker vessel 較弱的器皿 [7]

sweetness long drawn out 美妙樂聲久久不散

chief cook and bottle washer 校長兼撞鐘

7　Weaker sex和weaker vessel都指女性，是帶有貶意的舊有用語。

There are two guiding principles in the choice of words–*good use* and *good taste*. *Good use* tells us whether a word is right or wrong; *good taste*, whether it is adapted to our purpose or not.

A word that is obsolete or too new to have gained a place in the language, or that is a provincialism, should not be used.

Here are the Ten Commandments of English style:

(1) Do not use foreign words.

(2) Do not use a long word when a short one will serve your purpose. *Fire* is much better than *conflagration*.

(3) Do not use technical words, or those understood only by specialists in their respective lines, except when you are writing especially for such people.

(4) Do not use slang.

(5) Do not in writing prose, use poetical or antiquated words: as "lore, e'er, morn, yea, nay, verily, peradventure."

(6) Do not use trite and hackneyed words and expressions.

(7) Do not use newspaper words which have not established a place in the language.

(8) Do not use ungrammatical words and forms; as, "I ain't;" "he don't."

(9) Do not use ambiguous words or phrases; as–"He showed me all about the house."

Trite words, similes and metaphors which have become hackneyed and worn out should be allowed to rest in the oblivion of past usage. Such expressions and phrases as "Sweet sixteen"

有些過時、不該再用的舊有明喻包括：

sweet as sugar 甜如蜜

bold as a lion 勇如獅

strong as an ox 壯如牛

quick as a flash 快如閃光

cold as ice 冷如冰

stiff as a poker 僵硬如紙牌

white as snow 白如雪

busy as a bee 忙如蜂

pale as a ghost 蒼白如鬼

cross as a bear 脾氣壞如熊

還有更多類似的明喻，在此就不逐一列舉。

　　儘可能用原創方式表達自我。不要一昧延用舊有用語，試著用自己的方式表達。這不是要你自創風格，做些搞怪、標新立異的事，或是想辦法革新現存的慣例。原創並不一定就要推陳出新或開創先例，你的學識才能也不一定適合這麼做。這個意思是指在依循一般公認的語言大師的文風之餘，也可以在語言上表達原創性。試著用不同以往的方式去表達一個想法。如果你在講述或描寫舞蹈，不要用 trip the light fantastic toe（踩著輕盈夢幻的腳趾起舞）形容。這句話源自約翰・米爾頓（John Milton）的《歡樂頌》（L'Allegro），至今已經超過兩百年。你不是米爾頓，再說已有不下百萬人盜用米爾頓的這段描述，已經沒有再盜用的價值了。

"the Almighty dollar," "Uncle Sam," "On the fence," "The Glorious Fourth," "Young America," "The lords of creation," "The rising generation," "The weaker sex," "The weaker vessel," "Sweetness long drawn out" and "chief cook and bottle washer," should be put on the shelf as they are utterly worn out from too much usage.

Some of the old similes which have outlived their usefulness and should be pensioned off, are "Sweet as sugar," "Bold as a lion," "Strong as an ox," "Quick as a flash," "Cold as ice," "Stiff as a poker," "White as snow," "Busy as a bee," "Pale as a ghost," "Rich as Croesus," "Cross as a bear" and a great many more far too numerous to mention.

Be as original as possible in the use of expression. Don't follow in the old rut but try and strike out for yourself. This does not mean that you should try to set the style, or do anything outlandish or out of the way, or be an innovator on the prevailing custom. In order to be original there is no necessity for you to introduce something novel or establish a precedent. The probability is you are not fit to do either, by education or talent. While following the style of those who are acknowledged leaders you can be original in your language. Try and clothe an idea different from what it has been clothed and better. If you are speaking or writing of dancing don't talk or write about "tripping the light fantastic toe." It is over two hundred years since Milton expressed it that way in "*L'Allegro.*" You're not a Milton and besides over a million have stolen it from Milton until it is now no longer worth stealing.

用新字時也要小心。用原創方式建構和排列語言，但不要試圖發明單字，這件事交給語言大師去做吧。也不要搶先使用這類新字，等語言高手用過並評論過這些單字後再說。

古羅馬帝國修辭學家昆體良（Quintilian）說：「寧可選擇新詞之中最舊者、舊詞之中最新者。」亞歷山大・波普（Alexander Pope）重新詮釋這段話，至今仍很受用：「語言跟時尚有一條共通法則，太舊或太新的事物都不妥當，不要當第一個嘗新的人，也不要當最後一個棄舊的人。」

適當性

文風的「適當性」是指使用字詞的適當字意，跟純正度一樣，「用得好」是首要原則。許多單字在實際使用過程中，發展出與當初完全不同的意思。

prevent 原本是指「先於……」之意，這個意思來自其拉丁文字源；現在它指的是「阻止、妨礙」。想要擁有適當的文風，就要避免源自相同字根、容易造成混淆的單字，像是 respectfully（恭敬地）和 respectively（各別地）。在使用某個單字時，要用該單字的公認字義，或經日常用法認可的字義。

And beware of new words. Be original in the construction and arrangement of your language, but don't try to originate words. Leave that to the Masters of language, and don't be the first to try such words, wait until the chemists of speech have tested them and passed upon their merits.

Quintilian said—"Prefer the oldest of the new and the newest of the old." Pope put this in rhyme and it still holds good: In words, as fashions, the same rule will hold, Alike fantastic, if too new or old: Be not the first by whom the new are tried, Nor yet the last to lay the old aside.

PROPRIETY

Propriety of style consists in using words in their proper sense and as in the case of purity, good usage is the principal test. Many words have acquired in actual use a meaning very different from what they once possessed. "Prevent" formerly meant to go before, and that meaning is implied in its Latin derivation. Now it means to put a stop to, to hinder. To attain propriety of style it is necessary to avoid confounding words derived from the same root; as *respectfully* and *respectively*; it is necessary to use words in their accepted sense or the sense which everyday use sanctions.

簡潔度

　　風格的「簡潔度」是指選用簡單的字，並以不造作的方式呈現這些字。在能表達相同或幾乎相同的意思的前提下，應該優先使用簡單的字，而非合成詞或複合詞。英文裡的盎格魯撒克遜元素包含表達日常生活關係的簡單單字，這些字讀來鏗鏘有力、簡潔精練、富有活力，是市井小民在火爐邊、街上、市集和農田等日常環境中所使用的語言。這種風格正是《聖經》以及《天路歷程》、《魯賓遜飄流記》和《格列佛遊記》等許多偉大英文經典作品的特色。

明晰度

　　文風的「明晰度」是寫作新手必須注意的重點之一。務必避開所有隱晦、模稜兩可的字詞。如果某個句子或片語可能被解讀成與原意不同的意思，就該重寫成不會產生疑問的方式。意思相關的單字、片語或子句應該儘量放得近一點，以清楚呈現其相互關係。所有有助於完整表達想法的必要字詞不得省略。

SIMPLICITY

Simplicity of style has reference to the choice of simple words and their unaffected presentation. Simple words should always be used in preference to compound, and complicated ones when they express the same or almost the same meaning. The Anglo-Saxon element in our language comprises the simple words which express the relations of everyday life, strong, terse, vigorous, the language of the fireside, street, market and farm. It is this style which characterizes the Bible and many of the great English classics such as the "Pilgrim's Progress," "Robinson Crusoe," and "Gulliver's Travels."

CLEARNESS

Clearness of style should be one of the leading considerations with the beginner in composition. He must avoid all obscurity and ambiguous phrases. If he write a sentence or phrase and see that a meaning might be inferred from it otherwise than intended, he should re-write it in such a way that there can be no possible doubt. Words, phrases or clauses that are closely related should be placed as near to each other as possible that their mutual relation may clearly appear, and no word should be omitted that is necessary to the complete expression of thought.

統一性

　　文風的「統一性」是讓句中所有元素緊扣主旨，同時符合主旨的邏輯。有的句子結構能呈現想法的一體性，有的句子則結構鬆散，讓人感到困惑、不明確。彼此關係薄弱的想法應該分別在不同句子中呈現，而不是擠在同一句裡。

　　不要在句中加入長的插入語，如果句子已經結束，不要再加補充子句來繼續描述想法或概念。

張力

　　文風的「張力」賦予語言動感、活力和生氣，以維持讀者的興趣。就如身體需要營養的食物，語言也需要張力。如果缺乏張力，字詞就會顯得軟弱無力，難以讓人留下印象。想要創造張力，語言必須精練，意即言簡意賅、一針見血。反覆批判你的文章，刪掉無損句子明晰度或強度的單字、片語和子句，就能避免文章流於累贅、反覆、迂迴。前面章節說過，最重要的單字要放在最重要的位置，也就是句首和句尾。

UNITY

Unity is that property of style which keeps all parts of a sentence in connection with the principal thought and logically subordinate to it. A sentence may be constructed as to suggest the idea of oneness to the mind, or it may be so loosely put together as to produce a confused and indefinite impression. Ideas that have but little connection should be expressed in separate sentences, and not crowded into one.

Keep long parentheses out of the middle of your sentences and when you have apparently brought your sentences to a close don't try to continue the thought or idea by adding supplementary clauses.

STRENGTH

Strength is that property of style which gives animation, energy and vivacity to language and sustains the interest of the reader. It is as necessary to language as good food is to the body. Without it the words are weak and feeble and create little or no impression on the mind. In order to have strength the language must be concise, that is, much expressed in little compass, you must hit the nail fairly on the head and drive it in straight. Go critically over what you write and strike out every word, phrase and clause the omission of which impairs neither the clearness nor force of the sentence and so avoid

和諧性

　　文風的「和諧性」賦予句子流暢感，讓字詞讀來順暢悅耳。和諧性能讓讀音搭配得上意義。許多人在建構句子時沒有考慮到句子讀起來的感覺，以致寫出讀來刺耳不順的句子，例如：

> Thou strengthenedst thy position and actedst arbitrarily and derogatorily to my interests.
> 汝為鞏固地位，肆意貶損吾之利益。

　　貴格會所使用的人稱代名詞 thou（汝）常須搭配刺耳拗口的動詞形式，這個單字現在已遭到淘汰，一般使用複數形的 you 描述第二人稱單數。想要保持句子的和諧性，就該避免難讀的長字和詞組。

寫作者的表達形式

　　文風能夠表達寫作者的身分和特質。文章的結構代表寫作者的能力，文章的品質代表寫作者的本質。

redundancy, tautology and circumlocution. Give the most important words the most prominent places, which, as has been pointed out elsewhere, are the beginning and end of the sentence.

HARMONY

Harmony is that property of style which gives a smoothness to the sentence, so that when the words are sounded their connection becomes pleasing to the ear. It adapts sound to sense. Most people construct their sentences without giving thought to the way they will sound and as a consequence we have many jarring and discordant combinations such as "Thou strengthenedst thy position and actedst arbitrarily and derogatorily to my interests."

Harsh, disagreeable verbs are liable to occur with the Quaker form *Thou* of the personal pronoun. This form is now nearly obsolete, the plural *you* being almost universally used. To obtain harmony in the sentence long words that are hard to pronounce and combinations of letters of one kind should be avoided.

EXPRESSIVE OF WRITER

Style is expressive of the writer, as to who he is and what he is. As a matter of structure in composition it is the indication of what a man can do; as a matter of quality it is an indication of what he is.

文風類型

文風有許多種分類方法，難以逐一列舉，畢竟每個寫作者自有一套風格，不會有人跟別人的寫作形式一模一樣。儘管如此，我們或許能將不同作者的文風大致分為：枯燥、簡樸、俐落、典雅、華麗、浮誇。

枯燥風格撤除所有修飾用語，完全不求任何美感，只求正確表達想法。喬治・貝克萊（George Berkeley）是這種風格的代表人物。

簡樸風格也不注重修飾，而是追求清楚簡明地陳述，不雕琢潤飾。威廉・洛克（William John Locke）和理查・懷特利（Whatley）利屬於簡樸風格。

俐落風格只用極少的修飾用語，其追求的是正確的敘述、純正的措辭和清楚和諧的句子。戈德史密斯（Goldsmith）和格雷（Gray）是眾人公認的俐落風格高手。

典雅風格使用所有能讓文章變得優美的修飾用語，並避免會降低美感的措辭。麥考利和愛迪生被推崇為這種風格的王者，所有作家都要甘拜下風。

華麗風格過度使用多餘、膚淺的修飾用語，極力營造出多彩多姿的意象。《奧西安之詩》（The Poems of Ossian）屬於典型的華麗風格。

KINDS OF STYLE

Style has been classified in different ways, but it admits of so many designations that it is very hard to enumerate a table. In fact there are as many styles as there are writers, for no two authors write *exactly* after the same form. However, we may classify the styles of the various authors in broad divisions as (1) dry, (2) plain, (3) neat, (4) elegant, (5) florid, (6) bombastic.

The *dry* style excludes all ornament and makes no effort to appeal to any sense of beauty. Its object is simply to express the thoughts in a correct manner. This style is exemplified by Berkeley.

The *plain* style does not seek ornamentation either, but aims to make clear and concise statements without any elaboration or embellishment. Locke and Whately illustrate the plain style.

The *neat* style only aspires after ornament sparingly. Its object is to have correct figures, pure diction and clear and harmonious sentences. Goldsmith and Gray are the acknowledged leaders in this kind of style.

The *elegant* style uses every ornament that can beautify and avoids every excess which would degrade. Macaulay and Addison have been enthroned as the kings of this style. To them all writers bend the knee in homage.

浮誇風格的特色是過度使用單字、敘述和修飾用語，以致讓人覺得荒誕可笑、反感，就像馬戲團裡穿著鑲金絲服裝的小丑。狄更斯在《匹克威克外傳》（Pickwick Papers）裡，布茲福斯中士的演說中充分詮釋這種風格。

其他可能的文風類型包括口語、簡潔、簡明、晦澀、不連貫、流暢、古雅、精闢、花俏、薄弱、緊繃、強烈、做作，從這些形容詞就能看出這些文風的特色。

其實有多少人就有多少種寫作風格，因為風格表達的是寫作者的個體性。法國作家布馮（Georges-Louis Leclerc De Buffon）有一句話說得相當貼切：The style is the man himself.（文風即為人的本身）。

The *florid* style goes to excess in superfluous and superficial ornamentation and strains after a highly colored imagery. The poems of Ossian typify this style.

The *bombastic* is characterized by such an excess of words, figures and ornaments as to be ridiculous and disgusting. It is like a circus clown dressed up in gold tinsel Dickens gives a fine example of it in Sergeant Buzfuz' speech in the "Pickwick Papers." Among other varieties of style may be mentioned the colloquial, the laconic, the concise, the diffuse, the abrupt, the flowing, the quaint, the epigrammatic, the flowery, the feeble, the nervous, the vehement, and the affected. The manner of these is sufficiently indicated by the adjective used to describe them.

In fact style is as various as character and expresses the individuality of the writer, or in other words, as the French writer Buffon very aptly remarks, "the style is the man himself."

第十章
俚語

Slang

美國俚語和外來俚語

　　現今幾乎社會各種階層、各行各業多少都有俚語存在。俚語已經滲透我們的日常用語，它們如此悄然無聲地融入，以致大部分的人都沒察覺它們的存在，視之為正統用語，變成人人字彙庫的一部分。俚語被當成日常對話中的一般用語使用，藉以表達想法和意願，並向他人傳遞意思。事實上，在某些情況之下，俚語的實用程度甚至超過典型用語，在白話中占有一席之地，有時不用俚語反而難以表達意思。在許多情況中，俚語已經篡奪正規用語的地位，以其效力和影響力獨霸一方。

　　大部分的人常將行話（cant）和俚語（slang）混為一談，儘管兩者關係緊密，且都源自吉普賽民族，不過意思並不相同。行話是某個特定階層的語言，是某種工藝、行業或職業的特殊措辭或方言，除了該技藝、行業或職業的人之外，其他人無法輕易理解。行話的文法規則或許正確，但並不普及，只有特定領域和地區的人才使用，也只有這些族群才能理解。簡而言之，這是一種僅限於圈內人的語言，只有被傳授的人才懂。竊賊的黑話是一種行話，只有被教導其意義的竊賊才懂；職業賭徒發明的語言也是行話，只有職業賭徒才懂。

　　相反地，現今俚語不侷限於特定族群，而是廣泛分布，深入社會各個階層，並且被認可為日常用語，人人都能理解。當然，俚語的本質在極大程度上受到地域性的影響，因為俚語主要跟特定地區常見的口說用語或單字、片語有關，例如倫敦的俚語就跟

AMERICAN SLANG—FOREIGN SLANG

Slang is more or less common in nearly all ranks of society and in every walk of life at the present day. Slang words and expressions have crept into our everyday language, and so insiduously, that they have not been detected by the great majority of speakers, and so have become part and parcel of their vocabulary on an equal footing with the legitimate words of speech. They are called upon to do similar service as the ordinary words used in everyday conversation—to express thoughts and desires and convey meaning from one to another. In fact, in some cases, slang has become so useful that it has far outstripped classic speech and made for itself such a position in the vernacular that it would be very hard in some cases to get along without it. Slang words have usurped the place of regular words of language in very many instances and reign supreme in their own strength and influence.

Cant and slang are often confused in the popular mind, yet they are not synonymous, though very closely allied, and proceeding from a common Gypsy origin. Cant is the language of a certain class—the peculiar phraseology or dialect of a certain craft, trade or profession, and is not readily understood save by the initiated of such craft, trade or profession. It may be correct, according to the rules of grammar, but it is not universal; it is confined to certain parts and localities and is only intelligible to those for whom it is intended. In short, it

紐約的俚語有些微差異，某個城市中流行的某些用語，其他城市的人可能聽不懂。儘管如此，俚語可以說是普遍受到人們理解。to kick the bucket、to cross the Jordan 和 to hop the twig 等俚語都有死亡的意思，無論是在美國或澳洲的偏遠地區，或是在倫敦或都柏林，大家都能明白意思。

俚語是由意義被一般人接受的單字、片語組成，但不夠精緻優美，無法用於文雅的演說或文學。不過前面也提過，許多使用俚語的人渾然不知這是俚語，並將之融入日常口說和對話之中。

有些作家刻意在著作中使用俚語，藉此強調和增加作品的熟悉度和幽默感，不過新手不該如此仿效。狄更斯等文學大師這麼做無可非議，新手這麼做則不可原諒。

有一些屬於不同職業和社會階層的俚語，像是大學俚語、政治俚語、運動俚語等等。雖然俚語會在所有階層之間廣為流傳，不過這種語言形式分成好幾個種類，而且有分別對應的社會階層。俚語可以分成兩大類，一類是未受教育、思想粗俗的人使用的通俗俚語，一種是所謂上流階層、受過教育及富有人士使用的高雅俚語。鄉下的野丫頭跟閨房裡的淑女用的俚語不會一樣，不過兩者都會使用俚語，而且如果彼此相遇，也會了解對方富含表達性的俚語。因此，俚語或許可以分成未受教育和受過教育者的俚語，一種流傳於鄉野巷弄，另一種使用於大雅之堂。

在所有情況下，俚語的目的是用比標準用語更有力、活潑有味、精練的方式表達想法。一位女學生在讚美寶寶時會說：

is an esoteric language which only the initiated can understand. The jargon, or patter, of thieves is cant and it is only understood by thieves who have been let into its significance; the initiated language of professional gamblers is cant, and is only intelligible to gamblers.

On the other hand, slang, as it is nowadays, belongs to no particular class but is scattered all over and gets *entre* into every kind of society and is understood by all where it passes current in everyday expression. Of course, the nature of the slang, to a great extent, depends upon the locality, as it chiefly is concerned with colloquialisms or words and phrases common to a particular section. For instance, the slang of London is slightly different from that of New York, and some words in the one city may be unintelligible in the other, though well understood in that in which they are current. Nevertheless, slang may be said to be universally understood. "To kick the bucket," "to cross the Jordan," "to hop the twig" are just as expressive of the departing from life in the backwoods of America or the wilds of Australia as they are in London or Dublin.

Slang simply consists of words and phrases which pass current but are not refined, nor elegant enough, to be admitted into polite speech or literature whenever they are recognized as such. But, as has been said, a great many use slang without their knowing it as slang and incorporate it into their everyday speech and conversation.

Some authors purposely use slang to give emphasis and spice in familiar and humorous writing, but they should not be imitated by the tyro. A master, such as Dickens, is forgivable, but in the novice it is

Oh, isn't he awfully cute!
喔，他是不是很可愛啊！

只說「他很可愛」（he is very nice）語氣太弱，無法表達她的喜愛。路上出現一位美麗女孩時，愛慕者為了讚賞她的美麗，會說：

She is a peach, a bird, a cuckoo,
她是蜜桃、小鳥、杜鵑

等等可以突顯他對這位年輕女士評價的用語，這比起只說：

She is a beautiful girl. 她是一個美麗的女孩。
a handsome maiden 俏麗的少女
lovely young woman 可人的年輕女子

來得更強烈。政治人物打敗對手時，會用以下俚語來彰顯他贏得很輕鬆。

It was a cinch, 太簡單了。
He had a walk-over 他不費吹灰之力贏了。

有些俚語具有隱喻本質，比喻意味很強，例如：

To pass in your checks 死亡
To hold up 武裝搶劫
To pull the wool over your eyes 矇騙

396

unpardonable.

There are several kinds of slang attached to different professions and classes of society. For instance, there is college slang, political slang, sporting slang, etc. It is the nature of slang to circulate freely among all classes, yet there are several kinds of this current form of language corresponding to the several classes of society. The two great divisions of slang are the vulgar of the uneducated and coarse-minded, and the high-toned slang of the so-called upper classes—the educated and the wealthy. The hoyden of the gutter does not use the same slang as my lady in her boudoir, but both use it, and so expressive is it that the one might readily understand the other if brought in contact. Therefore, there are what may be styled an ignorant slang and an educated slang—the one common to the purlieus and the alleys, the other to the parlor and the drawing-room.

In all cases the object of slang is to express an idea in a more vigorous, piquant and terse manner than standard usage ordinarily admits. A school girl, when she wants to praise a baby, exclaims: "Oh, isn't he awfully cute!" To say that he is very nice would be too weak a way to express her admiration. When a handsome girl appears on the street an enthusiastic masculine admirer, to express his appreciation of her beauty, tells you: "She is a peach, a bird, a cuckoo," any of which accentuates his estimation of the young lady and is much more emphatic than saying: "She is a beautiful girl," "a handsome maiden," or "lovely young woman."

When a politician defeats his rival he will tell you "it was a

To talk through your hat 胡說八道

To fire out 開槍

To go back on 違背承諾

To make yourself solid with 獲得某人可靠的支持

To have a jag on 喝醉

To be loaded 喝醉

To freeze on to 堅持

To bark up the wrong tree 誤會、弄錯

Don't monkey with the buzz-saw 不要蹚渾水

In the soup 身處困境

　　多數俚語都有不好的起源，其中許多源自拉丁文中竊賊的行話，不過時間一久，這些俚語開始脫離為非作歹之輩，慢慢告別不光彩的過去，直到發展成為現今富有表達性的言語。不過，有些俚語則有相當體面的來源。

Stolen fruits are sweet（偷來的果子是甜的）的意思可以追溯到《聖經》〈箴言〉第九章第十七節的 Stolen waters are sweet（偷來的水是甜的）。

What are you giving me（你要給我什麼）應該是十足的美式用語，是根據〈創世紀〉第三十八章第十六節而來。[8]

8　該句是她瑪與猶大行房之前所講的話，當時猶大不知她瑪是自己的媳婦，以為她是妓女，要求與她共寢，她瑪於是要求猶大給她信物，做為日後自己被質疑時的證物。

cinch," he had a "walk-over," to impress you how easy it was to gain the victory.

Some slang expressions are of the nature of metaphors and are highly figurative. Such are "to pass in your checks," "to hold up," "to pull the wool over your eyes," "to talk through your hat," "to fire out," "to go back on," "to make yourself solid with," "to have a jag on," "to be loaded," "to freeze on to," "to bark up the wrong tree," "don't monkey with the buzz-saw," and "in the soup."

Most slang had a bad origin. The greater part originated in the cant of thieves' Latin, but it broke away from this cant of malefactors in time and gradually evolved itself from its unsavory past until it developed into a current form of expressive speech. Some slang, however, can trace its origin back to very respectable sources.

"Stolen fruits are sweet" may be traced to the Bible in sentiment. Proverbs, ix:17 has it: "Stolen waters are sweet." "What are you giving me," supposed to be a thorough Americanism, is based upon Genesis, xxxviii:16. The common slang.

A bad man 這個常見俚語原指西方暴徒，跟現在用的
「壞蛋」意思幾乎一樣，在史賓賽《仙后》、馬辛格劇
作《舊債新還》和莎士比亞《亨利八世》都可看到。

To blow on 意指告密，見於莎士比亞《皆大歡喜》。

It's all Greek to me（我無法理解）源自劇作《凱薩
大帝》。

All cry and no wool（只聽樓梯響，不見人下來）見
於塞繆爾‧巴特勒《胡德布拉斯》。Pious frauds 意
指偽善者，也是來自同一個出處。

Too thin 是指藉口薄弱，出自托比亞斯‧斯摩萊特《皮
可歷險記》，莎士比亞也用這種描述。

現代俚語有一大部分來自美國。

The heathen Chinee（異教徒中國佬）和 Ways
that are dark and tricks that are vain（黑暗的方
法和徒然的技倆）出自布雷特‧哈特《真誠的詹姆士》。

Not for Joe（不是給喬的）源自南北戰爭期間，一名
士兵拒絕給另一名士兵酒喝時說的話。

"a bad man," in referring to Western desperadoes, in almost the identical sense now used, is found in Spenser's *Faerie Queen*, Massinger's play "*A New Way to Pay Old Debts*," and in Shakespeare's "*King Henry VIII*." The expression "to blow on," meaning to inform, is in Shakespeare's "*As You Like it*." "It's all Greek to me" is traceable to the play of "*Julius Caesar*." "All cry and no wool" is in Butler's "*Hudibras*." "Pious frauds," meaning hypocrites, is from the same source. "Too thin," referring to an excuse, is from Smollett's "*Peregrine Pickle*." Shakespeare also used it.

America has had a large share in contributing to modern slang. "The heathen Chinee," and "Ways that are dark, and tricks that are vain," are from Bret Harte's *Truthful James*. "Not for Joe," arose during the Civil War when one soldier refused to give a drink to

Not if I know myself（我了解自己的話就不會）源自芝加哥。

What's the matter with...? He's all right（（某人）怎麼了？他沒事）也是來自芝加哥，原句是 What's matter with Hannah?，指一名懶惰的家僕。

There's millions in it（數不清的錢財）和 By a large majority（絕大多數）出自馬克·吐溫《鍍金時代》。

其他美式俚語包括：

Pull down your vest 管好你自己的事

Jim-jams 緊張兮兮

Got 'em bad 陷入熱戀

That's what's the matter 問題癥結

Go hire a hall 你話太多了

Take in your sign 不要誤導視聽

Dry up 枯竭

Hump yourself 埋頭苦幹

It's the man around the corner 在不遠之處的男人

Put up a job 設下圈套

Put a head on him 使他閉嘴

No back talk 不要頂嘴

Bottom dollar 最後的錢

another. "Not if I know myself" had its origin in Chicago. "What's the matter with–? He's all right," had its beginning in Chicago also and first was "What's the matter with Hannah." referring to a lazy domestic servant. "There's millions in it," and "By a large majority" come from Mark Twain's *Gilded Age*.

"Pull down your vest," "jim-jams," "got 'em bad," "that's what's the matter," "go hire a hall," "take in your sign," "dry up," "hump yourself," "it's the man around the corner," "putting up a job," "put a head on him," "no back talk," "bottom dollar," "chalk it down,"

Chalk it down 認同某事

Stave him off 阻擋某人

Make it warm 施壓

Drop him gently 委婉地告訴某人

Busted 逮到你了

Counter jumper 店員

Put up or shut up 要不就去做，要不就閉嘴

Bang up 監禁

Smart Aleck 自以為是的人

Chin-music 閒聊

Top heavy 頭重腳輕的

Barefooted on the top of the head 禿頭

A little too fresh 太缺乏經驗

Champion liar 大騙子

Chief cook and bottle washer 校長兼撞鐘

Bag and baggage 全副家當

Name your poison 想喝什麼酒

Died with his boots on 在仍活躍時死去；戰死沙場

Old hoss 老傢伙（用來暱稱馬）

Hunkey dorey 一切都好

Hold your horses 稍等，別急

Galoot 呆子

"staving him off," "making it warm," "dropping him gently," "busted," "counter jumper," "put up or shut up," "bang up," "smart Aleck," "chin-music," "top heavy," "barefooted on the top of the head," "a little too fresh," "champion liar," "chief cook and bottle washer," "bag and baggage," "name your poison," "died with his boots on," "old hoss," "hunkey dorey," "hold your horses," "galoot" and many others in use at present are all Americanisms in slang.

加州的比喻式用語尤其豐富。源自加洲的俚語包括：

Go off and die 滾去死吧

Don't you forget it 你可記好了

Rough deal 不公平的待遇

Square deal 公平的待遇

Flush times 豐裕歲月

Pool your issues 合作解決問題

Go bury yourself 去死吧！

Go drown yourself 去死吧！

Give your tongue a vacation 閉上嘴巴

A bad egg 混蛋

Go climb a tree 別來煩我

Plug hats 高禮帽

Dolly Vardens 花飾女帽

Well fixed 手頭寬裕

Down to bed rock 追根究柢

Hard pan 基礎，根本

Pay dirt 有利可圖的事物

Petered out 慢慢結束

It won't wash 禁不起考驗

Slug of whiskey 一口威士忌

It pans out well 報酬優厚

I should smile 樂意之至

美國俚語
和
外來俚語

406

California especially has been most fecund in this class of figurative language. To this State we owe "go off and die," "don't you forget it," "rough deal," "square deal," "flush times," "pool your issues," "go bury yourself," "go drown yourself," "give your tongue a vacation," "a bad egg," "go climb a tree," "plug hats," "Dolly Vardens," "well fixed," "down to bed rock," "hard pan," "pay dirt," "petered out," "it won't wash," "slug of whiskey," "it pans out well," and "I should smile."

波士頓俚語包括：

Small potatoes, and few in the hill 微不足道的事物

Soft snap 輕而易舉的事情

All fired 極度地

Gol darn it 該死的

An up-hill job 艱難的工作

Slick 狡猾的傢伙

Short cut 捷徑

Guess not 看來不行

Correct thing 恰當的事

美國南方用語包括：

Innocent 頭腦簡單的

Acknowledge the corn 承認錯誤

Bark up the wrong tree 誤會、弄錯

Great snakes 我的天吶！

I reckon 我估算

Playing possum 欺騙

Dead shot 神射手

以下用語出自紐約：

Doggone it 該死的

That beats the Dutch 怎麼可能

"Small potatoes, and few in the hill," "soft snap," "all fired," "gol durn it," "an up-hill job," "slick," "short cut," "guess not," "correct thing" are Bostonisms.

The terms "innocent," "acknowledge the corn," "bark up the wrong tree," "great snakes," "I reckon," "playing possum," "dead shot," had their origin in the Southern States.

"Doggone it," "that beats the Dutch," "you bet," "you bet your boots," sprang from New York. "Step down and out" originated in the Beecher trial, just as "brain-storm" originated in the Thaw trial.

You bet 當然
You bet your boots 肯定如此
Step down and out 時運不濟
（出自亨利・沃德・比徹的通姦案審判）
Brain-storm 集思廣益
（出自哈里・托爾的謀殺案審判）

源自英國的俚語包括：

Throw up the sponge 棄權，認輸
Draw it mild 不要誇大其詞
Give us a rest 別再打擾某人
Dead beat 游手好閒的人
On the shelf 嫁不出去的女人
Up the spout 出錯的，完蛋的
Stunning 極美的，極迷人的
Gift of the gab 能言善道

　　報紙上也有很多俚語。採訪記者、文字記者，甚至編輯經常寫些別人沒有說過的字詞，再說那是別人說的。紐約稱得上是俚語的大本營，尤其是包理街（Bowery）一帶。所有違反英文規則的錯誤用法都是來自這個不入流的街區，不過，其實住在第五大道的人們也一樣會用違反正規英文的用語。當地居民講的英文混雜外來語言，自然讓包理街有了這樣不光彩的名聲。不過跟紐

Among the slang phrases that have come directly to us from England may be mentioned "throw up the sponge," "draw it mild," "give us a rest," "dead beat," "on the shelf," "up the spout," "stunning," "gift of the gab," etc.

The newspapers are responsible for a large part of the slang. Reporters, staff writers, and even editors, put words and phrases into the mouths of individuals which they never utter. New York is supposed to be the headquarters of slang, particularly that portion of it known as the Bowery. All transgressions and corruptions of language are supposed to originate in that unclassic section, while the truth is that the

約其他地方一樣，這裡也不乏說白話的能言善道之士。只是，沒有經驗的報社記者都認為有必要把包理街當作笑柄，這些記者用自己有限的腦力擠出殘缺不全的英文（他們造字能力相當有限），再把這些亂七八糟的用語怪到包理街的人頭上。

報媒和作家也是這樣貶損愛爾蘭人。他們不了解愛爾蘭，卻把愛爾蘭人描繪成講話粗鄙的鄉下人，硬說一些荒唐用語是出自愛爾蘭人之口，其實這些用語愛爾蘭人聽都沒聽過。眾所皆知，愛爾蘭向來是世界上最有學問的民族，將近數千年來擁有許多優秀學者，而且如今世上沒有任何地方像這座西方小島一樣，能將正統英文說得如此純正。

日常時事常會產生出俚語，久而久之，這些俚語就像一般用語一樣，普遍出現在生活對話中，人們也忘了它們原是俚語。舉例來說，boycott（抵制）這個單字源自愛爾蘭土地聯盟時期一位不得人心的地主博伊卡的姓氏。當時人們拒絕替他耕種，任由他的作物腐爛。從那時起，就用 to be boycotted 形容不受歡迎、人人拒絕幫忙的人，boycott 這個單字也就變成放棄某人、不幫助某人以示懲罰的例子。起初這是一個不好聽的俚語，不過現在已是英文字典中的正規單字。

政治用語當中也有不少俚語，例如：

Dark horse 黑馬、爆冷門的人
The gray mare is the better horse 女人當家
Barrel of money 一大筆錢

laws of polite English are as much violated on Fifth Avenue. Of course, the foreign element mincing their "pidgin" English have given the Bowery an unenviable reputation, but there are just as good speakers of the vernacular on the Bowery as elsewhere in the greater city. Yet every inexperienced newspaper reporter thinks that it is incumbent on him to hold the Bowery up to ridicule and laughter, so he sits down, and out of his circumscribed brain, mutilates the English tongue (he can rarely coin a word), and blames the mutilation on the Bowery.

'Tis the same with newspapers and authors, too, detracting the Irish race. Men and women who have never seen the green hills of Ireland, paint Irish characters as boors and blunderers and make them say ludicrous things and use such language as is never heard within the four walls of Ireland. 'Tis very well known that Ireland is the most learned country on the face of the earth–is, and has been. The schoolmaster has been abroad there for hundreds, almost thousands, of years, and nowhere else in the world to-day is the king's English spoken so purely as in the cities and towns of the little Western Isle.

Current events, happenings of everyday life, often give rise to slang words, and these, after a time, come into such general use that they take their places in everyday speech like ordinary words and, as has been said, their users forget that they once were slang. For instance, the days of the Land League in Ireland originated the word *boycott*, which was the name of a very unpopular landlord, Captain Boycott. The people refused to work for him, and his crops rotted on the ground. From this time any one who came into disfavor and whom

Buncombe 胡說八道

Gerrymander 不公正畫分選區 [9]

Scalawag 南方佬 [10]

Henchman 黨羽

Logrolling 滾木立法，選票互助

Pulling the wires 套關係

Taking the stump 進行政治巡迴演說

Machine 領導核心

Slate 候選名單

金融市場則有下列俚語：

Corner 壟斷、囤積

Bull 牛市

Bear 熊市

Lamb 待宰羔羊，易上當受騙者

Slump 重挫

出於不同時代的習慣和時下表達方式的要求，即便最優秀的人在某些場合也得使用俚語。我們通常不知道這是俚語，就像小孩子講了粗話也不自知。我們應該儘量避免使用俚語，即使俚語能以強而有力的方式傳遞想法。如果某些俚語在時下對話中尚不普遍，那就不要使用。記住，大多俚語都是源自粗鄙下流的

9　1812年時任美國麻州州長埃爾布里奇‧傑利為了操縱選舉，將某個選區劃分成奇怪的樣子，狀似一條蠑螈，以求所屬的黨派獲勝。

10　意指支持美國南北戰爭後重建南方的白人。

his neighbors refused to assist in any way was said to be boycotted. Therefore to boycott means to punish by abandoning or depriving a person of the assistance of others. At first it was a notoriously slang word, but now it is standard in the English dictionaries.

Politics add to our slang words and phrases. From this source we get "dark horse," "the gray mare is the better horse," "barrel of money," "buncombe," "gerrymander," "scalawag," "henchman," "logrolling," "pulling the wires," "taking the stump," "machine," "slate," etc.

The money market furnishes us with "corner," "bull," "bear," "lamb," "slump," and several others.

The custom of the times and the requirements of current expression require the best of us to use slang words and phrases on occasions. Often we do not know they are slang, just as a child often uses profane words without consciousness of their being so. We should avoid the use of slang as much as possible, even when it serves to convey our ideas in a forceful manner. And when it has not gained a firm foothold in current speech it should be used not at all. Remember that most all slang is of vulgar origin and bears upon its face the bend sinister of vulgarity. Of the slang that is of good birth, pass it by if you can, for it is like a broken-down gentleman, of little good to any one. Imitate the great masters as much as you will in classical literature, but when it comes to their slang, draw the line. Dean Swift, the great Irish satirist, coined the word "phiz" for face. Don't imitate him. If you are speaking or writing of the beauty of a

用語，帶有粗俗的氣息。至於那些來源體面的俚語，可以的話也最好避而不用，因為它們就好比墮落的紳士，對任何人都沒什麼好處。盡量模仿大師的經典文學用語，至於他們用的俚語，還是敬而遠之。偉大的愛爾蘭諷刺作家史威夫特自創 phiz（相貌）這個單字來表示 face（臉龐）。不要模仿他。在講述或描繪美麗女子的臉龐時，不要稱之 her phiz。史威夫特是偉大學者，他的身分地位允許他這麼做，但你可沒有這樣的身分地位。莎士比亞用 flush（旺盛）暗指家財萬貫。記住，世界上只有一位莎士比亞，只有他有權這樣使用這個字。你絕對不會成為莎士比亞，別人也絕對不會——大自然在塑造這位才子時已經耗盡精力了。愛德華・鮑沃爾・利頓（Edward Bulwer-Lytton）用 stretch（延伸）代替 hang（吊死），例如 stretch his neck。不要像他一樣如此使用這個單字。最重要的是避開低級、下流、粗鄙的俚語，只有街頭賤民會覺得這樣是機智。說到某人昨晚死去，別說 He hopped the twig 或 He kicked the bucket。如果被迫聽人談他不了解的主題，別說 He is talking through his hat。描述自己曾跟羅斯福握過手，別說 He tipped me his flipper。描述一個有錢人時，別說 He has plenty of spondulix／the long green。這些俚語都很低級、下流、粗鄙，在任何場合使用都很不恰當。

如果要用俚語，就使用文雅的俚語，並且像紳士一樣使用，千萬不能傷害或冒犯他人。紅衣主教紐曼（John Henry Newman）曾說，紳士就是從不會施加痛苦在他人身上的人。使用俚語時請像紳士一樣，不要施加痛苦在他人身上。

lady's face don't call it her "phiz." The Dean, as an intellectual giant, had a license to do so–you haven't. Shakespeare used the word "flush" to indicate plenty of money. Well, just remember there was only one Shakespeare, and he was the only one that had a right to use that word in that sense. You'll never be a Shakespeare, there will never be such another–Nature exhausted herself in producing him. Bulwer used the word "stretch" for hang, as to stretch his neck. Don't follow his example in such use of the word. Above all, avoid the low, coarse, vulgar slang, which is made to pass for wit among the riff-raff of the street. If you are speaking or writing of a person having died last night don't say or write: "He hopped the twig," or "he kicked the bucket." If you are compelled to listen to a person discoursing on a subject of which he knows little or nothing, don't say "He is talking through his hat." If you are telling of having shaken hands with Mr. Roosevelt don't say "He tipped me his flipper." If you are speaking of a wealthy man don't say "He has plenty of spondulix," or "the long green." All such slang is low, coarse and vulgar and is to be frowned upon on any and every occasion.

If you use slang use the refined kind and use it like a gentleman, that it will not hurt or give offense to any one. Cardinal Newman defined a gentleman as he who never inflicts pain. Be a gentleman in your slang–never inflict pain.

第十一章
投書報紙

Writing for Newspapers

現在家家戶戶都有報紙，曾被視為奢侈品的報紙，如今已成為必需品。一個人再怎麼窮，也不會窮到買不起報紙，讓他不但能了解周遭事件，還有全世界發生的事。

　　無論是街頭工作的勞工或坐辦公室的銀行家，都能得知當天消息。透過報紙，人們可以感受國家脈動，了解國家的活力正在增強或逐漸削弱，也可以讀到時事，尋找個人關切的政治議題。

　　攤開報紙就能看到國外發生哪些事件，一瞥遠在地球其他地方發生的事。如果昨晚倫敦發生大火，紐約的人們在早餐桌上就會讀到這則新聞，說不定比倫敦人知道得更清楚。如果巴黎正在舉辦比賽，在參賽者離開賽場前，人們早就讀到所有內容。

　　美國有三千多家報社，其中超過兩千家在人口不到十萬人的城鎮發行。事實上，許多人口少於一萬人的地方也發行日報。在美國發行的週刊有超過一萬五千家。有些所謂的地方報紙在當地、甚至外地都相當具有影響力，透過發行量和廣告為報社業主和相關人士賺進利潤。

　　美國國內以報界相關工作維生的人數驚人。除了固定的勞工外，還有數以千計的人把報業相關工作當成副業，偶爾投稿日報、週報和月刊，為自己賺進一筆不小的額外收入。他們大多是能力一般的普通人，所受過的教育程度剛好足以讓他們寫出具有一定才智的文字。

The newspaper nowadays goes into every home in the land; what was formerly regarded as a luxury is now looked upon as a necessity. No matter how poor the individual, he is not too poor to afford a penny to learn, not alone what is taking place around him in his own immediate vicinity, but also what is happening in every quarter of the globe. The laborer on the street can be as well posted on the news of the day as the banker in his office. Through the newspaper he can feel the pulse of the country and find whether its vitality is increasing or diminishing; he can read the signs of the times and scan the political horizon for what concerns his own interests. The doings of foreign countries are spread before him and he can see at a glance the occurrences in the remotest corners of earth. If a fire occurred in London last night he can read about it at his breakfast table in New York this morning, and probably get a better account than the Londoners themselves. If a duel takes place in Paris he can read all about it even before the contestants have left the field.

There are upwards of 3,000 daily newspapers in the United States, more than 2,000 of which are published in towns containing less than 100,000 inhabitants. In fact, many places of less than 10,000 population can boast the publishing of a daily newspaper. There are more than 15,000 weeklies published. Some of the so-called country papers wield quite an influence in their localities, and even outside, and are money-making agencies for their owners and those connected with them, both by way of circulation and advertisements.

It is surprising the number of people in this country who make

許多人誤以為需要受過高等教育才能寫新聞文章。沒這回事！在某些情況中，高等教育反而是種阻礙，對寫新聞文章沒有幫助。

一般報媒要的不是學術論文或哲學理論；新聞報紙顧名思義，它要的是新聞，能夠吸引、激發、抓住讀者注意力的時事趣聞。從這點來看，一個小男孩寫的報導往往會比大學教授寫的更好。

教授的用字遣詞容易超出大多數讀者的能力範圍，而小男孩雖然不會這些字詞，但他會用所有人都懂的語句，直率地描述自己看到什麼、事件的嚴重程度如何、誰被殺害或受傷等等。

報界當然也有一些學識淵博的傑出人才，不過整體來說，業界享譽盛名的人士最初也是懵懂無知，從地方報紙出身。一些英美當前首屈一指的作家，最初也是透過投書地方報紙，才開啟他們的文學生涯。他們邊寫邊磨練自己，直到能在世界文壇打響名號。

如果你想投稿報紙或以報界工作維生，別因沒有大學學歷而卻步。前面章節說過，有些最偉大的英文文學大師並非靠著書本上的學問獲得優勢。

莎士比亞、班揚、伯恩斯等許許多多在名人榜上留下無法抹滅的名聲的人，本身沒有受過什麼值得炫耀的教育，但卻具備所謂的常識和對世界的了解。換句話說，他們了解人性，本身也很自然率真。

a living in the newspaper field. Apart from the regular toilers there are thousands of men and women who make newspaper work a side issue, who add tidy sums of "pin money" to their incomes by occasional contributions to the daily, weekly and monthly press. Most of these people are only persons of ordinary, everyday ability, having just enough education to express themselves intelligently in writing.

It is a mistake to imagine, as so many do, that an extended education is necessary for newspaper work. Not at all! On the contrary, in some cases, a high-class education is a hindrance, not a help in this direction. The general newspaper does not want learned disquisitions nor philosophical theses; as its name implies, it wants news, current news, interesting news, something to appeal to its readers, to arouse them and rivet their attention. In this respect very often a boy can write a better article than a college professor. The professor would be apt to use words beyond the capacity of most of the readers, while the boy, not knowing such words, would probably simply tell what he saw, how great the damage was, who were killed or injured, etc., and use language which all would understand.

Of course, there are some brilliant scholars, deeply-read men and women in the newspaper realm, but, on the whole, those who have made the greatest names commenced ignorant enough and most of them graduated by way of the country paper. Some of the leading writers of England and America at the present time started their literary careers by contributing to the rural press. They perfected and polished themselves as they went along until they were able to make

莎士比亞了解人類，因為他自己本身也是人。他以大師筆觸描寫人的感受、情緒和熱情，無論是宮殿中的國王或是小屋中的農人，都描述得如此真情流露。他心中的一把尺告誡著他，讓他知道是非對錯，就像老蘇格拉底所說，那個無時無刻在他耳邊低語，告訴他應該怎麼做的「惡魔」。

務農的伯恩斯以如此精湛的語言表達他構思的想法，任何飽讀學問的前人或後人都無法超越。這些人自然率真，正是這種臻至完美的自然性質，讓他們的盛名永垂青史。

若你想為報紙撰寫文章，必得自然率真，並用自己慣用、不帶矯飾的方式表達想法。不要模仿華麗修飾的風格，不要沉迷浮華或誇張的文筆，這樣不僅膚淺，也顯得愚蠢。日常報紙不刊這種文章。它要的是樸實無華、未經矯飾的事實。

的確，你應該閱讀大師作品，儘量模仿他們的風格，但不要試著逐字抄襲他們的字句。無論何時都要忠於自我。

names for themselves in universal literature.

If you want to contribute to newspapers or enter the newspaper field as a means of livelihood, don't let lack of a college or university education stand in your way. As has been said elsewhere in this book, some of the greatest masters of English literature were men who had but little advantage in the way of book learning. Shakespeare, Bunyan, Burns, and scores of others, who have left their names indelibly inscribed on the tablets of fame, had little to boast of in the way of book education, but they had what is popularly known as "horse" sense and a good working knowledge of the world; in other words, they understood human nature, and were natural themselves. Shakespeare understood mankind because he was himself a man; hence he has portrayed the feelings, the emotions, the passions with a master's touch, delineating the king in his palace as true to nature as he has done the peasant in his hut. The monitor within his own breast gave him warning as to what was right and what was wrong, just as the daemon ever by the side of old Socrates whispered in his ear the course to pursue under any and all circumstances. Burns guiding the plough conceived thoughts and clothed them in a language which has never, nor probably never will be, surpassed by all the learning which art can confer. These men were natural, and it was the perfection of this naturality that wreathed their brows with the never-fading laurels of undying fame.

If you would essay to write for the newspaper you must be natural and express yourself in your accustomed way without putting

Not like Homer would I write,
我不會學荷馬一樣寫作，

Not like Dante if I might,
不像但丁那般創作，

Not like Shakespeare at his best,
不似莎翁如此揮灑才華，

Not like Goethe or the rest,
不向歌德等輩模仿，

Like myself, however small,
我會寫出真我，無論多麼渺小，

Like myself, or not at all.
寫出真我，否則寧不提筆。

站在讀者的立場思考，寫你感興趣的主題，讓你的文字能流露你對事物的觀點。你是普羅大眾中的一員，因此在為報紙撰寫文章時，不要忘了自己是為大眾而寫，不是為了具有學識和美感高人一等的小眾而寫。

記住，你的讀者是市井小民，你想讓他們產生興趣，說服他們閱讀你的文章。這些讀者不要賣弄學問的作品，他們要的是與自己息息相關的新聞。你必須用樸實、單純的方式描述，就像跟他們面對面談話那樣。

on airs or frills; you must not ape ornaments and indulge in bombast or rhodomontade which stamp a writer as not only superficial but silly. There is no room for such in the everyday newspaper. It wants facts stated in plain, unvarnished, unadorned language. True, you should read the best authors and, as far as possible, imitate their style, but don't try to literally copy them. Be yourself on every occasion—no one else.

> Not like Homer would I write,
> Not like Dante if I might,
> Not like Shakespeare at his best,
> Not like Goethe or the rest,
> Like myself, however small,
> Like myself, or not at all.

Put yourself in place of the reader and write what will interest yourself and in such a way that your language will appeal to your own ideas of the fitness of things. You belong to the great commonplace majority, therefore don't forget that in writing for the newspapers you are writing for that majority and not for the learned and aesthetic minority.

Remember you are writing for the man on the street and in the street car, you want to interest him, to compel him to read what you have to say. He does not want a display of learning; he wants news about something which concerns himself, and you must tell it to him in a plain, simple manner just as you would do if you were face to

你可以寫些什麼？寫些可以成為時事新聞、當前重大事件的主題，任何可以吸引你所投稿報紙的讀者的題材。不管你住在什麼地區，當地有多落後，總能找到人們感興趣的主題。如果沒有什麼新聞，那就寫些吸引你的事情。人都是類似的，你感興趣的事情，別人很可能也感興趣。一般人都喜歡描述冒險的文章，寫些獵狐、獵獾或追捕大熊的故事。

如果你的住家附近有重要的製造工廠，那就描述一下，可以的話拍些照片，因為照片是現今新聞中的要素。如果某個家喻戶曉的大人物住在你家附近，就去採訪他，請教他對時下公共議題的觀點，描述他的居家生活、周遭環境和休閒嗜好。

試著寫些與時事相關、受到眾人矚目的事情。如果某位國外名人來訪，趁機描述他所來自的地方，以及在當地的事蹟。

舉例來說，如果蘇祿國的蘇丹來訪，便趁機描寫這個太平洋小群島。如果有人企圖炸毀停靠在薩摩亞阿皮亞港口的美國軍艦，藉機介紹薩摩亞和羅勃‧路易斯‧史蒂文森（Robert Louis Stephenson）。[11]

曼紐二世被迫退下葡萄牙王位時，正好可以介紹葡萄牙與其國內事務。如果國外發生重大事件，例如某國國王登基或君王遭到廢黜，那就介紹該國歷史，描述導致事件的前因。

11　史蒂文森是蘇格蘭旅遊作家，定居於薩摩亞並在當地過世。

face with him.

What can you write about? Why about anything that will constitute current news, some leading event of the day, anything that will appeal to the readers of the paper to which you wish to submit it. No matter in what locality you may live, however backward it may be, you can always find something of genuine human interest to others. If there is no news happening, write of something that appeals to yourself. We are all constituted alike, and the chances are that what will interest you will interest others. Descriptions of adventure are generally acceptable. Tell of a fox hunt, or a badger hunt, or a bear chase.

If there is any important manufacturing plant in your neighborhood describe it and, if possible, get photographs, for photography plays a very important part in the news items of to-day. If a "great" man lives near you, one whose name is on the tip of every tongue, go and get an interview with him, obtain his views on the public questions of the day, describe his home life and his surroundings and how he spends his time.

Try and strike something germane to the moment, something that stands out prominently in the limelight of the passing show. If a noted personage, some famous man or woman, is visiting the country, it is a good time to write up the place from which he or she comes and the record he or she has made there. For instance, it was opportune to write of Sulu and the little Pacific archipelago during the Sultan's trip through the country. If an attempt is made to blow up an

如果某個附屬地的野蠻部落之間爆發殘暴的動亂，例如菲律賓馬諾波族的起義事件，就是描寫這些部落和其周遭環境，以及反抗事件起因的大好機會。

　　隨時尋找符合時事的題材，每天閱讀日報，說不定你會在沒人注意的地方找到好文章的題材，或至少能提供你一點線索的事物。

　　慎選投稿報紙。了解該報紙的語氣和整體立場、社會傾向、政治關係和宗教屬性，所有可得的相關細節都要了解。無論是投稿拳擊比賽文章到宗教類報紙，或是投稿教會聚會報導到體育類報紙，都是欠缺周全思考的行為。

　　被退稿了也不必沮喪灰心。

　　比起其他領域，堅持不懈的精神在報界來說更是重要，也只有這種毅力才能帶來長遠的勝利。你必須培養韌性，被打倒了也要再站起來。無論遭到幾次拒絕都別沮喪，再接再厲、捲土重來。

　　如果你有這方面的能力，一定會被發掘，你的光芒不會在報界中一直被埋沒。如果你能寫出好的文章，很快地就會是各家編輯懇求你，而不是你懇求他們。他們一直都在尋找能寫出好文章的人。

American battleship, say, in the harbor of Appia, in Samoa, it affords a chance to write about Samoa and Robert Louis Stephenson. When Manuel was hurled from the throne of Portugal it was a ripe time to write of Portugal and Portuguese affairs. If any great occurrence is taking place in a foreign country such as the crowning of a king or the dethronement of a monarch, it is a good time to write up the history of the country and describe the events leading up to the main issue. When a particularly savage outbreak occurs amongst wild tribes in the dependencies, such as a rising of the Manobos in the Philippines, it is opportune to write of such tribes and their surroundings, and the causes leading up to the revolt.

Be constantly on the lookout for something that will suit the passing hour, read the daily papers and probably in some obscure corner you may find something that will serve you as a foundation for a good article–something, at least, that will give you a clue.

Be circumspect in your selection of a paper to which to submit your copy. Know the tone and general import of the paper, its social leanings and political affiliations, also its religious sentiments, and, in fact, all the particulars you can regarding it. It would be injudicious for you to send an article on a prize fight to a religious paper or, *vice versa*, an account of a church meeting to the editor of a sporting sheet.

If you get your copy back don't be disappointed nor yet disheartened. Perseverance counts more in the newspaper field than anywhere else, and only perseverance wins in the long run. You must become resilient; if you are pressed down, spring up again. No matter

一旦報紙刊載你的文章，這一仗就打贏了，你會受到激勵，繼續堅持並精進自己。重新看過自己寫的每篇文章，刪修文句，儘量讓文章更臻完美。拿掉所有贅字，仔細刪去所有含糊措辭和引述。

　　如果要為週報寫文章，記住它和日報有所不同。

　　週報不只要吸引一般男性，還要吸引家庭主婦，她們想看的是稀奇的事實、古怪的傳聞、名人或怪人的事蹟，精彩經歷的回顧，以及鮮為人知的生活趣事集錦。

　　簡而言之，任何能夠為這些主婦帶來娛樂、消遣和教導的事情都行。你的周遭隨時都有事情發生，某些能做為文章題材的有趣或驚人事件。

　　就像日報那樣，你必須了解你所投稿的週報的性質。舉例來說，《基督教先驅報》（The Christian Herald）雖然聲稱是一份宗教週報，但也刊載非宗教文章，以吸引所有讀者。在宗教的部分，該週報不分教派，廣泛報導世界各地基督教相關領域的新聞。在非宗教的部分，它以中立觀點報導人的事務，無論是屬於哪個階層、支持哪個教義的人，都有興趣閱讀這份週報。

how many rebuffs you may receive, be not discouraged but call fresh energy to your assistance and make another stand. If the right stuff is in you it is sure to be discovered; your light will not remain long hidden under a bushel in the newspaper domain. If you can deliver the goods editors will soon be begging you instead of your begging them. Those men are constantly on the lookout for persons who can make good. Once you get into print the battle is won, for it will be an incentive to you to persevere and improve yourself at every turn. Go over everything you write, cut and slash and prune until you get it into as perfect form as possible. Eliminate every superfluous word and be careful to strike out all ambiguous expressions and references.

If you are writing for a weekly paper remember it differs from a daily one. Weeklies want what will not alone interest the man on the street, but the woman at the fireside; they want out-of-the-way facts, curious scraps of lore, personal notes of famous or eccentric people, reminiscences of exciting experiences, interesting gleanings in life's numberless by-ways, in short, anything that will entertain, amuse, instruct the home circle. There is always something occurring in your immediate surroundings, some curious event or thrilling episode that will furnish you with data for an article. You must know the nature of the weekly to which you submit your copy the same as you must know the daily. For instance, the *Christian Herald*, while avowedly a religious weekly, treats such secular matter as makes the paper appeal to all. On its religious side it is non-sectarian, covering the broad field of Christianity throughout the world; on its secular side it deals with

月刊為文人志士提供另一個具有吸引力的領域。在此重申，不要以為非得是大學教授才能為月刊撰文。其實大部分一流的雜誌撰稿人沒有大學學歷，與大學的關係頂多是路過而已。但最重要的是他們經驗豐富，了解生活中有別於理論的實務面。

　　一般月刊刊載當前世人關注的主要議題、重大發明、偉大發現，或當前人們關切的事物，例如飛行載具、戰艦、摩天大樓、礦坑開採、開發新土地、政治議題、政黨領袖觀點、名人側寫等等。不過，在你投稿月刊、試試身手之前，先從寫日報文章磨練技巧會比較好。

　　最重要的是記住堅持不懈是開啟成功大門之鑰。堅持下去！如果遭到拒絕，不要灰心；相反地，把他人的拒絕當成繼續努力的動力。現代許多最成功的作家曾一再遭到拒絕。他們花幾天、幾個月甚至幾年，向一家又一家報章雜誌推銷自己的作品，直到有人願意採用。你或許是個孕育中的作家，但若不發揮自己的內在潛能，絕對不會萌芽，更不用說茁壯了。

　　給自己一個成長的機會，掌握每件能讓你拓展視野的事物。睜大眼睛，就能隨時看到讓你產生興趣、或許也能讓他人產生興趣的事物。

　　也要學習閱讀大自然這本書。石頭、小草、樹木、潺潺溪流和鳴唱鳥兒都有可以學習的地方。解讀你所學到的事物，再把它教給別人。永遠都要熱衷於自己的寫作，對其抱持堅決態度，不要膽怯畏縮，勇敢前進，始終如一。

human events in such an impartial way that every one, no matter to what class they may belong or to what creed they may subscribe, can take a living, personal interest.

The monthlies offer another attractive field for the literary aspirant. Here, again, don't think you must be an university professor to write for a monthly magazine. Many, indeed most, of the foremost magazine contributors are men and women who have never passed through a college except by going in at the front door and emerging from the back one. However, for the most part, they are individuals of wide experience who know the practical side of life as distinguished from the theoretical. The ordinary monthly magazine treats of the leading questions and issues which are engaging the attention of the world for the moment, great inventions, great discoveries, whatever is engrossing the popular mind for the time being, such as flying machines, battleships, sky-scrapers, the opening of mines, the development of new lands, the political issues, views of party leaders, character sketches of distinguished personages, etc. However, before trying your skill for a monthly magazine it would be well for you to have a good apprenticeship in writing for the daily press.

Above all things, remember that perseverance is the key that opens the door of success. Persevere! If you are turned down don't get disheartened; on the contrary, let the rebuff act as a stimulant to further effort. Many of the most successful writers of our time have been turned down again and again. For days and months, and even years, some of them have hawked their wares from one literary door

On the wide, tented field in the battle of life,
在生命之戰中，在布滿營帳的廣闊戰場上，

With an army of millions before you;
在數百萬大軍面前，

Like a hero of old gird your soul for the strife
要像古老英雄般武裝你的靈魂。

And let not the foeman tramp o'er you;
別讓敵人踐踏了你，

Act, act like a soldier and proudly rush on
行動，像士兵一樣行動，傲然前進，

The most valiant in Bravery's van,
勇者中的勇者。

With keen, flashing sword cut your way to the front
舉起鋒利閃亮的刀劍劈斬向前，

And show to the world you're a Man.
向世界證明你是一個男子漢。

　　如果你是男性，做任何事情都要達到「男子漢」一詞最高、最好的標準。這個頭銜遠比伯爵或公爵、皇帝或國王的稱號更加崇高。同樣地，「女子氣概」也是女性最崇高的榮耀。

　　當世人都嫌棄你，諸事不順時，要有耐性、期待更光明的日子來到。那天必會來到。在最陰暗的雲層背後，是一片陽光普照的風景。

to another until they found a purchaser. You may be a great writer in embryo, but you will never develop into a fetus, not to speak of full maturity, unless you bring out what is in you. Give yourself a chance to grow and seize upon everything that will enlarge the scope of your horizon. Keep your eyes wide open and there is not a moment of the day in which you will not see something to interest you and in which you may be able to interest others. Learn, too, how to read Nature's book. There's a lesson in everything–in the stones, the grass, the trees, the babbling brooks and the singing birds. Interpret the lesson for yourself, then teach it to others. Always be in earnest in your writing; go about it in a determined kind of way, don't be faint-hearted or backward, be brave, be brave, and evermore be brave.

On the wide, tented field in the battle of life,

With an army of millions before you;

Like a hero of old gird your soul for the strife

And let not the foeman tramp o'er you;

Act, act like a soldier and proudly rush on

The most valiant in Bravery's van,

With keen, flashing sword cut your way to the front

And show to the world you're a *Man*.

If you are of the masculine gender be a man in all things in the highest and best acceptation of the word. That is the noblest title you can boast, higher far than that of earl or duke, emperor or king. In the same way womanhood is the grandest crown the feminine head can wear. When the world frowns on you and everything seems to

當你的文章一次又一次地被退回，不要絕望，也不要認為編輯殘忍無情。他也有自己的事要煩惱。保持高昂士氣，直到接受最後的測試，再對自己的才能進行最終的分析，如果發現自己的文章就是無法被刊出，確定新聞寫作或文學作品不是自己的專長，那就轉向其他領域。

如果沒有更好的事情可做，試試做鞋子或挖水溝的工作。記住，正當的勞力工作無論多麼卑微，都是有尊嚴的。如果你是女人，把筆放到一旁，專心縫補兄弟、父親或丈夫的襪子，或穿上圍裙、拿起肥皂和水刷洗地板。無論你是誰，都要做點有用的事情。「人生來就該享福」這句古老謬論早就被戳破了。世界沒有欠你什麼，而是你該為世界努力工作。如果你不償還這份債務，就是辜負天意，沒有善盡自己的使命。

你要服務世界，讓它變得更加美好、光明、崇高、神聖、偉大、尊貴、豐富，因為你就生活在其中。無論命運賦予你什麼樣的地位，無論你是道路清潔工或是總統，都能做到這點。好好奮戰，取得勝利。

> Above all, to thine own self be true,
> 最重要的是要忠於自我，
>
> And 'twill follow as the night the day,
> 務必遵循這點，一如白晝黑夜，
>
> Thou canst not then be false to any man.
> 如此你將不會愧對他人。

go wrong, possess your soul in patience and hope for the dawn of a brighter day. It will come. The sun is always shining behind the darkest clouds. When you get your manuscripts back again and again, don't despair, nor think the editor cruel and unkind. He, too, has troubles of his own. Keep up your spirits until you have made the final test and put your talents to a last analysis, then if you find you cannot get into print be sure that newspaper writing or literary work is not your *forte*, and turn to something else. If nothing better presents itself, try shoemaking or digging ditches. Remember honest labor, no matter how humble, is ever dignified. If you are a woman throw aside the pen, sit down and darn your brother's, your father's, or your husband's socks, or put on a calico apron, take soap and water and scrub the floor. No matter who you are do something useful.

That old sophistry about the world owing you a living has been exploded long ago. The world does not owe you a living, but you owe it servitude, and if you do not pay the debt you are not serving the purpose of an all-wise Providence and filling the place for which you were created. It is for you to serve the world, to make it better, brighter, higher, holier, grander, nobler, richer, for your having lived in it. This you can do in no matter what position fortune has cast you, whether it be that of street laborer or president. Fight the good fight and gain the victory.

"Above all, to thine own self be true,
And 'twill follow as the night the day,
Thou canst not then be false to any man."

第十二章
用字遣詞

Choice of Words

前面章節說過，如果能用短字達到相同目的，就千萬別用長字。這裡要再次強調這個建議。在任何可能的場合中，都要避免長而艱澀、嘈雜的字詞，這些只會突顯膚淺思維和虛榮心態。

　　純粹論者、措辭大師、文風典範，使用人人都能了解的短字，意義不會模稜兩可的字詞。千萬記得，我們透過文字教導他人，因此使用對的語言是一項重責大任。我們必須謹慎小心，用清楚的方式思考和發言，不要使用易被誤解的字詞表達模糊不清的想法，以免造成他人錯誤解讀，或傳遞錯誤印象。

　　字詞讓我們的想法有了形體，如果沒有字詞，想法只是一個模糊概念，讓我們無法看出其薄弱或虛妄之處。我們必須努力使用對的字詞，以將我們心中的想法傳達到別人心中。

　　用他人能夠理解的清晰字詞表達想法是世界上最偉大的技藝。這是教師、部長、律師、演說家和商務人士必須掌握的技能，才能在各自領域獲得成功。如果對方本身不太了解你所使用的語言，確實很難向他表達某個想法、使他留下印象；不過，如果你用的字詞讓人無法理解，那就根本不可能傳達想法。

　　如果聽眾是一般民眾，我們卻用他們無法理解的字詞發表談話，這就跟向他們講外文沒有兩樣。用他們不明白的字詞傳達想法，他們根本無法從我們的談話中獲得任何好處。

In another place in this book advice has been given to never use a long word when a short one will serve the same purpose. This advice is to be emphasized. Words of "learned length and thundering sound" should be avoided on all possible occasions. They proclaim shallowness of intellect and vanity of mind. The great purists, the masters of diction, the exemplars of style, used short, simple words that all could understand; words about which there could be no ambiguity as to meaning. It must be remembered that by our words we teach others; therefore, a very great responsibility rests upon us in regard to the use of a right language. We must take care that we think and speak in a way so clear that there may be no misapprehension or danger of conveying wrong impressions by vague and misty ideas enunciated in terms which are liable to be misunderstood by those whom we address. Words give a body or form to our ideas, without which they are apt to be so foggy that we do not see where they are weak or false. We must make the endeavor to employ such words as will put the idea we have in our own mind into the mind of another. This is the greatest art in the world–to clothe our ideas in words clear and comprehensive to the intelligence of others. It is the art which the teacher, the minister, the lawyer, the orator, the business man, must master if they would command success in their various fields of endeavor. It is very hard to convey an idea to, and impress it on, another when he has but a faint conception of the language in which the idea is expressed; but it is impossible to convey it at all when the words in which it is clothed are unintelligible to the listener.

冗長、艱澀、直接擷自外語的字詞，只有受過高等教育的人才能理解。並非所有人都有這樣的優勢。

在我們偉大、榮耀的國家中，大部分的人很早就得開始為生活打拚。雖然大家都受過義務教育，不過大部分的人只具備閱讀、寫作和算數等基本技能。這些掌心長繭、肌肉發達的人是我們在日常生活中最常面對的人，他們為我們蓋房造路、駕駛車輛、耕種田地、收割作物，簡單來說，他們是社會的根基，讓世界正常運轉。他們要的不是大學程度的用語，沒有這些他們也能過得很好，因為他們的工作用不到這些字詞。

我們跟這樣的人打交道時，必須使用簡單易懂的日常用語，一般人從小就習以為常的用語。

無論一般人或學識豐富的人都能了解這些用語，那麼何不只用這些就好？何必事倍功半、只用所謂高學歷階層的人才懂的字詞？任何場合都用兩個階層都懂的語言不是比較好嗎？只要花點心思研究，就會發現最能影響群眾的演說家、律師、傳教士等公眾人物，都使用非常簡單的語言。

丹尼爾・韋伯斯特（Daniel Webster）是美國最偉大的演說家之一。他以滔滔不絕的口才打動國會議員和一般民眾的心。如果能用短字表達相同或相似的意思，他絕不使用長字。

If we address an audience of ordinary men and women in the English language, but use such words as they cannot comprehend, we might as well speak to them in Coptic or Chinese, for they will derive no benefit from our address, inasmuch as the ideas we wish to convey are expressed in words which communicate no intelligent meaning to their minds.

Long words, learned words, words directly derived from other languages are only understood by those who have had the advantages of an extended education. All have not had such advantages. The great majority in this grand and glorious country of ours have to hustle for a living from an early age. Though education is free, and compulsory also, very many never get further than the "Three R's." These are the men with whom we have to deal most in the arena of life, the men with the horny palms and the iron muscles, the men who build our houses, construct our railroads, drive our street cars and trains, till our fields, harvest our crops–in a word, the men who form the foundation of all society, the men on whom the world depends to make its wheels go round. The language of the colleges and universities is not for them and they can get along very well without it; they have no need for it at all in their respective callings. The plain, simple words of everyday life, to which the common people have been used around their own firesides from childhood, are the words we must use in our dealings with them.

Such words are understood by them and understood by the learned as well; why then not use them universally and all the time?

韋伯斯特在演講時，總是吩咐撰寫講稿給媒體的人刪掉所有長字。研究他的講稿，把他說過、寫過的東西看過一遍，就會發現他總是使用簡短、清楚、有力的詞彙。雖然有時為了音韻和演講效果，他會被迫使用較長的字，不過這並非出於他的意願。

　　有誰能像韋伯斯特如此生動地使用語言？他能如此清楚地描繪事物，讓聽眾彷彿親眼目睹。

　　林肯也是一位能夠激勵人心的人物，然而他不是演說家或學者，名字後面也沒有學士或碩博士等頭銜，因為他沒有任何學位。

　　他畢業於「社會大學」，當他成為美國總統時，他並沒有忘記這所嚴厲的「母校」。他還是跟當年在桑加蒙河邊劈柴、在船上工作時那樣簡樸謙卑。

　　林肯不用艱澀的字詞，而是將一般用語說得生動美麗。他的蓋茲堡演說（Gettysburg address）堪稱經典，是最偉大的英文演說之一。

　　短字未必就是意思清楚的字，不過幾乎所有意思清楚的字都是短字。此外，幾乎所有長字——尤其是外來語——都很容易被一般人誤解。使用這些長字的學者是否完全了解其在不同場合的意義，確實令人懷疑。這類長字多半有各種不同解讀方式。

Why make a one-sided affair of language by using words which only one class of the people, the so-called learned class, can understand? Would it not be better to use, on all occasions, language which the both classes can understand? If we take the trouble to investigate we shall find that the men who exerted the greatest sway over the masses and the multitude as orators, lawyers, preachers and in other public capacities, were men who used very simple language. Daniel Webster was among the greatest orators this country has produced. He touched the hearts of senates and assemblages, of men and women with the burning eloquence of his words. He never used a long word when he could convey the same, or nearly the same, meaning with a short one. When he made a speech he always told those who put it in form for the press to strike out every long word. Study his speeches, go over all he ever said or wrote, and you will find that his language was always made up of short, clear, strong terms, although at times, for the sake of sound and oratorical effect, he was compelled to use a rather long word, but it was always against his inclination to do so, and where was the man who could paint, with words, as Webster painted! He could picture things in a way so clear that those who heard him felt that they had seen that of which he spoke.

Abraham Lincoln was another who stirred the souls of men, yet he was not an orator, not a scholar; he did not write M.A. or Ph.D. after his name, or any other college degree, for he had none. He graduated from the University of Hard Knocks, and he never forgot this severe *Alma Mater* when he became President of the United

人們必須大量使用一個字，才會徹底熟悉它的意思。長字不僅無法傳達易懂、清楚的思想和概念，有時還容易造成混淆，進而產生不良後果。

舉例來說，我們能用長字掩飾犯罪行為，讓它看起來不像一件罪行。就連醜陋的罪孽披上這種字詞也會被美化。

當某個行員捲款上萬美元潛逃時，我們會禮貌地說這是「挪用公款」（defalcation），而不是直接說「偷竊」（theft）；我們也不叫他「小偷」（thief），而是拐彎抹角地說他是「挪用公款者」（defaulter）。

當我們看到某個富豪在時髦的大街上酒醉踉蹌，揮舞雙手、大聲咆哮，我們會笑著說：「可憐的先生，他有點『欣喜若狂』（exhilarated）」，或者更糟，說他帶了點「醉意」（inebriated）。

不過，當我們看到某個窮人因為貪戀杯中物而醉倒時，我們會用簡單字詞表達憤慨：「看看那個討厭鬼，他喝得爛醉（dead drunk）。」

States. He was just as plain, I just as humble, as in the days when he split rails or plied a boat on the Sangamon. He did not use big words, but he used the words of the people, and in such a way as to make them beautiful. His Gettysburg address is an English classic, one of the great masterpieces of the language.

From the mere fact that a word is short it does not follow that it is always clear, but it is true that nearly all clear words are short, and that most of the long words, especially those which we get from other languages, are misunderstood to a great extent by the ordinary rank and file of the people. Indeed, it is to be doubted if some of the "scholars" using them, fully understand their import on occasions. A great many such words admit of several interpretations. A word has to be in use a great deal before people get thoroughly familiar with its meaning. Long words, not alone obscure thought and make the ideas hazy, but at times they tend to mix up things in such a way that positively harmful results follow from their use.

For instance, crime can be so covered with the folds of long words as to give it a different appearance. Even the hideousness of sin can be cloaked with such words until its outlines look like a thing of beauty. When a bank cashier makes off with a hundred thousand dollars we politely term his crime *defalcation* instead of plain *theft*, and instead of calling himself a *thief* we grandiosely allude to him as a *defaulter*. When we see a wealthy man staggering along a fashionable thoroughfare under the influence of alcohol, waving his arms in the air and shouting boisterously, we smile and say, poor gentleman, he

當我們發現某人撒了漫天大謊，會用「閃爍其詞」（prevarication）這樣精心編製的外衣包裹謊言。莎士比亞說：「即便換了其他稱呼，玫瑰依舊芳香」，同樣地，就算換了一個名字，謊言依舊是謊言，應該受到譴責，那何不乾脆稱它「謊言」就好？言及所意，意及所言，說話直言不諱才是上策。

試著使用短字並避開長字，過一段時間後，你會發現自己能輕鬆做到。

有位農人帶一位城市來的紳士到草原去看一匹馬，馬兒被領入圍場中，一隻母豬也在裡面翻找食物。

城市人驚呼：「多麼棒的四足獸啊！」

農人問道：「你說哪一隻，豬還是馬？在我看來，兩隻都是很棒的四足獸。」

這位客人說的當然是馬，所以直接用簡單尋常的名字稱牠會比較好，才不會有語意不清的問題。他在這次事件中學到一課，之後就不再稱馬為四足獸了。

is somewhat *exhilarated*; or at worst we say, he is slightly *inebriated*; but when we see a poor man who has fallen from grace by putting an "enemy into his mouth to steal away his brain" we express our indignation in the simple language of the words: "Look at the wretch; he is dead drunk."

When we find a person in downright lying we cover the falsehood with the finely-spun cloak of the word *prevarication*. Shakespeare says, "a rose by any other name would smell as sweet," and by a similar sequence, a lie, no matter by what name you may call it, is always a lie and should be condemned; then why not simply call it a lie? Mean what you say and say what you mean; call a spade a spade, it is the best term you can apply to the implement.

When you try to use short words and shun long ones in a little while you will find that you can do so with ease. A farmer was showing a horse to a city-bred gentleman. The animal was led into a paddock in which an old sow-pig was rooting. "What a fine quadruped!" exclaimed the city man.

"Which of the two do you mean, the pig or the horse?" queried the farmer, "for, in my opinion, both of them are fine quadrupeds."

Of course the visitor meant the horse, so it would have been much better had he called the animal by its simple; ordinary name–, there would have been no room for ambiguity in his remark. He profited, however, by the incident, and never called a horse a quadruped again.

大多短小精簡、言簡意賅的優美單字，都屬於英文中純正的盎格魯撒克遜元素。天上星體（sun、moon、star）、四大元素中的三個元素（earth、fire、water）、四季中的三季（spring、summer、winter），其名稱都源自這個元素。

　　自然界所有時間畫分（除了 day 之外）也都來自精簡的盎格魯撒克遜單字，包括：night（夜）、morning（早晨）、evening（晚間）、twilight（黃昏）、noon（中午）、midday（正午）、midnight（午夜）、sunrise（日出）和 sunset（日落）。另外，light（光）、heat（熱）、cold（冷）、frost（霜）、rain（雨）、snow（雪）、hail（冰雹）、sleet（霰）、thunder（雷）、lightning（閃電），以及 sea（海）、land（土地）、hill（山丘）、dale（峽谷）、wood（森林）、stream（溪流）等用於形容美麗景致的單字，也都來自盎格魯撒克遜語系。

　　多虧了有這個語系，我們才有相關單字可以用來表達自然界中最早、最親密的關係，和最強烈、有力的感情，使得人們將這些字詞與最美好、神聖的事物聯想在一起。

　　這些字詞包括：father（父親）、mother（母親）、husband（丈夫）、wife（妻子）、brother（兄弟）、sister（姊妹）、son（兒子）、daughter（女兒）、child（孩子）、home（家）、kindred（相似的）、friend（朋友）、hearth、fireside（壁爐邊）、roof（屋頂）。

Most of the small words, the simple words, the beautiful words which express so much within small bounds belong to the pure Anglo-Saxon element of our language. This element has given names to the heavenly bodies, the sun, moon and stars; to three out of the four elements, earth, fire and water; three out of the four seasons, spring, summer and winter. Its simple words are applied to all the natural divisions of time, except one, as day, night, morning, evening, twilight, noon, mid-day, midnight, sunrise and sunset. The names of light, heat, cold, frost, rain, snow, hail, sleet, thunder, lightning, as well as almost all those objects which form the component parts of the beautiful, as expressed in external scenery, such as sea and land, hill and dale, wood and stream, etc., are Anglo-Saxon. To this same language we are indebted for those words which express the earliest and dearest connections, and the strongest and most powerful feelings of Nature, and which, as a consequence, are interwoven with the fondest and most hallowed associations. Of such words are father, mother, husband, wife, brother, sister, son, daughter, child, home, kindred, friend, hearth, roof and fireside.

Love（愛）、hope（希望）、fear（恐懼）、sorrow（悲痛）、shame（羞恥）等主要人類情感，以及 tear（眼淚）、smile（微笑）、laugh（笑）、blush（臉紅）、weep（哭泣）、sigh（嘆息）、groan（呻吟）等外在情感表徵，同樣出自這個語系的單字表達。幾乎所有普遍流通的諺語都來自盎格魯撒克遜語系；幾乎所有能以最生動的方式表達憤怒、蔑視和憤慨的字詞和片語也都源於它。

所謂的精英階層和上流社會在捨棄許多古老的盎格魯撒克遜字詞，揚棄這些服務過祖先的忠實朋友。這些自詡為文字權威的人士認為盎格魯撒克遜字詞俗不可耐，不適合他們富有美感的高雅品味，因此捨之不用，並以混雜外來語和未知來源的混種字詞取而代之。不過，對一般在街頭、農田、廚房或工廠工作的市井小民來說，這些字詞經過考驗，證實是受用的，應該像對待老朋友一樣珍惜，無論面對來自什麼背景的人，都要用這些字詞。

The chief emotions of which we are susceptible are expressed in the same language–love, hope, fear, sorrow, shame, and also the outward signs by which these emotions are indicated, as tear, smile, laugh, blush, weep, sigh, groan. Nearly all our national proverbs are Anglo-Saxon. Almost all the terms and phrases by which we most energetically express anger, contempt and indignation are of the same origin.

What are known as the Smart Set and so-called polite society, are relegating a great many of our old Anglo-Saxon words into the shade, faithful friends who served their ancestors well. These self-appointed arbiters of diction regard some of the Anglo-Saxon words as too coarse, too plebeian for their aesthetic tastes and refined ears, so they are eliminating them from their vocabulary and replacing them with mongrels of foreign birth and hybrids of unknown origin. For the ordinary people, however, the man in the street or in the field, the woman in the kitchen or in the factory, they are still tried and true and, like old friends, should be cherished and preferred to all strangers, no matter from what source the latter may spring.

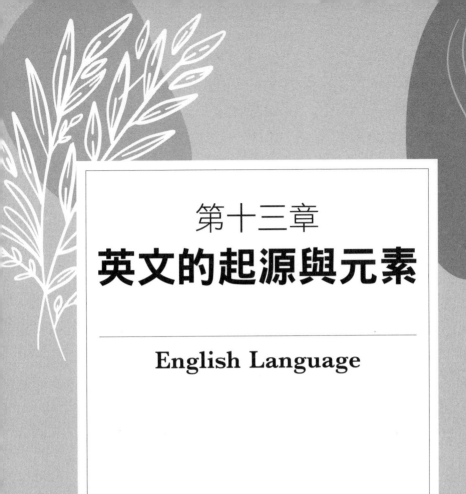

第十三章
英文的起源與元素

English Language

英文是目前流通於英國、英國海外領地和美國的語言。這個語言源自條頓人（Teutons）說的德文，該民族在羅馬人征服英國後來到這個國家。

　　條頓人由盎格魯族（Angles）、撒克遜族（Saxons）、朱特族（Jutes）和其他來自德國北部的多個民族組成。他們有各自的方言，不過在來到英國後全都混合在一起，成為盎格魯撒克遜文，是構成英文的主要基礎，現在仍是英文中的主要元素。

　　有些人試著拋棄某些純正的盎格魯撒克遜字詞，認為不夠精緻，無法表達他們富有美感的想法。然而，這些字詞是英文體系中重要部分的必要支柱，這麼做無疑是在破壞這些支柱。

　　盎格魯撒克遜元素提供必要的詞類、冠詞、各種代名詞、介系詞、助動詞、連接詞，以及將單字結合成句子，形成英文的骨架和血肉的質詞。它為英文字彙提供最不可或缺的單字（詳見第十二章）。

　　《主禱文》（The Lord's Prayer）最能闡述格魯撒克遜元素之美。文中計有五十四個單字為純正的撒克遜文，其餘單字也能輕易用撒克遜文取代。《約翰福音》（Gospel of John）是另一個幾乎都用盎格魯撒克遜文的範例。

　　莎士比亞寫得最好的文字，也使用盎格魯撒克遜文。以下引述《威尼斯商人》（Merchant of Venice）的一段文字，五十五字中有五十二字是盎格魯撒克遜文，其他三字則為法文：

　　The English language is the tongue now current in England and her colonies throughout the world and also throughout the greater part of the United States of America. It sprang from the German tongue spoken by the Teutons, who came over to Britain after the conquest of that country by the Romans. These Teutons comprised Angles, Saxons, Jutes and several other tribes from the northern part of Germany. They spoke different dialects, but these became blended in the new country, and the composite tongue came to be known as the Anglo-Saxon which has been the main basis for the language as at present constituted and is still the prevailing element. Therefore those who are trying to do away with some of the purely Anglo-Saxon words, on the ground that they are not refined enough to express their aesthetic ideas, are undermining main props which are necessary for the support of some important parts in the edifice of the language.

　　The Anglo-Saxon element supplies the essential parts of speech, the article, pronoun of all kinds, the preposition, the auxiliary verbs, the conjunctions, and the little particles which bind words into sentences and form the joints, sinews and ligaments of the language. It furnishes the most indispensable words of the vocabulary. (See Chapter 12.) Nowhere is the beauty of Anglo-Saxon better illustrated than in the Lord's Prayer. Fifty-four words are pure Saxon and the remaining ones could easily be replaced by Saxon words. The gospel of St. John is another illustration of the almost exclusive use of Anglo-Saxon words. Shakespeare, at his best, is Anglo-Saxon. Here is a quotation from the Merchant of Venice, and of the fifty-five words

All that glisters is not gold—
閃亮之物未必黃金，

Often have you heard that told;
這番話語人常耳聞，

Many a man his life hath sold,
多少人把靈魂出賣，

But my outside to behold.
只為一睹我的外貌，

Gilded tombs do worms enfold.
鍍金墳墓藏有蛀蟲，

Had you been as wise as bold,
若你智謀勇氣兼備，

Young in limbs, in judgment old,
四肢年輕，判斷老練，

Your answer had not been inscrolled–
則你毋須讀此卷軸，

Fare you well. Your suit is cold.
別了，你的機會已逝。

　　另外，哈姆雷特父親那番猛烈激動的話語——其絕妙程度僅次但丁在地獄之門上的題詞——其中有一百零八個盎格魯撒克遜文字，只有十五個拉丁文字。

fifty-two are Anglo-Saxon, the remaining three French:

> All that glitters is not gold–
>
> Often have you heard that told;
>
> Many a man his life hath sold,
>
> But my outside to behold.
>
> Guilded tombs do worms infold.
>
> Had you been as wise as bold,
>
> Young in limbs, in judgment old,
>
> Your answer had not been inscrolled–
>
> Fare you well, your suit is cold.

The lines put into the mouth of Hamlet's father in fierce intenseness, second only to Dante's inscription on the gate of hell, have one hundred and eight Anglo-Saxon and but fifteen Latin words.

現代英文的第二大構成元素是拉丁文，其中包含直接來自古羅馬文和間接來自法文的單字。前者是在十六世紀末葉，由奧古斯丁（Augustine）為首的羅馬基督徒帶到英國，主要跟教會事務有關，例如 saint（聖徒）來自 sanctus，religion（宗教）來自 religio，chalice（聖餐杯）來自 calix，mass（彌撒）來自 missa 等等。這類字其中有些源自希臘文，例如 priest（牧師）來自拉丁文 presbyter，這個單字又直接衍生自希臘文 presbuteros，deacon（助祭）也衍生自希臘文 diakonos。

最大的一類拉丁單字來自諾曼法文（Norman-French），又稱羅曼文（Romance）。諾曼人透過基督教，吸收了羅馬化高盧人（Gauls）和羅馬化法蘭克人（Franks）的語言、法律和藝術，並在定居法國一百多年後，於一〇六六年在征服者威廉（William the Conqueror）的帶領下成功侵略英國，展開新時代。法式拉丁文的差異可從單字拼法區別出來，例如 Savior（救世主）是由法文 Sauveur 而來，其又源自拉丁文 Salvator；judgment（審判）是由法文 jugement 而來，其源自拉丁文 judiclum；people（人們）是由法文 peuple 而來，其源自拉丁文 populuse，諸如此類。

長久以來，撒克遜文和諾曼文拒絕融合，有如兩股潮流一般涇渭分明。諾曼文是封建城堡、國會和法庭中貴族與男爵之輩的語言。撒克遜文是鄉間住家、農人和工坊中人們的語言。三百多年來，這兩個語系各自分流，最後終於交會，吸收了凱爾特文和丹麥文元素，成為文法變化簡單、字彙豐富的現代英文。

The second constituent element of present English is Latin which comprises those words derived directly from the old Roman and those which came indirectly through the French. The former were introduced by the Roman Christians, who came to England at the close of the sixth century under Augustine, and relate chiefly to ecclesiastical affairs, such as saint from *sanctus*, religion from *religio*, chalice from *calix*, mass from *missa*, etc. Some of them had origin in Greek, as priest from *presbyter*, which in turn was a direct derivative from the Greek *presbuteros*, also deacon from the Greek *diakonos*.

The largest class of Latin words are those which came through the Norman-French, or Romance. The Normans had adopted, with the Christian religion, the language, laws and arts of the Romanized Gauls and Romanized Franks, and after a residence of more than a century in France they successfully invaded England in 1066 under William the Conqueror and a new era began. The French Latinisms can be distinguished by the spelling. Thus Saviour comes from the Latin *Salvator* through the French *Sauveur*; judgment from the Latin *judiclum* through the French *jugement*; people, from the Latin *populus*, through the French *peuple*, etc.

For a long time the Saxon and Norman tongues refused to coalesce and were like two distinct currents flowing in different directions. Norman was spoken by the lords and barons in their feudal castles, in parliament and in the courts of justice. Saxon by the people in their rural homes, fields and workshops. For more than three hundred years the streams flowed apart, but finally they blended,

一般認為英文散文之父是約翰・威克里夫（John Wycliffe），他於一三八〇年翻譯《聖經》。在他之前的非宗教詩壇大師則是傑弗里・喬叟（Geoffrey Chaucer）。

除了德文和羅曼文這兩大英文組成要素之外，也有許多其他語言注入元素，其中又以凱爾特語歷史最悠久。受到凱撒侵略的英國人屬於凱爾特民族的一支。在威爾斯的威爾斯語（Welsh），以及愛爾蘭和蘇格蘭高地的蓋爾語（Gaelic）這兩種方言中，仍保留了凱爾特語的成語。英文中的凱爾特語相對較少，其中最常用的有：

cart 推車　　　　　babe 嬰孩
dock 碼頭　　　　　grown 成熟的
wire 金屬絲　　　　griddle 淺煎鍋
rail 橫木　　　　　lad 小伙子
rug 小毯　　　　　lass 小姑娘
cradle 搖籃

taking in the Celtic and Danish elements, and as a result came the present English language with its simple system of grammatical inflection and its rich vocabulary.

The father of English prose is generally regarded as Wycliffe, who translated the Bible in 1380, while the paternal laurels in the secular poetical field are twined around the brows of Chaucer.

Besides the Germanic and Romanic, which constitute the greater part of the English language, many other tongues have furnished their quota. Of these the Celtic is perhaps the oldest. The Britons at Caesar's invasion, were a part of the Celtic family. The Celtic idiom is still spoken in two dialects, the Welsh in Wales, and the Gaelic in Ireland and the Highlands of Scotland. The Celtic words in English, are comparatively few; cart, dock, wire, rail, rug, cradle, babe, grown, griddle, lad, lass, are some in most common use.

英文中的丹麥語元素可回溯到第九和第十世紀的海盜侵略潮，其單字包括：

anger 怒氣	jam 果醬	rug 小毯
awe 敬畏	kidnap 綁架	rump 臀部
baffle 困惑	kill 殺害	sale 出售
bang 猛撞	kidney 腎臟	scald 燙傷
bark 吠叫	kneel 跪下	shriek 尖叫
bawl 大喊	limber 靈活的	skin 皮膚
blunder 犯大錯	litter 亂丟	skull 顱骨
boulder 巨石	log 原木	sledge 大錘
box 盒子	lull 平息	sleigh 雪橇
club 棍子	lump 腫塊	tackle 對付
crash 撞擊	mast 桅杆	tangle 糾纏
dairy 乳品	mistake 錯誤	tipple 酒精飲料
dazzle 燦爛	nag 糾纏	trust 信任
fellow 傢伙	nasty 討人厭的	Viking 維京
gable 山牆	niggard 吝嗇鬼	window 窗戶
gain 獲利	horse 馬	wing 翅膀
ill 生病的	plough 犁	

The Danish element dates from the piratical invasions of the ninth and tenth centuries. It includes anger, awe, baffle, bang, bark, bawl, blunder, boulder, box, club, crash, dairy, dazzle, fellow, gable, gain, ill, jam, kidnap, kill, kidney, kneel, limber, litter, log, lull, lump, mast, mistake, nag, nasty, niggard, horse, plough, rug, rump, sale, scald, shriek, skin, skull, sledge, sleigh, tackle, tangle, tipple, trust, Viking, window, wing, etc.

英文從希伯來文中獲得許多專有名詞，包括：

Adam and Eve 亞當和夏娃	seraph 熾天使
John and Mary 約翰和瑪麗	hosanna 和撒那
Messiah 彌賽亞	manna 嗎哪
rabbi 祭司	Satan 撒旦
hallelujah 哈雷路亞	Sabbath 安息日
cherub 智天使	

　　許多術語和學科分支的名稱來自希臘文。其實幾乎所有學科和藝術，從字母系統到最困難的形而上學和神學，都是直接來自希臘文，數百種類似領域包括：

philosophy 哲學	mathematics 數學
logic 邏輯	arithmetic 算術
anthropology 人類學	astronomy 天文學
psychology 心理學	anatomy 解剖學
aesthetics 美學	geography 地理
grammar 文法	stenography 速記法
rhetoric 修辭	physiology 生理學
history 歷史	architecture 建築學
philology 文獻學	

From the Hebrew we have a large number of proper names from Adam and Eve down to John and Mary and such words as Messiah, rabbi, hallelujah, cherub, seraph, hosanna, manna, Satan, Sabbath, etc.

Many technical terms and names of branches of learning come from the Greek. In fact, nearly all the terms of learning and art, from the alphabet to the highest peaks of metaphysics and theology, come directly from the Greek–philosophy, logic, anthropology, psychology, aesthetics, grammar, rhetoric, history, philology, mathematics, arithmetic, astronomy, anatomy, geography, stenography, physiology, architecture, and hundreds more in similar domains; the subdivisions and ramifications of theology as exegesis, hermeneutics, apologetics, polemics, dogmatics, ethics, homiletics, etc., are all Greek.

exegesis（註釋）、hermeneutics（詮釋學）、apologetics
（護教學）、polemics（論證法）、dogmatics（教義學）、ethics
（倫理學）、homiletics（講道學）等神學的子類和分支也都是
希臘文。

荷蘭文提供某些現代航海術語，例如：sloop（單桅帆
船）、schooner（雙桅縱帆船）、yacht（遊艇），以及boom
（隆隆聲）、bush（灌木）、boor（鄉下人）、brandy（白蘭
地）、duck（閃躲）、reef（縮褶帆面）、skate（冰鞋）、
wagon（貨運馬車）等其他用語。曼哈頓島的荷蘭人提供boss這
個名詞，用來表示雇主或工頭，另外還有coleslaw（由切碎的捲
心菜和醋做成的涼拌沙拉），以及一些地理術語。

英文中許多悅耳的單字，尤其是音樂相關用語，直接來自義
大利文，包括：

piano 鋼琴	piazza 廣場
violin 小提琴	gazette 報紙
orchestra 管弦樂隊	umbrella 傘
canto 曲調	gondola 貢多拉船
allegro 快板	bandit 強盜

The Dutch have given us some modern sea terms, as sloop, schooner, yacht and also a number of others as boom, bush, boor, brandy, duck, reef, skate, wagon. The Dutch of Manhattan island gave us boss, the name for employer or overseer, also coleslaw (cut cabbage and vinegar), and a number of geographical terms.

Many of our most pleasing euphonic words, especially in the realm of music, have been given to us directly from the Italian. Of these are piano, violin, orchestra, canto, allegro, piazza, gazette, umbrella, gondola, bandit, etc.

西班牙文提供的單字包括：

alligator 短吻鱷	hurricane 颶風
alpaca 羊駝	mosquito 蚊子
bigot 頑固者	negro 黑人
cannibal 食人者	stampede 奔逃
cargo 貨物	potato 馬鈴薯
filibuster	tobacco 菸草
阻撓議事的漫長演說	tomato 番茄
freebooter 劫掠者	tariff 關稅
guano 海鳥糞	

來自阿拉伯文的單字包括一些數學、天文、醫學和化學術語，例如：

alcohol 酒精	cipher 密碼
alcove 壁龕	elixir 萬靈藥
alembic 蒸餾器	harem 閨房
algebra 代數學	hegira 伊斯蘭教紀元
alkali 鹼	sofa 沙發
almanac 天文年曆	talisman 護身符
assassin 刺客	zenith 天頂
azure 蔚藍色	zero 零

Spanish has furnished us with alligator, alpaca, bigot, cannibal, cargo, filibuster, freebooter, guano, hurricane, mosquito, negro, stampede, potato, tobacco, tomato, tariff, etc.

From Arabic we have several mathematical, astronomical, medical and chemical terms as alcohol, alcove, alembic, algebra, alkali, almanac, assassin, azure, cipher, elixir, harem, hegira, sofa, talisman, zenith and zero.

來自波斯文的字有：

bazaar 市集	scarlet 緋紅色
dervish 苦行僧	shawl 女用披巾
lilac 紫丁香	tartar 酒石
pagoda 寶塔	tiara 寶石頭飾
caravan 商隊	peach 桃樹

Turabn（女用頭巾）、tulip（鬱金香）、divan（長沙發椅）和 firman（詔書）是土耳其文。drosky（無頂四輪馬車）、knout（笞刑）、rouble（盧布）、steppe（乾草原）、ukase（敕令）是俄羅斯文。

印地安人對英文貢獻匪淺，提供極為悅耳動聽的單字，例如以下河流和州名：

Mississippi 密西西比州	Ohio 俄亥俄州
Missouri 密蘇里州	Massachusetts 麻薩諸塞州
Minnehaha 明尼哈哈河	Connecticut 康乃狄克州
Susquehanna 薩斯奎哈納河	Iowa 愛荷華州
Monongahela 莫農加希拉河	Nebraska 內布拉斯加州
Niagara 尼加拉河	Dakota 達科塔州

Bazaar, dervish, lilac, pagoda, caravan, scarlet, shawl, tartar, tiara and peach have come to us from the Persian.

Turban, tulip, divan and firman are Turkish.

Drosky, knout, rouble, steppe, ukase are Russian.

The Indians have helped us considerably and the words they have given us are extremely euphonic as exemplified in the names of many of our rivers and States, as Mississippi, Missouri, Minnehaha, Susquehanna, Monongahela, Niagara, Ohio, Massachusetts, Connecticut, Iowa, Nebraska, Dakota, etc. In addition to these proper names we have from the Indians wigwam, squaw, hammock, tomahawk, canoe, mocassin, hominy, etc.

除了這些專有名詞之外，來自印地安人的單字還有 wigwam（棚屋）、squaw（美洲原住民女性 [12]）、hammock（吊床）、tomahawk（戰斧）、canoe（獨木舟）、mocassin（莫卡辛鞋）、hominy（玉米粥）等等。

　　英文中有許多混種字詞，也就是來自兩種或以上不同語言的字。其實英文吸納所有語言來源，每天都在增加原已龐大的字彙；不僅如此，它還擴散到世界各地，可能很快就會將全體人類收服其下。許多人認為英文即將成為通用語言。歐洲各國和世界各地所有商業城市的頂尖大學都將英文納入高等教育的一環。在亞洲，英文追隨英國的統治和商業的腳步，遍及擁有兩億五千萬名異教人士和伊斯蘭教徒的遼闊東印度地區。日本和中國海港大量使用英文，也有越來越多當地人民學習英文。英文也在南非、賴比瑞亞、獅子山以及印度洋、南洋許多島國紮穩根基。英文是澳洲、紐西蘭和塔斯馬尼亞省的語言 [13]，基督教傳教士也將英文帶到玻里尼西亞所有島嶼。英文或可說是北美洲的現行商用語言，從巴芬灣 [14] 到墨西哥灣，從大西洋到太平洋都能流通，許多南美洲共和國也使用英文。它的足跡不受限於經緯線的畫分，因為英國和美國這兩大英語國家將英文傳到世界東、南、西、北各個角落。

12　此字帶有貶意。
13　位於澳洲近海，是澳洲唯一的島州。
14　巴芬灣是大西洋西北部界於格陵蘭島與巴芬島之間的延伸部分。

There are many hybrid words in English, that is, words, springing from two or more different languages. In fact, English has drawn from all sources, and it is daily adding to its already large family, and not alone is it adding to itself, but it is spreading all over the world and promises to take in the entire human family beneath its folds ere long. It is the opinion of many that English, in a short time, will become the universal language. It is now being taught as a branch of the higher education in the best colleges and universities of Europe and in all commercial cities in every land throughout the world. In Asia it follows the British sway and the highways of commerce through the vast empire of East India with its two hundred and fifty millions of heathen and Mohammedan inhabitants. It is largely used in the seaports of Japan and China, and the number of natives of these countries who are learning it is increasing every day. It is firmly established in South Africa, Liberia, Sierra Leone, and in many of the islands of the Indian and South Seas. It is the language of Australia, New Zealand, Tasmania, and Christian missionaries are introducing it into all the islands of Polynesia. It may be said to be the living commercial language of the North American continent, from Baffin's Bay to the Gulf of Mexico, and from the Atlantic to the Pacific, and it is spoken largely in many of the republics of South America. It is not limited by parallels of latitude, or meridians of longitude. The two great English-speaking countries, England and the United States, are disseminating it north, south, east and west over the entire world.

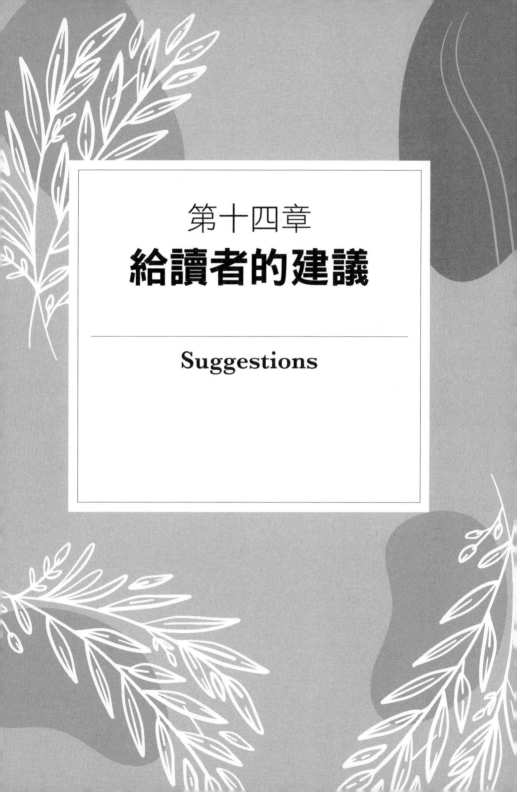

第十四章
給讀者的建議

Suggestions

文法和修辭規則有其作用，必須遵守這些規則，才能正確表達思想和概念，以令人愉悅、為人接受的方式傳遞確切意思。不過光是遵守固有規則，無法讓人變成一位作家。能讓人變成作家的只有大自然，誰也不能取代它的地位。如果自然沒有賦予某人將想法訴諸適當文字的能力，他就無法做到。

一個人可能沒有值得記錄下來的想法，而如果沒有想要表達的想法，就無法做表達。這些東西不能無中生有。寫作者必須先有思想和概念，才能用文字表達之。

思想和概念是與生俱有以及後天孕育而生，透過學習以發展、強化。有一句拉丁古話這麼形容詩人：「詩人是天生的，不是養成的。」這句話也適用於寫作這件事。

有些偉大學者飽讀詩書，卻無法用像樣的文章表達自我。他們的知識就像鎖在箱子裡的黃金一樣，對個人或社會沒有半點貢獻。

學習寫作最好的方法是提筆去寫，就像學騎腳踏車最好的方法是坐上腳踏車開始騎。先從稀鬆平常的熟悉事物寫起，例如寫一篇關於貓的文章，談些貓的特性。別寫「幼貓很愛玩耍，成貓比較穩重。」這種描述有太多人寫過了。寫寫你家的貓做過的事，例如牠如何在閣樓抓老鼠，抓到以後又怎麼做。

熟悉的主題最適合初學者。如果你沒去過澳洲，對這個國家一無所知，就別試圖描述澳洲的景致。

Rules of grammar and rhetoric are good in their own place; their laws must be observed in order to express thoughts and ideas in the right way so that they shall convey a determinate sense and meaning in a pleasing and acceptable manner. Hard and fast rules, however, can never make a writer or author. That is the business of old Mother Nature and nothing can take her place. If nature has not endowed a man with faculties to put his ideas into proper composition he cannot do so. He may have no ideas worthy the recording. If a person has not a thought to express, it cannot be expressed. Something cannot be manufactured out of nothing. The author must have thoughts and ideas before he can express them on paper. These come to him by nature and environment and are developed and strengthened by study. There is an old Latin quotation in regard to the poet which says "Poeta nascitur non fit" the translation of which is–the poet is born, not made. To a great degree the same applies to the author. Some men are great scholars as far as book learning is concerned, yet they cannot express themselves in passable composition. Their knowledge is like gold locked up in a chest where it is of no value to themselves or the rest of the world.

The best way to learn to write is to sit down and write, just as the best way how to learn to ride a bicycle is to mount the wheel and pedal away. Write first about common things, subjects that are familiar to you. Try for instance an essay on a cat. Say something original about her. Don't say "she is very playful when young but becomes grave as she grows old." That has been said more than fifty

不用苦思寫作主題，你身邊多的是可以寫的題材。描述你昨天看到的事，例如火災、脫逃的馬、街上打架的狗。

你的描述要有原創性，可以模仿最優秀作家的文風，但不要模仿他們的原話。不要因循守舊，走出自己的路。

務必遵守這條金科玉律：了解自己寫的事物，寫自己了解的事物。想要了解事物，你就必須讀書。

世界是一本打開的書，任誰都能閱讀。自然是一本大書，無論平民或貴族都能閱讀。研究自然的意境和時序，因為那遠比文法的語氣和時態更為重要。透過書本學習是最理想的，但那畢竟只是理論而非實踐。

在英文中——事實上，在任何語言中——最偉大的託寓出自一位人們口中沒受過教育、名為約翰・班揚的補鍋匠之筆。莎士比亞並不符合我們今日所認定的學者標準，然而他闡述想法的能力可謂前無古人，後無來者。他只是閱讀了自然之書，將之透過自己出眾的聰明才智詮釋出來而已。

不要誤以為唯有受過大學教育才能成為成功的作家。完全不是這麼回事。有些唸過大學的人只是死腦筋的呆子、社會的寄生蟲，不但對社會沒有貢獻，對自己也是一無是處。

thousand times before. Tell what you have seen the family cat doing, how she caught a mouse in the garret and what she did after catching it. Familiar themes are always the best for the beginner. Don't attempt to describe a scene in Australia if you have never been there and know nothing of the country. Never hunt for subjects, there are thousands around you. Describe what you saw yesterday–a fire, a runaway horse, a dog-fight on the street and be original in your description. Imitate the best writers in their *style*, but not in their exact words. Get out of the beaten path, make a pathway of your own.

Know what you write about, write about what you know; this is a golden rule to which you must adhere. To know you must study. The world is an open book in which all who run may read. Nature is one great volume the pages of which are open to the peasant as well as to the peer. Study Nature's moods and tenses, for they are vastly more important than those of the grammar. Book learning is most desirable, but, after all, it is only theory and not practice. The grandest allegory in the English, in fact, in any language, was written by an ignorant, so-called ignorant, tinker named John Bunyan. Shakespeare was not a scholar in the sense we regard the term to-day, yet no man ever lived or probably ever will live that equalled or will equal him in the expression of thought. He simply read the book of nature and interpreted it from the standpoint of his own magnificent genius.

Don't imagine that a college education is necessary to success as a writer. Far from it. Some of our college men are dead-heads, drones, parasites on the body social, not alone useless to the world but to

有的人就像裝飾用的花瓶，沒有半點價值。一般來說，裝飾用的物品沒有太多用處。有的人什麼都知道，卻什麼都只知道一點。這句話乍聽之下相互矛盾，但經驗證明此話所言不假。

　　如果你出身貧困也無妨，這樣反而對你有利無害。貧困是人們努力的動力，不是一種缺點。比起含著金湯匙出生，帶著一顆有用的腦袋出生要來得好多了。如果世界是靠這些幸運寵兒在支撐，那早就完蛋了。

　　從貧困的泥淖、從苦難的境地、從疏於照顧的破敗小屋、從默默無聞的林中房舍、從飽受迫害的小巷和小路、從在陰暗骯髒的閣樓和地下室永無止境的勞力和苦役中，出現造就歷史的男男女女。他們的存在讓世界變得更光明、美好、崇高、神聖，讓世界變成一個適合安身、值得死去的地方。世界因這些男男女女的足跡而變得神聖、因他們的存在而變得偉大，並在許多情況下，因他們的鮮血而變得崇高。

　　如果施加在對的人身上，那麼貧困就是來自天父的祝福和恩典，而非詛咒。貧困非但沒有阻礙文學發展，反而提升各個時代的文學水準。

　　荷馬是個失明的乞丐，靠著吟唱詩歌乞求人們施捨。偉大的睿智先知老蘇格拉底，儘管因貧窮而經常三餐不繼，卻教育著雅典城的年輕學子。神聖的但丁不過是個無家可歸、沒有朋友，浪跡義大利各處的乞丐，但他寫下永垂不朽的詩篇。

themselves. A person may be so ornamental that he is valueless from any other standpoint. As a general rule ornamental things serve but little purpose. A man may know so much of everything that he knows little of anything. This may sound paradoxical, but, nevertheless, experience proves its truth.

If you are poor that is not a detriment but an advantage. Poverty is an incentive to endeavor, not a drawback. Better to be born with a good, working brain in your head than with a gold spoon in your mouth. If the world had been depending on the so-called pets of fortune it would have deteriorated long ago.

From the pits of poverty, from the arenas of suffering, from the hovels of neglect, from the backwood cabins of obscurity, from the lanes and by-ways of oppression, from the dingy garrets and basements of unending toil and drudgery have come men and women who have made history, made the world brighter, better, higher, holier for their existence in it, made of it a place good to live in and worthy to die in,–men and women who have hallowed it by their footsteps and sanctified it with their presence and in many cases consecrated it with their blood. Poverty is a blessing, not an evil, a benison from the Father's hand if accepted in the right spirit. Instead of retarding, it has elevated literature in all ages. Homer was a blind beggarman singing his snatches of song for the dole of charity; grand old Socrates, oracle of wisdom, many a day went without his dinner because he had not the wherewithal to get it, while teaching the youth of Athens. The divine Dante was nothing better than a beggar, houseless, homeless,

米爾頓儘管失明，卻敢望向天使畏懼之處，在窮困潦倒時寫下崇高之作《失樂園》。莎士比亞曾在白馬戲院外替看戲的顧客照顧馬匹，以賺幾個銅板買麵包吃。羅勃‧伯恩斯在農忙之餘，唱出永垂不朽的詩歌。

　　可憐的海因里希‧海涅（Heinrich Heine）在巴黎的那段歲月備受冷落、一貧如洗，還因疾病終日困在他口中的「床褥之墓」，卻讓祖國德國的文壇多了一位文學大師。在美國，伊萊休‧伯里特（Elihu Burritt）在從事鐵匠工作之餘，也自學成為一位精通多種語言的大師，成為當代美國文學巨擘。

　　在其他領域，貧困是激發行動的動力。

　　拿破崙出生貧寒，是落後的科西嘉島上一名收入勉強糊口的書記之子。林肯是美國引以為傲的偉人，他讓美國「這片土地變得如此炎熱，教奴隸制度沒有立足之地」，但他也是出身於俄亥俄州偏遠地區的小屋。詹姆士‧加菲爾德（James A. Garfield）情況相同。

　　尤利西斯‧格蘭特（Ulysses Grant）出身皮革工廠，後來成為世界上最偉大的將軍。湯瑪士‧愛迪生（Thomas A. Edison）原本也只是火車上的報童。

　　這些都是貧困激發行動的例子。貧困非但沒有阻礙他們，反而讓他們奮發向上。因此，如果你出身貧困，就把環境當作達成目的的手段。要有雄心壯志，堅守目標，並竭盡全力達成目標。

friendless, wandering through Italy while he composed his immortal cantos. Milton, who in his blindness "looked where angels fear to tread," was steeped in poverty while writing his sublime conception, "Paradise Lost." Shakespeare was glad to hold and water the horses of patrons outside the White Horse Theatre for a few pennies in order to buy bread. Burns burst forth in never-dying song while guiding the ploughshare. Poor Heinrich Heine, neglected and in poverty, from his "mattress grave" of suffering in Paris added literary laurels to the wreath of his German Fatherland. In America Elihu Burritt, while attending the anvil, made himself a master of a score of languages and became the literary lion of his age and country.

In other fields of endeavor poverty has been the spur to action. Napoleon was born in obscurity, the son of a hand-to-mouth scrivener in the backward island of Corsica. Abraham Lincoln, the boast and pride of America, the man who made this land too hot for the feet of slaves, came from a log cabin in the Ohio backwoods. So did James A. Garfield. Ulysses Grant came from a tanyard to become the world's greatest general. Thomas A. Edison commenced as a newsboy on a railway train.

The examples of these men are incentives to action. Poverty thrust them forward instead of keeping them back. Therefore, if you are poor make your circumstances a means to an end. Have ambition, keep a goal in sight and bend every energy to reach that goal. A story is told of Thomas Carlyle the day he attained the highest honor the literary world could confer upon him when he was elected Lord

關於湯瑪斯‧卡萊爾被選為愛丁堡大學校長，獲得文學界最高榮譽那天，傳了這麼一段故事。結束就職演說之後，他穿越學校廳堂，遇到一位看起來正埋首苦讀的學生。這位人人口中的「赤爾西賢者」用他特有的唐突、粗暴口吻問這位年輕學生：「你讀書是為了以後要做什麼？」年輕人回答：「我不知道。」

卡萊爾厲聲說道：「你不知道。年輕人，你真愚蠢。」然後解釋他為何說出這番激烈的話：「孩子，我在你這個年紀的時候，在鄧弗里斯郡的埃克爾費亨這座小村莊過著貧窮清苦的生活。在這個窮鄉僻壤中，只有牧師和我能讀《聖經》。雖然貧困卑微，在我心裡卻有一張椅子擺在名人殿堂等著我，於是我日以繼夜、夜以繼日地苦讀，直到今天坐上那張椅子，成為愛丁堡大學校長。」

另一位蘇格蘭人羅勃‧布坎南（Robert Buchanan）是知名小說家，他從格拉斯哥前往倫敦時，口袋裡只有一個錢幣，但他立志能像其他文學名家一樣，被安葬在西敏寺大教堂的墓園。儘管他稱不上是學者，他的雄心壯志讓他努力不懈，成為這座世界大城中的文學巨擘之一。

亨利‧史坦利（Henry M. Stanley）是救濟院裡的孤兒，本名叫做約翰‧羅蘭茲。雖然在威爾斯的救濟院長大，但他懷有遠大目標，後來成為偉大的探險家、作家、國會議員，並受到英國國王封為爵士。

Rector of Edinburgh University. After his installation speech, in going through the halls, he met a student seemingly deep in study. In his own peculiar, abrupt, crusty way the Sage of Chelsea interrogated the young man: "For what profession are you studying?" "I don't know," returned the youth. "You don't know," thundered Carlyle, "young man, you are a fool." Then he went on to qualify his vehement remark, "My boy when I was your age, I was stooped in grinding, gripping poverty in the little village of Ecclefechan, in the wilds of Dumfriesshire, where in all the place only the minister and myself could read the Bible, yet poor and obscure as I was, in my mind's eye I saw a chair awaiting for me in the Temple of Fame and day and night and night and day I studied until I sat in that chair to-day as Lord Rector of Edinburgh University."

Another Scotchman, Robert Buchanan, the famous novelist, set out for London from Glasgow with but half-a-crown in his pocket. "Here goes," said he, "for a grave in Westminster Abbey." He was not much of a scholar, but his ambition carried him on and he became one of the great literary lions of the world's metropolis.

Henry M. Stanley was a poorhouse waif whose real name was John Rowlands. He was brought up in a Welsh workhouse, but he had ambition, so he rose to be a great explorer, a great writer, became a member of Parliament and was knighted by the British Sovereign. Have ambition to succeed and you will succeed. Cut the word "failure" out of your lexicon. Don't acknowledge it. Remember

"In life's earnest battle they only prevail

立下成功的野心，你就會成功。將「失敗」這兩個字從你的字典裡拿掉。不要認輸。記住：「在人生的奮戰中，只有日日向前、不言失敗的人才能勝出。」將每個阻礙變成讓你不斷進步、邁向成功的踏腳石。

身處困頓時，要有克服困境的決心。班揚是在貝德福德的監獄中，在只吃麵包配水、快要餓死的情況下，在包裝紙碎片上寫下《天路歷程》。命運多舛的美國才子愛倫坡是在紐約福德漢姆街區的一間小屋中，在最窮途末路的情況下，寫下《烏鴉》（The Raven）這首英文文學中最美妙、最具美感的詩歌。在他短暫卻精彩絕倫的寫作生涯中，可憐的愛倫坡從來沒有賺進一分一毫屬於自己的錢財。不過除了時運不佳，這也是他自己造成的，因此他是一個負面教材。

不要以為必須博覽群書才能成為成功的作家。太多書往往讓人感到迷惑。只要精通幾本好書，好好將其讀透，就能得到所有寫作必備技巧。一位偉大的專家曾經說道：「要小心只讀一本書的人。」意思是只讀一本書的人已把書中內容讀到通透。有人主張只要徹底掌握《聖經》中的知識，就能成為文學大師。的確，《聖經》和莎士比亞的作品濃縮了必要知識的典範。莎士比亞匯集前人成果，並為後人播下種子。他是知識之海，其浪潮席捲所有思想大陸。

Who daily march onward and never say fail."

Let every obstacle you encounter be but a stepping stone in the path of onward progress to the goal of success.

If untoward circumstances surround you, resolve to overcome them. Bunyan wrote the "Pilgrim's Progress" in Bedford jail on scraps of wrapping paper while he was half starved on a diet of bread and water. That unfortunate American genius, Edgar Allan Poe, wrote "The Raven," the most wonderful conception as well as the most highly artistic poem in all English literature, in a little cottage in the Fordham section of New York while he was in the direst straits of want. Throughout all his short and wonderfully brilliant career, poor Poe never had a dollar he could call his own. Such, however, was both his fault and his misfortune and he is a bad exemplar.

Don't think that the knowledge of a library of books is essential to success as a writer. Often a multiplicity of books is confusing. Master a few good books and master them well and you will have all that is necessary. A great authority has said: "Beware of the man of one book," which means that a man of one book is a master of the craft. It is claimed that a thorough knowledge of the Bible alone will make any person a master of literature. Certain it is that the Bible and Shakespeare constitute an epitome of the essentials of knowledge. Shakespeare gathered the fruitage of all who went before him, he has sown the seeds for all who shall ever come after him. He was the great intellectual ocean whose waves touch the continents of all thought.

現在的書相當便宜，多虧了有印刷技術，所有人都能讀到最偉大的著作。只要是值得一讀的書，讀得越多越有益。就像食物一樣，有時人們讀了毒害思想的東西卻仍不自知，其不良作用很難擺脫，因此要慎選讀物。

如果買不起大量的書——前面也提過沒這必要——那就挑選幾本大師的偉大著作，將之消化吸收，豐富你的文學知識。前面章節中也介紹了一些世界名著，任君挑選。

你的大腦是一間寶庫，不要在裡面擺滿沒用的家具，以致放不進有用的東西。只放有價值、有用途的東西，方便你隨時取用。

閱讀最傑出的著作，才能成為作家；同理可證，學習最優秀的講者，才能說得對、說得好。

想要說得對，就得模仿演說大師。聽口才最好的人如何表達自我。聽最好的講座、演說和布道。不用模仿他們演說時的手勢，雄辯家和演說家是先天造就而非後天養成的。

你該注意的不是演說家「如何」表達自我，而是其所使用的語言和使用的方式。你聽過時下演講大師的演說嗎？過去也有不少大師，只是再也聽不到他們演說，只能讀到演說內容。

不過，你還是可以聽到尚在人世的大師的演說魅力。對許多人來說，當年聆聽的已逝大師絕妙演說仍迴盪耳邊。

Books are cheap now-a-days, the greatest works, thanks to the printing press, are within the reach of all, and the more you read, the better, provided they are worth reading. Sometimes a man takes poison into his system unconscious of the fact that it is poison, as in the case of certain foods, and it is very hard to throw off its effects. Therefore, be careful in your choice of reading matter. If you cannot afford a full library, and as has been said, such is not necessary, select a few of the great works of the master minds, assimilate and digest them, so that they will be of advantage to your literary system. Elsewhere in this volume is given a list of some of the world's masterpieces from which you can make a selection.

Your brain is a storehouse, don't put useless furniture into it to crowd it to the exclusion of what is useful. Lay up only the valuable and serviceable kind which you can call into requisition at any moment.

As it is necessary to study the best authors in order to be a writer, so it is necessary to study the best speakers in order to talk with correctness and in good style. To talk rightly you must imitate the masters of oral speech. Listen to the best conversationalists and how they express themselves. Go to hear the leading lectures, speeches and sermons. No need to imitate the gestures of elocution, it is nature, not art, that makes the elocutionist and the orator. It is not *how* a speaker expresses himself but the language which he uses and the manner of its use which should interest you. Have you heard the present day masters of speech? There have been past time masters

也許你仍沉醉於亨利·沃德·比徹（Henry Ward Beecher）和詹姆斯·塔瑪格（Thomas De Witt Talmage）的演說中。他們兩人的演說振奮人心，贏得無數人的喝采。他們都能言善道，精於修辭，演說起來宛如向聽眾拋出美妙花束，聽眾則將其視為珍寶般謹記在心。他們都是學者和哲學家，不過他倆遠遠不及查爾斯·司布真（Charles Spurgeon）。

司布真是一個普通人，沒受過太多現今社會所認定的教育，卻靠著演講吸引上千人到他的禮拜堂聽講。新教徒、天主教徒、土耳其人、猶太人和回教徒爭相聆聽他的布道，陶醉在他的話言中。

另一位同樣傑出的是德懷特·萊曼·穆迪（Dwight L. Moody），他是世界上最偉大的布道者。穆迪不是學者，起初在芝加哥賣鞋，但沒有人像他一樣，能夠吸引大批聽眾如癡如醉地聆聽他的演說。

你會說這只是個人吸引力使然罷了，但並非如此。是他們口中吐出的熱烈話語，以及他們使用這些話語時的方式、舉止和張力吸引群眾前來聽講。他們的成功與個人吸引力或外表無關。論起長相，他們都有一些缺陷。司布真是一個矮胖的小傢伙，穆迪像個鄉下農夫，塔瑪格穿著一襲大斗蓬，樣貌十分邋遢，只有比徹算得上文雅、有紳士氣質。

but their tongues are stilled in the dust of the grave, and you can only read their eloquence now. You can, however, listen to the charm of the living. To many of us voices still speak from the grave, voices to which we have listened when fired with the divine essence of speech. Perhaps you have hung with rapture on the words of Beecher and Talmage. Both thrilled the souls of men and won countless thousands over to a living gospel. Both were masters of words, they scattered the flowers of rhetoric on the shrine of eloquence and hurled veritable bouquets at their audiences which were eagerly seized by the latter and treasured in the storehouse of memory. Both were scholars and philosophers, yet they were far surpassed by Spurgeon, a plain man of the people with little or no claim to education in the modern sense of the word. Spurgeon by his speech attracted thousands to his Tabernacle. The Protestant and Catholic, Turk, Jew and Mohammedan rushed to hear him and listened, entranced, to his language. Such another was Dwight L. Moody, the greatest Evangelist the world has ever known. Moody was not a man of learning; he commenced life as a shoe salesman in Chicago, yet no man ever lived who drew such audiences and so fascinated them with the spell of his speech. "Oh, that was personal magnetism," you will say, but it was nothing of the kind. It was the burning words that fell from the lips of these men, and the way, the manner, the force with which they used those words that counted and attracted the crowds to listen unto them. Personal magnetism or personal appearance entered not as factors into their success. Indeed as far as physique were concerned, some of

與許多人的看法相反，外表並非他們吸引聽眾的關鍵。愛爾蘭政治人物丹尼爾‧歐康諾（Daniel O'Connell）是個其貌不揚、笨拙難看的人，但他的演說吸引數百萬人支持，他也成為英國國會議員。他是語言大師，知道要說什麼才能擄獲聽眾的心。

　　在幾乎所有場合中，真正重要的是字詞和其擺放位置。無論一個人在其他方面多麼優秀，如果他用字遣詞不對，沒有按照適當的句構表達自己，就會令你產生反感。

　　相對的，一個人用字遣詞得當，依循良好演說法則使用語言，那麼無論他的地位多麼卑微，都會吸引你並對你產生影響。

　　好的講者、對的講者永遠都能吸引別人注意，機會大門為之敞開，其他沒有能力表達自我的人則無從得到機會。

　　能言善道、切中要點的人永遠不必擔心沒有工作。幾乎各行各業都需要這樣的人才，世界隨時需要這種人。雇主隨時都在尋找善於表達，能用語言的力量吸引、說服群眾的人。

　　有的人或許具備能力、受過教育、富有學養、品格高尚，卻沒有能力表達自我、妥善地用言語適切闡述個人觀點，這樣的人只能站到一邊，讓能力遠低於他，卻能立即而有效地傳達想法的人上場。

　　你也許又會說，口齒流利的講者是先天造就，而非後天養成的。這句話大致上沒錯，不過「正確」的講者是可以「養成」的，說話正確就能說得流利。只要堅持不懈、下點功夫和心力，任何人都能成為正確的講者。

them were handicapped. Spurgeon was a short, podgy, fat little man, Moody was like a country farmer, Talmage in his big cloak was one of the most slovenly of men and only Beecher was passable in the way of refinement and gentlemanly bearing. Physical appearance, as so many think, is not the sesame to the interest of an audience. Daniel O'Connell, the Irish tribune, was a homely, ugly, awkward, ungainly man, yet his words attracted millions to his side and gained for him the hostile ear of the British Parliament, he was a master of verbiage and knew just what to say to captivate his audiences.

It is words and their placing that count on almost all occasions. No matter how refined in other respects the person may be, if he use words wrongly and express himself in language not in accordance with a proper construction, he will repel you, whereas the man who places his words correctly and employs language in harmony with the laws of good speech, let him be ever so humble, will attract and have an influence over you.

The good speaker, the correct speaker, is always able to command attention and doors are thrown open to him which remain closed to others not equipped with a like facility of expression. The man who can talk well and to the point need never fear to go idle. He is required in nearly every walk of life and field of human endeavor, the world wants him at every turn. Employers are constantly on the lookout for good talkers, those who are able to attract the public and convince others by the force of their language. A man may be able, educated, refined, of unblemished character, nevertheless if he

容我再次強調下列良好建議：

一、聆聽最優秀的講者，仔細注意讓你印象最深刻的字詞。

二、隨身攜帶筆記本，寫下出色、超乎尋常的單字、片語和句子。

三、聽到某個不太明白意思的單字就查字典。

四、許多同義字意思幾乎一樣，不過仔細檢視就會發現意思不盡相同，而且有些意思非但不同，反而相差甚遠。要小心這些單字，找出確切的字意，學會正確使用它們。

以開放心胸面對批評，不要對批評感到不滿，而是要歡迎他人指教，將之視為指出你的缺失、好讓你改過的朋友。

lack the power to express himself, put forth his views in good and appropriate speech he has to take a back seat, while some one with much less ability gets the opportunity to come to the front because he can clothe his ideas in ready words and talk effectively.

You may again say that nature, not art, makes a man a fluent speaker; to a great degree this is true, but it is *art* that makes him a *correct* speaker, and correctness leads to fluency. It is possible for everyone to become a correct speaker if he will but persevere and take a little pains and care.

At the risk of repetition good advice may be here emphasized: Listen to the best speakers and note carefully the words which impress you most. Keep a notebook and jot down words, phrases, sentences that are in any way striking or out of the ordinary run. If you do not understand the exact meaning of a word you have heard, look it up in the dictionary. There are many words, called synonyms, which have almost a like signification, nevertheless, when examined they express different shades of meaning and in some cases, instead of being close related, are widely divergent. Beware of such words, find their exact meaning and learn to use them in their right places.

Be open to criticism, don't resent it but rather invite it and look upon those as friends who point out your defects in order that you may remedy them.

第十五章
英文文學
大師和鉅作

Masters and Masterpieces
of Literature

《聖經》是世界上最偉大的書籍，它除了是神聖的天啟之書，也是現存最完美的文學作品。

除了《聖經》之外三部最偉大的作品，分別出自荷馬、但丁和莎士比亞之手，其次則是維吉爾（Virgil）和米爾頓的作品。

■ 書架必備著作

荷馬、但丁、塞萬提斯、莎士比亞和歌德作品。

適合一般讀者閱讀的荷馬英譯本首推查普曼的版本。另也推薦諾頓翻譯的但丁作品，和泰勒翻譯的歌德作品《浮士德》。

■ 優良藏書

除了上述作品，也應儘量收藏下列書籍：

普魯塔克的《希臘羅馬名人傳》、馬可斯·奧理略的《沉思錄》、喬叟作品、耿稗思的《師主篇》、傑若米·泰勒的《神聖生死》、《天路歷程》、麥考利散文、培根散文、艾迪生散文、查爾斯·蘭姆的《伊利亞隨筆集》、雨果的《悲慘世界》、卡萊爾的《英雄與英雄崇拜》、帕爾格雷夫的《英詩金庫》、華茲華斯作品、《維克菲德的牧師》、喬治·艾略特的《亞當·比德》、薩克萊的《浮華世界》、司各特的《艾凡赫》、奧爾巴赫的《在高地》、巴爾扎克的《歐也妮·葛朗台》、霍桑的《紅字》、愛默生散文、鮑斯威爾的《約翰生傳》、格林的《英國人民簡史》、《世界史大綱》、《物種起源》、蒙田隨筆、朗費羅作品、丁尼生作品、白朗寧作品、惠蒂埃作品、拉斯金作品、赫

The Bible is the world's greatest book. Apart from its character as a work of divine revelation, it is the most perfect literature extant.

Leaving out the Bible the three greatest works are those of Homer, Dante and Shakespeare. These are closely followed by the works of Virgil and Milton.

■ INDISPENSABLE BOOKS

Homer, Dante, Cervantes, Shakespeare and Goethe.

(The best translation of *Homer* for the ordinary reader is by Chapman. Norton's translation of *Dante* and Taylor's translation of Goethe's *Faust* are recommended.)

■ A GOOD LIBRARY

Besides the works mentioned everyone should endeavor to have the following:

Plutarch's Lives, Meditations of Marcus Aurelius, Chaucer, Imitation of Christ (Thomas a Kempis), *Holy Living and Holy Dying* (Jeremy Taylor), *Pilgrim's Progress, Macaulay's Essays, Bacon's Essays, Addison's Essays, Essays of Elia* (Charles Lamb), *Les Miserables* (Hugo), *Heroes and Hero Worship* (Carlyle), *Palgrave's Golden Treasury, Wordsworth, Vicar of Wake field, Adam Bede* (George Eliot), *Vanity Fair* (Thackeray), *Ivanhoe* (Scott), *On the Heights* (Auerbach), *Eugenie Grandet* (Balzac), *Scarlet Letter*

伯特‧史賓賽作品。

　　最好能有一部優良的百科全書，一本可靠的字典也是不可少的。

■ 美國文學鉅作

　　《紅字》、帕克曼的史學著作、莫特利的《荷蘭共和國崛起》、格蘭特的《回憶錄》、富蘭克林的《自傳》、韋伯斯特的演說集、洛威爾的《比格羅詩稿》和《批判性文集》、梭羅的《湖濱散記》、惠特曼的《草葉集》、庫柏的《皮襪子故事集》、《早餐桌上的獨裁者》、《賓漢》，以及《湯姆叔叔的小屋》。

■ 美國十大詩人

　　布萊恩特、愛倫坡、惠蒂埃、朗費羅、洛威爾、愛默生、惠特曼、拉尼爾、阿爾德里奇，以及斯托達德。

■ 英國十大詩人

　　喬叟、史賓賽、莎士比亞、米爾頓、伯恩斯、華茲華斯、濟慈、雪萊、丁尼生，以及白朗寧。

■ 英國十大散文作家

　　培根、艾迪生、史蒂爾、麥考利、蘭姆、傑佛瑞、德昆西、卡萊爾、薩克萊，以及馬修‧阿諾德。

(Hawthorne), *Emerson's Essays, Boswell's Life of Johnson, History of the English People* (Green), *Outlines of Universal History, Origin of Species, Montaigne's Essays, Longfellow, Tennyson, Browning, Whittier, Ruskin, Herbert Spencer.*

A good encyclopedia is very desirable and a reliable dictionary indispensable.

■ MASTERPIECES OF AMERICAN LITERATURE

Scarlet Letter, Parkman's Histories, Motley's Dutch Republic, Grant's Memoirs, Franklin's Autobiography, Webster's Speeches, Lowell's Biglow Papers, also his *Critical Essays, Thoreau's Walden, Leaves of Grass* (Whitman), *Leather-stocking Tales* (Cooper), *Autocrat of the Breakfast Table, Ben Hur* and *Uncle Tom's Cabin.*

■ TEN GREATEST AMERICAN POETS

Bryant, Poe, Whittier, Longfellow, Lowell, Emerson, Whitman, Lanier, Aldrich and Stoddard.

■ TEN GREATEST ENGLISH POETS

Chaucer, Spenser, Shakespeare, Milton, Burns, Wordsworth, Keats, Shelley, Tennyson, Browning.

■ TEN GREATEST ENGLISH ESSAYISTS

Bacon, Addison, Steele, Macaulay, Lamb, Jeffrey, De Quincey,

■ 最佳莎劇

按優秀程度排列，依序為：《哈姆雷特》、《李爾王》、《奧賽羅》、《安東尼與克麗奧佩托拉》、《馬克白》、《威尼斯商人》、《亨利四世》、《皆大歡喜》、《冬天的故事》、《羅密歐與茱麗葉》、《仲夏夜之夢》、《第十二夜》，以及《暴風雨》。

■ 只讀好書

如果無法大量收藏偉大著作，至少也要擁有幾本。仔細閱讀，加以思考，藉以豐富自己的文學視野。記住，好書值得一讀再讀，劣書則要敬而遠之。文學跟其他事情一樣，都該唯善是舉。

Carlyle, Thackeray and Matthew Arnold.

■ BEST PLAYS OF SHAKESPEARE

In order of merit are: *Hamlet, King Lear, Othello , Antony and Cleopatra, Macbeth, Merchant of Venice, Henry IV, As You Like It, Winter's Tale, Romeo and Juliet, Midsummer Night's Dream, Twelfth Night, Tempest.*

■ ONLY THE GOOD

If you are not able to procure a library of the great masterpieces, get at least a few. Read them carefully, intelligently and with a view to enlarging your own literary horizon. Remember a good book cannot be read too often, one of a deteriorating influence should not be read at all. In literature, as in all things else, the good alone should prevail.

i生活14

像樣的英文，這樣寫，這樣說
用英文思考，掌握正確的文法與字彙；不再背公式，擺脫不道地的中式英文

作者　約瑟‧德夫林　譯者　楊雅琪
封面設計　柳佳璋　責任編輯　洪翠薇　內文排版　游淑萍
副總編輯　林獻瑞　印務經理　黃禮賢

社長　郭重興　發行人兼出版總監　曾大福
出版者　遠足文化事業股份有限公司 好人出版
新北市新店區民權路108之1號8樓
電話02-2218-1417#1282　傳眞02-8667-1065
發行　遠足文化事業股份有限公司
新北市新店區民權路108-1號8樓
電話02-2218-1417　傳眞02-8667-1065
電子信箱service@bookrep.com.tw　網址http://www.bookrep.com.tw
郵政劃撥　19504465　遠足文化事業股份有限公司
法律顧問　華洋法律事務所　蘇文生律師
印製　成陽印刷股份有限公司　電話02-2265-1491

初　　版　2020年9月9日　定價　450元
初版三刷　2022年9月2日
ISBN　978-986-98693-6-2

HOW TO SPEAK AND WRITE CORRECTLY by JOSEPH DEVLIIN. Traditional Chinese
edition copyright © 2020 by Atman Books, an imprint of Walkers Cultural Co., Ltd. ALL
RIGHT RESERVED

國家圖書館出版品預行編目(CIP)資料

像樣的英文，這樣寫，這樣說：用英文思考，掌握正確的文法
　與字彙；不再背公式，擺脫不道地的中式英文／約瑟‧德夫
　林作. 楊雅琪譯. -- 初版. -- 新北市：好人，2020.09
　面；　公分. --（i生活；14）
　ISBN　978-986-98693-6-2（平裝）
　1.英語　2.讀本
805.18　　　　　　　　　　　　　　　　　109012088

讀者回函QR Code
期待知道您的想法